LIFE C
DEAT

# BOOKS BY CHRIS MERRITT

*Bring Her Back* — 1
*Last Witness* — 2

# CHRIS MERRITT

# LIFE OR DEATH

bookouture

Published by Bookouture in 2019

An imprint of StoryFire Ltd.

Carmelite House
50 Victoria Embankment
London EC4Y 0DZ

www.bookouture.com

ISBN: 978-1-78681-679-5
eBook ISBN: 978-1-78681-678-8

*To Kate Mason – first reader, fiancée, friend.*

# PROLOGUE

The gunshot stops him dead. Its echo dissipates quickly but the ringing left behind continues: a piercing monotone blocking out all sound, consuming the silence. The smell of gunpowder drifts across the large open room. He knows the pain of being shot: shocking, insistent heat like a flame on your skin, coupled with unbearable pressure. But that feeling doesn't come.

Seconds later he realises: he wasn't hit. Assumes it was a deliberate miss, a warning shot. Guesses that if he runs any further, the next one will be for real. A bullet to the leg, probably. Not a kill shot, though. Not yet. That would defeat the purpose of bringing him here. Defeat the purpose of using the most precious thing in his life to get him to this exact place, at this exact time. He thinks he knows the reason he's here now.

Detective Inspector Zachariah Boateng can't see the person who fired from the darkness. But he knows there's someone in the shadows. And the ear-splitting volume of the gunshot tells him this person isn't far away. He steadies his breathing, lets his eyes adjust. The blackness appears to part and, peering into it, he can just make out a human form. The shape, the outside of this figure, is about all that's recognisably human; what's inside is not. The mind, the motivation, the emotion – or lack of it – belong to some other species.

In the Met Police, they call these people meat eaters. Predators who base a life on exploiting others. They like to use violence to get what they want. Boateng isn't one of them but, given the slightest chance, he'd kill this assailant with his bare hands. He knows who it is before the shooter steps forward and the light picks out those familiar features. And, he acknowledges with a stab of guilt, he's brought this on himself. On his family. On his colleagues. On everyone and everything that matters.

As the figure advances, these thoughts vanish. The pistol's muzzle is suddenly at his eye level. Then a new possibility dawns on him: maybe there is no purpose. Maybe there won't be any explanation.

Maybe there's just a kill shot.

# EIGHT DAYS EARLIER

# CHAPTER ONE

**Monday, 20 August 2018**

The scream woke Zac Boateng from a light sleep. He stared into the gloom. The cry came once more – anguished, tormented – making him wince. It was the sound of visceral pain. And it was coming from his garden. In his state of semi-consciousness, it took a moment before he knew what was happening.

Bloody urban foxes.

Zac lay in bed, listening to the London night. A siren rose and fell somewhere in the distance. He wondered which of his colleagues were out there, what they were responding to at 1 a.m. Serious violence or simply neighbours arguing over a stereo playing too loudly? In this city, either possibility was just as likely. Next to him, his wife, Etta, was breathing with the steady rhythm of deep slumber; something which had eluded Zac for some time. He had just closed his eyes again in the hope of drifting off when he heard the noise.

A dull, heavy thud from downstairs.

He tensed, a little stab of adrenalin rippling through his belly, making his hands tingle. He glanced across at Etta. She hadn't stirred. Again: scrape, thud. He wasn't imagining it. Zac exhaled slowly. *Think.* If they were being burgled, the safest thing to do was stay up here. Let the guy get on with it, take the PlayStation, iPad and whatever else he could carry and leave. They had insurance for exactly this situation. Unless the intruder was crazy or high, he wouldn't risk coming upstairs to look for jewellery. Best stay put.

But Zac had always had difficulty taking his own advice. And someone threatening his family, in their home, was a red line. He wasn't having it.

He slid out of bed.

Zac reached up to the top of the wardrobe, grasped the baseball bat. He stepped onto the landing; his eleven-year-old son Kofi's door was ajar as usual, the night light on. Zac crept down, using the edge of the stairs to avoid any creaks that might signal his approach. Sounds of human movement came from behind the closed living room door. He reached for the handle, fingers trembling slightly.

He threw the door open and charged into the light. The shriek was followed by a crack and tinkle of glass. Next to the bookshelf was a chair. On the chair stood his son, staring down at the shattered photo frame which lay on the wooden floor.

'Kofi! Jesus.'

'Sorry, Dad.'

Zac tossed the bat onto the sofa then walked over and hugged his boy. 'Scared the hell out of me. What're you doing down here?'

'I couldn't sleep.'

Zac rubbed Kofi's back. 'Me neither.' He looked over his son's shoulder to the broken frame: the photograph of Zac and Etta's daughter, Amelia, was intact beneath jagged pieces of glass.

'I just wanted to see her picture,' said Kofi, quietly. 'I didn't mean to—'

'Hey, don't worry about it.'

The boy sniffed. 'I miss her.'

'Yeah, me too, mate.' Zac squeezed his son a little tighter.

'Is it weird to want to talk to her, even though she's dead?'

'Nope. I do it sometimes.'

At length, Kofi spoke. 'Someone killed her, didn't they?'

His son was old enough to understand what that meant. 'Yes.'
'Who was it?'

'A man.' Zac paused, unsure what else to say. 'But he didn't just kill Amelia. He shot two other people that day, too. One of them was the person he was after. Your sister was just in the wrong place when he opened fire.' His voice caught slightly and he took a breath. 'And he hit her.'

Kofi pulled back from the hug and searched Zac's face. 'Did you catch him?'

'I did.' But Zac knew that wasn't the whole story. He'd nearly lost his own life last summer, trying to find the person responsible after a new lead had come his way during a separate murder case. Despite his efforts to investigate – most of which were unofficial – no one had been convicted for his daughter's killing, no evidence found for the crime. And it seemed like someone else had been involved in the shooting too, behind the scenes; invisible as a puppet master. Someone, known only as Kaiser, who was still out there.

The intelligence on Kaiser was thin, and sourced exclusively from an incarcerated murderer named Darian Wallace, who refused to cooperate any further. Not exactly reliable information. Still, the prospect of its truth niggled at Zac. And not just because the victim had been his daughter. According to Wallace, Kaiser was a police officer. One of his own.

●

Two a.m. This was what they meant by the dead of night. No moon and virtually no people. Just the roads of south London flashing past, the darkness punctured by street lamps and car headlights. Jermaine heard the passenger beside him flick the safety catch off the gun on his lap, then back on again. Off, on. Click, click. He glanced across. The guy's finger was on the trigger. Jermaine tried to keep his eyes ahead, his hands on the wheel.

'Can you put that under the seat or something?' he said. 'Making man nervous.'

'Pussy.'

Jermaine was no expert on guns, but his passenger had spent the past five minutes explaining how the Heckler & Koch MP5 Kurz was the sickest weapon he'd ever held. How it could unleash its entire thirty-round magazine of ammunition in two seconds. How the short barrel meant the shots weren't accurate, but that was the whole point. It was the reason they called the MP5 Kurz the 'crowd pleaser'.

'Why'd you have to bring it anyway?' Jermaine scowled.

'Protection.'

'For us?'

'For our cargo. *His* cargo,' the guy corrected himself.

The cargo that was making the VW Golf which Jermaine had borrowed ride low, accelerate more slowly. Jermaine had some idea what was in the heavy bags he'd seen being loaded into the back. But he hadn't asked too many questions. Not when he'd been given five hundred quid upfront with the promise of more on delivery. That money would pay the bills for months. 'I thought we were supposed to keep a low profile,' he said.

'We are.'

'In that case, turn the damn music down.'

The man beside him reached over and nudged the volume higher. The grime beats were making the car windows vibrate. Jermaine sucked his teeth and snatched another look sideways. Aaron Collins was someone he used to roll with a lot. But now Jermaine was at college studying business, their paths didn't cross much. Aaron had his own business, if you could call it that. Judging by his wide eyes and faster speech, he was sampling his own product too often.

'How much've you had?'

'It's just a little taster.' Aaron grinned. 'No big thing.'

'Foolishness.' Jermaine shook his head, kept driving. Something caught his eye in the rear-view mirror, before it disappeared as they rounded a bend. 'Yo,' he said. 'Was that…?'

The road straightened out. No mistake. Cop car.

'Oh fuck.' Jermaine gripped the wheel tighter.

Aaron turned to check. 'Relax, mate. Why would they be interested in us? We're just a couple of lads out for a drive.'

'At two o'clock in the morning.'

'So what?'

The lights on the police car were flashing now, although they hadn't hit the siren. Trying not to piss off the local residents.

'Just chill and let them go past, yeah?' Aaron slunk lower in his seat.

Jermaine could feel his heart beating faster and a twisting sensation somewhere below his stomach. The police accelerated and pulled out to overtake. Jermaine stared straight ahead, but the car didn't appear in front. It remained alongside them. One howl of a siren got his attention. He turned to see an officer motioning to him. He hesitated, then slowed and pulled into the kerb behind the swirling police lights that bathed everything in blue.

'What now?' Jermaine hissed.

'Be ready.' Aaron's right knee was jiggling.

Both officers exited the vehicle and began walking towards them. Aaron flicked the safety catch off the Kurz, adjusted his grip. A film of sweat had formed between Jermaine's hands and the steering wheel. The cops were almost at their car. One raised his palm in a 'stay there' sign.

'Showtime,' whispered Aaron.

'No way. You crazy motherfu—' Jermaine stopped himself. Dropped the handbrake slowly. Knocked the gearstick back into first. Then stamped on the accelerator and yanked the wheel right. They shot forward, back into the road, as one officer dived aside. Then the houses were flying past, blurring left and right.

Jermaine felt the engine growl, saw the needle reach fifty mph. Heard Aaron laughing.

'Where do I go now?' he barked.

'I don't know.'

'Think!'

'OK. We're a mile from the garage. Take some side roads and we'll get there before they catch up with us.'

'Side roads?'

'I'll navigate.' Aaron produced his phone, tapped a few times. 'Left up here.'

Jermaine had just begun turning when an identical siren whooped and he clocked a vehicle speeding towards them from the new road: unmarked, blue lights behind the grille. He spun the car back, tyres screeching, and accelerated again as another siren came from somewhere off to the right. Checked the rear-view: the original cop car was behind them.

'They're everywhere!' Jermaine gripped the wheel, pressed his foot down. 'How did they know?'

'Who'd you borrow this car off, again?'

'My boy.'

'I'm guessing your boy's got some kind of record then. Or maybe he's a snitch. Either way, we're fucked.' Aaron checked over his shoulder. 'Come on, man, faster!'

Jermaine swerved instinctively as a 4 x 4 came at them from the right, then sped up. Now the two cars were side by side, the cops driving in the wrong lane. *Shit, shit, shit.* He braked hard and skidded left into a smaller road, losing the 4 x 4, which couldn't turn quickly enough. Then they were alone.

'Yes!' cried Aaron, turning in his seat. 'Now cut back this way.' He jabbed left. 'There.'

Jermaine followed the instruction and heard the sirens recede. He slowed to quieten the engine and cut the headlights. Reached forward and turned the music off. Blew out his cheeks, blinked.

'Now where are we?' The terraced houses all looked the same around here.

'Give me a second.' Aaron dipped his head to the phone screen.

Jermaine checked his right-hand wing mirror. The street was empty, barely lit. Curse that damned money, he didn't want it any more. If he could—

The impact from the passenger side snapped his neck, the seat belt locking as the steering wheel turned against his grip. He tried to recover but the 4 x 4 was blocking them. He fumbled for reverse, missed, dropped the clutch again and found the gear. Turned to look over his shoulder. Then stopped as another car squealed to a halt behind them. They were trapped.

'Armed police!' came the shouts from all sides.

'Get your hands up!' bellowed one voice, as dark shapes moved behind the 4 x 4 headlights that now shone full beam into their vehicle.

Jermaine raised his hands, his breathing ragged. He looked left. Aaron was still smiling. And he was holding the Kurz in his lap.

'Let it go, Aaron!' Jermaine gasped. 'Put your hands up.'

'We have to fight.'

'What're you talking about? We're surrounded. Just do what they say or they're gonna shoot you.'

'It's too late.' Aaron flicked the safety catch once more. Fully automatic.

The dark shapes in front fanned out, repeated their commands.

'Fuck's sake!' spat Jermaine. 'Put it down. Do you want to die?'

'Remember whose stuff we're carrying.' Aaron swallowed, exhaled. 'We're already dead.' His finger curled around the trigger.

'No, wait!'

'He'll find you, J. Anywhere.' Aaron's body tensed.

'Don't!'

Aaron raised the Kurz to the windscreen. Jermaine ducked below the steering wheel as the deafening rattle was followed by hot casings spraying inside the car, pinging off the windows and dashboard. Several struck him, one scalding the back of his neck. Then a volley of shots came from outside, cracking through glass and metal, and ceased just as fast. Jermaine twisted his neck sideways and up. Aaron was slumped back in his seat, still holding the gun, mouth half open, a small black hole in his cheek. He wasn't moving.

A high-pitched tone was ringing in Jermaine's ears.

'Hands in the air!' came the shout, followed by another, more urgent. 'Officer down!' A radio bleeped and crackled and a voice gave a badge number and street name, demanded an ambulance.

Jermaine raised both trembling hands and slowly uncurled his body. He saw a figure and a gun muzzle through the window before his door was yanked open. A thick arm reached in and undid his seatbelt.

'Get on the fucking ground!'

He did as he was told and lay on his stomach, arms out in front. The tarmac was rough and warm, hard against his ribs. He began to cry, like he had no control over it. As one figure squatted next to him, pulling his hands behind his back and cuffing him, another stepped around him to the rear of the car. He heard the boot pop and the whine of its door rising. Then the sound of long zips unfastening: the bags. For a few seconds, there was only silence beyond the monotone filling Jermaine's head. Then one of the officers spoke.

'Jackpot.'

# CHAPTER TWO

Boateng marched down the corridor towards the interview rooms at Lewisham police station. He was clutching a manila folder containing what they knew about the shootings and arrest last night. It was pretty thin. Detective Sergeant Kat Jones strode alongside him.

'I watched it on the news this morning,' she said.

'So did half of London,' he replied. 'You saw the crowd outside the station? They're not happy.' He'd been told the first protesters had arrived just after 8 a.m., brandishing placards about the police murdering civilians, demands for justice. Their numbers had swelled as the morning went on, and the TV cameras had followed.

'Who's the guy they arrested?' asked Jones.

'Jermaine…' Boateng flipped the folder open. 'Mensah. Nineteen years old, Brixton resident.' He paused. 'Do Lambeth know about this? He's from their patch.'

'Not yet. No one else has got his name – you know, because of the deaths. I'll call the MIT straight after.'

'Great.' They stopped outside a door and Boateng gripped the handle. 'Ready?'

She nodded.

'OK.' He flashed a smile. 'Let's see what he has to say.'

They stepped into the interview room. In front of them, a young man in a grey T-shirt sat on the other side of a plain table, beside a thin, older guy in a suit: the lawyer. Neither one looked like he'd slept last night.

Boateng started the recording and made the introductions. Noted Mensah's flash of recognition at his Ghanaian family name. That common ground was a first step. Then he removed a photograph from the folder and rotated it on the table towards the detainee. The flash-lit image showed a VW Golf, its left-side panels caved in, the windscreen a spider's web of fractured glass through which a corpse was just visible in the passenger seat. Boateng watched his suspect; his reaction would tell him a lot.

Mensah closed his eyes, his lower lip curling a fraction. OK, some emotion. That was another step.

'What can you tell me about this, Jermaine?'

The young man's head dropped. His lawyer leaned across, whispered something to him.

'No comment,' mumbled Mensah.

'You were in the car when it happened, weren't you?'

Mensah was still looking down, but he gave a single tiny nod. The guy wanted to talk, but he was scared.

Boateng leaned forward, clasped his hands together. 'Was he your friend?'

The question made Mensah's eyes screw shut.

'Is that why you helped him?'

'No comment.' The response was barely audible.

'Decent cash, was it?'

No reply.

'Must've been,' said Boateng. 'To take the risk of carrying this lot.' He produced a second image, showing the contents of the boot. Mensah raised his head and Boateng watched his eyes widen.

'Forty Škorpion machine pistols. Czech-made. They could've done a lot of damage on the streets. Worth about two grand each.'

He let Mensah absorb the photograph and its implications.

'Did you know what was in those bags?'

Mensah shook his head, pinched the bridge of his nose. The lawyer leaned in again, cupping his hand to Mensah's ear. Boateng could see his resolve was weakening; the guy wasn't a gangster. Probably just hard up and loyal to his old mates – a dangerous combination when certain people wanted jobs done. The tipping point of the interview was coming.

Boateng carefully placed a third image on the table. It showed a muscular middle-aged man supine on the road. Blood had pooled around his head and shoulders. A paramedic sat on the ground at the edge of the frame. She had evidently given up trying to resuscitate the man.

'This is Sergeant Toby Sullivan,' said Boateng. 'He died at 2.15 a.m. today from a single 9 mm bullet wound to his neck.'

Mensah's lips drew back in horror.

'That's murder.' Boateng knew that proving Aaron Collins had intended to kill a police officer, rather than simply wound, would be extremely difficult. But he was banking on Mensah not knowing the distinction between murder and manslaughter. Even if his lawyer tried to explain the nuances to him, the seed of panic was already sown. 'That makes you an accessory.' He let the words sink in.

Mensah had started twisting his fingers, picking at his nails. He didn't reply.

'You're not a killer, Jermaine. I've met a lot of psychopaths in this job, and that's not you. But a jury might not see it that way. You don't want to go to prison for fifteen years, do you?'

'No,' whispered Mensah. His eyes were wet.

'I can help you,' continued Boateng. 'We can offer you protection. Just tell me who's behind this.'

The lawyer shifted, murmured something else. Boateng caught the words 'no obligation' and 'deal'.

Mensah shook his head. 'I can't.'

Boateng studied the young man as he stared down at the table. A tattoo on his forearm read 'Effi' in copperplate script. Effi? From Efua, most likely. A Ghanaian woman's name. Sister?

Mensah had a simple thread wristband on the other arm, the sort made by a child. Younger sister. One he cared about.

'It's not just you, Jermaine. You have to think about your family now. We can protect them too. Your mum.' He paused. 'Your sister.'

The lawyer extended a palm towards Boateng. 'I'd like a moment in private with my client, ple—'

'You can?' Mensah had raised his head, his gaze unfocused.

Boateng nodded. 'If you help us.'

'OK.'

'Who's behind this, Jermaine? Who brought those guns into London?'

'I don't know him.'

'What do you know about him?'

'Only what Aaron called him.'

'Alright.' Boateng glanced at Jones. 'What did he call him?'

Mensah swallowed, blinked and met Boateng's eyes. 'Kaiser.'

•

Susanna Pym glanced at her watch. The slender hands below the word 'Cartier' were touching XI and II: 11.10 a.m. She was late. Her appointment had been scheduled for 11 a.m., but it had taken forever to part the sea of tourists when she arrived, and even longer for the security procedures. Her host was a stickler for punctuality in others, though she nearly always ran late. That was the case today, so Pym hoped she'd get away with it.

Only three days into her new job, Pym was still desperate to make a good impression. She disliked the idea of being desperate for anything – it was so undignified – but at this precise moment, it was true. She was desperate for approval and the opportunities it could afford her.

Pym had just been seated in a comfortable chair in a well-appointed anteroom, and was ignoring the eighteenth-century oil paintings around her in favour of an iPad. Irritatingly, they'd taken her mobile at the door and offered her a 'secure' tablet for web browsing. She was using it to read every news article she could find about the police officer who'd been shot dead in the early hours. Technically, he was one of her employees. Last week it would have been down to someone else to deal with the unfortunate incident. Now, it was up to her. Of course, she'd been fully briefed by the head of the Metropolitan Police, in person, first thing that morning. She was aware of information that the press had not been given. What she wanted to see was the journalistic opinion, the editorial lines, the media spin. And the pieces she'd read so far didn't look good. As Pym heard footsteps approaching, she closed the browser window.

'Sorry for the delay, minister,' said a besuited middle-aged man who didn't sound sorry at all. 'The prime minister will see you now.' As she stood, the man introduced himself only as Donald. He gave no further details – classic self-importance. Pym guessed he was one of the private secretaries and she would be expected to know his name, to have done her homework. She handed the iPad to a nearby flunkey, smoothed her skirt and followed him down a hallway, trying to breathe slowly. He rapped on the door and immediately admitted her. Before she had a chance to take in the room, Pym was offered a chair and found herself sitting opposite the PM. Neither woman apologised for being late. The PM didn't need to, and Pym didn't want to draw attention to her own tardiness.

'How are you finding the new role, Sue?' asked her boss.

Pym fought back the grimace; she hated being called Sue. It was Susanna. Nobody called her Sue. The PM probably thought it indicated intimacy. If anything, it demonstrated the opposite. Normally, Pym would have pulled someone up on that immediately. But this was the PM. So she let it slide.

'Well, it's early days, Prime Minister,' she replied. 'But I plan to get out from behind the desk as much as possible. Meet the troops on the ground, as it were.'

'Quite right. Minister for Policing and the Fire Service is a challenging role. When I was Home Secretary, it was one of the trickiest portfolios in our department. I want you to know that you have my full support.'

Pym wasn't sure what that might entail, but she offered her thanks anyway. She had begun to crave a cigarette.

'You'll be aware that there are certain sensitivities around our policing strategy, particularly in light of recent events.' The PM's tone had shifted, become more serious.

'Naturally.'

'A shooting on the streets of our capital in which a young man and a police officer are both killed is a recipe for significant unrest. I've just seen on the news that crowds are protesting outside a local police station, not far from here.'

Pym nodded.

'We don't want a repeat of 2011,' continued the PM. 'Accusations that we've lost control of London while I'm off in Europe trying to negotiate our—' She paused, shook her head. 'Never mind. Let's just say that people are watching how we respond to this, both here and abroad. I can't stress how important it is that we get it right.'

'Absolutely.' Pym interlocked her fingers; the communications guy had said that was both authoritative and calm, though she felt neither. 'In fact, I see the current situation as an opportunity to show just how effective our police force is. Firm but fair. A British approach to law enforcement. Dialogue and communication with the public.' Pym had borrowed the last line from Met Police Commissioner Cressida Dick, who had used it in their meeting two hours earlier.

The PM smiled. Pym couldn't tell if it was in agreement or amusement.

'Of course. You're right, Sue,' said the PM. 'And if you handle this incident correctly, people will certainly take notice.'

Pym imagined they'd also take notice if things went tits up. Nevertheless, these were the words she wanted to hear: the hint of an invitation to the top table. To a position in the cabinet. To bigger and better things. Her hands were suddenly clammy.

'Well, I'm afraid I must go; I'm expecting a phone call any moment.' The PM stood and proffered a hand. Pym casually brushed her palm over her skirt on the way up to shake it, hoping the fabric would absorb the sweat. 'I'm told the media are already giving us a hard time,' added the PM. 'The last thing we want is a riot on top of that.'

'Well, I promise not to start one.' Pym regretted the humour immediately. 'I'll keep you updated.'

'Wonderful,' said the PM, guiding her back towards the door. 'You can speak to Donald and he'll make sure I'm in the loop on major developments.'

*Donald.* The private secretary. Great. No direct line to the PM then. Not yet at least. Pym needed to show some initiative.

'I was thinking… if we were to demonstrate the extent of the criminality behind the operation in which those two men were shot last night, it might turn the public opinion in our favour.'

The PM inclined her head slightly. 'Good idea.'

'My plan is to form a small task force to find the arms importer as quickly as possible.'

'Fine.' The PM wafted a hand. 'Do whatever you need to do, just…' She stopped before fixing Pym with a stern gaze. 'Don't let me down, Sue.'

Pym swallowed, nodded and mumbled a goodbye. Day three and already the sword of Damocles was hanging over her. Fortunately, she knew a man who could stop it falling. She resolved to call him as soon as she left. Once they'd given her bloody phone back, obviously.

# CHAPTER THREE

'Welcome to Operation Pluto,' said Detective Chief Inspector Siân Krebs, gesturing around her. 'This is the base from which you will find the people who brought that shipment of weapons to the UK and onto our streets in London.'

Kat Jones looked around the incident room at Lewisham police station. If not well staffed, it was at least well equipped: there were more telephones, computers and white boards than there were people. Six of them were assembled around the meeting table, Boateng alongside her. She'd flushed with pride when he'd asked her to help him on the new, temporary task force. She also knew it would piss off DS Patrick Connelly, who had been left back in the MIT, Lewisham's Major Investigation Team. The Irishman saw himself as Boateng's right-hand man, and senior to her in age and experience if not rank. Jones had dealt with a year of mild cynicism from him since she'd joined the MIT, wrapped up in casual sexism. Fundamentally, she believed Connelly was a good guy. He just had a funny way of showing it. She smirked at the thought of him being given her paperwork while she got the exciting gig.

'Most of you will know DI Zac Boateng,' said Krebs, gesturing towards him. 'He's senior officer investigating the killing of Sergeant Toby Sullivan, committed shortly after 0200 today by Aaron Collins, who was also shot dead during the operation to seize imported weapons.'

A snort came from across the table and Krebs paused. Jones glanced over to its source: DCI Dave Maddox. The burly Lambeth officer had a rugby player's build and permanent stubble beneath his broken nose. She'd met him twice before and both times he'd been abrupt, even aggressive. Nothing she wasn't used to. The only difference between him and the rest of the Met's macho men was his rank.

'Everything alright, Dave?' asked Krebs.

'You said "killing",' he replied. 'Let's call it what it was: murder.'

'Well, we have to be very careful with our choice of words at this stage.'

'Right.'

'Anyway,' continued Krebs. 'We're very fortunate to have DCI Dave Maddox from Lambeth assisting on Op Pluto. As you know, both young men involved last night are – were – residents of Lambeth. So, welcome, DCI Maddox.'

Maddox grunted.

'This is a perfect opportunity to demonstrate inter-borough cooperation.' Krebs surveyed them one by one.

Nobody responded.

'Good.' Krebs indicated a sweaty, slightly overweight man in a dark polo shirt and jeans who had not yet spoken. His face was young, almost babyish, but the grey hair at his temples suggested he was probably mid-forties. 'This is DI Will Chambers, brought on to the team by DCI Maddox. They used to work together. DI Chambers is one of the senior Trident officers in Southwark, well versed in gang activity across south London. He'll bring expertise in handling sources. By tapping into that network, we should get upstream intelligence on arms imports and movement.'

Chambers nodded sagely without making eye contact with anyone. Jones wondered how he built any rapport with his informants. Boateng shifted in his seat and Jones turned to see him staring at Chambers. She knew her boss well enough to spot the hostility.

'Anything you'd like to say, DI Chambers?' asked Krebs.

'Not really,' he replied, cracking chubby knuckles. 'We know what we need to do. I've sent you a request for some operational expenses. Covert payments, that sort of thing.'

'OK, I'll take a look after the meeting and sign it off. Right.' Krebs held out a hand towards Kat. 'This is DS Kat Jones, also from Lewisham MIT. She has a background in Cyber Crime and will quarterback our electronic investigations.'

*Quarterback?* Krebs must have heard an American police officer use the word. She hoped it was in real life rather than on TV.

'Good to meet you all,' said Jones. 'Looking forward to working together.' She knew that was a platitude, but it seemed the safe option when others weren't exactly throwing themselves into the new team. Perhaps they were just in a post-lunch slump.

'We're also joined by Detective Constable Rajiv Patel and Amy Goodhew, who is a civilian analyst. They will provide operational support and develop leads. Welcome to you both.' The junior staff members nodded their appreciation and Patel looked poised to speak when the door flew open. An athletic man of about forty with a gelled quiff and tanned face bowled into the room.

'Traffic on Westminster Bridge was a big fat bitch,' he announced, taking a seat and tugging the lapels of his navy-blue suit, which Jones noticed was tailored. 'I don't normally have to come this far out.'

Krebs narrowed her eyes slightly. 'Well, I'm sure you'll get used to it. I'm DCI Siân Krebs, head of Lewisham MIT, and you must—'

'Kevin Harper, National Crime Agency.' He sniffed, his gaze sweeping the assembled officers and alighting on Jones. She tried not to take an instant dislike to him. Looking away, she saw Maddox and Boateng exchange a smirk.

'You used to work here, I believe.'

'Not *here*,' replied Harper, wrinkling his nose at the surroundings. 'In the Met, yeah. Major narcotics, vice. Talent-spotted to the NCA, jumped ship three years ago.'

'Well, you'll be familiar with our working practices and systems then, although I dare say they've been updated in that time. Mr Harper is our expert on arms importation and will coordinate any international angles to Op Pluto. The arms importer who is our target may be a foreign national.'

'Most of 'em are,' said Harper, adjusting a gold signet ring on his pinkie finger.

Boateng seemed about to say something when Krebs spoke again. 'Now, I'm aware that this is a somewhat disparate group of officers, which brings its challenges, but the hope of our senior command is that you will exemplify the values of cooperation and teamwork which the Met, and our agency partners' – she nodded at Harper – 'consider vital to our success. Particularly in such difficult times of budget reductions, and with a new Minister for Policing. We must show that our ability to detect and counter serious crime together is second to none.'

Krebs did have something of the politician about her, but the words sounded sincere enough to Jones.

'So top brass is watching.' Maddox leaned back in his chair. 'Don't screw up.'

'Thank you, Dave. I wouldn't have put it exactly like that, but it's accurate to say there is a certain amount of scrutiny on this operation from a very high level.'

'And from the street outside the station,' said Boateng.

'Not least,' acknowledged Krebs.

'Will you be in charge day-to-day, ma'am?' asked Jones.

'No. I'll have strategic oversight, but daily tactical command will lie with DCI Maddox, as senior officer present.'

'Surely I'm senior?' Harper placed his palms on the table.

'DCI Maddox is our senior *police* officer.' Krebs's tone left no room for argument. Jones liked her more for shutting Harper down so confidently.

'Thank you, Siân. In that case,' said Maddox, loosening his tie even further. 'I suggest we make a start. Zac, do you want to brief us on Jermaine Mensah?'

Boateng summarised the interview; Jones chipped in with a few details.

'So we're looking for a man named Kaiser,' stated Chambers, stroking his fleshy chin. 'And if Kaiser's an alias, he could be literally anyone in London, or outside the city.'

Boateng shrugged. 'Mensah hadn't met him. Collins might have done, but he's dead, so we can't ask him.'

'And did Mensah say anything else about Kaiser?' asked Harper. 'No.'

Harper arched a well-groomed eyebrow. 'Nothing off record?' 'No.'

'And do we know anything else about Kaiser?'

Jones noticed Boateng hesitate for a fraction of a second. 'No.'

⁘

'Can we read one more chapter, Dad? Please. Mum?' Zac's eleven-year-old son grinned hopefully.

Zac closed the *Black Panther* storybook and placed it on the bedside table. 'Time for lights out, mate.'

'I'll head downstairs,' said his wife, Etta. 'Goodnight, Ko. Sweet dreams.' She planted a kiss on his forehead.

Kofi groaned in disappointment.

'I'll be down in a minute, love,' said Zac. He stayed perched on the edge of Kofi's bed for a moment. 'You OK, son?' he asked, after Etta had left.

Kofi shrugged.

'What's up?' said Zac, gently.

The boy pushed out his lower lip.

'Is it your new school?'

'Maybe.'

Zac put an arm around his son's narrow shoulders. 'I'll tell you something. I had to start a new school too, when I was your age. It was massive, full of huge teenagers. They all smelled terrible.' Zac pinched his nose and Kofi giggled. 'But I got used to it pretty quickly. And before I knew it, I was one of those big teenagers.'

'Were you scared, Dad?'

'Yes, I was.'

'So what did you do?'

'Well, I had my pal Jonny, like you've got your friend Neon. That helped a lot.'

'What else? I mean, what did you do when you were frightened?'

Zac stroked the soft curls of Kofi's hair. 'Do you promise not to tell anyone? It's a secret.'

Kofi nodded quickly.

'OK. I imagined myself as a superhero.' He nodded at the book. 'Like Prince T'Challa, the Black Panther.'

Kofi frowned. 'But Dad, *Black Panther* wasn't out when you were at school.'

'Hey! I'm not that old. The film wasn't out. Comic book was.'

'Did it work?'

'Oh yeah. You know how Prince T'Challa makes a drink from the magic herb and gets the power of the Black Panther? In my mind, I did the same thing. Magic flower, super power!'

Kofi beamed.

'Try it next time you feel a bit scared, son. Imagine yourself as the Black Panther. Then just start doing the thing that's scaring you, and pretty soon you won't feel frightened any more.'

'OK.' The lad seemed to relax a bit.

'And you've got your new phone too, if you need to call us, right?' Zac and Etta had debated the pros and cons of getting their son a mobile – including the perils of exposure to social media – but in the end pragmatism had won out and they'd bought him a simple pay-as-you-go.

'Yeah.'

Zac held out his palm and Kofi slapped it. 'That's my boy.' He kissed the top of Kofi's head and switched off the bedside lamp. 'Goodnight, Prince Kofi.' Zac stood and crossed his forearms over his chest like the Black Panther.

Kofi smiled and repeated the gesture. 'Night, Dad.'

Pulling the bedroom door almost shut, Zac stepped onto the landing. He was hungry and wanted to share his day with Etta. But first, he needed to make a phone call.

●

Kat Jones stood in a housing estate courtyard in Vauxhall, steadying her breathing. She stared up at the wall in front of her. Ten feet high, she reckoned. Impossible.

'You've got this, Kat.' The instructor clapped his hands. 'Just commit to it. All in.'

Easier said than done. But that was the point of a challenge, wasn't it? Despite the fear, this was why Jones loved parkour classes. Since her last romantic disappointment, she'd needed something new in her life. So, at the start of the year, she had begun training with Parkour Generations, and found herself getting stronger and more agile every week. She'd learned to vault, climb, jump and swing from walls, stairs, scaffolding and railings. Moving in new ways. Building herself up physically as well as psychologically. Some coppers had given her stick for it: jokes about superwoman outfits and leaping over piles of paperwork. She ignored the piss-taking. Jones had already chased a couple of suspects since joining the MIT and she was determined to give herself every advantage the next time.

It was a chase that had sown the seed for her future Met career. When she was ten, her father – a police officer in the north London borough of Haringey – had been run down by a car while in pursuit of robbers fleeing a post office. For a while, she couldn't accept that her indestructible old man had died, making her mum hide his photos at home. But, gradually, she got used to him not being there, and his pictures reappeared around the house. As a teenager, she found a better way to cope. Jones wrote a promise to him in a card, vowing to join the Met. She placed it on his grave and swore to continue the work he believed in: protecting the city that was her birthplace and their family's home. She owed it to her dad to train as hard as she could. When she thought about that, even the toughest parkour drill seemed a bit easier, had a bit more purpose.

'Right, left, kick, reach,' said the instructor.

She flexed her hands, wiped them on her T-shirt. Then launched herself into a sprint, planted a foot on the brickwork and stretched upwards. For a second, she felt weightless before her hand hit the wall, about six inches below the top. Her palm raked down the rough surface and she fell to the ground, letting out a growl and inspecting the blood that was seeping out where the skin had come off her fingers.

'You OK, Kat?'

'Fine. Just need a plaster or two.'

Jones went over to her bag and was just applying the third Band-Aid when her mobile rang. She checked the caller: Boateng.

'Zac, what's up?'

'Am I interrupting?'

'Not really. I'm at parkour. You should come to a session.'

He chuckled. 'Not sure I'm really built for that, you know.'

'Anyone can do it.'

'I'll take your word for that.' He coughed. 'Listen, I couldn't tell you back in the office, but I do know something more about this guy Kaiser.'

'What?' she exclaimed, before lowering her voice. 'But we were together in the interview room with Mensah the whole time this morning. He didn't say anything else.'

'It wasn't Mensah who told me.'

Jones was struggling to understand. 'Then who?'

'Darian Wallace.'

'Wallace?' Jones had worked with Boateng last year as they tracked Wallace for a string of murders in south-east London. 'How? Was Kaiser involved in—?'

'Yup. Gun supply. And there's more.'

'Go on.'

'He's one of us.'

'Police?'

'Yes. According to Wallace.'

'Jesus.'

'I'm telling you because I trust you, Kat. And I need your help.'

Jones glanced round, checked no one was in earshot. Others were trying the wall jump. 'You can't do this alone,' she whispered. 'Trying to find the guy who killed Amelia nearly got you murdered. It changes everything if Kaiser is someone in the Met. We'd need the Directorate of Professional Standards to run an investigation. It would—'

'But we haven't got a clue who he is. He could be in the DPS, for all we know. We need to find him.'

'Look, Zac.' She chose her words carefully. 'I know finding Kaiser is about as personal as it gets, but you're taking a huge risk if you don't let anyone else in on that.'

'I am letting someone else in. You.'

A cheer went up. Jones saw someone had cracked the jump and was standing triumphantly on top of the wall.

Jones sighed. If she helped Boateng off the books, he wouldn't be the only one taking a risk. 'I appreciate you telling me. I'll keep it to myself, obviously.'

'Thanks, Kat. See you tomorrow.' He rang off, leaving her with a slight sense of unease as she considered his disclosure. Now wasn't the time to think about that, though. She replaced the phone in her bag, fixed the final plaster over her cuts and stood up. Then she jogged across to take on the wall again.

●

Kaiser had a serious problem. No, that wasn't accurate. Two problems.

The first was the shipment of Škorpions that had been taken. Forty pistols, two grand each after Kaiser's mark-up. Shouldn't have trusted the job to amateurs. That was eighty grand down the plughole, and there were some hard bastards in Prague who were owed twenty grand for the consignment. Hard bastards who charged a lot of interest when they didn't get paid. And who, needless to say, had access to a lot of weaponry.

The second problem was Zac Boateng. Kaiser had been made aware that the copper – with whom Kaiser shared both a professional and personal history – had interviewed that little scrote Mensah in custody. He was a tenacious bastard, Boateng, and now he'd sniffed out a lead, Kaiser knew that he would keep chipping away until he'd found out more. And there was a lot to find.

But perhaps there was a way to deal with both problems in one fell swoop, so to speak. The expression was apt. Not only did it describe a bird of prey descending on its victim, but its first recorded use was in Shakespeare, when Macbeth seeks out his enemy's weak point: his children. Children were certainly Boateng's weak point. That dealt with problem number two.

And as for problem number one, Kaiser could rely on the commodity with consistently high financial value: human life.

# CHAPTER FOUR

**Tuesday, 21 August 2018**

Boateng had skipped breakfast and arrived at work early, using the back entrance to avoid the protesters who had already set up for the day. He'd decided to visit Jermaine Mensah first thing, without stopping by the Pluto incident room. Find out what else Mensah knew about Kaiser before he was forced to join the team effort upstairs. He'd sweet talked the custody sergeant, apologised for the short notice, stressed the urgency. Some fuss had been made about lawyers, but Mensah agreed to see him alone for an unrecorded meeting, aka an 'intelligence interview'. Nothing said could be used as evidence, but that was fine by him. He just wanted leads.

Boateng studied Mensah as he was brought into the small room. Looked like he'd been awake more than forty-eight hours straight. Kid was probably getting the fright of his life being in here. But prison would be worse. Boateng asked the custody officer as nicely as he could for two cups of tea. Pushing his luck, but sometimes it was small things that made a difference to a detainee choosing whether to cooperate or just sit there repeating the words 'no comment'. The constable scowled but Boateng's winning smile and promise to owe him a proper drink seemed to change his mind.

'How's it going, Jermaine?' asked Boateng when they were alone.

'Shit.'

Boateng nodded. No point trying to dress it up. 'This is a tough situation. You got a cell on your own at least?'

'Nah, I'm sharing. Big brer. Snores like a' engine.'

Boateng allowed himself a small laugh. 'Once we know what's happening, we can arrange for your mum and sister to come visit, either here or…' He tailed off, not wanting to mention prison. 'And anyone else.'

'It's just us.'

'Right.' Boateng had suspected Mensah's father wasn't around. He'd seen it far too often: young men and their mothers let down.

'I want them to know I'm OK, though.'

'We can arrange for a call,' said Boateng. 'So, is your family from Ghana?'

'My mum is. Don't know about my dad.'

'Ever been there?'

'Spent two years at school in Kumasi, back in the day.' Mensah's expression lightened. 'Mum thought I was missing out on the motherland.'

Boateng smiled. 'Yeah, my parents said the same thing.'

'For real? They sent you there?'

'Kind of. I went to Accra for a bit after college, worked in my uncle's business.'

There was a knock at the door. The custody officer entered and placed two polystyrene cups of tea on the table. Boateng thanked him and slid one across to Mensah.

'But the tea wasn't as good as it is here. So I came back.' Boateng took a quick sip as Mensah smiled. There was a brief silence before the young man spoke.

'Yesterday you said you could help me. Like, protect me. And my family.'

'I can.' Boateng had argued for an extension to hold Mensah for up to thirty-six hours before charging him. The request had been granted because there was a chance Mensah could assist with Op Pluto, which was being given every priority by top brass. Boateng wasn't complaining: for once his requests were being actioned quickly. But no charge had been agreed yet for Mensah; there were those who wanted accessory to murder or joint enterprise, throwing the book at him. Boateng hoped to use that to cut a deal. But he only had about six hours left.

'How?'

'If you help me find Kaiser, we can take that into account when considering what crime you're charged with, arrange for you to be transferred to a special wing while you're on remand, negotiate a substantial reduction in any sentence. We—'

Mensah held out both hands. 'OK. But I don't know anything about him. I never met him, I don't even know what he looks like. So how can I help you?' The lad cast his eyes down. 'And what'd happen if he found out I'd snitched?'

'We can take care of that, Jermaine. We'll keep your information completely secure. Just tell me anything you can think of.'

'Is this on the record?'

'No.'

Mensah blew on his tea, blinked. 'Snitching,' he said, eventually.

'What?'

'Aaron said that Kaiser had killed a snitch. Or that was the rumour, anyway.'

'Who was the victim?'

'Dunno.'

'Could he have been trying to scare you?' suggested Boateng. He needed something more concrete. 'You know, make sure you didn't get any ideas.'

'Maybe. Aaron told me it was a few years back, in our ends, he said. South London. Kaiser did it personally. Like, executed him.'

Boateng processed the implications of that. 'So he got away with it.'

'Yup.' Mensah's eyes were wider, his nostrils flaring. He was processing the implications too. For his own safety.

'Anything else?'

'Nope.'

'Can you try to find out more?' Chances of that were slim to none while Mensah was in here. But if he were bailed, could be a different story.

Mensah rubbed his chin. 'Dunno. Maybe.'

'It would go a long way to helping your cause.'

The young man looked up and met Boateng's eyes. 'Am I gonna be safe?'

'Yes,' he replied, too quickly. 'You're in police custody. It's the safest place you could be right now.' Boateng heard the uncertainty in his own voice.

They drank their tea, Mensah staring into his cup between sips.

There was another knock at the door. It opened immediately and DI Will Chambers strode in, face flushed. A sheen of perspiration lay on his top lip and at the sides of his nose, dark circles around the armpits of a fresh polo shirt.

'What's going on?' he demanded.

Boateng bit his lip. This was exactly the kind of interference he'd wanted to avoid. 'How did you know I was here?'

'Never mind. Are you speaking to a source without me?'

'Jermaine and I were just having a cup of tea.'

'I can see that, son.' Chambers glared at the detainee.

'And a little chat.'

'You know that running operational sources is my responsibility.' Chambers squared his shoulders, though the effect wasn't physically intimidating. 'I'll need to brief the team on what you've done. What were you talking about, anyway?'

Boateng glanced at Mensah, then shrugged. 'Ghana.'

Darian Wallace sat at the desk in his cramped prison cell. Lying down was more comfortable, but he didn't want to spend all day on a plastic-covered mattress. And the desk was in front of the window, which allowed strips of natural light to filter between the bars. Better than nothing. At least he had his own cell: a perk of the seriousness of his conviction, if you could call it that. Three counts of murder, representing three traitors he'd dealt with, and thirty years before a parole hearing. That was 10,957 days, including leap years. He'd served 419 of them. He paused, calculated: 252,912 hours left. Yup. Hadn't lost the knack for maths. But that was a hell of a lot of hours to fill. Wallace scratched the scar under his collarbone. He'd needed surgery last summer to remove the bullet that had clipped his lung. He had a brer named Zac Boateng to thank for being shot, even though it wasn't the copper who'd pulled the trigger. A year later, the skin over the wound was tight and uncomfortable. On the cold winter days, he'd noticed it was harder to breathe. Not that he got out of breath often, in here.

And he'd been so close to getting away. Then it had all turned to shit, and now here he was: Her Majesty's Prison Belmarsh, in the High Security Unit. Wallace knew he'd been destined for so much more – that he still was, if only he could find a way out. But in nearly fourteen months spent here – broken only by court appearances for his trial – he hadn't yet identified an exploitable weakness in the system. Reckoned his best chance was bribing a guard, but he had no money. He could threaten one of them instead, but he had no one on the outside to follow through with their family. Fraud was an option too, but prisons were wise to scams after the guy who'd faked his own bail letter and walked out of HMP Wandsworth a couple of years back. There had to be a way. He'd find it. Just had to keep thinking.

In the meantime, Wallace was reading every book he could get hold of, trying to occupy his mind, stop himself going nuts with all those hours. He'd nearly finished *Sapiens* by Yuval Noah Harari. The guy argued that it was the ability to believe in shared fiction, like the value of money, that had enabled humans to cooperate and become the dominant animal on the planet. Wallace wasn't convinced. Life had taught him the opposite. Shared belief in money, power and success only made people compete, trying to become the dominant *individual* on the planet. Survival of the fittest. Literally, in his experience.

A heavy knock was quickly followed by the grate sliding up on his door. 'Letter for you, Wallace,' said the screw, placing the already opened envelope on the shelf before slamming the grate shut again. Wallace walked over and examined the front: a woman's script. Not his mum's; in any case, her dementia was surely worse now, and he doubted she was capable of writing coherently. He unfolded the paper inside, smoothing it against the back of the door, and read:

*Dear Darian,*

*You're probably surprised to hear from me after what happened. To be honest, I'm surprised to be writing to you, but I had to. There's something I have to tell you. After you stayed with me last summer, I realised about a month later that I was pregnant. It was a really hard choice but I decided to keep the baby, and now we – that's right, we – have a son. He's five months old. I know he's definitely yours because I wasn't sleeping with no one else at the time. So, you're a dad! I thought you should know. Sorry it's taken so long to write to you but after you left I was so scared I didn't want to be in touch with you at all. Later on I thought you had a right to know, and maybe you said things to me at the time that you didn't mean. Anyway, it's so exciting that little Reece (by the way he's not so little any more!) has a brother. I'll teach them to play nicely together when they're old enough. I've*

*named our son Leon, after your mum, because I know how
special she is to you. They've told me I can visit you if I want,
once I've done some security checks and stuff. I don't really
want to bring Leon (and Reece) into a prison, but I will if I
have to. I want you to meet your son, and I hope you want
to meet him too. He's beautiful. Write back to me if you can.
      Jas (and Leon)
      x*

Wallace rubbed his eyes, blinked. He was grateful for the
isolation; no one could see him crying. He pictured Jasmine
Fletcher, his ex, cradling their baby. The woman who had dumped
him the previous time he'd been to prison, but who'd never
completely broken away. Wallace was too analytical to believe in
fate or anything similarly vague and metaphysical, but he felt an
opportunity had been gifted to him: the chance to be a father,
to help and teach his son; not mete out abuse like his own dad,
the drunk, aggressive soldier who'd breezed in and out of the flat
then fucked off back to his hometown in Scotland when Wallace
was a teenager. When he was home, Wallace's dad had slapped
both him and his mum around. His poor mum, Leonie, who had
emigrated from Jamaica to escape the violence. Now, for Wallace,
a son of his own was a chance to do something different with his
life. Or, it would be, if he wasn't in here.

He folded the letter into the envelope, wiped his eyes with the
back of his hand and walked across to the window. Stared out
through the wire mesh shutters on the outside of the bars. His
gaze travelled over a small park, past another building to the high
perimeter wall and into the world beyond. Now everything had
changed.

He had to get out.

# CHAPTER FIVE

Susanna Pym had left work at 8 p.m. She was beginning to realise that, in her new job, that counted as an early night. She'd taken a black cab from Westminster to the Oxford and Cambridge Club on Pall Mall. She could easily have walked it, but the car was more private; these days you never knew who was watching, photographing, filming, uploading. Careers could be ruined in seconds, with a single post on social media. And she didn't want her next meeting to be captured in any format.

At the reception she showed her tatty old membership card and watched the doorman squint at it then glance back up to her. The photo was twenty years old, but she still thought there was a strong likeness. Besides, there was no point getting a new card; she barely ever came here. Only when she needed to meet someone – how to put it? – discreetly. She asked to see the guest register and spotted the name John Archer, his sign-in time fifteen minutes ago. Since you weren't allowed to smoke in the Smoking Room, she knew where she'd find her visitor.

Pym emerged onto the roof terrace and spotted the lone figure on the far side, puffing away, his head wreathed in grey ribbons. Neither of them had switched to e-cigarettes or vapes. In that respect, they shared an affinity for the authentic, the old school. But that was where the similarities stopped. He turned as the door shut behind her.

'Mr Archer.' She nodded, taking a seat beside him and extracting a packet of cigarettes from her handbag.

'Your ladyship,' replied the visitor.

Pym tutted. 'Please don't call me that.' She put a cigarette to her lips and the man held out a lighter. Pym inhaled deeply, closing her eyes.

'Fine. Sue.'

'Or that.'

'Only joking.' The man grinned. 'Susanna.'

'Thank you.' She took another drag. 'How's it all going then? Op Pluto.'

'Well, considering we've got coppers from three different boroughs and the NCA, it's a roaring success. We haven't killed each other yet.'

'Very funny. Any leads that haven't been briefed to the Home Office?'

The man stubbed out his own cigarette, reached down for a whisky glass and took a sip. Then immediately lit another cigarette. 'We've made inquiries with the Czech police about the suppliers. Don't hold out much hope there, though. The pistols could've passed through a middleman in any country between the Czech Republic and here.'

'Fine. What about the young chap in custody? Has he been charged?'

'Yeah, very quietly. Possession of firearms. Didn't shift the crowds outside Lewisham station, though. And a lot of police are pissed off, reckon he should've got something much more serious.'

'Does that mean he's cooperating?'

'Seems to be, but I don't reckon he knows much about Kaiser.'

'He's a dead end then?' She realised that was an unfortunate metaphor in the circumstances.

'Probably. We'll see.'

'What else?'

'Techies are trying to get phone data off the dead guy's mobile. Aaron Collins. Might tell us who he was in touch with, where he was going. Unless they were comms savvy. Kid they've charged claims he was in the dark. He says Collins was navigating and he didn't know where they were headed. Smart.'

Pym felt the frustration growing – a tightness in her jaw and shoulders that seemed to have come with her new job. 'So how close are we to finding this Kaiser fellow?'

'Not very, by the look of it. In fact, barring some miracle off that dead fella's phone, you might want to focus your attention on other things. Stuff where you've got a chance of success. Like improving our pensions, for example.'

'Ask the Treasury about that.'

The man grunted; it might've been a laugh. 'Talking of money…'

Pym tutted. 'You'll get it.'

'I'm sticking my neck out, passing you material from a live investigation like this. It's a risk.'

'You're not the only one taking a risk,' replied Pym sharply. 'Don't forget, it was me who put you on that task force. You'll benefit from it.'

'Well.' The man paused, blew a cloud of smoke upwards. 'We're both screwed if our arrangement gets out.'

'I'm well aware of that.' She tried to relax, took a long drag. Mutually assured destruction. She seemed to have a habit of getting into those relationships.

'We've managed it for years with no problems, though,' said the man, suddenly turning to look her in the eye.

'Let's hope it stays that way.'

'Some money would help maintain the status quo.'

'Message received.' Pym stubbed out the cigarette harder than was necessary. 'Anything else? Anything at all? I'll be damned if I'm letting some journalist get one over on me tomorrow.'

The guy cracked his knuckles. 'There is one thing I'm not sure about.'

'Right.'

'There's a DI on the Pluto team called Zac Boateng. Lewisham, Major Investigations. He's a good bloke, but this morning he met the kid arrested at the shoot-out, Mensah, alone.'

Pym shrugged. 'You said he was cooperating. Perhaps this chap Boateng was just cutting a deal.'

'Maybe. But he didn't share anything from the interview with us.'

'Look at the recording.'

He rolled his eyes. 'Yes, thank you. That had occurred to me. It wasn't recorded. A so-called intelligence interview – with no product.'

'Hm. So what are you saying? You don't trust Boateng?'

The man blew out his cheeks. 'He's a nice guy, and a solid copper. But he knows something about this that he isn't telling us.'

'Well, keep an eye on him, will you?'

The man nodded, puffed on his cigarette.

Pym wasn't quite sure how these things worked. She was paying a man to snoop. That man was an official. Technically, she supposed it constituted corruption. On the other hand, the ultimate aim was making the streets of London and the wider UK safe. No one could argue with that intention. So, if a little chat here or there helped achieve that, and some expenses were incurred along the way, then that was defensible, wasn't it?

She felt the urge for another cigarette.

⦿

Zac knew it wasn't advisable, but he did it anyway. Leaning right over the bubbling pot of jollof rice on the hob, he inhaled deeply through his nose. A cloud of steam stung his face and made his eyes water, but it was worth it. The aroma was incredible: hot pepper, tomato, garlic. He tasted the mixture and added a touch more curry powder and salt. He was ravenous, eager to dive straight in, but that was the dilemma with jollof: the longer you let it stew, the better the flavour. Like the self-control test for kids he'd learned for his psychology degree at night school: can you resist eating one marshmallow for ten minutes if you get two at the end? It was all about patience and discipline, which didn't always come naturally to him. In any case, he couldn't start without Etta. She was upstairs making sure Kofi brushed his teeth properly.

In the meantime, he cracked open a pale ale from the local brewery and poured his wife a glass of wine. Dizzy Gillespie was working his magic on trumpet through the stereo. Jollof, beer, music, family. Ordinarily, all of this would have meant life was good. It *was* good. But Zac's thoughts kept returning to Kaiser: to the prospect of finding him and the possibility that he might have got away with another murder, maybe even on Zac's turf in Lewisham. He'd wanted to jump in and start investigating this morning, check unsolved cases that might have matched the victim Mensah talked about. See if that could lead them to Kaiser. But like the marshmallows or the jollof, it'd be better if he waited. Made a plan. Particularly when he didn't know who he could trust. He'd not had a chance to tell Jones about it privately yet. He'd ask for her help tomorrow.

'Smells amazing, love.' Etta walked into the kitchen, planted a kiss on his neck and reached for her glass of wine. She'd let her hair down and changed into jeans. Zac thought she looked great. 'Thank you for dinner, Chef Boateng,' she said, holding out the glass. He chinked his beer bottle against it then made an expansive gesture towards the cooker.

'Tonight, madam, we have roasted vegetables served on a bed of traditional Ghanaian jollof rice, and—'

'Er…' She held up a finger. 'Don't you mean Nigerian?'

'Like I said, Ghanaian.'

'Everyone knows where jollof really comes from.'

'What, Senegal?'

She laughed and took a sip of wine.

'Anyway,' he continued. 'If you visit a Ghanaian restaurant, you should expect Ghanaian dishes, that's all I'm—'

She leaned in and kissed him. Zac smiled. He'd managed not to think about work for nearly a whole minute.

Etta grinned and tilted her head to one side. 'Got any specials on the menu?'

'Depends on whether you want dessert,' he replied.

'Reckon I do.'

The doorbell rang.

Etta checked her watch. 'Expecting anyone?'

'Nope. You?'

'Don't think so.' She shrugged, put her glass down. 'I'll see who it is. Probably neighbours.'

'I'll plate up,' he said, grabbing a serving spoon as Etta padded down the hallway. A high-pitched engine revved out in the street and faded. He heard the front door open as he began heaping jollof onto their plates. But no voices followed. He paused, listened. 'Who is it, love?' he called.

The front door shut.

'Etta?'

'No one,' she said casually, walking back down the hallway. Zac heard the crackle of plastic as Etta reappeared in the kitchen, clutching a large bouquet of flowers.

He frowned. 'Who was it?'

'There was no one there,' she said. 'These were lying on the doorstep. A scooter was driving off, I think, but I didn't get a proper look at it. Probably the delivery guy. That's kind of lazy, just buzzing the door and leaving.'

'Yeah.' Zac wasn't so sure. 'Can I see?'

He dropped the serving spoon back in the jollof, went over to her and peered into the bouquet. The flowers were lilies. Traditional at funerals. People said the white petals symbolised the innocence of the departed soul. He sometimes put them on Amelia's grave during their weekly visits.

'There's a card,' said Etta, reaching into the bunch. She held it up, turned it over. '"Sorry for your loss."'

'What?'

'That's what it says. "Sorry for your loss."' Etta handed him the card. 'What a shame. I guess they were meant for someone else. Could be one of the neighbours, I suppose. But we can't exactly go round asking if they've had a bereavement, can we?' She groaned. 'If only the delivery guy had waited, we could've told him.'

Zac examined the card. It was handwritten in capitals, just those four words. Nothing else. The reverse was blank. 'Did you see the person on the scooter?'

'No. I told you, I just saw it going around the corner. It's a mistake, that's all.'

'Maybe not.'

'What d'you mean?' She paused, glanced at the card. 'You think this is about Amelia?'

'I don't know.'

'Zac?'

He didn't want to tell her what he really thought: that it was unlikely to be a botched delivery, an accident. And if it was deliberate, then it was about Amelia. About their murdered daughter, who had simply been in the wrong place at the wrong time. But that wasn't all. The card must have come from someone who knew about Amelia – and who wanted to be anonymous. That probably made it about the person – or people – who had got away with killing her. And, with a message delivered to their home, it was also about them. About Etta, Kofi and him. There was a small chance that Etta was right and the bouquet was intended for another house, but in his mind, the more likely explanation was that the flowers had come from the one person who connected Amelia to the case that Zac had started working yesterday.

Kaiser.

He took the lilies from Etta and put the card back inside. He might need to submit it as evidence down the line. Not that he expected it to yield anything traceable. Kaiser was too smart for that. As far as Zac was concerned, though, Kaiser had given him proof of one thing: six years after their paths had first crossed, Zac was on his radar again. And so was Zac's family.

# CHAPTER SIX

**Wednesday, 22 August 2018**

Boateng glanced around the canteen, checked they weren't in earshot of anyone else. 'So, what do you think?' he asked quietly, rotating the cardboard coffee cup with his fingertips while he waited for an answer. He'd filled Kat Jones in on Mensah's private disclosure, Chambers's interruption of the interview and the bunch of flowers that had arrived on his doorstep last night.

Jones took a swig of coffee, shook her head. 'I think it sounds dangerous to go it alone, for a start.'

'Kaiser's trying to threaten me,' said Boateng. 'But I'm not backing down. I won't be intimidated.' His jaw was set.

'Look, I know this is personal for you, Zac. But you can't keep it that way. If this guy has killed before, then he's capable of killing you, your family, Jermaine Mensah, any of us.' Boateng understood what she meant by those final words. If she helped him, she'd be at risk too. He knew he was asking a lot.

Boateng tapped his cup on the table. 'Then we stay alert, watch our backs. So, you in?'

Jones sighed. 'Then there's the question of professional integrity. Or lack of it. We can't withhold what Mensah told you. We should get everyone else in on this.'

'All I'm suggesting is that you and I do a bit of digging around,' he said casually. 'Just to start things off.'

'I know you better than that. You want to solve this supposed murder and find Kaiser in the process.' She stared at him.

He hesitated, then nodded his acknowledgement.

'And you want to do it unofficially,' she added.

'If we start a new murder inquiry connected to Pluto, or reopen an old case, then it's on the system, maybe even in the news. Kaiser can stay ahead of the game. Do whatever he needs to do: destroy evidence, intimidate or eliminate witnesses, frame someone else. We can't let him know we're investigating.' He spread his hands. 'Can't you see?'

'Yeah, I get that, but…' Jones took a deep breath, blew out her cheeks. 'Ah, I don't know.'

'I thought that if anyone could understand a family reason for investigating a crime, it'd be you,' blurted Boateng. He knew he'd crossed a line as soon as the words were out.

She held up a finger. 'Don't you dare bring my dad into this.'

'Sorry.'

They sat in silence, each sipping their coffee.

'Listen,' Boateng said, his tone more measured. 'Kaiser's been doing this for years and getting away with it. In *our* force. Now we've got a chance to nail him. We're lucky to even be in this position. He doesn't make a lot of mistakes, but this time he did. Or the people working for him did.'

'And two men died.'

'I know. I'm guessing Kaiser wasn't too bothered by that loss of life. And it would've been a hell of a lot worse if those Škorpions had made it to the street. That's why we need to get him this time. Put him away. Imagine that on your CV.' Boateng drained the rest of his coffee and slapped the cup down. 'We won't get a better opportunity.'

Another silence hung between them.

'Why me, Zac?' She bit her lip, paused. 'Why do you want *my* help?'

'You mean apart from the fact that you've done some bloody great work on murders in the past year?'

She gave a small laugh of embarrassment. 'Yeah, apart from that.'

'Because I trust you. And you've got good instincts. You think outside the box.'

'Thanks.'

'And besides,' he added, 'six years ago, when Amelia was killed, you hadn't even joined the Met. So, you're the only person I'm sure can't be Kaiser.'

They stared at one another for a second before both cracked a smile. Jones wiped a hand over her face. 'OK. Just tell me what you're suggesting, and I'll think about it.'

He leaned in. 'We check all unsolved murders in the past five years in south London. Look for any that have the hallmarks of an execution – close-range gunshot as cause of death, restraint, isolated location. We profile the victim – I'd expect it to be a young man with some gang affiliation. I can cover Lewisham and Croydon. You could do Southwark and Lambeth. Then we move out to other boroughs as needed.'

'What if Mensah's wrong, or Kaiser was lying? Or it's true but the body hasn't been found?'

He'd considered that. *Then we're screwed.* 'We have to start somewhere,' he replied, trying to sound upbeat. 'If it turns into something where we need forensics, we go back to see Mensah in prison and confirm it with him. Then we can make it official.'

Jones sipped her coffee.

'Alright,' she said, eventually. 'I'm not promising all my spare time on this. But I'll start looking at the records later on. Once we've had that conference call with the Czech police.'

'You're a legend.' He smiled.

'Easy.' Jones sat back, crossed her arms. 'Don't push your luck.'

'It's true.'

'Just tell me one thing,' she said. 'Why were you giving Chambers the evil eye yesterday in Krebs's briefing?'

Boateng pressed his lips together. Knew he had to be straight with her. 'When Amelia was killed, Chambers was one of the investigators. He was on the Southwark murder squad at the time, mostly covering gang violence alongside the Trident team. Very good at his job, by all accounts. But somehow he got absolutely nowhere with working out who shot Amelia.'

'That's because Kaiser destroyed evidence, right?'

'Maybe.'

'What do you mean?' Jones's gaze flicked around. 'You think Chambers might be Kaiser? Or working for him?'

'I didn't say that.'

She was about to respond when his phone rang. It was Krebs. He showed the screen to Jones, pulled a face and answered.

'Morning, ma'am,' he said cheerfully.

'Zac. I'm sure you've seen the protesters that are still camped outside our station.'

'You can hear them even if you use the back entrance.'

'Right. Well, the crowd isn't getting any smaller. They're all over social media, using a hashtag about justice for Aaron Collins. And word from the top is that we need something to quell public anger. The Chief Super is going to do a statement about the inquiry into Collins's shooting, how the firearms officer who shot him is being assessed, body cam footage reviewed, et cetera. I need you to do a press briefing later, focusing on the weapons smuggling. Potentially even go out and engage with the protestors.'

'But, ma'am, surely it's a better use of my time to—'

'What are you doing now, by the way?'

He hesitated. 'Talking through some operational ideas with DS Jones.'

'In the incident room?'

'Er, no.' He scanned around in case she was watching. 'In the canteen.'

'Canteen?'

'We're just getting some coffee.'

'Hm.' Krebs paused. 'Well, we need you both back up in the Pluto room for a briefing in five minutes, please. And everyone needs to get their shifts up on the ops board.'

'Ma'am.'

She rang off and Boateng pocketed the phone. Shook his head. Jones was grinning. 'Piss off,' he said. 'Just wait till you're a DI.'

•

'You wanted to see me, ma'am?' Kat Jones shifted her weight from one foot to the other. She didn't know why she was here, standing in front of Krebs's desk. She felt as though she was about to receive a detention from the headmistress. But maybe that was just her guilty conscience after agreeing to help Boateng.

'Have a seat, Kat,' said Krebs pleasantly.

Jones took the chair, tried to relax.

'How are you finding Op Pluto?'

'It's challenging work, ma'am. A complex operation. But I'm enjoying working with some new people, bringing our expertise together. Hopefully we'll nail Kaiser.'

'Mm, that's the spirit. Is everything OK in the team?'

'Yes, fine.'

Krebs steepled her fingers. 'I know that when officers of different backgrounds are asked to work together, certain tensions can arise.'

Jones gave a small shake of her head. 'Not sure what you mean, ma'am.'

'It's been brought to my attention that DI Boateng is being particularly proactive in his inquiries.'

'That's his style, and it's probably a good thing.' Jones was a bit uneasy about where this was going.

'It's just that, well, his communication is somewhat less enthusiastic than his investigative efforts.'

Jones didn't say anything.

'I've been told, in confidence,' continued Krebs, 'that DI Boateng spoke to the young man detained at the shooting incident. Privately.'

'I don't know, ma'am.' Jones sensed she was now on dangerous ground.

'It's imperative in an investigation of this strategic significance that all – and I do mean all – information is shared fully within the Pluto team. That includes me.'

Jones shifted slightly in her seat. 'We have the daily briefings, the—'

'I'm talking about off-record material too. Things that are not being shared with the main investigation.'

Her heart was beating a bit faster now.

'You've mentioned your concerns about DI Boateng to me before,' continued Krebs. 'In December last year, you remember?'

'Yes, but that was because—'

'You and I both know, Kat, that DI Boateng is a talented and experienced detective. But he also has a tendency to – how shall I put it? – go off on his own a bit, doesn't he?'

That was true. Jones nodded once.

'Now, I don't need to remind you how important this inquiry is. Two people have been shot dead, the new Minister for Policing is taking a personal interest, senior management in the Met are requesting updates and' – she gestured to the outside of the building – 'the public is watching us very closely indeed. Pluto is the kind of operation that could define a career.' Krebs raised her eyebrows, which Jones took to mean *your* career.

'But how it defines a career,' Krebs went on, 'depends on our choices. And it depends on us all playing by the same rules.'

'Of course, ma'am.'

'So if we have anyone on our team who is playing by a different set of rules – their own rules – then it rather spoils the game for everyone else. Don't you agree?'

It was a leading question if ever Jones had heard one. 'I suppose so.'

'You've had a stunning career so far, Kat.'

Jones felt herself redden slightly at the praise.

'You're one of the youngest detective sergeants we have in the whole of the Met. Impressive work under your belt already – in Cyber Crime and now here in Major Investigations. You apprehended a killer last summer and—'

'That was really DI Boateng's collar. He was the one who—'

'You found the evidence that proved decisive in the December murders, too. What I'm saying is you have the potential to go very far in this organisation, Kat.' Krebs tilted her head. 'All the way to the top, on the fast track. You're bright, motivated and capable.'

'Thank you, ma'am.'

'I know you're close to DI Boateng, and he's something of a mentor to you. But it would be a terrible shame if your progress was impeded by some of his more... let us say, rash decision making, don't you think?'

'Um, perhaps, yes.' What was Krebs getting at?

'Therefore, I'd like to ask you, in confidence, to let me know personally if DI Boateng is crossing any procedural red lines in his work.'

Jones wasn't sure how to reply. Spying on Boateng?

'I will, of course, treat anything you tell me in the strictest confidence,' added Krebs.

'Mm.'

'We have to consider the impact on the team's work, as a whole, on the force. I know it might seem awkward coming directly to me, and a bit irregular, but we can't have lone operators damaging high-level work, can we?'

'No, ma'am.'

'So, will you do that for me, Kat?' Krebs fixed her with a level gaze.

The silence grew uncomfortable.

'Yes, ma'am,' she replied quietly. There wasn't much else she could say.

•

'You haven't touched your sandwiches, Zac.'

Boateng looked up from the briefing notes. Maddox was pointing at the triangular packet on the table between them. It lay unopened, alongside Maddox's demolished counterpart.

'You have them, Dave.'

'Sure?'

'Yeah, I'm not hungry right now.'

'Few nerves about the press conference, is it? Gotta have something in your belly before you go in front of that pack of wolves.' Maddox grinned and reached across to grab Boateng's unwanted lunch. 'Do you want a hand? After the Chief Super, we could go Krebs, me, you – split it up.'

'Thanks, I've got it.'

'OK.' Maddox tore open the packet and took a bite before immediately speaking with his mouth full. 'If you get any awkward questions about Aaron Collins's death, you know the lines that the lawyers agreed?'

Boateng tapped the paper with his biro. 'Body cam footage records him opening fire on the officers first. There's a brief delay and they return fire. Even if they had been able to assess that his magazine was empty, there was every chance he was reloading and still therefore posed immediate threat to life. All within standard rules of engagement.' He hoped that was true, though he had no way of knowing for sure.

'Spot on.' Maddox swallowed, shook his head. 'Can you believe they're trying to pin that "unlawful killing" bullshit on us? Sergeant Sullivan was murdered by that little wanker. Unlawful…' he repeated, as if the words tasted unpleasant.

'There's no doubt Collins murdered Sullivan. But the crowds are on to the timing of the shots.' Boateng wagged the pen at him. 'It's trending on Twitter.'

'So you're going to hold them off and remind them why the hell we pulled those guys over in the first place. The Škorpions are going to be displayed alongside you to emphasise the point. Just don't be tempted to use one on the media.' He grunted a laugh and took another bite of sandwich. 'You've done this loads of times, Zac. You're in charge.'

'Well, Krebs is—'

'Yeah, she's in charge-charge, that's why she's topping and tailing the press conference. But you're the one who knows the granular detail. They'll listen to you. And seriously,' he added with a half-smile, 'could you imagine Harper or Chambers doing a better job?'

Boateng began to relax. He reached across and took the packet back from Maddox. 'Actually, I will have the other half.'

*

Darian Wallace closed one eye and took aim. Then he smacked the cue ball into the stripe at the far end of the pool table. It missed the pocket and rebounded off the cushion, tapping the black into a side pocket.

'Unlucky,' said the bearded man he was playing.

Wallace grunted and passed the cue to the next guy. This was about exciting as it got during 'association time': the five hours a day they were obliged to spend with each other in communal areas. The Muslim guys chatted away, walked and prayed together, or just played table football and pool. The older guys sat in the library. The gangsters lifted weights, got big. Wallace drifted between all of it, not feeling part of any group. He hadn't made any friends, but that was OK by him. People knew what he was in for and gave him a bit of distance. In any case, he had a lot to think about now. Like being a dad.

And getting out of here.

Apparently, no one had ever escaped from Belmarsh prison. Attempts had been made and foiled, but the countermeasures were tight. Fourteen locked doors between his cell in the High Security Unit and the outside world. Facial ID, X-ray scanners and metal detectors for anyone coming in, including staff. Staff rotated out regularly to prevent them being manipulated by inmates. Inmates rotated to new cells every few months, presumably to stop a *Shawshank Redemption*-style breakout. This was why the HSU at Belmarsh was called the 'prison within a prison'. Even so, there had to be a way.

The TV caught Wallace's eye.

It was running BBC News on mute, the closed captions informing him that a major shipment of firearms had been intercepted on the streets of south London. Video footage ran above the headlines, the camera panning over a large table where dozens of identical weapons had been laid out. Wallace recognised them as Škorpion machine pistols. He'd been offered the chance to buy one, once, by Kaiser. He didn't like them personally: they were too big to hide in your clothing; better suited to scaring people. Still, the Škorpion was a serious piece. And there were a lot of them on display. He grabbed the remote, took the TV off mute.

Wallace heard the word 'Lewisham' seconds before the video cut to a press conference. The backdrop was a tiled set of Met Police logos with some slogan about working together to make

London safe. Cameras clicked and flashbulbs popped, and in the middle of it all was a man he recognised all too well.

Zachariah Boateng.

The detective was talking about a police officer who'd been shot dead in the early hours of Monday morning. Wallace hadn't been paying much attention to the news that day – must've missed it. And a young man had also, regrettably – according to Boateng – been shot and killed. Someone called Aaron Collins. A mugshot of a young white guy with a shaved head flashed up. Wallace didn't know him. Some footage played of crowds outside Lewisham police station; maybe a couple of hundred people, with placards and everything. A woman at the front had a megaphone and was leading chants about justice and saying no to a police state. The feed cut back to Boateng, who was talking about arms smuggling and the danger it posed to the community. He didn't look like he wanted to be in front of the cameras.

Wallace became aware that a few other inmates were standing around him, watching too. He began to think. Škorpion weapons smuggled into south London. Had to be Kaiser; he was the only person Wallace knew who could get hold of the Škorpion. A police officer and a young man dead. A lot of public interest. Boateng working on the investigation. Wallace handed the remote control to the guy alongside him. Then he went over to the window and let the sunlight warm his face.

There might be a way out after all.

# CHAPTER SEVEN

Boateng cast around the Pluto incident room to check no one was paying attention to him, then pulled a chair up to Jones's desk. She had a map of south London on the screen and what looked like mobile cell site data alongside it.

'Got anything?' he asked quietly.

She hesitated, had a little glance behind her, then flipped some pages in her notepad and showed him. 'There's been nearly eight hundred recorded homicides in London since 2011,' she began, tapping the digits with her biro. 'Seventeen of those were gunshot victims in the four boroughs we're checking. Twelve of those cases are solved. The convictions seem legit – solid forensics, known rivalries or vendettas. I've made a list of the unsolved ones here.' She lifted the page and Boateng saw five names.

'Nice work, Kat.' It was better than he'd hoped for; she'd even managed to cover the two boroughs he'd been planning to search.

'It's a start.' Jones kept her voice low. 'Like we said, assuming Mensah's story is even true, Kaiser might have covered his tracks in any number of ways. Unconventional method, destroyed the body, hidden it, framed someone for the crime. It could still be a missing person case, for all we know.'

'Yeah, but this gives us something to work with. Can I?' He angled the pad, produced his own notebook and began copying the names.

Jones didn't say anything else. 'You OK?' asked Boateng, pausing to look at her.

'Yeah, fine.'

'Sure?'

'Why wouldn't I be?'

'Well…' He nodded at the notebook. 'This isn't strictly official. But I really appreciate the help.'

She waited for him to finish writing and then flipped the pages back to cover her list. 'What happens now?'

He pushed out his lower lip, considered the options. 'With five cases, we can study the files, maybe add in a couple of extra gunshot murders to hide our interest. Let's see if there was anything unusual about the scenes, the victims, the progress of the cases. Evidence going missing, witnesses changing their stories. If it doesn't feel right, flag it. Then we go from there.'

Jones didn't reply.

'Kat?'

She seemed about to speak, but the heavy footfall made them both turn. Kevin Harper was striding over. He wore a crisp white shirt that was slightly too tight. Boateng guessed the colour was designed to show off his tan, the size to show off his muscles.

'How's it going?' said Harper, focusing his attention on Jones.

'Fine,' she replied cautiously.

'Alright, Kev.' Boateng nodded.

'Kevin. Not Kev.'

'My bad,' said Boateng. He couldn't resist a little prod. 'I thought that's what everyone call—'

'It's Kevin.' Harper sniffed. He looked pissed off.

'It's just that I heard—'

'You know, this is one of the reasons I left the Met. People not giving me the respect I deserve.'

'Sorry, Kevin, I didn't mean to…' Boateng trailed off when he saw Harper's grin.

Teeth gleaming, he pointed at Boateng. 'Ah! Got you!' He clapped Boateng on the shoulder, harder than necessary. 'Chill out, yeah?' He shook his head, turning to Jones. 'His face, eh? Course that's not why I left.'

Boateng forced a laugh. He was glad Harper wasn't taking himself quite so seriously, but his initial assessment had still been on the money: Harper was the kind of guy who felt the need to dominate any situation. That's why he didn't like the fact that Maddox was in charge of Pluto, and he didn't like Boateng undermining him. Harper was a self-styled alpha male, a silverback. Or, to use the technical term, a twat. Jones looked bemused by the whole performance. If Harper was trying to impress her, he was going about it the wrong way.

Harper surveyed their workspace. 'So, what are you two working on?'

Boateng exchanged a glance with Kat. She pointed at her computer screen. 'Mapping the route taken by Collins and Mensah on Sunday night,' she replied. 'Trying to work out where they might've been headed.'

'Had Collins put anything into Google Maps on his phone?' asked Harper.

Jones shook her head. 'Not for that night. I'm trying to cross-reference with his location history, but it's patchy.'

'Great stuff.' Harper's gaze lingered on her. He placed a hand on her shoulder briefly. 'Keep it going.' Then he swivelled towards Boateng.

'Listen, Zac, I've got a job for you. Ballistics lab on Lambeth Road have started looking at the MP5 Kurz they found on Collins. I need you to go down there and get the results of their tests immediately. Expedite the analysis; make sure they haven't missed anything. Then Patel or Goodhew can check it against the databases, including the European ones I can access, to see if the weapon's been used before.'

It was a key investigative angle, but Boateng bristled at being given orders by Harper. The guy wasn't in charge. He wasn't even in the Met any more. 'Does it need to be me?' He checked his watch: just after 4 p.m. 'I've got to pick up my kid in half an hour.' He'd planned to come back to the station after Etta got in from work, if needed.

'I can go,' offered Jones.

'We need you here, Doris,' said Harper, tapping the top of her monitor. 'This is critical.'

'Doris?' she frowned.

'Sorry. Kat.' Harper corrected himself and gave her what Boateng presumed was meant to be a winning smile. His teeth were whiter than his shirt. The guy had the vibe of a cut-price professional footballer. Boateng hoped Jones knew better than to fall for it.

'I could do it,' she said, flicking her eyes from Harper to Boateng and back. 'I've not been to that lab yet. I want to learn a bit more.'

'I asked Maddox, and he thought it was best you go, Zac. He said you've got more experience than the rest of us with ballistics evidence.'

'Seriously,' said Jones. 'I don't mind. I can—'

'No, it's fine, Kat. I'll go.' Boateng took out his mobile. 'I'll just tell Kofi to wait at the school. He's had a kids' activities club there all day, finishes at four thirty. Got to put him somewhere in the summer holidays, you know?'

'Lovely,' said Harper. 'Right. Let me know what you find, Zaccy boy. I'm off out again.' He took a final look at Jones and walked away.

They turned back to the screen and Boateng made a face of mock confusion. 'Since when have I been "Zaccy boy"?'

'Never mind that – why am I Doris?'

Boateng grimaced. 'Doris Day, good lay. Old-school police slang.'

'Prick.' She wrinkled her nose in disgust.

'I'd better go then,' said Boateng. 'Team spirit and all that.'

'Why don't I come too?' Jones spun her chair to face him.

'Harper's probably right: it's more important for you to work on this.'

She narrowed her eyes. 'You want me to carry on with those checks, don't you?'

'I didn't say that,' he protested. 'Just a question of division of labour.' He shrugged.

'Fine.' She held up a finger of warning. 'But I want to get some ballistics experience at some point.'

Boateng reckoned that was just a matter of time.

'Zac?'

'Yeah?'

'You'll let me know what you're doing, won't you? I don't want to get caught out here.'

'For sure.'

Boateng sent a text to tell Kofi he'd be half an hour late and that his son should follow the usual routine in this situation: get a snack from the vending machine, wait at the school, read a book. He hesitated a moment before hitting send, recalling the flowers on their doorstep last night. No, he was overreacting. There were plenty of grown-ups there to supervise the kids. And they didn't let anyone leave without an adult. It was fine.

Sent.

●

'And that is why we must' – Susanna Pym emphasised the final word with a vertical movement of her fist, thumb on top, firm without being aggressive – 'I repeat, *must* be resolute in the face of this threat from individuals who seek to bring a gun culture to *our* Britain.'

She was on fire: the moment was hers.

Journalists were assembled outside the Home Office entrance. The block placed behind Pym's lectern elevated her slightly above them all. Subtle assertion of command – planned in advance, of course. She briefly pictured herself at the main speaker's box in the House of Commons, shooting down the Corbynistas with polished rhetoric to rapturous applause from her own benches.

'I am making it a personal priority to disrupt arms smuggling to our shores. And I know that the prime minister shares my vision,' she continued, making eye contact with several key reporters whom her communications director had individually invited to ensure favourable coverage. They all nodded enthusiastically.

Pym had already batted away a few alarmists from the left-wing press asking about the crowds outside Lewisham police station, the protests for justice, the social media trending. Her answers flowed as if she were reading from an autocue: 'In a democracy, citizens have the right to free speech; it is precisely these values we are protecting from those who would threaten our way of life with firearms, and I have full confidence in our highly trained officers to facilitate the demonstrations without escalation.' Before the naysayers had a chance to respond, she hit them with the synergy line:

'Earlier this week, weapons smuggling led to tragic loss of life on the streets of our capital. But out of that, new operational work has arisen, its aim to identify and apprehend those responsible. Our security forces are establishing new partnerships and developing existing ones. We will emerge from this challenge surer, safer, stronger.'

*Surer. Safer. Stronger.* The three words that she wanted the hacks to quote. Three words she wanted associated with her tenure in the Home Office. Associated with her as a politician. As a person. She pressed her lips together and gave a single nod; it had been agreed before that a smile wouldn't be appropriate.

Pym thanked the assembled media and stood for a few moments, angling her best side to the cameras. She focused on a point across the road; far-sighted, but still grounded. She collected up her notes at the lectern, ready to re-enter the building. Just a little longer here. Cameras were clicking and an appreciative murmur was running through the assembled reporters. Pym felt the buzz grow in her and had to suppress a grin. This was why, despite all the shit she had to shovel, she loved politics. She'd just started to turn towards the main doors when a voice she associated more with market trading than journalism piped up:

'Is it true that the Met has given immunity to the gun-runner arrested at the shooting in exchange for his cooperation?'

Pym froze. This was not public knowledge. And it was definitely not in the script. She identified the source of the question: a tall, red-headed woman with broad shoulders and a distracting number of tattoos. Pym cleared her throat.

'Did you authorise that personally, minister?' continued the redhead. 'How do you respond to calls for an inquiry into that decision?'

'Ah, I…'

'Has there been an offer of immunity? Yes or no?' The woman had a tough face and clearly wasn't intimidated by status. Pym tried to juggle a dozen possible responses, but none was a clear winner. Just like that, she was losing her grip on the situation. Had the police failed to brief her on such a significant decision? Where had this reporter got her information from?

The chatter rose among the crowd and Pym spotted some cameramen switching their equipment back on as she scanned the mob for an ally.

'I can neither confirm nor deny those rumours,' she replied, hearing the tremor in her own voice.

Pym snatched her notes and turned away from the media, aware that the last image captured of her was a gormless, open-mouthed fish face of shock and uncertainty.

As the automatic doors parted to admit her into the cool lobby, she knew one thing for sure: she needed to speak to her man again. And – with every irony in a case about firearms – blast him with both barrels.

●

Kofi Boateng hung out just inside the school gates. The activities club had finished slightly early and some of the other kids had already been picked up. A few had permission to leave without an adult. He didn't have that yet but hoped he would soon. He'd tried to tell his mum and dad last week that his friend Neon was allowed to walk home on his own. Every eleven-year-old should be, he'd argued. But they hadn't changed their minds, so here he was again, waiting.

Kofi knew that his parents worked hard. His mum was a lawyer in an office at London Bridge and had to make all kinds of important decisions about things. Go to court and stuff like that. And his dad was basically Batman, out fighting the bad guys all the time, even at night. Sometimes *actually* fighting them. A lot of the bad guys had weapons but that didn't scare Dad. Kofi always asked him for cool stories about chases and arrests. Sometimes Dad told him, but when it was really serious he wasn't allowed to talk about it. The only problem was that both Mum and Dad often worked late. Usually, one of them was around to pick him up. This morning, he was sure that his dad had said he would be there at four thirty. He'd meet him at the gates. But there was no sign of him.

Kofi reached into his bag, took out his new mobile phone. No! The battery was dead and he hadn't even realised. Must've run out when they were playing football. Mum and Dad would kill him; they'd told him to keep it charged. But even if he'd remembered the low battery, he'd forgotten the charger. He pressed the power button extra hard, just to make sure, but it didn't come back on. Definitely dead.

He glanced back towards the main doors. The teacher they all called 'Mrs Fatty' was talking to Sayid's mum, while Sayid chased his little sister in circles. Maybe Kofi could just walk home on

his own. It wasn't *that* far, and he knew the way. That was what
the bigger boys all did.

'Want a lift, mate?'

Kofi looked up at the man. He didn't recognise him, but he was
smiling. What were Mum and Dad always telling him about strangers?

'Er… No, thanks. My dad's coming.'

The man shook his head, lips pressed together. 'No, he isn't.'

'Um, I'm supposed to wait—'

'It's OK, buddy. I work with your dad.' The man produced
the silver badge in a little black wallet, the exact same one his
dad carried around.

'Oh,' said Kofi. If he was a friend of Dad's, that was different.

'Your old man's tied up with something and he's going to be
late. So I said to him that I'd come and pick you up, take you to
see him at the station.'

'Really?' Maybe Dad had sent him a message about it.

'Yeah. And as a special treat, you can come and check out our
operations room. Where we're tracking the people with all the
guns. We've got twenty big TV screens together on one wall.'

'Wow.'

'What do you think about that?' The man's face lit up. He
looked kind. 'If you like, we can put the siren on when we drive.'

Kofi felt his excitement grow, but he stayed rooted to the
spot. It was just a small feeling, but he recognised it: the one
where you think maybe you shouldn't be doing something, but
you're not sure. He checked over his shoulder again. Mrs Fatty
was still talking, her back to the gates. He reached into his bag.
His phone was still dead.

'You're not scared, are you?' said the man with a frown.

Kofi swallowed. 'Course not.'

'Cos if you're scared, then—'

'I'm not scared.' Kofi stood up straight, took a step forward.

'Alright then.' The man waved an arm towards a car. 'Let's go.'

# CHAPTER EIGHT

Zac was feeling pretty good as he pulled up outside the school. His mood had risen with the visit to the ballistics lab and had been boosted further by listening to Little Richard batter the piano keys through his car stereo on the drive back. The Lambeth Road technicians had made a significant finding: the barrel of Collins's MP5 Kurz had been machine-tooled to remove its rifling. The weapon would've lost some accuracy – not that the Kurz offered much anyway – but gained anonymity by preventing forensic links to any previous shootings. Although that seemed like a dead end, it was in fact a new lead. Modifying gun barrels was a specialist's job. If they assumed Collins had sourced the gun from Kaiser, then it meant Kaiser was either doing the modification personally or had a confederate. And a place where it was done. It lent new aspects to the investigation: profiling the few people with those skills, the locations where it could go unnoticed. He'd already called the incident room and given Patel the headlines, sharing his excitement with the young DC before cranking up the rock and roll as Little Richard sang about having some fun tonight.

Zac scanned the gates, but Kofi wasn't in his usual spot. He turned down the music and reached for his mobile. Dialled Kofi's new phone. Straight to voicemail. Zac sighed; maybe the kid had got bored and decided to call someone. More likely he'd switched the thing off or forgotten to charge it. Zac got out and walked over to the school gates. A slight worry popped into his head: what if Kofi hadn't received his message? If his battery had died before

Zac texted, over an hour ago, he wouldn't have known Zac was running late. *Calm down.* He was probably just waiting inside.

There was no sign of Kofi in the main entrance and the receptionist had already gone home. Zac began to move more quickly now, marching down the corridors, checking rooms with open doors as he headed towards the hall where the activities group was based. Inside, two kids sat at a table. One was drawing, the other playing on a phone. Neither one was Kofi. Behind them, a large lady Zac recognised as Dawn Clarke – the one the kids all called Mrs Fatty – was tidying colouring pens into a plastic tub.

'Dawn!' he called. 'Have you seen Kofi?'

The woman looked up, startled. 'Er, no.' She pushed a pair of glasses up the bridge of her nose. 'He was waiting at the gates earlier…'

'Well, he's not there now. Has he come back inside?'

She shook her head, cheeks wobbling. 'Not that I've seen. He could be in the cafeteria.'

'Right, I'll check there. You didn't let him leave, did you?'

'Well, I… He knows not to go without an adult. Our procedures aren't quite the same during summer sessions as they are in term time, though. With so few children, we don't have a staff member at the gate.'

Zac didn't reply; she clearly had no idea where Kofi was. He hurried to the canteen, redialling Kofi's number with the same result: voicemail. The canteen was empty, silent, the lights off. Zac went through and rounded the next corridor out into the playground. A lone, skinny black kid was playing basketball at a hoop on the far side. Zac closed his eyes, exhaled slowly. Thank God.

'Kofi!' he called, and the kid turned.

He was a long way off, but Zac knew immediately. It wasn't his son.

'Have you seen Kofi?' he yelled. The boy shook his head.

'Damn,' he muttered, sweeping across the playground and back towards reception. 'Kofi!' he shouted across the grounds, left and right, his voice rising each time. 'Kofi!'

There was no response.

Could he have…? No, there had to be a straightforward explanation. *OK, think.* There was the possibility that Kofi had misunderstood and walked home, or forgotten about the pickup arrangement with Zac and gone to his pal Neon's house. He hoped.

With no sign of Kofi back at the main entrance, Zac returned to the hall and left his number with Dawn Clarke in case she saw his son. He asked the other two kids if they knew where Kofi had gone. They didn't.

He fought down the dread creeping into his stomach as he jogged back to the car. *Make a plan*: Neon's house, their own home, search a few local roads between those two places.

If that didn't turn up anything, he'd have to do the unthinkable.

Call his wife and make sure that Kofi wasn't with her.

Then tell her that their son was missing.

•

Kat Jones handed the glass of white wine to her friend Georgie, placed the well-earned pint of pale ale in front of her own seat and dropped the packet of crisps between them. The pub in Kennington was busy, but they had their own little table. And the bus ride up from Lewisham was worth it to put some space between her and work. Her mate raised the wine for a 'cheers', then took a gulp and closed her eyes in a moment of satisfaction.

'Thanks, Kat. It's so great to see you! Come on, then – first things first. Any men in your life?'

Kat shook her head, sipped the beer. 'I'm taking a break from them for a while.'

'Right. That's what I said a couple of years ago, then I met Max.' Georgie grinned and placed her left hand on Kat's arm.

Kat's gaze travelled down and she zeroed in on the diamond engagement ring Georgie was wearing. She wiggled her fingers. 'And look what happened.'

'That's so cool about you guys,' said Kat, forcing a smile. 'Congratulations, by the way. Don't think I've seen you since it happened.' Kat recalled that, even back at university, Georgie had always been keen to settle down. Her job in PR was never a real priority.

'Aww, thanks. Anyway, never say never.' Georgie tilted her glass towards Kat, just to be clear that meant her. There was a certain smugness with some people who'd just got engaged, like they'd accomplished the one thing in life that counted. The implication was that others could get there too, if they tried a bit harder or had better luck. The expectation of receiving your most enthusiastic praise. Despite that, Kat couldn't begrudge her friend the happiness. Max was a nice enough bloke, the ring was suitably sparkly and Kat would probably want to show off a bit if she was engaged to someone she loved. But having quit Tinder and basically stopped looking for dates, the prospect of an eligible man was somewhat distant. In any case, she was only twenty-seven. No rush.

'I'm not really up for it that much at the moment,' she said. 'We've got a big operation going with this new task force, and I'm doing a lot of parkour training.'

'Oh my God, yeah!' Georgie's eyes widened. 'I saw something you put on Facebook about that. Jumping off buildings and stuff, isn't it?'

'Not exactly. Don't think I'd still be here if it was.' She chuckled. 'Great all-round training, though. You should try it.'

'Er, maybe not.' Georgie gave a lopsided grin. 'How's work going then, Detective Jones?'

'Pretty good.' Kat took a drink, wondering how to explain it to her friend. 'But it's not easy.'

Georgie tore open the crisp packet. 'What do you mean? That's the point, isn't it? Brain like yours, I thought you'd love the challenge. Solving crimes and all that stuff.'

'I do,' said Kat. 'It's more like the politics. The personalities.'

'Know what you mean.'

'You do?'

'Yeah, basically everyone in my company hates each other, so it's kind of hard to know who to side with.'

'What do you do then?' Kat reached for some crisps, hoping her voice didn't betray how keen she was to get some advice.

'Try and stay out of it!' laughed Georgie.

'What if you can't?'

Her friend pondered this with a mouthful of wine. 'Then I go senior. Boss is the one with the most power, right? So if you want to keep your job, follow them, not the people in between.'

'Mm. Bit cold, isn't it? I mean, say you're close to your team. The people you work with every day.'

Georgie pushed out her lips. 'Nah. You've got to look after yourself. S'pose it all depends on your office, though. Mine's dog eat dog. Maybe in the Met there's a bit more cooperation, people looking out for each other and stuff.'

'Not always.'

'Huh. I imagined you lot being all matey. Us against the criminals, that kind of thing.'

Kat gave a tiny shake of the head. 'You'd think so, wouldn't you? But at the end of the day, the Met's just like anywhere else. We're all human beings: helping others is usually about your own survival.'

'Damn straight.' Georgie and Kat were both modern Darwinians at heart, the result of the human sciences degree they had studied together.

'What if,' began Kat, hesitating slightly, looking at the top of her pint, 'someone you really liked – and respected – was making a bad call. Like, actually breaking the rules. You knew why they were doing it, but it didn't feel right. And you'd be in the shit if it came out.'

Georgie gave a wry smile. 'When you say "you", you mean *you*.'

Kat blinked.

'Depends if you want to keep your job,' said Georgie. 'You love the Met, and you're smashing it so far. You don't want to ruin that over one workmate. A career in the police force is always going to be more important. When you're running the show in twenty years' time, you'll be glad you sacrificed a bit of loyalty to that person now.' She leaned in conspiratorially. 'Who's breaking the rules then?'

Before Kat had a chance to reply, her phone rang. Speak of the devil.

'Zac, how's it going?'

There was some silence, then a long breath. 'Not good,' he said.

•

'I'm so, so sorry, love. I just don't know how it could've happened.' Zac stopped pacing around the kitchen and came to sit beside her at the dining table.

Etta sniffed, wiped her eyes with both palms. She didn't say anything, but Zac knew exactly what she'd be thinking. That he'd lost their other child, too. Amelia had been with him the day she died, six years ago. That Saturday morning, they'd been going to the newsagent to get sweets. Clutching her pocket money, Amelia had run ahead and straight into the middle of a revenge shooting by a gang member. No one could have foreseen that, but the implication hung between Zac and his wife. If he'd kept her with him…

'The squad cars have all got Kofi's picture, techies are watching to see if his phone pings, and Pat and Nas are already registering a missing person case. He's a child with no history of running away, which makes it top priority. That's everything we can do for now.'

Etta simply shook her head, her face creasing up with a new
stab of anguish. Zac wanted to cry too, or punch the walls, flip
the dining table over, smash a chair through the window. But he
knew the only way out of this was logic. That and some luck. He
checked his phone to see if there were any new messages. Nothing.

Zac shuffled his chair across and put his arm around Etta,
held her tight. But her body was rigid and didn't soften with
the contact.

When she eventually spoke, her voice was a whisper. 'Has
someone taken him? Be honest with me, Zac.'

It was true that Kofi had been more anxious than usual lately,
his impending move to secondary school filling him with fear. But
that was relatively normal, and there had been nothing to suggest
it would make him run away from home. He'd never done that
in the past. Taken alongside the reappearance of Kaiser this week
and the flowers on their doorstep last night, abduction was the
most likely explanation. Technically, a missing person case didn't
become a kidnap until word was received from the abductors.
But Zac thought it was a reasonable assumption.

If that was right, then Zac anticipated the worst was yet to
come. Kaiser would use Kofi to get what he wanted. Specifically,
he'd use the threat of violence towards him. He tried to push down
the rage and think it through. Kaiser would know that he was
the subject of a major inquiry, and he was clearly aware that Zac
was on the investigative team. He could have learned that just
from watching the news. So what did he want? Cash? Immunity?

Zac bit his lip, felt the tears prickling his eyes. 'Probably.'

Etta let out a wail from deep inside, thumping her fist on the
table, her mouth contorted.

'I'll find him. I promise,' said Zac. As far as he could see, the
only proactive way to do that was to find Kaiser. And right now,
if he did find him, Zac would kill him.

'Not on your own.' Etta finally turned to look at him.

'Course. The others are already on working on it, trying to figure out where he is.'

'Don't put our boy in any more danger.' She spoke quietly, but there was no mistaking the pain in her voice.

·

As far as Kaiser was concerned, it couldn't have gone more smoothly. The boy had got in the car with almost no hesitation, and hadn't shown any reaction when the doors were locked as they pulled out from the school. It was only when the kid noticed they were driving away from Lewisham that he'd asked a question about where they were going. He was placated by the simple explanation of a 'stop-off', and by the time they'd rolled into the garage and the automatic door had been shut behind them, there was no way out.

Kaiser regretted the need for the kid to be electrocuted with a stun gun when he tried to get away, not least because he'd pissed his pants and it stank. But the boy had quickly got the message, offering no further resistance when he was dragged through the empty house and handcuffed to a radiator pipe in the bathroom. His skinny little arms weren't strong enough to pull the pipe out, and a strip of duct tape over his mouth ensured he wouldn't be squealing to the neighbours.

Kaiser knew it was a risk, abducting Boateng's boy. But it was a calculated one – potential profit versus estimated costs. Boateng preferred doing things off the books, and – if Kaiser guessed correctly – he wouldn't go to the Met's Kidnap Unit if he suspected that Kaiser was in the police. Particularly not if he had been warned of the consequences for his son. In any case, Kaiser didn't expect to have to keep the kid alive very long.

Now, while one problem was being solved, Kaiser needed to fix another related issue. He selected a new burner phone. He'd drive somewhere else to make the call, just to be on the safe side.

But there was nothing really to worry about. His number was untraceable. So was the miniature handset he'd be calling. And no one would be looking at that end. After all, mobile phones weren't supposed to exist in prison.

# CHAPTER NINE

Thursday, 23 August 2018

'You've let me down.' Susanna Pym glared at the man across the table from her. He held her gaze a moment, then stopped a passing waitress and ordered a bacon sandwich – white bread, brown sauce. The waitress frowned, then smiled, dipped her head and departed towards the kitchens.

'Bit posh, isn't it?' he said, scanning the room.

Pym had to admire anyone who had the balls to ask for a bacon sandwich in a Michelin-starred restaurant, but this wasn't the time to let him know that.

'And a pain in the arse to get to,' he added.

She took a sip of coffee. 'Not for me.'

'Right.'

The Céleste at The Lanesborough on Hyde Park Corner was a brief stroll from her London pied-à-terre off Belgrave Square, but a long and tedious rush-hour car journey through the congestion zone if, like the man opposite her, you lived south of the river. It had been her intention to make it inconvenient for him. She needed to show who was in charge.

'As I was saying, you've let me down.'

'How's that?' He frowned, swigged his black coffee.

'You failed to inform me that the young man arrested at the shooting earlier this week had been offered a deal for his cooperation.'

'He hasn't.'

'Really?' Pym gave him a withering look. 'Then why are journalists embarrassing me at press conferences by claiming that he has?'

'First I've heard of it.'

Pym leaned in. 'Don't give me that bollocks,' she hissed. 'It's your job to know everything that goes on in that operation. It's the whole reason I put you on the team. To stop the sort of thing that happened yesterday.'

He smirked. 'Yeah, I saw that on the TV.'

'So?'

The man made a show of remembering, his eyes flicking up to the left and then the right. 'Come to think of it, I do remember that offer being discussed in a briefing.' He shrugged. 'Must've forgotten to pass it on.'

'Don't bloody well let it happen again!' Pym checked herself. Fortunately, there was no one next to them. Their corner table was discreet, but she needed to keep her voice down. 'You want more money, is that it?'

'I want *some* money. That'd be a start.'

She sighed. 'I told you, I'll make the transfer soon.'

He stared at her.

'Today,' she added. 'With some extra.'

His face cracked a smile. 'Outstanding.'

'Just remember what your job is, OK? And whoever's leaking to the press, get a lid on it.'

The man nodded, but she knew he wouldn't be remotely worried. On paper she might be the more powerful of the two of them, but he had a trump card, one that could topple her, depending on how he played it. As long as that existed, her threats were largely empty. She was all carrot, no stick.

Pym needed to find a way out of this, to change the game, assert her control. That was what politics was all about, wasn't it?

'Suppose I'd better get moving then,' he said.

'Good idea.'

The man stopped the waitress again and asked for his bacon sandwich to go.

Boateng showed his warrant card to the woman on the front gate and the barrier lifted for him to drive through into the almost empty car park. He brought his Audi to a stop outside the main reception of HMP Belmarsh. Boateng didn't want to be visiting a prison right now; he wanted to be out looking for Kofi, scouring the streets, getting everyone in Lewisham station on the hunt. Going house to house personally till he found his son. But he knew that, even if it were possible, that would be futile. Kofi's disappearance was no accident and he wouldn't be found by chance.

Since his boy had gone missing, Boateng had felt nothing but a crippling mixture of anxiety and fury, present to the point that he could barely tell them apart. He sat in the car a moment before getting out, massaging his eye sockets with his fingertips. His whole body was humming with nervous energy. The frequent bouts of nausea were a reminder of the danger Kofi could be in. A reminder of everything Boateng could have done differently. Everything he *should* have done differently. Each stab of guilt recalled his failure in the most basic of parenting tasks: protect your child. He took a few deep breaths through his nostrils. Ruminating wouldn't do any good; he needed action. That's why he was here. He forced himself out of the car and into the building.

'DI Boateng,' he announced to the man on reception. 'I called last night. Here to see an inmate.'

'Just you?'

Boateng nodded. He'd not told Jones he was coming, despite his earlier promise to keep her in the loop. He thought it'd be easier to conduct his business here one to one, and it might be better for her if she didn't know his whereabouts. That way, she wouldn't need to lie when their Op Pluto colleagues asked what he was doing.

The guy scrutinised Boateng's warrant card, noted the details and checked his system. He asked Boateng to look at a small camera, which would no doubt capture every line and shadow of insomnia. He was handed a visitor pass and then buzzed through a door. After a set of scans that seemed tighter than airport security, Boateng was shown to a waiting room. Ten interminable minutes later, a woman walked in. Not a prison officer, as he'd been expecting, ready to escort him to a meeting room, but a manager in a suit. She introduced herself as May McClintock, the deputy governor.

'DI Boateng,' she said. 'Please, join me in my office.'

He stood and shook her hand. 'Thanks, but I'm pretty tight on time, so if you don't mind, I'd like to get to work.'

'About that.'

'Yes?'

She pressed her lips together. Paused. 'I'm afraid I have some bad news for you.'

⁕

'Where is he then?' demanded DI Will Chambers.

Kat Jones spun her chair round to see Chambers and Kevin Harper standing over her. They made a comical pair, side by side: Harper carefully preened, looking like he was ready for a night out; Chambers with no effort made to conceal his flab or sweat, let alone style his hair or clothes. She casually rested her arm on the list of unsolved murder cases, tried to slow her rising pulse.

'Who?' she asked.

'Your boss, Boateng. What've you done with him?' Harper made the question sound like an innuendo.

'I haven't done anything with him,' she replied evenly.

Chambers made a show of checking his watch – a big, ugly gold thing. 'It's nine thirty and he's not here yet. We're working a major investigation. He's going to miss the morning briefing. What's he doing?'

'I don't know,' said Jones. 'Have you tried calling him?'

She'd already attempted that twice since arriving in the Op Pluto incident room an hour ago. Both times it'd gone to voicemail. Jones knew that Boateng's son, Kofi, had gone missing yesterday, and that he'd be doing everything he could to find him. When Boateng had called her last night, she'd offered to help, but he'd said the most useful thing she could do was continue to follow up on the unsolved murders. Anything that might help identify Kaiser. She sympathised with Boateng, of course, but bristled slightly at what felt like emotional blackmail. This morning, she suspected that Boateng was off alone, and she had a fair idea where he'd gone. Somewhere you weren't allowed phones.

'Yeah, I called him.' Chambers looked at her as if she were a moron. 'Surprise, surprise, he's not answering.'

Jones shrugged. 'I know we work together, but that doesn't mean I know what he's up to 24/7.' She held back from telling them about Boateng's son. He'd asked her to keep that close as well, while their MIT colleagues Connelly and Malik built a missing person case. If, as they expected, it turned into a full kidnap operation, it wouldn't stay secret long.

'You know he spoke to a source without telling us?' said Chambers.

She pushed out her lips, shrugged. 'Which source?'

'Mensah, the kid arrested with the guns,' replied Harper.

'Is he a source?' asked Jones.

Chambers squinted at her. 'What's Boateng up to?'

'Don't know,' she replied. 'Could be a personal thing.'

'What, a personal thing on this case?'

'Your guess is as good as mine, sir,' she said pleasantly.

Harper put his hands on his hips, his groin uncomfortably close to Jones's eye level. 'Well, when you see him, tell him that we'd appreciate his participation in Operation Pluto. If he's got time,' he smirked.

'Will do.' She flashed a smile and returned to her computer screen, watching the reflections of the two men diminish as they walked off. She couldn't begin to imagine what Boateng was dealing with – especially after what had happened to his daughter – but at the same time, Jones was struggling to cover for him. Particularly when he wasn't telling her what he was doing.

She glanced around the room again and saw DCI Krebs in the doorway, watching her.

●

'A drug overdose?' The news was like a punch in the solar plexus. Boateng knew he wasn't thinking clearly, but he definitely didn't believe this explanation.

'Unfortunately, that's what it looks like,' said May McClintock, the deputy governor, and clasped her hands.

'What happened?'

'Well, as we understand it, Jermaine Mensah's cellmate alerted a prison officer before breakfast, saying that Mr Mensah was unresponsive to wake-up calls. Staff went into the cell, examined him and found that he wasn't breathing.' She glanced down at some notes. 'They radioed a code-blue emergency to bring nurses from the medical wing and called for paramedics. The officers attempted initial resuscitation before the defibrillator arrived with the nurses, but the machine couldn't find a pulse to shock. Paramedics got here pretty fast, but unfortunately it was already too late. They pronounced him dead shortly before 8 a.m.'

'The cellmate doesn't know anything more?'

'No. Neither does anyone else.'

'Hm.' Boateng was totally unconvinced. The rage was rising inside him and he wanted to break something. He gripped the chair arms hard. He needed to keep it together, for Kofi.

'We're interviewing other inmates, obviously. Anyone who may have been in contact with Mr Mensah during association time yesterday.'

Boateng took a deep breath. 'Why do you think drug overdose?'

McClintock inclined her head, sighed. 'We do our best to keep the prison clean, to ensure the only drugs within our walls are those given on prescription and administered under supervision, but I won't pretend that inmates aren't using illicit substances. In the last month alone we've found heroin, crack cocaine and LSD inside the prison, as well as newer synthetic cannabis products. And one of our biggest problems is with diverted medications.'

Through the fog of his anger and confusion, Boateng tried to focus on her words. He was familiar with the issue. In prison, you could get opiate substitutes like methadone or Subutex on prescription if you were part of a drug rehab scheme, same as in the outside world. But inside, where supply was low and demand high, those drugs had serious value. Inmates constantly came up with new and creative ways to 'divert' their medication: receiving but not taking it, then trading or selling it on to another prisoner.

'We found paper cups with a green residue among Mr Mensah's personal possessions,' continued McClintock. 'So our current thinking is that he obtained some liquid methadone from another inmate, then either he got the dose wrong or it reacted badly with something else he'd taken. You know, painkillers, that kind of thing. We'll have to wait for the report.'

'Was he in the methadone programme?'

'No.'

Boateng shook his head. 'This is bollocks. Jermaine Mensah wasn't a drug user.' He was confident of that; no way an opiate addict could've gone thirty-six hours in their custody cells without getting the sweats and shakes of withdrawal, and there hadn't been any evidence of that. Of course, it was possible that Mensah had obtained drugs simply to deal with the stress of being in prison. Understandably, he was scared shitless of Kaiser. But there was another, more likely explanation: that Kaiser had found a way to get to Mensah. The idea made Boateng feel sick, and he noticed his hands were trembling.

'There'll be an inquest, obviously,' said McClintock. 'Southwark Coroner's Court. And a full toxicology report. But I'd be surprised if that turned up anything other than a toxic level of methadone in his blood.'

'Is his body here?'

'Taken to Greenwich Mortuary already.'

Boateng wondered if that meant Dr Mary Volz would be performing the post-mortem. If there was any solid evidence that Mensah's death was a homicide, the cool-headed pathologist would find it. Then he remembered the family of which Mensah had spoken. 'Does the mother know?'

'Family Liaison Officer should be on the way now.'

Boateng's chin dropped to his chest and his body suddenly felt heavy and sluggish. A new feeling was starting to take hold: defeat. Kaiser was too quick, too far ahead of him. Op Pluto's star witness was dead, any further leads he could provide severed. Leads on Kofi, perhaps. And Mensah's death resonated for Boateng. In another life, the young British-Ghanaian lad could've been his own son. Someone whom he'd promised – and failed – to protect in return for his cooperation. Guilt hit him once more, and he vowed to visit Mensah's mum when the time was right, to offer his condolences in person, for what they would be worth to a grieving parent.

Mumbling his goodbyes to McClintock, Boateng made his way out of the prison. He had to show his face at work now. And he had to keep going, to find a new way to his son and to Kaiser. Through the pain, a small idea had formed. It wasn't one he wanted to pursue. A pact with the Devil. But with Mensah gone, there wasn't much alternative.

·

In a quiet corner of the cafeteria, Jones put another call through to Boateng's mobile. It rang a while, and she was just about to give up when he answered.

'Yeah?' he said. Sounded like he was driving.

'Where've you been, Zac?' she blurted. Jones knew that accounting to her for his whereabouts wasn't his top priority, but she was feeling the pressure in the Pluto incident room.

'Out,' he said, simply.

'Where?' She could hear the irritation in her own voice. 'I'm taking some shit for you here.' That was verging on insubordinate, but he had to know.

Boateng didn't reply. But he didn't hang up either.

'Zac?'

'I'll tell you later.'

'Right.' Jones tried to keep control, keep in mind what he was going through. She took a breath. 'Any news?' she asked. 'On Kofi?'

'Nope.'

Silence.

'Nothing at all?'

'No.'

She waited, but he didn't elaborate. 'OK then,' she said.

He rang off without another word. She sat down, alone. Started to think about what she was doing. About what her dad would have done.

Jones knocked on the open door and stepped half inside.

DCI Krebs stopped typing and glanced up at her.

'Kat,' she said. 'How can I help?'

Taking another step, Jones closed the door behind her. 'I've got something to tell you, ma'am.' She spoke quietly but clearly.

Krebs turned away from her computer, gestured towards the empty chair in front of her. 'Please.'

Jones couldn't swear to it, but as she sat down, she thought there was the hint of a smile on Krebs's face.

# CHAPTER TEN

Detective Sergeant Patrick Connelly watched his boss trudge across the MIT office towards the desks, where he sat alongside Detective Constable Nasim Malik. Boateng and Kat Jones had been away from their team for just a few days, seconded to the fancy new Operation Pluto task force, but to look at Boateng, you'd think he'd worked every hour since then without a wink of sleep. Connelly knew the reason for that.

As soon as Boateng had called him last night, he'd dropped his tools on the allotment in Herne Hill and left his strawberries to enjoy the last of the warm summer evening on their own. He'd driven straight to Lewisham police station and opened the missing person case for Boateng's wee boy, Kofi. Connelly's kids were grown up now – long since left home and made their own lives – but you never lost a father's protective instinct. He was determined to do whatever he could to help find Kofi, even if it meant going without sleep, too. Boateng was a damned fine boss and Connelly wanted to repay every ounce of faith the fella had shown in him over the years.

'Alright, Pat? Nas.' Boateng nodded at Malik as both men stood to shake hands with him.

'Aye, Zac, we're grand. How're you coping?'

Boateng shook his head. No other answer required. 'You boys got any news?'

Connelly pulled up another chair between him and Malik, and the three of them sat down. 'We've been back to the school, canvassed for witnesses. It's possible one of the other kids saw him leave. Waiting for anything to come through, then we can head down and speak to them. Our man Nas is doing the CCTV side of things.'

Malik rotated a laptop running split-screen video footage of roads. 'Looking at the area around the school in the forty-five-minute window between the activities club ending and you arriving. Slow progress, but there's a chance we might catch something.'

Connelly was confident that if a single frame of Kofi existed, Malik would spot it. The lad was thorough. You first noticed it with his meticulous personal grooming: never a hair out of place, the short beard always perfectly trimmed. That same precision and care extended into his police work. Not all the youngsters in the Met were that diligent.

'No CCTV of the main gate?' said Boateng.

'Sorry, boss,' replied Malik. 'Only inside the school. We've got him walking out of the reception at four twenty-five, but that's the last time he appears there.'

'And you said he's never run away before?' It was a sensitive question, but Connelly had to ask. 'Nothing like that?'

'Never.'

Connelly understood what that probably meant, though he didn't want to voice it. The thought had already crossed his mind a few times since last night. *Abduction.* Boateng had made a fair number of enemies over the years, mainly because he was a bloody good copper. Tenacious, too. Could it be that one of those cases had come back to him now? You heard stories about fellas orchestrating all kinds of stuff from inside prison...

'No word from the lad, I assume?' said Connelly. 'Emails or anything, even from before he was last seen?'

Boateng sighed. 'No. What about his phone?'

'Off since 3 p.m. yesterday,' answered Malik.

'And no contact from anyone else?' Connelly raised his bushy eyebrows.

'No,' replied his boss.

Connelly waited to see if he'd say any more. If Kofi had been abducted, the bastards would be in touch soon, to set out their demands. But at that point, the case would automatically be transferred to the Met's Kidnap Unit, miles away, in a different borough, and Connelly and Malik wouldn't be involved any more – professionally at least. Obviously, they'd do whatever they could for Boateng on a personal level. Anything from taking him for a pint to saying a few prayers to the Holy Mother on the boy's behalf. But the development of a proven kidnap would be a double-edged sword.

In missing person cases, the longer someone was absent – especially a kid – the less likely it was that they were coming back. That was the sad fact of it, and the statistics didn't lie. On the other hand, if a ransom arrived, it'd normally come with proof that the victim was still alive, but then you were into entirely new territory. Pay up, or… Connelly wasn't going there yet. It was bad enough when threats were made by criminals against one of their own. But a kid? That was sick.

Connelly flexed his hands as he tried to contain the anger. Face-to-face with anyone who'd kidnapped a child, he'd rediscover his old boxing skills pretty fast. The fists that had brought him a dozen knockouts in amateur fights when he was a young man. He could only guess what kind of rage Boateng must be feeling. Was his son's disappearance connected with his work? Connelly knew that his boss got into some scrapes, normally with good cause. And it wasn't entirely impossible that, if the right intelligence came his way, he'd try to rescue the lad on his own without telling a soul.

'What do you two think?' Boateng flicked his eyes back and forth between Connelly and Malik. 'Has he been kidnapped?'

Connelly blew out his cheeks. 'I can't say.'

This wasn't Colombia, where wealthy kids were routinely abducted and ransomed back to their families. Or Iraq, where Malik's parents came from and where kidnapping was basically a full-time job for some people. Occasionally, in London, someone from a rough part of town flashed about too much wealth and got snatched by a gang. In those cases, the typical threat was hurting the victim if a ransom payment from their family was late. Fortunately, that didn't happen very often. But if Kofi had been targeted by an abductor, Connelly suspected it wasn't for financial reasons alone. Boateng would be aware of that, no doubt.

'Is there anyone you can think of who might want to get at you through Kofi?' asked Connelly.

Boateng shrugged. 'Probably lots. But no one who's said anything about it. And I've checked with all his friends, our other relatives. Extended family, even. Nothing.' His leg was jiggling and he picked at his nails. Deep bags lay under his bloodshot eyes. The poor fella was a wreck.

'Is there anywhere else he might have gone?' said Connelly. 'Anywhere at all you can think of?'

Boateng shook his head, then shut his eyes and pinched the bridge of his nose. When he took his hand away, Connelly could see that his boss was crying. He put a hand on Boateng's shoulder.

'Don't worry, Zac. Krebs is letting us work this full time. We'll do everything we can. And I mean that.'

•

Kofi woke with a start. He was sitting on the floor and his shoulders felt numb and prickly. In the near darkness, it was a few seconds before he worked out what was going on. Realised that his nightmare about not being able to move hadn't been just a dream. That the things that had happened to him yesterday weren't simply his imagination. He didn't know what time of day it was, only that he'd been uncuffed earlier and allowed to eat and drink something, and then to use the toilet next to him, before the tape and handcuffs were replaced and he was back on the floor again with the lights off.

He shuffled himself forwards slightly and yanked at the pipe behind his back. But the thick metal didn't budge. The only result was more pain in his wrists where they'd rubbed on the cuffs and gone sore. He worked his lips and jaw as much as he could, with no success. The big strip of tape was too tight. In any case, he didn't really want to take it off, because of what the man would do when he came back and found out.

At least his pants were drier than yesterday. But they were still damp where he'd peed in them, and the skin stung on the insides of his thighs. It smelled horrible. He felt like such a loser – a bigger boy would never pee himself. Everyone would think he was a baby if they knew. But he'd had no control over it when the man had jabbed the black box thing into him. It had made his whole body go rigid and it'd felt as if his skeleton was going to rip out of his skin like in the *Mortal Kombat* video game that he played at Neon's house, even though his parents told him not to because it was too violent. The man said that every time he did something wrong, he'd get the black box. Kofi was a quick learner and he decided after that to do whatever the man said. Even thinking about it now, his tummy felt all wriggly, like there were loads of worms inside trying to get out.

He'd been so naughty, so stupid. He shouldn't have gone off with the man in the first place. Mum and Dad had told him never to go anywhere with someone he didn't know, but he thought he could trust the police officer. The guy had the badge and everything; said he knew Dad. He'd be in so much trouble when he got home.

*Home.*

He pictured his bedroom, where he felt snug and safe, especially at night when Mum or Dad came in to read him a story. If he was lucky, they'd both be there. Kofi knew it wouldn't be much longer before he was too old for these stories at bedtime, but right now he'd give anything to be tucked up with Mum and Dad next to him. All of a sudden, sadness surged through him and he started to sob, tears filling his eyes and running down his cheeks, catching on the tape. Snot was trailing out of his nose. *Come on!* He pulled his legs up and wiped his face on his knees. What had Dad told him the other day? Imagine you're a superhero.

Kofi closed his eyes and pictured himself as Prince T'Challa, the Black Panther. Breaking open the handcuffs, smashing his way out of this tiny bathroom. Then jumping into his special jet, collecting his dad from the roof of the police station and flying off together. He imagined them finding the man who had done this to him and getting their own back. When he thought of that, it wasn't so bad. His tummy wriggled a bit less.

He kept his eyes shut.

•

Boateng took in the face of the man sitting opposite him. He'd lost some weight since the last time he'd seen him, in the dock at the Old Bailey earlier that year. His high cheekbones stood out more than ever, the light skin of his Jamaican-Scottish parentage paler than before. The changes weren't surprising: neither food nor sunlight were abundant in the High Security Unit of Belmarsh prison. But one feature that remained the same for Darian Wallace was his eyes. Dark, distant, with a single black tear tattooed under the right one. Boateng knew it was a mistake to equate the lack of life in those eyes with a lack of activity behind them.

Wallace was one of the smartest criminals he'd ever hunted. Statistically speaking, he was probably among the most intelligent people in the country. Ten years ago, an educational psychologist had tested him at school – before he got thrown out – and estimated Wallace's IQ at 155. That put him in the cleverest 0.01% of the population. Most tests didn't even measure beyond 160. Wallace had chosen to turn his extraordinary brain to crime, but his powerful analytical capabilities were unable to master the rage that Boateng suspected would always live somewhere inside him.

'I knew you'd come.' Wallace nodded. 'Soon as I saw it on the TV.'

'Yeah?' Boateng assumed he was talking about the press conference.

'You turned up quicker than I expected, though. Didn't even give me a chance to contact you.' He chuckled briefly, narrowed his eyes. 'So, something must've changed. Let me guess: your snitch on the Škorpions ain't talking no more.'

Boateng didn't reply, hoped his expression wasn't giving anything away.

Wallace tilted his head, studied him. 'No, wait a second. I know. He's dead, innit?'

They held eye contact as Wallace's smile gradually formed. He wagged a finger at Boateng, the movement limited by his handcuffs. 'The overdose brer on the other side in the main section. Heard about it at lunch. Shame, the drugs got the best of him. Seen a lot of man go that way in here.'

'What do you know about Kaiser?' said Boateng.

The smile grew. Wallace looked away, his eyes flicking around the corners of the small room in which they sat. 'So, you want my help?' he said, eventually.

Something held Boateng back from a simple affirmation. 'What loyalty have you got to him?' he asked. 'Now you're in here.'

Wallace arched his eyebrows. 'You think it matters that I'm in prison? If anything, that makes it easier for him to get to me.'

'You're frightened of him then?' Boateng hoped the challenge would force a reaction.

'Did I say that?' Wallace reached down, pulled his T-shirt up to reveal a wiry abdomen with a six-inch scar running above his hip bone. 'Defended myself inside before, you know. Ask the brer who did that to me.'

'So if you're not scared, then you're open to assisting us on Kaiser?'

Wallace sniffed. 'Maybe.'

'OK.' Boateng knew there'd be a massive quid pro quo. Some kind of favour. He wondered what he could live with providing in exchange for valuable information. What the Pluto team would countenance.

'I've got a kid,' said Wallace. 'Few months old.'

'Congratulations.' Boateng's voice was flat. He did the calculations; it must've happened when Wallace was out last summer.

'I wanna go and see him.'

Boateng frowned. 'Given your charges, you won't be permitted a day release, even for one trip. We can arrange for him to visit you here, though. Depending on what you can tell us about Kaiser.'

Wallace sucked his teeth. 'Nah. A visit's my right, anyway. I want to see my son *outside*. Don't want to bring a kid in here.'

'He's a baby. He won't know where he is.'

'That's not the point.' Wallace shook his head. 'Would you want to meet your boy for the first time in prison?'

'What kind of question's that?'

'A hypothetical one.'

Boateng snorted. 'I'm not serving a life sentence.'

'That's what I'm saying. It's theory of mind. You studied psychology, right? You should get that. Use your imagination. Would you want to be on lockdown the first time you ever saw your son? For that to be his only real image of you?'

Boateng could understand it. He fought back a picture of his own boy, reminded himself why he was in here with Wallace.

He inhaled deeply and let out a long breath through his nose. 'For me to even make a case for that, you'd need to give me something damned good on Kaiser.'

'Oh, I've got that, don't you worry.'

Boateng felt a flutter of excitement, but he tried not to show it. 'What do you know?'

Wallace grinned. 'What he looks like, for a start. We can do one of them e-fit things. You might even know him.'

Boateng blinked. 'OK. What else?'

'Lots more besides. I met him four, five times, back when we were dealing. Anything you wanted, he could get it.'

'Be more specific.' Boateng could feel his frustration building.

'I know where he gets his weapons from.'

'So do we.'

'Really? How come you ain't found him then, if the trail leads there?' Wallace tutted. 'You being here means you got nothing else. You need me. And I want to see my son. Outside. I'm sure you can arrange that. Maybe speak to that politician on TV who's banging on about gun crime and whatnot. The one in the Home Office. She'll give you lot permission.'

'We can arrange a visit.'

'Like I said: outside. A park would be good.'

'Look around you,' said Boateng, gesturing to the breeze-block walls. 'You're not in much of a position to negotiate.'

'Neither are you.' Wallace smirked and leaned back in his chair. 'It's a nice little trip out to see my son – or nothing. You decide, big man.'

*

Jones shut her eyes and tried to block out the pain. She'd been hanging from a scaffolding bar in Vauxhall for thirty seconds and the agony in her fingers was getting too much to bear. This was a standard drill in parkour training, a challenge of last one left. Six people had already dropped, and there were five of them still up there. Each hoping the others would break first.

Jones must have done this exercise a dozen times. But tonight, the self-imposed punishment in the name of strength felt like a penance. She'd vacillated, going back and forth in her own mind, about going to Krebs and telling her about Boateng. In the end, she'd decided that his solo efforts were just too much on this occasion, too dangerous for others. The greatest good for the greatest number – that was an ethical principle, wasn't it? And unfortunately, in this situation, it was achieved by letting Krebs know what Boateng was doing.

A guy fell off the bar beside Jones, his failure drawing her attention to the burning sensation in her own hands. She gritted her teeth and held tight.

She hadn't told Krebs everything, just some key parts. Like how Boateng had discovered from Darian Wallace that Kaiser was in the police, and how Kaiser was connected to the death of Boateng's daughter. Those two pieces of information accounted for Boateng's secrecy and obsession, respectively. She hadn't mentioned the unsolved murders they were checking out. But perhaps that sliver of loyalty was just self-preservation.

The pain in her fingers was becoming unbearable now. A woman on a parallel bar a metre in front of her let go, leaving Jones and two others hanging.

Krebs had remained silent, steepling her fingers and nodding thoughtfully. Then she'd thanked Jones for her disclosure, telling her she'd done the right thing. Jones had asked what action she'd take; Krebs had smiled and said none, for now. Jones presumed she would wait until the time was right for intervention. She left Krebs's office with a slight sense of relief at not being dropped in it immediately. One thing was clear though: Jones was under instructions to continue reporting on Boateng.

Without warning, her fingers uncurled. She had a second to register the fall before her feet hit the concrete, followed by her backside. The two people who'd beaten her hung on for another thirty seconds or more.

Jones blew out her cheeks, flexed her hands. There was some way to go.

# CHAPTER ELEVEN

**Friday, 24 August 2018**

'Here you are, love.' Zac put the mug of coffee down in front of his wife, but she didn't move. Just sat at the kitchen table with her head in her hands. Last night was the second since Kofi's disappearance and, again, neither of them had slept much. They each spent the night shifting around, getting up, fetching water, checking their phones. At one point, Zac must have drifted off, because when he woke again it was past 3 a.m. and Etta wasn't beside him. He'd found her sitting on Kofi's bed, smoothing the Spider-Man duvet cover with her fingers. When he sat down next to her, she got up and went back to their bedroom without a word.

Etta had been given leave from work today on compassionate grounds, and her parents were coming to their house to keep her company. Zac was glad of that; he hated the thought of her ruminating on Kofi's disappearance all day long on her own. There was no way he could stay with her, despite also being offered time off by Krebs; he had too many leads to follow up. Part of him hoped he could set out for work before Etta's mum and dad arrived. Zac's relationship with the in-laws had been cordial enough in recent months, but he suspected they still hadn't completely forgiven him for Amelia's death. He knew what they'd think this time: his fault, again.

'I'll just leave it there for you,' he said, sliding the mug slightly closer to his wife.

She murmured an acknowledgement.

Zac glanced at his watch: 7.35 a.m. Time to get moving. He'd see how Connelly and Malik were getting on, and then check in with Jones and plan how to develop their investigation on the unsolved murder. But that would come after his best chance to fix all of this: a deal with Darian Wallace to identify Kaiser. He'd already set the wheels turning yesterday, as soon as he'd got back to Lewisham from Belmarsh. He'd run it past Krebs, telling her about the Wallace-Kaiser link. After bollocking him for not sharing that information earlier, she'd given him the go-ahead to draft a submission for the Home Office Minister for Policing, Susanna Pym. A Met motorbike rider had couriered it to her London home last night. He hoped to get the sign-off first thing today, then get in touch with Wallace's ex-girlfriend Jasmine Fletcher and set up the visit for that afternoon.

Krebs had made it clear that anything that happened to Wallace while he was outside of prison was Boateng's responsibility. He'd tried to mitigate the risks as much as possible, but even with a small firearms escort team, it was still a gamble. When he'd put Darian Wallace away for a string of murders that took place last year, he'd hoped it'd be the last Wallace ever saw of the outside world. Now, he was begging for him to be let out for the day.

'I've got to head in now,' he said gently. 'I'll message you with any updates, soon as we know anything at all. We've got the—'

*Bing.*

Zac stopped as the tone chimed in his trouser pocket. He and Etta looked at one another. Her face was drawn and lined with fatigue, but her eyes widened slightly. He whipped out the mobile, stabbed at its screen.

One new message. He didn't recognise the number.

Zac felt the adrenalin pulse around his ribs as he sat down next to her. He opened the text. They both looked at the screen for a few seconds, then Etta unleashed a howl. He gulped, put his arm around her and read it again:

*£20k in cash to get your boy back. Delivery instructions to follow. You have two days. Tell anyone and he loses fingers.*

Zac stared at the message, his lips and jaws working to hold back the tears. Then he leaned into his wife as they grasped each other, and he stopped fighting it.

•

For a few seconds, Darian Wallace felt like a free man. He stepped out of the prison gates, the mid-afternoon summer sun beating down on him. He tilted his face up and closed his eyes. Hands on each arm kept him moving towards the waiting line of three unmarked cars. The air was thick and stuffy, but Wallace smiled to himself as he took a lungful of it. He flexed his hands in front of him, the cuffs on his wrists a further reminder that he was still a prisoner, held at Her Majesty's Pleasure. Weird phrase, that. Like the Queen took some personal enjoyment in him being locked down.

Wallace opened his eyes as they approached the cars. He surveyed the escort that stood beside their vehicles watching him: two armed feds per car, front and back, plus drivers. Looked like a driver plus one more armed guy in the middle car. And he could guess who'd be in the back seat of that vehicle. The hands on his arms shifted to his back and head, pushing him down and through the open car door. Zachariah Boateng was inside. The man looked like shit warmed up.

'Lovely day for it,' said Wallace, flashing Boateng a grin as the door slammed shut behind him. Locks clunked shut and two slaps sounded on the roof. 'Summer vibes.'

'It's a half-hour drive from here to Camberwell,' replied Boateng, turning in his seat to face him. 'So you've got plenty of time to tell me everything you know about Kaiser.'

The cars pulled away in convoy, speeding up immediately. Trees flashed past as they exited the prison approach road, heading for Greenwich. Wallace glanced at the armed cop in the front. He was holding his weapon across his chest and his jaws worked ferociously at some gum. The brer was stressed. Understandable.

Wallace spread his hands as much as the cuffs would allow. 'Where do I start?'

•

'Stay here,' Boateng told Wallace as the cars pulled up outside Ruskin Park in Camberwell. It was a normal day in south London: buses roaring past on Denmark Hill, overground trains rumbling on the tracks cut lower into the hillside, pedestrians coming and going at the hospitals down the road. The park was quiet, and local colleagues had closed off a section of it, enabling them to control the environment as much as possible.

Across the grass he could see a young woman he recognised from last summer. She stood alone. Her long, dark hair was down, framing her face, and she'd dressed up in a skirt and heels. A sling was wrapped around her chest and over one shoulder. Boateng could make out the shape of a baby beneath it. Jasmine Fletcher was holding the child tightly and rocking it side to side, whispering something Boateng couldn't lip-read. What would you say to your kid when he was about to meet his dad for the first time?

He was thankful that Fletcher had agreed instantly to meet Wallace. He knew that she'd experienced violence and coercion at his hands. The last time Boateng had seen her, she was in pieces after a threat Wallace had made – one his form had suggested he would follow through. But a lot appeared to have changed since then, not least that they'd had a child. Boateng had seen the unfortunate pattern too many times to mention: an abused woman taking back the man who mistreated her, a tie she just couldn't break despite all her bad experiences. Maybe that's what had happened here. Fletcher and Wallace had been in communication by letter, Boateng was aware of that. But he couldn't rule out the young woman being here under duress, part of some set-up. He had to be vigilant.

When the minister had signed off the submission late last night, possibly after a glass of wine, her handwritten note had read: *Extract maximum intelligence refs Op Pluto and do NOT take your eyes off this man for a moment. S.P.*

It was Boateng's name on the document, his head on the block. There could be no room for error here, no lapses of security. The armed lads from the Tactical Firearms Team gave him some confidence on that score at least. And so far, the exercise had been worth it: Wallace had given details of how Kaiser procured some of the weaponry he sold to the streets of London. He'd also described what Boateng believed was the unsolved murder Kaiser had committed four years ago, mentioned by Mensah. It was enough to work with, officially and otherwise. Boateng just hoped Jones was still on board with helping him. The real breakthrough would come after the meeting with Fletcher, when Wallace would do the e-fit of Kaiser's face. That was the best that Boateng could negotiate.

'Hi, Jasmine,' said Boateng as he approached her.

'Alright?' she replied, looking cautiously at the armed officer who had followed Boateng across the park.

'Thanks for agreeing to meet.'

'I wanted to. It's Darian's right to see his kid. I respect him for choosing to do it out here, too.' She jerked a head to their surroundings. 'He knows how I feel about prison.'

'Sure. Well, we appreciate it.'

'Is he helping you lot then?'

'I can't discuss that, I'm afraid.'

'Nah, course not.' She smiled. 'Whatever. We're just happy we can see him. Aren't we?' She jiggled the baby as her voice rose an octave. 'Yes. We're going to see Daddy.'

'So we'll stay inside this part of the park, but you guys can walk around a bit, OK?'

'Yeah. Bit weird, isn't it? Having blokes with guns and that watching us. And them guys on the gates over there.'

Boateng held eye contact. 'You know that Darian Wallace was convicted earlier this year on three counts of murder. He killed three men. A jury found him guilty of those crimes, beyond reasonable doubt. There aren't many people who've done something that serious that see another day outside of prison. In his case, the judge recommended life without parole. He's lucky to be out here today.' He was laying it on a bit thick, but he was familiar with cases like this, where the ex-partner refused to believe that her – it was usually a her – man couldn't have done the things of which he was accused. A fit-up by the police, a miscarriage of justice. Boateng wanted to remind Jasmine that Wallace was capable of serious violence.

'Well, he must be giving you something special then, mustn't he? Can we see him now?'

Boateng nodded. 'Come with me.'

•

She was as sweet-looking as Wallace remembered – maybe better, the way she'd done her hair, all straight and shiny and glinting in the light. There was a lot he could have done differently in life, and one of those things was Jasmine Fletcher. To think he'd screwed up with her not once but twice, and despite all his dicking around, now she was his baby mum. The mother of his son. Whatever happened, they were bound together by that, forever. Like a wedding vow neither of them had wanted to take.

'Jas, damn girl,' he said, and she gave him that wide smile in return – the sexy one, with her head tilted. As if nothing had ever gone wrong between them. Wallace's mind started racing, and memories weren't the only thing stirring. Needless to say, he wasn't getting any on lockdown, except from his own hand. But he reminded himself why he was here: the little bundle strapped to her chest.

'Hi, Darian.' She sounded a bit nervous.

'Is this him?' Wallace stepped towards her, dimly aware of the armed coppers discreetly surrounding him in a triangle. He knew the others were positioned further away, by the entrances, the drivers ready in their cars alongside the park. He'd insisted on this place: near Jas's house, nice and outdoorsy, space to walk. About as different from Belmarsh as you could get. No one seemed to have questioned his choice. Maybe Boateng was just keen to get on with the deal.

'Yeah,' she giggled. 'Leon, meet Darian. Darian, this is Leon.' She peeled back the muslin to expose the tiny, wrinkled head of a baby, a few random curls of hair sticking up. Its eyes were barely open, the miniature nose and mouth twitching. His first thought was that it didn't look like him at all. Was she having him on? Then again, it didn't look much like her either. Didn't look like anything, really, except maybe an alien. At the sound of a train's horn from beside the park, one little hand reached up from inside the cloth, grasped the air and came to rest on Jas's shoulder.

'Hello,' she cooed. 'Are you waking up, mister?'

Wallace raised his cuffed hands slowly towards the kid, and in the corner of his eye he saw the feds move closer. They'd be watching to make sure Jas wasn't passing him something; that the baby didn't have a gun or whatnot hidden inside its little suit thing. Boateng would've checked already, most likely, before he let Wallace out of the car. He could understand their caution, but they had nothing to worry about.

'Hello, lickle man,' he said, stroking the kid's head with the back of his fingers. It was weird; Leon didn't *feel* like his baby. Maybe because he hadn't known he'd existed until the start of this week. Wallace hadn't been through the pregnancy, the birth, the long nights and nappy changing. None of it. But now, here he was: a ready-made son. Leon. Wallace smiled; his mum would love the fact her grandson was named after her. He'd probably never get the chance to tell her, though, what with her being stuck in that care home. And even if he did, she wouldn't understand what he was on about. He wondered whether his own dad had been there when he was born. Anyone's guess, really.

'D'you wanna hold him?' asked Jas.

Wallace flicked his eyes to her and back to Leon. 'Yeah. But I can't really do it with these on.' He nodded at his wrists.

'No, it's OK. Go like this,' Jas crossed her wrists and held her forearms up. Wallace copied, his arms forming a cradle. She unwrapped the muslin and lifted Leon out, carefully placing him between Wallace's forearms and his chest. 'Got him? Watch the cuffs don't stick in his arm.' She gave a small laugh. 'There you go. Aww, look. Leon, it's your daddy. Here he is. Yes.'

Leon grizzled and whined a bit, but settled down once Wallace held him closer. His little body was warm and soft. He opened his eyes wide and looked up at Wallace. At that moment, Wallace thought he could see some likeness of himself in the expression. And he wondered if things could change. If he could ever be a normal dad. OK, maybe not normal. But a dad; there for his son at least. He felt his throat getting a bit tighter.

'Shall we walk him?' he asked, getting to his feet. 'What's the time?'

She took out her iPhone. 'Just gone three.'

'What time exactly?'

Jas frowned. 'Seven minutes past. Did they say you had to go back at a certain time?'

'No, just, you know. Wanted to know.'

They arced round across the grass towards the perimeter of the park. The traffic noises grew, and the armed coppers followed them. Wallace sat on a bench under a big, old tree and Jas joined him, so close their skin was touching and he could smell her perfume. He started getting aroused again and tried to calm himself down. Tried to concentrate on what he was doing.

'He likes being out in the open air,' she said.

'Same as me,' grinned Wallace. They sat like that for a while, both gazing at Leon, at the life they'd created. Wallace never liked to show his emotion – usually, that was a sign of weakness – but there was something magical about this. He didn't want to leave just yet. But Leon had other ideas and started to cry.

'D'you want me to take him?' said Jas.

'Nah, it's cool,' replied Wallace, standing and trying his best to rock Leon despite his handcuffs.

'He might need feeding.'

'Let me hold him a bit longer, yeah?' They began walking towards the far side of the park, where the grass ended abruptly at a wall that overlooked the train tracks. 'So, what you been up to?'

Jas told him about how her older boy, Reece, was doing at school. Wallace remembered him: a sweet little kid who loved toy cars. She said it was getting a bit cramped in their flat now with the three of them, and told him about another place she was hoping the council could give them in Clapham: a two-bed. Better schools around there as well, she said. Better than the one Wallace had gone to in Brixton, probably.

Wallace came to a stop with his back to the wall. The coppers were still there, in their triangle. Boateng was watching him too, a bit further away. But they didn't seem as stressed as when they'd arrived. Everyone looked kind of relaxed. Maybe it was the summer afternoon, maybe the fact that he hadn't tried to take Jas hostage the minute he'd arrived. He was about to ask her what time it was, again, when a horn in the distance told him. It was time.

Still holding Leon, Wallace quickly placed an elbow on the wall and sprang up so he was sitting on it. There was a ten-metre drop over his shoulder to the train tracks.

'Darian, what you doing?' said Jas. 'Get down.'

'It's cool, babes.' Wallace glanced over his shoulder, shuffled himself along a bit.

'Give him here,' she said, approaching with her arms out. There was urgency in her voice, desperation.

'Wallace!' cried Boateng.

The armed police drew their pistols.

'Get on the ground!' barked one of them, and Wallace saw Jas drop to the grass. He stayed up on the wall, holding the baby. The rumble of engine and wheels grew from his left, and the horn sounded again.

'Don't do anything stupid, Darian!' shouted Boateng.

'Get down from the wall!' yelled the armed officer in the centre of the triangle.

'Chill, yeah?' Wallace smiled and lifted Leon slightly. 'You'll wake him up.'

The armed officers got closer, maybe just five metres away now. All three had their guns raised at his lower body, aiming away from the baby.

'Put the kid down and step away!'

The growl of the train was louder. He glanced to his left and saw its engine barrelling through Denmark Hill station towards them.

'If you do not follow the order, we will shoot.'

Wallace reckoned the feds wouldn't risk it, so long as he held the kid.

'I can put one in your leg from here,' said the lead officer.

'Have a go, big man,' said Wallace, drawing his feet up slowly so that he was squatting on the wall.

Boateng was on the outside of their triangle now, his palms raised. 'Darian, come on.' He had to shout over the thundering train. 'It's not worth it. Don't wreck this. If you get down now, you'll still be able to see Leon.'

Wallace paused. Maybe Boateng was right. He could be a father to his boy.

'Alright,' he said. One of the coppers had his pistol trained on Wallace's face. The guy was confident. 'OK. Just relax, yeah?' He spread his hands and gently leaned forwards to place Leon on the wall. Looked at his son for a moment.

Then he rolled backwards and felt himself falling.

●

'Stop!' screamed one of the firearms team as they all surged forward, but it was too late. Fletcher leapt up and grabbed Leon, while another officer sprinted to the wall and climbed onto it. His weapon was pointing down at the tracks and he took aim. But he didn't fire. Boateng planted his hands on the brickwork and looked over.

Ten metres below, on the metal rails, a yellow freight train hurtled away from them. Its open-topped wagons were filled with sand.

And there was no sign of Darian Wallace.

# CHAPTER TWELVE

'So is it true, Kat?' Patel looked up at Jones, wide-eyed, and extended the packet of chocolate biscuits towards her. 'You were the one who arrested this guy that's got away?'

Jones wasn't expecting the question and suddenly felt uncomfortable. The news of Wallace's escape was still vague, and she hadn't yet processed its implications. She looked around to see who was in earshot. Apart from her, Patel and Goodhew, the only other people in the Pluto room were Chambers and Harper, who were conferring quietly at a whiteboard by the far wall.

'Yeah, sort of,' she replied, taking the packet. She plucked a biscuit out and offered the packet to Goodhew, who was sitting at the desk next to Patel.

'Holy shit. Amazing!' Patel's face lit up. He shook his head in awe. 'That's exactly the kind of thing I want to be doing: nicking suspects; getting out there, where the action is.'

Goodhew crunched into her biscuit and swept the crumbs off her trousers. 'Wouldn't catch me getting involved with all that.' She pulled a face of horror. 'Way too dangerous. I've got a two-year-old.' She held up her mobile and showed them the screensaver: her and a man with a little girl perched between them on some grass. 'Holly.'

'Sweet,' said Jones through a mouthful of biscuit.

'My husband's an accountant,' continued Goodhew. 'He thinks working at a computer in the Met is risky enough.' She laughed.

'You're missing out, Amy.' Patel took the packet back from her and helped himself to another one. 'What about before you settled down?'

'There's a reason I joined as an analyst. Give me some data and a nice cup of tea and I'm happy.'

'Come on.' Patel spread his hands. 'What about the buzz?'

'I get a buzz from finding a decent lead on here,' replied Goodhew, gesturing to her monitor. 'Thank you very much.'

'I'm talking about the *real* buzz.'

Jones knew what he meant, but she still wanted to offer a few words to curb his exuberance. Christ, did that mean she was getting old? Before she could calibrate her response, footsteps sounded from the corridor. She looked over her shoulder to see Boateng enter the Op Pluto incident room, his head bowed like a condemned man's. Just behind him came Maddox and Krebs, both ashen-faced. Maddox told them all to gather round. Jones imagined the dressing-down the two DCIs would've just given Boateng, after what happened. The team had only caught a few snippets in the office, and she could barely believe what she'd heard. Details were hazy, but the headline was clear.

'Darian Wallace, a convicted murderer, has escaped.' Krebs bit her lip, shook her head briefly and glanced at Boateng. 'He was under the supervision of a Tactical Firearms Team and DI Boateng during a visit from HMP Belmarsh High Security Unit to Ruskin Park, Camberwell. The minister had signed off for Wallace to visit his baby son, in exchange for information that might help us to identify and apprehend Kaiser.'

'Pardon my French,' said Kevin Harper, 'but how the fuck did that happen?'

Maddox thrust his hands into his pockets, rocked back and forth. 'Zac, would you care to explain for the benefit of this lot?'

Boateng ran a hand over his face, swallowed. 'I don't...' he began. 'He was holding the baby and everything seemed fine. We had all the park exits covered. Then, the next minute, he was up on a wall using the baby as a shield. Firearms guys couldn't risk a shot, not even an immobilising one.'

'Wallace must've known that,' observed Chambers.

'Then he agreed to put the kid down,' said Boateng. 'But the second he did, he dropped backwards off the wall.'

'Onto… what exactly?' said Harper.

'The wall by the train tracks?' Chambers frowned. 'It's miles off the ground. How did he survive that?'

'He landed in a freight wagon full of sand,' replied Boateng, closing his eyes in what Jones took for disbelief.

'We managed to stop the train two miles west of Denmark Hill,' said Krebs. 'One of our helicopters was rerouted from another job to survey the area.'

'Let me guess. He wasn't found.' Chambers looked from Krebs to Boateng and back.

'Nope.'

'I'll repeat my question then,' said Harper, his voice rising. 'How did that happen?'

'He must've known, somehow.' Boateng rubbed his eyes.

Harper snorted. 'What, he knew there was a train full of sand coming past at that exact moment?'

'Clever bastard,' said Chambers, massaging his double chin. He pulled the shirt away from his armpit, where the material had stuck to his skin.

'Maybe he knew the timetables?' offered Patel.

'It's possible,' said Maddox. 'Are they online?'

Goodhew tapped away at her computer for a few seconds, clicked a couple of times. 'Yes. Freight timetables for the whole country are on the Network Rail website.'

'He could have accessed the web in prison,' said Maddox. 'Smuggled smartphone, maybe. Explains why he chose that location.'

'Sorry, sir,' said Boateng. 'I didn't predict that at all. I just never thought – I mean I didn't even see…' He sat down heavily. 'I thought that if we controlled the environment, that'd be enough.'

'Look at this.' Goodhew rotated her screen and scrolled down pages of times and locations. 'This is just one line. There are at least twenty freight lines running through London alone. How could he have memorised that?'

Boateng looked up. 'This is a guy with an IQ of 155.' He bashed the heel of his hand against his head. 'I'm such an idiot; I should've thought of it.'

'Well,' said Krebs, 'the inquiry will determine that.'

'Hang about,' interjected Harper. 'How did this fella know about Kaiser, anyway? How did we know that he'd know?'

'DI Boateng?' Krebs raised her eyebrows.

Boateng coughed. 'He'd told me before.'

'What?' said Harper. 'When?'

'Last year,' replied Boateng quietly.

'Jesus Christ.' Harper threw his arms up, rocked back in his chair. 'You knew about this and you've said nothing all week while we've been running around like twats trying to catch this guy. What the hell, Zac?'

'I just… He told me under duress, and there was no evidence. It could've been rumour, or whatever he wanted me to hear.'

'Even so,' said Krebs, towering over him, 'you had a duty to report that. At the very least once this investigation started.'

'Well, if he went to see this Wallace guy in prison, then he must've been working on it already.' Chambers leaned forward.

Boateng didn't respond. Jones felt for him; he'd obviously screwed up big time, but she understood the motivation that had led to his choices. Seeing his dejected expression and defeated body language now, she felt some niggling guilt about reporting to Krebs about him. And she knew the DCI would expect an update on his reaction to today's events.

'I'll draw my own conclusions then.' Chambers tapped his biro on the table, shaking his head.

'Anything else you're not telling us, Zaccy boy?' said Harper, surveying the room for approval.

'What do you mean?' asked Boateng, glancing up.

Harper pointed a finger at him. 'How do we know you didn't orchestrate the whole bloody thing with Wallace? How do we know he isn't chilling round at your gaff right now with a six-pack of beers and a box set?'

'And if Wallace is connected to Kaiser, where does that put your loyalty on this op, son?' inquired Chambers, staring Boateng down.

'Will.' Maddox's tone was cautionary.

'You've got some serious questions to answer, Zac.' Harper leaned forward, his chest puffed out. 'Will's right. Can we trust you?'

Boateng didn't reply.

'Come on,' said Maddox. 'Take it easy. We're all on the same side. Zac's just been under a lot of pressure the past twenty-four hours. Right, Zac?'

Boateng rubbed his legs and looked around the assembled group. 'Er, yeah. Yesterday afternoon my kid went missing.'

Chambers narrowed his eyes. 'What, ran off? Or kidnapped?'

'I don't know,' said Boateng. His voice was barely audible and his leg was jiggling.

'I'm sorry to hear that,' said Harper, without a trace of sympathy. 'But the fact is, you've lied to us and let a murderer loose in south London. Is there anything else you're hiding?'

'That's enough, Kevin,' said Maddox. He loosened his tie even further. 'Zac informed DCI Krebs and me that, prior to his escape, Wallace gave him some useful intelligence on Kaiser. Tell them what you told us, Zac.'

'Wallace said that Kaiser doesn't just source his weapons on the continent. He gets them here, too.'

'Impossible.' Harper cracked his knuckles.

'A lot closer to home than you'd think, too,' said Maddox. 'Go on, Zac.'

'Wallace said that Kaiser is able to get firearms from the Met's destruction depot. God knows how. He must have an insider there. Smuggles out confiscated guns before they get chopped up – a few every month. Apparently, they do around a hundred weapons a week, so I guess one or two can slip through unnoticed.'

'We need to take a quiet look at the depot,' said Maddox, nodding. 'See whether any guns have gone missing – confirm what Wallace says. Then check the staff lists, draw up some profiles. Amy, Raj?'

'Sir,' they said as one.

'Kaiser lost a load of firearms when we nabbed his Škorpions on Sunday night, so he'll be looking for new supplies to make up for it.' Maddox surveyed them. 'This could be our chance to get him. And let's keep that within these walls, please. Zac obtained the ballistics report yesterday on the Kurz used by Collins. Kaiser's obviously got a man somewhere who redrills the barrels for him. He could be converting replicas or breaking the link between a weapon and its history. That's a decent lead, too.'

Maddox distributed some more actions and wrote a few notes on their team whiteboard.

Jones raised her hand and Maddox nodded at her. 'Kat.'

'Sir, what about Wallace?' Her question was partly motivated by the fact that she'd played a significant part in his arrest last year. And by her knowledge that Wallace was a man who took revenge.

Maddox blew out his cheeks. 'Better pray we find him.'

•

Connelly took a deep pull on his Guinness, closed his eyes and swallowed. Pretty bloody good. Not the same as you'd get up in Camden, where the best Irish pubs were, let alone County Cork, where he'd grown up, but alright for England. And well earned after a long day looking for Boateng's boy. Well, sort of. He'd give himself A for effort, E for attainment. A lot like his old school reports. Except for the A part.

'Alright, Pat?' Boateng clapped a hand on his shoulder and took the bar stool next to him.

'Aye, grand.' He didn't even ask this time. As if anything would be better twenty-four hours later. He tilted the glass towards Boateng. 'Can I get you one?'

'No, thanks, mate. I've gotta head home in a bit, see how Etta's doing.'

Connelly looked sideways at his boss. Raised his big grey eyebrows.

'OK then.' Boateng shook his head. 'Christ knows I need it.'

Connelly called the order to the barman. 'I saw the alert on Wallace.'

'It's gone out to every station in London,' said Boateng. 'And surrounding counties.'

'Jeez.' Connelly gave a low whistle, stared into his pint. 'I mean, how did he—'

Boateng held up a hand. 'Do you mind if we don't, Pat?'

'Yeah, course.'

The new pint was placed down and Boateng drank half of it in one go before letting out a huge breath.

'Cheers,' said Connelly. 'Bad luck if you don't.'

Boateng stared at him a second. Then he laughed and clinked his glass against Connelly's. 'My bad. Don't know whether I'm coming or going.'

Connelly was about to say that he felt like that most days, but he didn't want Boateng to think he was taking the piss. So he just sipped his Guinness instead.

'Anything today then?' There was optimism in Boateng's tone, but his voice was strained.

'Well,' began Connelly. Boateng would be aware that if he or Malik had made a major breakthrough, they'd have been on the phone straight away. What he was after was details. Connelly couldn't blame him; if one of his kids went missing, he'd want to know every damn keystroke and handwritten note the police made about it. 'We've checked all the CCTV. Nothing that gives us a clue about where he went. Phone's still off – no activity there.'

Boateng's head sank nearer to his pint.

'But there was one thing. Small, mind you. Came in late today.'

His boss perked up. 'What?'

'A kid at the school activity club thinks she saw Kofi getting into a car.'

'What kind of car?'

'She, ah…' Connelly flapped a hand. 'You know, you have to be so careful about the way you ask the wee ones questions, you don't want to—'

'I know, make them think they have to agree with you, bias their response, all of that. What did she say?'

'She thought the car was grey.'

'OK.' Boateng looked hopeful.

'Or silver.'

'Right.'

'Or white.'

Hope turned to pain on his boss's face. 'Damn.' He took another gulp of his pint. 'And she only *thinks* it was Kofi?'

'That's right, boss. She can't be sure, it's—'

'She see anyone with him?'

'Aye, but she said it was just for a second. An adult.'

'What?' spluttered Boateng. 'An adult driving a fucking car? Of course it was an adult.'

'Easy now, Zac. The wee lass is seven years old. You can't pressure them into saying anything at that age. They send you on the wrong lines cos you hint this or that and you're up shit creek.'

'She say anything else?'

'Just, a big adult.'

'Big? Jesus. Like, what? Tall, fat, muscle, what?' Boateng was getting frantic.

'Alright, let's just…' He held both hands out. 'All she could say was big, like me.'

'No offence, Pat, but you're not that big.'

'None taken. Five feet ten inches is the average height for a man in this country.'

'So what she means is an adult.'

'Yup.'

'Hair?'

'Hat.'

'Male?'

'She's not sure. Like I said, it was just a glimpse, by the sounds of it.'

Boateng sighed. As thin and potentially unreliable as it was, they were both aware what it implied. What suspicions it confirmed. Abduction. But Connelly knew it remained a missing person case in the absence of any communication from those responsible. Or the absence of a more definitive eyewitness statement.

'Malik's still in the office,' said Connelly. 'Running the CCTV again.'

'Now?' Boateng checked his watch. 'Did they authorise the overtime?'

'Nope. He's just a good lad.'

'True.'

They both drank.

'But we shouldn't get our hopes up with that description of the car. It's so vague that we probably—'

'Pat.' Boateng was looking him square in the eye. His boss was a friendly man, but sometimes his expression could make even an ex-fighter like Connelly shit himself. 'I'm gonna show you something. But I want you to promise you won't tell a damned soul. You promise?'

'Aye.'

'Swear?'

Connelly crossed himself. 'On the Holy Mother.' That was as good an oath as an Irishman could make.

Boateng produced his phone, tapped the screen and turned it to Connelly. He read it twice.

'Jesus, Zac. You've not told anyone?'

'Like it says.'

Connelly inclined his head. 'I get that.'

'Is there anything you can do with it?' asked Boateng. 'I mean, without it going to the kidnap team?'

A moment passed while Connelly sipped his drink, flicking his eyes from Boateng to the phone screen and back. Then he reached for a little white napkin from the bar, produced a pen from his rucksack and wrote down the number.

●

'We've got five grand, split between our different savings accounts,' said Etta, laying out some bank statements on the kitchen table. 'Mum and Dad will give us another ten, they said.'

Zac nodded, glancing at the statements. 'I've got a few hundred in my personal account.'

'I was thinking of asking the church for the rest. They keep a lot of cash from the collections at services. You know, just until we can pay it back. He said two days, didn't he?' She was speaking quickly, her fingers drumming on the wooden tabletop.

'Yeah.'

'And he hasn't sent anything else? About when and where, anything like that?'

'No.' Zac didn't expect the delivery instructions to come until the eleventh hour. Kaiser was too smart for that. Even if Zac followed the order not to tell anyone – which he'd already broken – then Kaiser would know that the extra time would give him the chance to plan, to set something up, an ambush or whatever, at the handover. He wouldn't take that chance. He hadn't stayed under the radar for so long by taking chances.

'I told Pat,' he said.

Etta's eyes widened and she slapped the table. 'Why did you do that? He said not to tell *anyone*. That's what he said. He said that if we tell anyone, Kofi loses his, his fi…' Her voice caught. 'Fingers.' She pinched her eyes.

'I know, but we can trust him. He'll see if they can get anything on that number, quietly. Even the smallest detail might help us. I didn't take it to the kidnap team. They'd be all over it, trying to communicate back, messing it up and God knows what else. Maybe even going to the media if they thought that'd help. Pat's discreet.'

'You're sure we can trust him?'

'Etta! Jesus. Pat's a good guy. I've worked with him five years.'

'All I'm saying is' – her voice was rising – 'we don't know the first thing about this person who's taken our son.'

He laid a hand over hers, felt it trembling. 'That's not true. We know he wants money. That's a weakness. And we think that's because his guns were intercepted and he needs to pay a supplier.'

'You don't know for sure that it's even the same guy!' she blurted. 'This Kaiser – we don't know that it's him who's got Kofi.'

'Has to be. It's personal. He knows I'm looking for him.' Boateng felt his own frustration growing. 'Who else could it be?'

'I don't know, Zac! I don't bloody well know anything any more. I don't know left from right or up from down. Some other enemy you've made, maybe?'

'Oh, so it's my fault either way then? That what your parents said, is it?'

She didn't reply.

Zac withdrew his hand. 'Well, thanks for the vote of confidence. I'm busting my balls trying to catch this guy and find our boy and this is how—' He stopped himself when he saw she was crying.

Etta leaned over, put her head on his chest. He wrapped his arms around her.

'I'm sorry, love,' he whispered.

'Me too,' she replied.

They sat like that for a minute before Etta sat up again and wiped her eyes.

'Look, let's make a call to the pastor tonight,' she said. 'Tomorrow morning, we go to the bank and draw out everything we can. Get it ready in a packet or whatever. Then we wait until this evil bastard tells us where to take it. We do what he says, and we get Kofi back. Simple. Then we worry about everything else later.'

Zac never ceased to be amazed by his wife's strength, her resilience. Like she'd shown so many times. Maybe it was as simple as she'd just stated; Zac wished it was. But even if they got Kofi back, he doubted Kaiser would allow himself to be caught. And it wasn't just Kaiser they had to worry about. Now, of course, Darian Wallace was out there, too.

Somewhere.

# CHAPTER THIRTEEN

Jones stared down at the glass on the table; her third beer. It was probably an error to have drunk two pints in less than one hour, and on an empty stomach. She'd considered another parkour training session tonight, but the draw of alcohol was too strong. She didn't particularly want to be here – a bog-standard pub in Ladywell with a random bunch of colleagues – but after the past week, she needed to let off some steam. Booze was the easiest way to deal with the stress of keeping secrets. And she told herself that accepting the invitation was the sociable thing to do. She'd even taken a group selfie of them all at the beginning, then WhatsApped it to Boateng with a short message: *You're not missing much*.

The Op Pluto lot were getting on it, now that Maddox and Krebs had left. The two DCIs had bought a round each for the team and then buggered off, presumably having bigger and better plans for their respective Friday nights. That was standard for senior officers; they wouldn't want to have their authority dented by the team seeing them pissed. At least Maddox had lasted two rounds.

In their absence, Kevin Harper had assumed the alpha position. He was loudly telling Patel and Goodhew a story from his Met days about arresting a pimp who'd got stuck trying to climb out of a window during a house raid. The pair of them were enthralled: Patel was riveted while Goodhew giggled. She said she'd got the night off, with her husband looking after their toddler, and she was putting away the white wine. Jones watched Harper's theatrical performance, his muscular movements. OK, he was a bit slimy, for sure, but he wasn't *un*attractive… and the snippets she could catch of his anecdote were quite funny. Had she been too quick to judge him, or was she just starting to get beer goggles?

Only Boateng was absent. Jones wondered where he was, what he was doing. With Kofi still missing, it was understandable that he wasn't coming to the pub with them. But she knew her boss. And somehow, she doubted he'd be sitting quietly at home, waiting for news. She imagined him off pursuing a lead on Kaiser, putting himself in harm's way again, with determination that shaded all too quickly into stubbornness and obsession. She'd definitely made the right call. His actions were getting dangerous. Yet after reporting on him to Krebs, the guilt nibbled at her with the low-level but constant discomfort of an insect bite.

Jones took another swig of her drink. She felt it go straight down and hit her stomach. She needed some food to soak up the beer. Cheeseburger and chips? Yeah, that'd do the trick. Just as she was about to get up and head to the bar, Chambers blocked her exit and sat down heavily beside her, a fresh pint in one hand, two shot glasses in the other. He slurped the foamy top off his lager and placed the shots in front of them. He smelled of cigarettes; Jones hadn't realised he smoked.

'Alright?' he said, without looking at her.

'Er, pretty knackered, actually.' That was usually a good way to put off unwanted men.

'Get this down you,' he said, sliding the shot glass in front of her pint. 'It'll help.'

'I don't know, sir, I'm not—'

'Call me Will. Come on, let's do it.' He raised the glass.

Jones glanced around but there was no help coming. Normally, she wouldn't accept a drink that she hadn't seen poured, or from a guy she barely knew. She couldn't reasonably turn this down, though. 'OK, thanks.' She lifted the shot and caught a sickly whiff of aniseed. Sambuca? Jesus, Chambers really was stuck in the noughties.

'Cheers.' Chambers necked the shot, belched into his fist and rubbed his belly. He nodded towards the others. 'You know, Harper's not the big man he says he is. And just cos he's studied economics or whatever, it doesn't make him smarter than the rest of us.'

Jones didn't reply. She just took a sip of beer to get rid of the sambuca taste. But that made it even worse.

'Reckons he's the dog's,' said Chambers. 'You know what his nickname was when he was in the Met?'

'No,' said Jones. She had to admit, she was intrigued.

'Kev the Tosser.'

She laughed out loud and, somewhat unsubtly, looked over to Harper. They made eye contact briefly and Jones caught a snatch of his conversation. He'd moved on to telling Goodhew and Patel about his motorbike.

'I've got a bike, too,' said Chambers, watching Harper mime a throttle movement. 'And my engine's bigger than his,' he added, with no trace of irony.

Jones glanced sideways at him. Yup, he was serious about the engine size.

'Kev the Tosser, that's what we all called him,' continued Chambers. 'Not to his face, mind. He had another nickname too. One he supposedly started himself.'

'Which was?'

'Shagger.' Chambers slurped his beer. Jones could see a film of sweat on his face.

'Lovely.'

'Yeah, he used to work with hookers. Vice squad. You know what that lot were like, ten, fifteen years ago.' Chambers raised his eyebrows.

'Um, no, I don't.' She would've been at school at the time.

'Dodgy as hell. Used to run prostitutes as informants. There were all kinds of rumours. I steered clear of that work myself, you know? I've got standards. But some of those vice coppers used to take a cut from the hookers they were running, collect debts on their behalf. Even use their services personally. Then put it down on expenses.'

Jones pulled a face of disgust. Three beers in, it was getting harder to mask her reactions.

'And you know he's not telling the full story about that pimp.' Chambers pointed at Harper. Belched again. 'When they arrested the geezer, one of the lids on the scene said there was a trunk with about ten grand in it, cash. The takings. Vanished from the pimp's home. Then the lid changed his story, said he must've made a mistake and there was no cash to begin with.' Chambers shook his head. 'I've had offers like that. "Get yourself a drink," they always say. But it ain't right. You've just gotta turn them down. Doesn't matter if you get labelled a grass eater.'

'Grass eater?'

'Yeah. A copper who won't take a bung or shave a bit off on the side. As opposed to the meat eaters, who chew up everything they can get their hands on. Like Harper.'

'Right.' At least the secondment to Op Pluto was expanding her Met vocabulary.

'Or Boateng.'

'Look, Will, I don't think Zac is—'

'Where is he tonight, by the way?'

'At home with his wife?' she suggested.

'He was just coming back into the office when I left.' Chambers took a big gulp of lager.

'I don't know. Looking for his son then?'

'All I'm saying is, be careful.' He reached down to his trousers and ran a hand around the inside of his belt, where his stomach was spilling over it. 'You want another shot?'

'No, thanks,' she said. 'I mean, I need to head off. Got to meet some friends.'

'Oh. Where?'

'Shoreditch,' she replied quickly, collecting her things. 'Birthday drinks for an old uni mate.'

Jones surprised herself with how easily she'd managed to lie. Maybe she was getting used to it.

●

Darian Wallace had waited in the trees until the light faded. Friday night outside a student hall of residence; it was just a matter of time. He heard the chatter of young voices, the thump of bass speakers, the clink of bottles. He'd been hiding here about an hour. His stomach was hollow and he still had sand in places he couldn't reach. Worse, his left arm hurt like a bitch from the second drop, off the freight train and onto the ground. With the cuffs on, there'd been no way to catch himself. But at least he was free. That was the main thing. He'd work out the rest later.

His first task had been to find a thin piece of metal and pick the ratchet on his handcuffs. Getting hold of the material was easy enough; he'd found some stiff wire in a junkyard next to the railway line where he'd jumped off the train. The picking itself wasn't a problem, either; there were a ton of YouTube videos he'd watched while inside that showed you how to do it. It was trickier with both wrists in the cuffs, but even so, the job took less than a minute. He'd cut one wrist in the process, but it had stopped bleeding now. Cuffs off, the next thing he needed was cash and a change of clothes. Couldn't walk around in prison-issue grey sweatpants and T-shirt. Might as well put a flashing light on his head. That was why he'd come here, watching and waiting for someone he knew wouldn't risk reporting a crime.

Finally, he saw what he'd been waiting for: a lone youth coming up the road, probably seventeen or eighteen, by Wallace's estimate. The guy stopped short of the building. Took out an old Nokia-style phone and dialled. Wallace knew he wasn't a student from the way he hesitated, hovering a few metres before the entrance, away from any cameras or lights. He didn't belong there. The little black bag hanging from a shoulder strap to his hip was a giveaway. Damn, had these guys learned nothing? Wallace recognised an earlier version of himself, though this guy's hair wasn't as good. He wondered whether this kid would go down the same path he had. Or get his shit together and go to uni, like the floppy-haired, skinny boy bounding towards him from the halls, desperate to get his hands on the gear. Floppy-hair gave the younger kid some notes; the kid handed over a bag. Simple as that. A transaction that was done thousands of times across London every day.

Wallace watched Floppy-hair skip back towards his front door and the dealer turn around and walk off into the shadows, the way he'd come. Wallace emerged from the trees and quickened his pace. Had to break into a jog to close the gap. The dealer heard something and began to turn just as Wallace wrapped the crook of his right elbow round the guy's neck from behind. He squeezed to cut off the oxygen, then kicked the back of the kid's knee to make him drop. Wallace folded his left arm around his own right hand, forming a scissor around the neck. Finally, his left hand pressed the dealer's head forward. The guy's arms flapped about before his body went limp, and then Wallace dragged him sideways into the trees. The whole thing had taken twenty seconds. His victim would probably be out for about the same time.

Working fast, Wallace took the kid's bag and top off. Pulled his hands behind his back and cuffed them. Then he removed the dealer's shoes and moved up to his trousers. Wallace was undoing the belt when he heard a gasp and saw the kid had woken up. His eyes were darting all over the place. The brer looked terrified, probably thinking he was about to get batty-raped or something.

Wallace smiled. The guy began to speak but Wallace was on him again, turning him onto his stomach, elbow round neck, head forward, back to sleep. The next time he woke up, Wallace had his trousers off.

'D'you wanna be put down again, big man?' asked Wallace.

The guy shook his head.

'Then keep quiet, yeah?' Wallace began putting on the new clothes.

The dealer nodded once, glanced around. A dribble of spit had leaked down his chin.

'You can keep your boxers,' said Wallace. 'Probably got skid marks in 'em now, anyway.'

'What crew you with?' whispered the kid.

Wallace didn't reply. He just separated the cash out of the bag. Probably a couple of hundred quid there.

'Who you shottin' for?' said the dealer.

Wallace grinned as he flung the bag of drugs back at the guy and stood. 'Myself.'


Wallace pushed open the door. This was like stepping back to a time before smartphones. Against the left wall, two guys sat in separate booths, each jabbering away into a receiver. The first sounded like he was speaking Somali. Wallace didn't recognise the second language. On the right, three more brers sat at a long table divided by plywood screens. One was Skyping with a headset and the other two were on chat forums. The hawala man at the money transfer counter nodded Wallace towards a free terminal and he sat down. Fired up the web browser and went to Gmail. A minute later he had a new email address in a fake name.

He hit 'Compose' and began typing.

Boateng stopped typing, leaned back in the chair and rubbed his eyes. He reached for his coffee and took a swig: stone cold, and not even decent stuff. The only good thing was the mug. It was his favourite: a present from Kofi though, since he'd only been three at the time, Etta had bought it. The mug carried a commemorative 2010 World Cup image of the Ghanaian national football team. The first World Cup in Africa, and the furthest Ghana had ever reached in the tournament. They'd made progress that no one had thought possible. But they'd come up short at the final hurdle, losing their composure at the last minute. He couldn't make the same mistake, let his emotions get the better of him when it really mattered. Let Kaiser get away with wrecking lives for his personal gain. Let him get away with taking Kofi. But until the instructions for delivering the ransom money arrived, the best thing he could do was keep digging.

Wallace had given Boateng a name that he hadn't yet shared with anyone else: Leonard Bray. A guy with form for armed robbery. According to Wallace, Bray had purchased several firearms from Kaiser back in 2014. In order to pay debts of his own, Bray had then threatened to turn Kaiser over to the police, claiming he had recorded their transaction. Kaiser notionally agreed to pay and the two arranged a meeting. The rest was obvious, Wallace said. And he was right: Bray was one of the five names on Jones's list of unsolved murders in south London.

Boateng had the report and crime scene photos up on his screen now. Bray had been shot twice in the chest and once in the face, his body left where it had fallen between two shipping containers on a building site in Tooting. There were no witnesses, no CCTV and no shell casings found at the scene. Plenty of DNA had been found in the vicinity, but all of it was from construction workers who were cleared. One thing stuck out for Boateng: three 9 mm slugs were recovered from the industrial unit, but in the week following the murder, the bullets were lost before any analysis of them could be conducted. An unnamed detective's note speculated that human error by the ballistics lab or couriers was responsible. Further investigations, which looked half-hearted at best, had failed to identify any viable suspects from Bray's recent activities. They obviously hadn't found out that he'd just bought a load of weapons. The case was shelved a year later. He'd hoped there would be some detail in the notes to point him in the right direction. But he hadn't found it yet.

It was nearly 10 p.m. and Boateng knew he should head home to see how Etta was doing. Perhaps he'd just look at a few more entries from the Bray murder file before he called it a night. He told himself he wasn't simply delaying the inevitable confrontation with Etta's parents.

He finished the coffee, grimaced and carried on reading.

●

Kaiser finished his double espresso and stared at the laptop screen. Normally, coffee at this time of night was a bad idea. But there was work to do and a sharpener was required. It had taken longer than usual to travel home; after drinking earlier, the bike was off limits, which meant using public transport. Kaiser had been impatient to get back, but even after the time-consuming journey, nothing had arrived. Then, ten minutes ago, a message had dropped into the old 'ColonelKurz21' Gmail inbox: the communication Kaiser had been expecting for several hours, since news of the escape had come through.

Wallace's options were limited. His face would be everywhere: at transport hubs, in the London papers, on the news. Kaiser was probably one of the few people he could trust not to turn him in. It was logical that Wallace would set up a new account and contact the email address he had for Kaiser. The one they'd used when Kaiser had supplied weapons to Wallace and his friends. A different email for each customer, that was the rule. So Kaiser had known which one to check. The only surprise was how long it had taken Wallace to make contact.

The message itself was simple, economical:

*I need money K. Hook me up. Any odd jobs you need doing? D*

Wallace was exceptionally smart. But he was also a volatile young man and Kaiser didn't trust him; a mutual feeling, no doubt. The convicted murderer had clearly traded information on Kaiser to get out of prison for the day. That was the kind of betrayal that was usually punished swiftly, to make sure others knew the price for snitching. However, they shared a common enemy: Boateng. The detective would be doing everything he could to identify Kaiser. The others in that team weren't as motivated. That was understandable; they hadn't lost children. Wallace's intel would have brought Boateng a step closer, and with the bit between his teeth now, he wouldn't give up. The only logical solution was to remove him altogether, once the ransom payment had been made.

So if Wallace was looking for cash, Kaiser could think of a way for him to earn it. A call would need to be made to the Quartermaster to get Wallace the equipment he needed. But that was the easy part. Kaiser hit reply and began typing:

*I've got just the thing for you...*

# CHAPTER FOURTEEN

**Saturday, 25 August 2018**

Seven days ago, life had been so much simpler. Then, Susanna Pym had been just one day into her new ministerial appointment and chock-full of enthusiasm. Crucial to that optimism was the fact that there hadn't really been time for anything to go wrong. Now, in an astonishingly short period, it all seemed to have gone tits up. The Home Office policing portfolio was supposed to be her ticket to the grown-ups' table. Instead, it was looking like the last act in a political career that observers would ultimately sum up as 'rather disappointing', if they bothered to comment on it at all.

Pym's gaze travelled from the television and across the dining table to her husband. He was gawping at the news coverage of Darian Wallace's escape, his flabby chops open like a bulldog waiting for its breakfast. Sidney had been a different man when she'd married him, twenty-six years ago. Young, vigorous, charming. He hadn't been so... How could she put it? Fat. That was it. Or boring. Perhaps three decades in private banking did that to people. Too many client dinners, too much discussion of wealth management. And not enough sex. Not with your wife at least.

'Good lord,' he exclaimed, reaching for more toast without taking his eyes off the screen. 'Have you seen this, darling? Well, of course you have. Your bag now, isn't it? This sort of thing.'

'Mm.' She took aim at the boiled egg and brought the back of her spoon down on it with a satisfying crack. 'It's a bloody great mess, that's what it is.'

'If this chap kills anyone else, then you'll probably be—'

'Yes. Out of a job. Thank you for reminding me.'

Ordinarily, her husband had the political acuity of an amoeba, but even he could see the writing on the wall in this case. *Out of a job.* Those were effectively the PM's words when she'd heard the news late yesterday and telephoned Pym. Well, that wasn't strictly true. It was her private secretary, Donald, who had made the call. The bastard had barely been able to disguise his glee at taking her down a peg or two. *Bigger picture… public interest… reshuffling the portfolios… safe pair of hands… a fresh approach.* As he'd reeled off a series of clichés and euphemisms for her potential sacking, she'd noticed her jaw, neck and shoulders becoming tighter, until it felt as if something in her head was going to snap. This sensation was accompanied by a fantasy of using one of those Škorpion guns on the self-important little shit delivering the message of impending doom. Something had to change. *She* had to change something.

As she picked the shell off her egg, Pym wondered if it was worth it. The stress, the conniving, the humiliation. Sidney was a few years off retirement, their children had grown up and left home and they had no mortgage. She didn't *need* to work so hard. Maybe she could engineer a cushy little board membership, just to pay for holidays. Or chuck the grind in altogether and retire early, perhaps? Take up a new hobby, like sex.

And yet, the top tier was within reach. First class, the upper deck. True, the killer to whom they had given a day release in exchange for helping catch an arms dealer had escaped. But the situation could still be retrieved if this Wallace chap could be caught or some clever spin put on the whole unfortunate business. You could even argue that the higher stakes meant the pay-off for success was larger, the reputational gain greater. If the alternative to sorting this out was resigning, then she might as well go down in flames. Then, the idea came to her. All of a sudden, she felt rather better. Perhaps her career wasn't over after all.

Pym polished off the egg and took her phone out to the garden, grabbing her cigarettes on the way. Her husband would notice the smell when she returned, but she didn't care. She sat on the bench at the bottom of the lawn, lit up and dialled her man. Drew deeply on the fag before he picked up.

'What can you tell me about this escaped prisoner?' she asked. 'Wallace.'

'Not a lot. The MIT are trying to find him.'

'It was Boateng's name on the submission,' she said between puffs. 'Was he with Wallace when he got away?'

'He was there, but so were a bunch of firearms officers, so you can't really—'

'You said you don't trust Boateng,' she interjected.

'No. His police work's alright; I just said there's something he wasn't telling the rest of us.' He paused. 'But *you* obviously trusted him, if you signed off his submission.'

'Anything that would help us catch Kaiser – that was my guiding principle. I thought you lot would be able to stop a man in handcuffs slipping away in a large open park with police officers on the exits. Obviously, I was wrong.'

'Well, I wasn't there.'

She paused, lowered her voice. 'Do you think there's a chance Boateng was complicit in Wallace's escape?'

'Zac? No way. He does his own thing sometimes, but he's not bent.'

Pym took a couple of drags. 'You know, everyone has started to point the finger at me for this series of cock-ups. If you fail to find Kaiser, and Wallace isn't caught again, then people will want someone to blame. I won't let it be me.'

'Hang on,' he said. 'Are you talking about me?'

'The thought had occurred to me.' She chuckled. 'No. I rather think Boateng should take the rap, don't you?'

The man was silent.

'Makes sense, doesn't it?' she added.

'Look, he's put in his time. He doesn't deserve—'

'It's heart-warming that you have some loyalty for him. But think about yourself. You don't want his failure tainting your career, do you?'

There was a long silence. 'Suppose not.'

'What else can you tell me about Boateng?'

'Well,' he began, before clearing his throat. Pym was enjoying his discomfort. 'That young guy Boateng visited in prison croaked. I've still not worked that out, but Boateng went to see him without telling the rest of us.'

'Hm.' She inhaled deeply on the cigarette, watched the ash tip glow and fade. 'All the more reason to suspect him. Keep a close eye on him, will you, please?'

'OK. Thanks for my money, by the way.'

'Welcome,' she forced herself to reply.

There was a strained silence. Pym realised she was expected to say something else.

'I'll pop some more through,' she added.

'Lovely.'

She rung off, took a final draw and stubbed out the fag. If these botched police operations went on much longer, it was going to get expensive. And in the short term, there was no easy way out. Even if she publicly divulged the incident in which this man had caught her using cocaine nineteen years ago and managed to keep her job, there was bribery in there now, too. Unless she could call it a consultancy fee. She'd check the rules about that.

Pym reclined on the bench and reached for another cigarette. There was no rush to get back inside.

It'd been an error to go hard last night. Looking at the bunch of zombies in the Op Pluto room this morning, Kat Jones knew that she wasn't the only one nursing a hangover. Krebs and Maddox had had the right idea, leaving after one and two drinks respectively. They hadn't confirmed until 8 a.m. today that the team's services were required for overtime. No one wanted to turn that down – they were all determined to nail Kaiser, and the money was decent – but few of them were up to it. Chambers seemed to be sweating alcohol; one pass of his desk had been enough to make Jones steer clear of the man and the smell that hung off him. Goodhew was popping paracetamol and ibuprofen, resting her head in her hands between attempts to rehydrate. Jones guessed that, with a young kid, her boozy nights out were few and far between. Patel had lost his usual enthusiasm, and even after several suspiciously long toilet breaks, he was no closer to getting it back. The only one who looked OK was Harper. Somehow, he appeared energised and alert.

Down the corridor, Jones knew that several members of the Major Investigation Team were also in, overtime having been authorised for the operation to find Darian Wallace, too. Apparently, it was coming right from the top: the Minister for Policing. Jones didn't envy Malik and Connelly working on that: extensive media coverage of the escape would mean sifting through hundreds of calls, emails and alleged sightings. A ton of chaff for every bit of wheat, if there was any wheat at all. Wallace was frighteningly smart and not likely to reveal himself easily.

Malik had told Jones that some basic surveillance had been placed on Wallace's ex-girlfriend, Jasmine Fletcher, who denied any knowledge of his current whereabouts. Jones still remembered seeing Fletcher in pieces last year, after Wallace had stayed with her. She suspected Fletcher was a lost cause in terms of finding him; he'd know they'd be all over her. By now, Wallace could be anywhere. Jones just wished the MIT guys would hurry up and find him, for her own safety as much as anyone else's. She'd played a big part in catching him last year and knew he was one to hold grudges.

'Kat,' came a voice from behind her. She started and turned, head throbbing, to see Krebs. 'How are you doing?' said the DCI.

Jones sat up straight. 'Fine, ma'am. I'm just going through the Police National Computer. Looking for anyone capable of drilling gun barrels who we might have come across before. You know, following up on Wallace's lead to DI Boateng.'

'Good, good.' Krebs nodded quickly. 'Can I have a word, please? Privately.'

Jones followed Krebs down the corridor to her office. Once inside, Krebs shut the door but didn't invite Jones to sit. Instead, she stood, pinning her in the corner. It was easy to forget how physically imposing Krebs was: well over six foot in her heels; lean and strong from her obsessive cycling. Normally the epitome of authority, something in her boss's manner this morning was distracted, her movements tense and agitated.

'DI Boateng was here last night,' began Krebs. 'Late. Apparently he came back in after the rest of us left and spent three hours or more on the Crimint system.' She held eye contact with Jones. 'Any idea what he might've been doing?'

'I'm afraid not, ma'am.'

'Hm. Well, I'm very grateful for the information you've given me so far. And I'd just like to emphasise that you've made entirely the right decision. We can't have lone operators jeopardising the success of our work and the safety of our personnel, not to mention the public.'

'Boateng was unlucky yesterday,' said Jones. It felt easier than blaming him directly.

'He's on very thin ice. In fact, the only reason he isn't suspended after the Wallace debacle is so that we can keep an eye on him here. All of us.' She inclined her head to underline the collective responsibility. 'We have more control over DI Boateng – over his actions – if he's here, working with us, rather than outside, where we have no knowledge of what he's doing.'

Jones was reminded of that expression about tents and pissing but thought the better of quoting it.

'So, any sense what he might be up to, generally?' said Krebs. 'You're closer to him than anyone.'

An uncomfortable silence ensued. The room seemed overheated and Jones was finding it hard to think. 'He…'

'Yes?'

'He's looking into an unsolved murder, ma'am.'

'What? Whose murder?'

'I'm sorry, I don't know.'

Krebs put her hands on her hips. Her gaze lost focus a moment. 'So, what *do* you know about it?'

Jones swallowed. Her throat felt thick and dry and she was desperate for some water. 'Only that, um, it's an old case, which DI Boateng thinks may have been interfered with, ma'am. The investigation, I mean. By Kaiser.'

Krebs narrowed her eyes. 'Kaiser impeded a murder investigation?'

Pressed into the corner like this, Jones didn't feel as if she could stop there. 'Not just that, ma'am. Kaiser may have committed the murder himself. And got away with it.'

Krebs put a hand to her mouth and took a step back. Jones felt like she could breathe a bit more easily, though she didn't feel at all well.

'And how did DI Boateng discover this?' asked Krebs.

'He, er, I think the detainee from the shoot-out told him. Jermaine Mensah. But I'm not certain,' she added hastily.

Krebs was silent for a while. She turned; paced to one side of the room. Inspected the framed photograph of herself with Met Commissioner Cressida Dick. Then came back over to Jones.

'And he isn't sharing this with anyone else because, as you told me before, he believes Kaiser is in the police,' stated Krebs.

'I think that's right, ma'am.'

Krebs cleared her throat. 'That is one possibility, of course.'

Jones didn't respond. Her brain felt like a wet sponge and she was beginning to feel nauseous. A bottle of whisky on a shelf behind Krebs caught her eye, the thought of its alcohol smell making her guts lurch.

'The other possibility,' Krebs resumed, 'is that he's covering something up. Something he's been involved in personally. It wouldn't be the first time.'

'Well, I mean, it's—'

'I'd like you to offer your help to him, Kat. Off the record. See what he's doing. Find out which murder he thinks was carried out by Kaiser.'

'I...' Jones had no choice but to agree. It was basically what she'd been doing for the last week anyway. 'OK.'

'Good. Do you know where he is at the moment?'

'No, ma'am.' Something was moving in her stomach and she could taste bile.

'Me neither. I suggest you give him a call.' Krebs stepped forward and clasped Jones's arm in one hand. Her grip was surprisingly strong. Suddenly, the room felt even hotter. 'And get involved in whatever he's up to.'

Jones mumbled something affirmative, then slipped out and raced down the corridor. She just made it to the ladies' toilet before her breakfast came back up.

⬤

Kofi was thirsty. He couldn't remember ever feeling this thirsty before. It was hot in the little bathroom and, even though the window was open a crack, it didn't cool the place down one bit. His mouth was dry all the time and his throat felt like paper. Often, he'd find himself dreaming of a big glass of cold Coca-Cola, full of ice cubes, with tiny drops on the outside like in the adverts. The water he'd been given wasn't enough: a cupful or two, twice a day with his food, when the man came in.

Those visits were the only way that Kofi had to keep track of time. He thought he'd been here three nights – at least, he reckoned it had been night outside the window three times – but he couldn't be sure. There were moments when he felt scared – mainly when he heard the man stomping up the stairs towards him. Each time, he'd wonder if he was going to get that black box stabbed into him again. It'd only happened once, but that was all he needed to know that he never wanted to be touched by it a second time. Other than that, he mostly felt bored. So he'd close his eyes and make up stories, like the ones Mum and Dad read to him at night.

He'd drifted into a daydream in which he was flying through space in a special suit like Iron Man when he heard the front door shut downstairs. The heavy steps came up and then the door was thrown open, the lights were on and he was blinking, trying to see what was happening. This didn't seem like the normal time for food or the toilet. But maybe he'd got confused. Hands reached down, unlocked the cuffs behind his back and ripped the tape off his face. The skin around his mouth stung.

'Get up.'

Kofi tried to stand but his legs were all wobbly and he had pins and needles in his bum. He held on to the radiator.

'Stand the fuck up,' barked the man. He reached into his pocket and produced the black box. Its metal prongs looked like a pair of devil's horns. Kofi worked harder, pulling himself up with his arms and trying to straighten his legs, but there was no strength in them.

'I can't,' he said.

'Come here.' The man grabbed him by the arm and Kofi thought he was going to be electrocuted, but instead he was pushed through the bathroom door and onto the landing. 'Downstairs,' ordered the man.

Kofi held tight to the bannister and stepped down sideways, trying to keep his footing on the thick carpet. His hands ached and his thighs were shaking. 'Elvis legs', his old football coach used to call that – when your muscles gave up. He wished he was playing in the park right now. Then his knee gave way and he reached out for the rail but missed, and he was falling forwards, tumbling, until he hit the ground. His ribs and hip hurt where they had smashed into the bottom steps, but he was OK. With his hands free, he'd at least managed to catch himself, to shield his head.

'Clumsy bollocks,' said the man, hauling him to his feet. 'Get in here.'

Now he was in a new room he hadn't seen before. A living room. It was pretty empty; just two sofas and a small table. Nothing on the walls: no pictures or ornaments or books or anything. It was like a fake house that no one lived in. He sat down on a sofa, happy to give his legs a rest. Rubbed his side where it had hit the stairs. On the table in front of him was a newspaper.

'We haven't got much time,' said the man. 'So don't fuck about.'

Kofi nodded.

The man took a seat alongside him. He produced a phone from his jacket pocket, tapped at the screen and rotated a voice recording app towards Kofi. Then he produced a piece of paper, which he unfolded and slid across the table. 'Read this.'

Kofi took the paper, his hands trembling, and began scanning the text. It was a letter to Mum and Dad, but he hadn't written it.

'Read it aloud, you twat.' The man tapped the phone screen and a red dot appeared. Recording. He put the phone on the table.

Kofi gave a dry cough. 'Um, dear Mum and Dad. I am fine and being looked after.' He broke off and glanced at the man, who scowled and pointed at the letter. 'I can prove that it is Saturday the twenty-fifth of August,' he continued, 'because the headline in *The Times* is…' The man held up the newspaper for him. Kofi read the biggest writing on the front before the man put it back down on the table.

'I have not been hurt,' he said, carefully following the message text again. 'But if you don't obey these instructions exactly, I will be. I want to have all my fingers, so please—'

He stopped, processing the words. Suddenly, his tummy felt all wriggly again. The man glared at him, jabbed a finger at the script. Kofi finished reading it and looked down at his own hands, imagined them just as blobs on the end of his arms. *All my fingers*. If he didn't have all his fingers, he wouldn't be able to write, draw or play video games. And that wasn't even the worst of it. Last year, he'd sliced into a fingernail when he was cooking with his dad. That was so painful, and it was just a little cut. Surely having your fingers sliced off was the most painful thing that could happen? Maybe even more painful than the black box. Now the worms in his tummy were moving loads.

Kofi studied the man. Gone was the kindness in his face from that first time he'd seen him, outside the school. Now, he looked like someone who might enjoy cutting off your fingers. Kofi hoped Mum and Dad would just pay the money. He willed them to pay it. They had to. Then he'd be allowed to go home.

'Wait here,' the man told him as he got up and went out. Kofi heard some doors opening and closing. It sounded like the man was in the garage that joined on to the house. Kofi glanced over at the mobile phone on the table. It wasn't recording any more, but the screen wasn't locked. Could he quickly make a call? He knew his parents' number from the days before he had a mobile of his own; they'd made him memorise it. Or he could just dial 999. He shuffled closer to it, keeping an eye on the doorway. The man was still doing something in the garage, moving stuff around. Kofi stretched a hand towards the phone.

Then he pulled up short. What would he say? He didn't know where he was.

Sounds were still coming from across the hallway, in the garage.

Maybe he didn't need to say anything, except his name and that he needed help… It could be like in one of those films where they trace the call and find out where the person is. Then Dad might come and rescue him! On the other hand, if the man caught him on the phone, he'd get hit with the black box again… But there was a chance that this would help. And it was what a superhero would do if he couldn't use any other magic powers. He reached out once more, grasped the mobile phone and picked it up slowly while watching the hallway, his hands shaking.

Then the door from the garage slammed and Kofi dropped the phone. It thudded on the carpet by his feet. The man was coming back. He reached down and grabbed the phone. The footsteps were getting closer. Kofi threw it onto the table and sat back on the sofa as the man appeared in the doorway.

The man looked down at Kofi and scanned the table. He was just about to speak when the mobile rang. Kofi could see that the screen said 'Private number'. The man narrowed his eyes at Kofi, then snatched the phone and answered it. He told whoever was on the other end something about being ready right now and then he hung up.

'Let's go,' he said, jerking a thumb towards the doorway.

Kofi stood, pushing himself up on the sofa.

'Come on, I haven't got all fucking day.'

They had just gone through the door into the hall when the man stopped.

'Wait,' he said.

Kofi froze. Was he going to ask about the phone? The man grabbed Kofi's arm and pulled him back to the living room. Kofi's heart was beating really fast.

'Bring the paper,' said the man.

Kofi reached forward and picked it up. Then the hands were gripping him, marching him through the house and into the garage. Tape was stuck across his mouth and his hands cuffed again before he was lifted into the boot like a bag of shopping. Then the lid came down and everything went dark.

# CHAPTER FIFTEEN

Boateng drummed his fingers on the steering wheel and gazed up through his windscreen at the massive art deco building while he waited for the gates to open. Tooting police station was one of those old-fashioned nicks, built between the wars, when architects had an eye for grandeur and the Met had a bit of money. These days, the government's austerity plans meant both were in short supply, and like many other pieces of Met real estate, the place was destined to be sold off. Most likely, it would end up turned into flats to soak up some of London's insatiable demand for homes. Where the proceeds of that sale would go, Boateng had no idea. Not to fund more police work, he guessed. The melancholic jazz of Miles Davis on his car stereo seemed somehow appropriate, although the choice hadn't been deliberate.

What was deliberate, however, was the decision to come here. Boateng knew that if he wanted to make any progress investigating the murder of Leonard Bray, he had to find out what had happened to the slugs recovered from the construction site in 2014. There was nothing to be gained by visiting the scene of the murder: a brief check on Google Maps had shown it was now a supermarket, and the crime scene had been thoroughly documented in the file. The tampering had occurred later, perhaps in this police station. Three little pieces of compressed metal had disappeared; finding out what had happened to them could be the key to identifying Kaiser. And that possibility made this exercise the single most useful action he could take towards finding Kofi, too.

Since Boateng had woken up from another fractured night's sleep, he'd barely taken his eyes off his phone, waiting for another message from Kaiser about the ransom money and its delivery. He expected that it would be last minute, to avoid giving him any time to plan a countermove. They would be as ready as they could be, though; Etta was at the bank in Brixton right now. The amount she wanted to withdraw was so large that they'd had to call the manager from a bigger branch to authorise its release.

However, they both knew the cost was immaterial; they would give anything to get their boy back. Kaiser had just chosen to be realistic about his demands. The money would probably be heading straight to Europe to pay the suppliers of those intercepted Škorpions. Maybe even used as a down payment on a replacement lot. Boateng couldn't quite get his head around the twisted economics: in Kaiser's mind, Kofi was worth the same as a bagful of machine pistols. And all Boateng and Etta could do was accept it, if they wanted to stop any harm coming to their son. The impotence made rage flare in Boateng's belly. Was the search for these bullets a waste of time? A way to fool himself into believing that he was achieving something? Just as he was winding up to take his frustration out on the steering wheel, the gates slid open.

Inside, a special constable who'd drawn the short straw for Saturday duty showed Boateng down a corridor to a door which he unlocked, opening it with a broad grin and the invitation for Boateng to 'knock himself out'. As the strip lights flickered on, Boateng took in the size of his task: cardboard boxes shelved floor to ceiling around all four walls, with a few piles in the middle of the room for good measure. They didn't appear to be labelled. Another fine by-product of decommissioned police stations – whack everything from the CID filing cabinets in a big cupboard and pretend none of it existed. He was just wondering where the hell to start when his phone rang. It was Jones.

'Hey, Zac, how's it going? Anything on Kofi?'

He sighed. 'Pat and Nas are working their arses off, but there's nothing new. Thanks for asking, though.'

'What about you? What you up to?'

He surveyed the boxes. 'Well, I'm looking for something, and right now I don't think "needle and haystack" quite captures it. A haystack's way too small. You? How were those drinks?'

'Don't ask. I feel like shit.' Jones could obviously mask a hangover well; she sounded pretty chipper for someone who'd had a heavy Friday night.

'That makes two of us,' he replied. 'Only I don't have the excuse of boozing.'

'Do you need a hand?'

'Sure.' He paused. 'Aren't you working on Pluto?'

'Yeah, but I'm guessing you are too.'

'I hope I am.'

'Right,' she said. 'Where are you?'

'Tooting police station – the old one. I'm warning you, though, Kat. This could be the most boring thing you've ever done in your life.'

'There isn't much chance of that. I spent a year updating local crime reports in Croydon.'

He laughed, realising that he hadn't done that very much lately.

'I'm on my way,' she added, and rang off.

Boateng was pleased that Jones had offered to help, and not just because he needed another person on this mammoth task. He'd also sensed recently that she was lukewarm about getting involved with his private inquiry, but maybe she'd had a chance to think about it, to weigh up her options and make a decision. With two of them here, they'd get the search done twice as fast. And he'd have the privacy to fill her in on Leonard Bray and the missing bullets, picking up where they'd left off a couple of days ago. Suddenly, he didn't feel quite so alone.

Boateng turned a full circle, taking in the boxes once more. The scale of the task was overwhelming. But the mental image of his son was all he needed to start. He selected a blues playlist on his phone to keep him company. Then he went to the nearest box, removed the lid and began to examine the paperwork inside.

●

Three racks wasn't much. Three thousand pounds. About a month and half's wages for the average person in Britain. That was the value of Zac Boateng's life. Or the price Kaiser was willing to pay for his death. Low.

It wouldn't be the first time Darian Wallace had killed someone, but it would be the first time he'd ever been paid to do it. He wasn't going to lie: he'd expected a higher fee. Then again, it wasn't a lengthy job. If the whole thing only took a couple of hours, then you were looking at a rate of twelve grand for a working day. That was sixty thousand pounds a week. He did the maths: £3,120,000 a year. Premier League footballers' wages. Maybe it wasn't such a bad offer.

Not like Wallace had much say in the matter, anyway. Right now, it was his only source of income beyond robbing drug dealers. He'd got away with that once. Second time he might not be so lucky. All it'd take would be one guy carrying acid or a shank or some other tool and Wallace would end up in hospital. Assuming he survived, medical staff would identify him, and before he knew it, he'd be back inside. In solitary with no parole. From that angle, doing this was a question of survival.

In purely mechanical terms, taking out Boateng was easy. All he had to do was collect the equipment later today, wait in the right location at the appointed time and pull the trigger. It was the philosophical side that was more complex.

True, Boateng had tracked Wallace down for a string of murders last year and was therefore directly responsible for his incarceration. Responsible for the endless days in his cell without much sunlight or fresh air. If someone had asked him a year ago, Wallace would've offered to kill the detective for free, and without hesitation. But things had changed. Now, he shared something with Boateng: they were both dads.

Wallace had obviously taken a risk with his Leon's life yesterday in the park, but it was a calculated one. It didn't mean he was trying to harm his son or that he didn't care. He had to acknowledge that he felt something for Boateng, and for his son, who'd be left without a father if Wallace took him out. He wouldn't want his own kid growing up like that. Wallace had felt the lack of a male role model at home when he was a teenager, though absence was better than presence as far as his dad, Craig – the alcoholic soldier who used to beat him and his mum – was concerned.

And it wasn't just paternal empathy that made him question Kaiser's request.

Last year, Wallace had come to understand something for the first time: revenge didn't always help. Maybe you kept your reputation intact, but for that to happen, you had to tell people what you'd done. And that meant the chance of being caught increased exponentially. It meant people coming for you, keeping your eyes open all the time. And it caused a whole lot of pain to people who'd done nothing wrong. Was it worth it? Maybe he needed to be more like his mum's favourite musician, Bob Marley: love, peace, feeling irie and all of that. Didn't make you weak; it just meant you were growing up, you had new priorities.

But that was the problem for Wallace. His priority right now was money. With everyone looking for him and the greyhound track shut down, this job was his best option for cash. His only real option. It was business, pure and simple. He couldn't get sentimental about it. This was what Kaiser had asked him to do. And when Kaiser asked you to do something, you did it. Even Wallace accepted that. He looked again at the screen and the email from ColonelKurz21, wondering about his employer's choice of alias.

'Colonel Kurz' was surely a mash-up of the weapon, the MP5 Kurz and the character called Colonel Kurtz in the film *Apocalypse Now*. That film was based on a book: *Heart of Darkness*. Wallace remembered getting it in the prison library and reading it in a day. Its author, Joseph Conrad, was right: whatever their original intentions, humans had the capacity to be corrupted. Was Kaiser admitting his corruption with the film reference? Bragging about it, even?

Maybe Kaiser had started off his police career by travelling into that darkness like Kurtz, the brer in the story, hoping to make the world a better place or some other bollocks. If so, then he'd obviously realised pretty quickly that the mobsters, gangsters and badmen he was meant to be stopping represented a massive untapped market for another kind of work: arms dealing. And if one criminal in London had a gun, everyone else wanted one too. So Kaiser began selling. Who better to source tools than a fed? Kaiser's ability to supply had made him a kind of god in the darkness, like Kurtz in the book. A god armed with an MP5 Kurz. The brer had some sense of humour at least.

Wallace checked over his shoulder. Behind his little desk, the Somalian hawaladar was engrossed in something on his phone, and everyone else in the call shop appeared to be on some kind of private business. No one seemed to have recognised him off the news, and they hadn't batted an eyelid when he walked in off the street looking rough, having slept behind some bushes in a park like a tramp. He clicked reply and typed:

*OK. I'll do it. You gonna be there?*

He sent the email and was leaning back in his chair, wondering if he should check the latest headlines on the search for Darian Wallace, when the reply dropped into his inbox, almost instantly.

*Maybe. 1000 upfront, 2000 more when it's done. I don't need*
*to tell you what happens if you fuck up.*

Wallace stared at the screen as a chill prickled his skin. There
weren't many people that scared the shit out of him. But he knew
Kaiser was for real. There was no way back for Wallace now.

And there was no way out for Boateng.

●

Pat Connelly couldn't remember having been this busy for a
while. He and Malik had worked every angle they could on
Kofi's disappearance, pushed as much as possible, but there was
still no result. No magical CCTV image of a car with Kofi in
the passenger seat and a nice view of the number plate. No new
eyewitness statement to give a better description of the person
who may have met him outside the school. There was nothing
left to investigate. Not officially, anyway.

The ransom text message Boateng had showed him in the pub,
though, had been clear enough. So Connelly had added the sender
to their missing person request, filling Malik in discreetly, with
Boateng's consent. They'd described it as another mobile used by
Kofi, rather than giving its true origin. Boateng said he'd take the
rap for that if it ever came out in the wash. This way, Connelly
hoped, they could have the best of both worlds: a chance to get some
intel on Kofi's kidnapper without any harm coming to the lad. The
only trouble was that without being an abduction case, the phone
activity was further down the pecking order. Right at the bottom, in
fact. Unsurprisingly, there'd been no word yet. Connelly tried to be
optimistic. Maybe Boateng would be able to deal with the kidnap
personally – pay the guy off and get his wee boy back with no bother.

And maybe there was a little person at the end of the rainbow
with a pot of gold.

'D'you believe in leprechauns, Nas?'

Malik spun his chair towards Connelly. 'Lepre-whats?'

'Leprechauns.'

'Is that like a skin disease?' Malik frowned.

'You're thinking of leprosy.'

'Right.'

'Leprechauns are the little people. Sort of like magical spirits – only, in Ireland.'

'Ah. Jinns, you mean?'

'Jinns?'

'Yeah, spirits. That's what my parents call them. It's where the word genie comes from.'

'No, it's not.'

Malik raised his palms. 'I swear. Genies, lamps, Aladdin. They're Arabian stories, mate.'

'Well, if I had a magic lamp right now, I know what I'd wish for.'

'Apart from a million quid?'

Connelly snorted. 'Apart from that. Wish one: find Boateng's kid. Wish two: find Darian Wallace.'

'What's wish three?'

'That's easy.' Connelly smirked. 'Infinite wishes.'

Without much more to do on Kofi's abduction, the two of them had been putting in the overtime – authorised, though they would've done it for free – on Wallace. The cheeky bastard had given them the slip too often. Boateng should never have got him out, but Connelly guessed the boss had had his reasons. Wallace's escape had caused all sorts of panic. Connelly wondered if the brass were more worried about the public's judgement of their failure than about the harm Wallace might do at large. Whatever the motivation, it was one hell of an operation that had kicked off yesterday. Right on time for everyone's weekend.

Officers had been drafted in from across south London for the manhunt. They had sniffer dogs out, not that the poor mutts were much good at finding people in cities. Ports and train stations were alerted. Associated addresses had been searched, known communications checked. And the media were all over it – or at least they had been for a few hours, until they'd got bored and the latest balls-up over Brexit had taken centre stage. But none of that activity had resulted in a whiff of Wallace. He was a sly one. Connelly wondered how many of the Met's forty-three thousand men and women would need to be looking to give them a chance of finding him.

He was just thinking about a tea break when the desk phone rang. He snatched it up.

'Connelly.'

'This is the telecoms centre. You initiated a geolocation request yesterday on a handset ending 7819?' The guy sounded bored, but maybe that was just his voice.

'Aye, I did.' He guessed they were about to tell him they'd taken it off altogether, the penny-pinching wankers.

'It's been active at an address in Tulse Hill.'

Connelly stood up. 'You're shittin' me?'

The person on the other end coughed. 'No, DS Connelly, I'm not.'

'How recently?'

'About an hour ago.'

'And you're only just telling us now?'

'It's category four. You're lucky we're telling you at all.'

'Jeez.' Connelly waved across at Malik. 'And the handset's still active?'

He heard a computer keyboard clicking in the background. 'Yes.'

'Alright, what's the address?'

The analyst read out the details and Connelly repeated them aloud. Malik was already tapping and searching before Connelly had hung up.

'No trace on PNC,' said Malik. 'Let me try Crimint.' He punched a few more keys and waited. 'Yes. Here we go: 79

Romola Road, SE24. It's in the system. But there's nothing on it.' He frowned, turned to Connelly.

'What's the file code?'

Malik's finger hovered over the screen. '3-G-T slash 8.'

'Let me see.' Connelly skimmed the entry. No mistake. But it didn't make sense. Unless… 'Oh, Christ.'

'Pat? What's going on?'

Connelly lowered his voice. 'You know what that code means on a property?'

Malik shook his head.

'It's a safe house, lad.'

'How do you—'

'Some old work I did.'

'Right. So that means—'

'Aye,' whispered Connelly. 'It belongs to us.'

# CHAPTER SIXTEEN

Jones had helped Boateng search the archives at Tulse Hill police station for over three hours without finding anything useful. Despite that, she still counted the visit a success. Boateng had told her about his new obsession: Leonard Bray. A man supposedly executed by Kaiser on a building site four years ago. Jones recalled his name from the list of unsolved cases, but that didn't mean that investigating his murder would lead them anywhere. Boateng was right about needles and haystacks. At least she had something to tell Krebs that would keep the DCI at bay for a while.

Jones still felt awful about reporting to her on Boateng, but she didn't think she could refuse, not when he was operating outside regular channels and – more selfishly – her own career was at stake if she insisted on protecting him. She'd started to feel tense around him, imagining that he'd somehow see through her questions. She'd been relieved when DCI Maddox had called and asked her to accompany him to the Met's firearms destruction depot as part of the Pluto investigation. She'd made her excuses and left Boateng in the cramped storeroom, still searching. There was a kind of frantic energy about him, even though she guessed he hadn't slept properly for days. Perhaps it was simply one of a range of responses to your child going missing – diving headlong into some task or other to take your mind off it. Jones didn't have children, but she understood from personal experience that the emotions brought up by family crises could be the strongest of all.

When she arrived, Maddox was waiting for her outside the warehouse. She'd never been here before; in fact, she hadn't even known the place existed. The building was like a corrugated iron fortress, with sheer walls and small, boxlike windows set high off the ground. Only a 'Private Property' sign and nest of CCTV cameras hinted at its purpose; otherwise, the depot was unmarked. They held their IDs up to a camera at the outer fence and the gate was opened for them.

'Zac and I were chatting yesterday after the team meeting. He said you wanted to learn more about ballistics,' said Maddox, as he buzzed the intercom on the warehouse door.

'Yes, sir.' Now she felt even worse; Boateng had gone to the trouble of creating this opportunity for her, despite everything else on his plate.

'Don't worry about the "sir",' said Maddox. 'Dave's fine.'

'Sorry,' she said, but it was lost in the voice crackling through the intercom. Maddox gave their names in reply.

'I feel for him. Zac.' Maddox shook his head briefly. 'He's had some bad luck. He doesn't need wankers like Harper giving him a hard time.'

'I know.' And he didn't need her spying on him.

The door whirred and clicked. Maddox pushed it open. He turned to her as they entered. 'You OK with the plan here?'

She nodded. He'd briefed her by phone on the way over.

'Alright then,' he said. 'Let's go.'

Inside, a man in overalls with a double chin and beer belly was walking over to them. Jones guessed he was in his early fifties. He removed a hard hat and proffered a pudgy hand to Maddox only, introducing himself as Terry.

'Welcome to the chop house,' he said with an expansive gesture, turning to Jones. 'We don't see a lot of ladies here.'

'Well, get used to it, Terry,' replied Maddox. 'They let women join the Met these days, and some of them are even allowed to be detectives.' There was just the right amount of sarcasm in his voice, and Jones fought back a smirk. Terry didn't reply; he just looked confused.

'Thanks for taking the time on a Saturday,' said Maddox, smiling at their host.

Terry shrugged. 'We've got so much work on at the moment, the place runs six days a week.'

'We're here about some weapons confiscated last year that ended up here,' Maddox continued briskly. 'I can't say too much, but a source mentioned them.'

'Right. This way then.' Terry spun round and waved over his shoulder. They followed him across the warehouse. The place was full of workbenches, tools and tall storage cabinets with combination locks. As they rounded a corner and came into a new section, Jones stopped and stared. A giant yellow machine sat in the middle of the space like a monster in its lair. A younger man who looked remarkably similar to Terry was setting something on it using a large pair of blacksmith's tongs. Another chunky guy in a high-vis vest was watching him, holding a clipboard. Jones wondered if the body shape was compulsory in order to work here.

'Ah, you've found Bertha then,' observed Terry.

Jones turned to him. 'Bertha?'

'Yeah, you know, Big Bertha?' He rolled his eyes. 'Never mind. Do you wanna see her in action?'

She shrugged. 'Sure.' The three of them went over to the machine.

'That's my lad Gaz there, on the controls,' said Terry, pointing to the younger version of himself. 'And Joey, of course,' he added, indicating the man with the clipboard and chuckling. 'He records everything we feed Bertha.'

On the machine plate, Gaz had placed a pump-action shotgun, which he clamped in the tongs. He stepped back and pressed some buttons. Jones watched as the hydraulics whirred and a metal claw descended, pinning the shotgun to the plate. Gaz checked its position and pressed another button, whereupon a second, even bigger claw came down slowly and smoothly alongside the first. Jones noticed its huge steel blade just before the metal bit through the shotgun barrel. It sliced six inches off the gun as if it were a salami. Gaz repositioned the weapon and repeated the process, chopping off another six-inch piece. Joey made a note on his clipboard, nodding with satisfaction.

'This way, it can't ever be used again,' commented Terry. He jerked a thumb at the severed pump-action. 'Remington 12 gauge. It's American-made. God knows how that one made it into the country.'

They carried on into Terry's office, and Jones and Maddox took seats opposite his desk.

Maddox produced a small notebook from his trouser pocket. 'Our covert source claimed they got hold of a weapon confiscated by the Met Police.'

Terry frowned, his lips pursed. 'From here?'

'It's a possibility,' said Maddox. 'And quite serious, if he's on the money. So we have to look into it.'

'Obviously. But it's impossible.' Terry shook his head.

'Why impossible?' asked Jones.

'Well, apart from our security arrangements, every weapon has a serial number, love. If it's a replica without a serial number, we brand it with a unique code when we take delivery of it. Then, when it comes to destroying the firearm, we check the serial of the weapon we're cutting against our delivery record. And we always have two men doing that for every firearm – you saw the lads out there – so there's no mistakes. Every weapon's accounted for.'

'So you haven't lost any then?' asked Maddox.

'Not one,' replied Terry. He spread his hands. 'I can't say what happened before I was here, but I'm proud of the fact that we haven't had a single firearm go walkabout in the last eight years.'

They asked a few more questions about bookkeeping and the surveillance cameras, but Terry's answers seemed legit. A check of the logbooks – both the hard copies and their electronic counterparts – suggested everything was in order.

On their way out, Jones registered Joey watching her over his clipboard. Working around a lot of blokes, she'd learned not to pay too much attention to that; it was just how some guys were – silent and starey. She wondered if the men who did that had ever actually spoken to a woman.

Maddox tucked his notebook back into his pocket as they walked over to the cars. 'What do you think?'

Jones considered the facts. 'Seems like they've got a decent system for registering the guns. It's not like they're lying around the warehouse and anyone could just walk in off the street and take one. Security's pretty tight.'

'So?'

'Well, it makes me wonder how Kaiser's doing it, in that case. Maybe he's paying off the guys who work there?'

'Come on, Kat. What's the other explanation? The more obvious one.'

She paused, then it struck her. She felt like an idiot for being so credulous. 'Wallace was making it up?'

'Maybe.'

'What do you think?' she asked.

Maddox paused, scratched his stubble. 'I don't really know what to think any more. All I know is that Wallace wanted to engineer a chance to escape, and he did it. Unless I'm mistaken, the guy has a track record of lying. And if you wanted to negotiate your way out of Belmarsh, you'd tell a copper whatever they wanted to hear. Especially one as' – he searched for the diplomatic word – '*motivated* as Zac.'

'What's your theory then?'

Maddox pressed his lips into a flat line and tugged at his loose tie. 'Well,' he said, 'I wouldn't go as far as Harper, who reckons Zac might've set the whole thing up with Wallace; or Chambers – but we know he and Zac don't see eye to eye. That's a step of paranoia too far for me. Those two have got it in for Zac, but I know him and he's a good bloke. We've worked together before. He can be a bit reckless, and he might've held back his old intelligence about Wallace, but you can see why he did that. And I trust him. So, assuming Zac's reported what Wallace said accurately, the doubt has to be with Wallace. He's a convicted murderer who had more to gain than anyone by lying. You want to know my personal view?'

Jones's eyes widened. 'Yeah.'

'I'm wondering if Kaiser even exists.'

She frowned. 'What do you mean?'

He leaned against the car and took out his cigarettes. 'OK. There's obviously someone who arranged for those Škorpions to come in from Europe. But if we put too much weight on what a couple of street-level scrotes tell us, we're fools. Everything Mensah knew about Kaiser was second hand off this Collins guy. And we don't know that Wallace actually met Kaiser. Even if he thought he did, how does he know that person wasn't just an emissary sent to let the real Kaiser hide his face? Or hers?' Maddox held a fag between his lips and sparked the lighter.

'Hers?'

'Women can sell weapons too, Kat,' he said, blowing a cloud of smoke away from her. 'Have a look online. There have been a few female arms dealers convicted in recent years. Jamaica, Korea, the US – why not here, too?'

Jones counted herself as a feminist, but she wasn't sure arms dealing was something to celebrate among women's recent achievements. She tried to process the idea of Kaiser being female. Had she – like Boateng – been too focused on the assumption that Kaiser was a man?

'There are other options, of course,' continued Maddox. 'It may be that "Kaiser" is the collective identity of a group of people, or even that it's Wallace himself.'

'But the deal with the Škorpions took place while Wallace was in prison,' she protested.

'Doesn't matter,' countered Maddox. 'Have you seen those new miniature mobile phones? They're the size of a KitKat finger. You could fit two up your arse – at least. Someone as sharp as Wallace could've got hold of one and arranged it from his cell. Think about it – it's the perfect plan. You set up a deal, tip the authorities off about it, then from prison you offer them intel in exchange for a trip outside that gives you the chance to escape. Eventually they forget about you, cos they're all looking for the bigger fish. Only that guy doesn't exist. You've just led everyone a merry dance.'

Jones hadn't even considered these possibilities, but she had to admit they made sense. She'd been looking at the problem in too linear a fashion. Normally, of course, it was Boateng who provided the creative thinking in their work. But perhaps he'd lost that ability because of his personal proximity to the case. 'Have you told anyone else in the team about this theory?'

'Only DCI Krebs,' he replied. 'So keep it between us for now, yeah? I don't want the others losing their fight if they believe we haven't got a clue who we're looking for – or a chance of finding them.'

Jones nodded.

Maddox opened the door to his car. 'You want to know what I really think?'

She waited while he took another drag.

'Whoever Kaiser is, I reckon they're long gone. Probably sat on a yacht off Saint-Tropez. Reading the news and laughing at us lot chasing around London like a bunch of blue-arsed flies.'

'OK, but what about the MP5 Kurz that Aaron Collins used? The ballistics lab found that its barrel had been redrilled. Wallace couldn't have done *that* inside Belmarsh.'

Maddox snorted a small laugh. 'Fair enough.'

'So even if Kaiser is a myth, there's definitely one person we're still looking for in Op Pluto: whoever did the drilling. Find them and we can shut down their operation to put guns on the streets. That's got to be worth doing. And they might even tell us who Kaiser is.'

The DCI slid into his seat and dropped the window. 'I can see why they promoted you so fast, Kat. Great instincts. Maybe we should focus on this tinker character then. That might give us something to show for Op Pluto at least. You heading back to the office?'

Jones checked her watch. It was after 5 p.m. Maddox clearly sensed her hesitation.

'Call it a day,' he said. 'Back in tomorrow morning.'

'Sure. See you then.'

As Maddox pulled away and Jones walked across to her own car, she felt a little swell of pride in her chest at his praise. She wished her dad could've seen her following in his footsteps. He would've been proud of her, too.

●

Zac sat next to his wife at the kitchen table. They were both gazing at the A4 manila envelope, which contained twenty thousand pounds in cash.

'It's not as big as I thought it'd be,' said Etta quietly.

'Four hundred fifties.'

'I can't believe we scraped it all together.' She shook her head. 'Mum and Dad were amazing. The church, too.'

'We owe them.'

'There's no debt, Zac,' she said irritably. 'They've given us the money.'

'I just meant—'

'It's not some debit and credit system for our son's life!'

Unfortunately, for Kaiser, that's exactly what it was: a transaction. Cold, calculated. Designed to prey on their emotions, on the most important person in their world. Zac had done his best to keep those feelings under control. He knew they weren't useful. They'd only cloud his judgement and block his thinking, and he needed every bit of both in order to help bring Kofi back.

Nevertheless, as he saw his wife's trembling fingers trace the contours of the notes bundled into the envelope, a familiar anger began to well inside him. The blind rage that accompanied a father's protective instinct. He knew that feeling all too well. It'd been triggered time and again since they'd lost Amelia, resurfacing on Monday morning when Mensah mentioned Kaiser in his custody interview. It had quadrupled in intensity on Wednesday evening, when Kofi went missing. And when the ransom message arrived yesterday morning, it had gone off the charts.

The anger was a visceral experience. His heart beat faster, his lip quivered, he began to sweat and his limbs felt shaky and hollow. It was a lot like panic, but for one key effect: tunnel vision. When the rage came for Zac, it was like the sides of his vision whited out, and all he could see was whatever was in front of him that represented his pain. It was rising now, quicker than he could control. In the absence of a face to put to Kaiser, the focus of his fury became the envelope of money. Before he knew it, he'd stood and swung his fist down hard on the table.

'Fuck this guy!' he yelled. 'Who does he think he is, doing this to us?'

Etta looked up at him through wet, bewildered eyes.

'I'll fucking kill him!' bellowed Zac, winding up again and banging his fist against the table once more. He held up a quivering forefinger. 'I swear to you, Etta, if that bastard has touched one hair on our son's head, God help me, because I will not be responsible for what I do to him.'

'Zac,' she appealed, standing too.

'He thinks he can play with people's lives like this and get away with it. When I find him, I'm going to—'

'Zac! Stop.' She held her palms up to him, then her arms fell limp by her sides and she began to sob. 'It's not g-gonna help,' she stammered. 'We just… need to… get him back.'

The rage dropped away as quickly as it had come on, and Zac found himself automatically reaching out and pulling Etta into a hug. His heartbeat began to slow as they held one another, the insistent pulse in his temple receding.

Etta wiped her eyes on her sleeve and took some deep breaths. Eventually, she spoke. 'How do you know we can trust this person, Zac? I mean, how do we know they'll give us Kofi back?'

'Whoever took him is obviously professional,' he said. 'Once they've got the money, there's no more reason for them to hold on to him. As long as we do what he says—'

'But we can't be sure.' She searched his face for a few seconds before her mouth twisted in a new paroxysm of grief. 'Can we?'

Zac drew her tighter, placing a hand on the back of her head. There were no more words of reassurance he could offer sincerely. He knew she was right. Then his phone began to vibrate in his pocket. Etta could feel it too, and they parted as Zac fished it out, swiping the screen to answer.

'Pat,' he said. 'Any news?'

'Maybe, boss. Don't go gettin' carried away now.'

Zac had worked with the Irishman long enough to recognise the optimism in his voice. But there was something else there too. Caution. 'What is it?'

'It's early days,' replied Connelly. 'But I think we might have something.'

# CHAPTER SEVENTEEN

Connelly checked his watch: 10.06 p.m. It'd taken just under four hours to set this up. Not bad for a Saturday night. The duty magistrate had raised an eyebrow at the Met's request to storm one of its own safe houses, but she'd signed it off anyway. Connelly had raced over to Brixton and briefed the Met's Territorial Support Group, the TSG. And the telecoms centre had just confirmed that the target mobile phone was still active inside the location. Local Lambeth units had already sealed off each end of Romola Road. Now, TSG was ready to put the door in. The boys and girls were clad in their dark blue overalls and black body armour, faces obscured by helmets bearing each officer's unique code. They had fanned out from the door in two lines, the man closest holding the red 'enforcer' battering ram – just in case whoever was inside didn't feel like opening up to a polite knock.

'Lights are on,' observed Malik, sitting alongside him in their unmarked vehicle across the street.

'Probably a good sign,' Connelly whispered. The curtains were all shut, so it was impossible to tell if they'd been spotted. It wasn't easy getting two dozen coppers into position without making some kind of racket. He hoped they still had the element of surprise.

'Funny, isn't it?' said Malik, without breaking his gaze on the house.

'What is? Your face?'

'No funnier than yours, mate.'

'Oi. These fine features are the result of a long and successful boxing career.'

'Can't have been that successful if you kept getting punched in the face.'

Connelly glanced at him. 'Have you seen Rocky?'

'He's not a real boxer, Pat.'

'Fair one,' conceded Connelly. Malik was right: in reality, a few strong head shots would put most people on the canvas. He thought of Boateng, on the ropes. Wondered if he was just a couple more blows away from knockout.

'Nah, I mean it's funny about raiding one of our own places,' continued Malik. 'I never thought I'd be doing that when I joined the Met.'

'Me neither.'

'So, come on then. You ever been tempted? Take a bribe or whatever.'

'I'm not answering that.'

Malik grinned. 'You have!'

'Jeez, keep your voice down.'

'Hope you said no.'

'What do you think?'

They watched the house in silence.

'D'you think he's in there?' asked Malik.

'Bloody well hope so.'

Then the TSG sergeant turned towards their car and held up a hand. Connelly was just about to give him the signal when he heard footsteps hammering down the pavement towards them, bursts of shouting.

'Is it a resident?' asked Malik, dropping his window and craning his neck out to get a look. 'I thought the lids had sealed off the road.'

'They have,' replied Connelly. 'To the public. Christ almighty,' he sighed, as the figure got closer. 'I'll deal with this.'

Connelly held up a palm to the TSG sergeant, noticing that the officers had all turned at the sound. He slid out of the car and half-closed the door, jogging across to intercept the uninvited guest.

'Zac! What are you doing here?'

'Where is he, Pat? Is he here?' Boateng's eyes were wild, his chest heaving up and down. He was scanning the street, searching over Connelly's shoulder. Without waiting for an answer, he tried to get past.

Connelly grabbed his boss by the arms and pulled him behind a vehicle. 'Zac, you can't be here,' he hissed. 'The door's about to go in.'

'It's my son in there,' cried Boateng.

'Shh.' He clamped his hands tighter around Boateng's arms. The fella was a bag of nerves. 'Take it easy.'

'I need to see him.'

'I know.' Connelly tried to deploy a soothing tone, though he couldn't help thinking that Boateng was about to balls up his operation. 'But you've got to let them enter first, Zac. I shouldn't have given you the details of this place until after we'd executed the warrant.'

'Thank God you did, Pat.'

'Aye, well. Look, don't drop me in the shit, here. Just come over and watch from inside the car, yeah?'

Boateng nodded and some of the tension dropped from his body. Connelly led his boss over to the car and opened a rear door for him. Then he gave the signal to the TSG sergeant, who stepped forward and knocked on the door.

No answer.

'Open up, it's the police.'

Nothing.

'If you don't answer, we will break the door down.'

Silence.

Connelly watched as the sergeant stepped back and chopped his hands towards the door. The enforcer smashed straight through it and officers poured in. Then he realised Boateng was out of the car and sprinting towards the house like a man possessed.

'Zac, wait!'

Connelly chased after him as the shouts rose from inside the building.

                               •

Wallace surveyed the outside of the Flaxman Sports Centre in Camberwell. He could see why Kaiser had chosen this place: quiet road; concealed entrance; a low-profile public building. And there was every reason for Wallace to be here. Fifteen minutes before closing time on Saturday night and it was dead. So dead, in fact, that he thought he might be too late. Had there been a mistake in the opening hours listed on Google? He cursed under his breath, wondering if he'd screwed up. But as he got closer, he saw a couple of low lights through the tinted glass and a lone figure behind the reception desk.

He pushed open the door and turned on his charm for the young lady in the hijab who was sitting at a computer.

'Wa gwan,' he beamed at her, swaggering slightly, as if rocking up there was an everyday event for him. 'I was here earlier. Left some of my stuff in the changing rooms.' He kept back a bit to minimise the chance of her smelling his body odour.

'OK.' The woman shrugged and pressed something under the counter. A gate swung open to let Wallace through. He kept his head down as he went in. Knew he'd be on CCTV, briefly, but that was the trade-off for security of the transaction. He imagined Kaiser wouldn't be on camera, though. Wallace wasn't used to one-sided relationships – at least not where he was the disadvantaged one. He sucked his teeth as he walked down the corridor, looking for the men's.

The changing rooms smelled of sweat and mould and cheap deodorant. Wallace was relieved to see there was no one in the main area, but he heard the spray of a shower and someone whistling in a cubicle around the corner. He briefly considered taking a shower, but thought better of it. Moving across to the lockers, he scanned the banks of doors until he found the right number. It was sealed with a combination padlock, just as the email had said. He spun the number dials to the four digits he'd been given, and the shackle popped up. Checking once more over his shoulder towards the shower, he eased the locker open and peered in. A small rucksack was stuffed into the tight space. Wallace extracted the bag, unzipped it and examined the contents.

Even in shadow, he could make out the contours of a 9 mm pistol. He'd inspect it more closely later, but from the shape he guessed it was an old Beretta. Old as in antique. It had towel grip tape wrapped around the handle, presumably to stop prints getting on it. The muzzle had a bit sticking out, like maybe something had been done to the barrel. Wallace wasn't going to lie: it looked like a piece of shit. Not what he would've chosen for the job. But Kaiser knew what he was doing, didn't he? As long as it could put a bullet in Boateng, that was all he needed. There was some other stuff in the bag, too. Box of ammo, beanie hat, burner phone with charger… but no money. Where was the money?

He heard the shower turn off.

Wallace rummaged in the bag and his fingers connected with something small, flat and hard. He ran his thumb across the raised letters and numbers: a bank card. What was going on? Why use a card when cash was virtually untraceable? Was Kaiser trying to play him for a fool?

Wallace's thoughts were broken by the rip of a shower curtain being pulled aside, the slap of sliders approaching. He zipped up the bag and turned, realising too late that the door was on the other side. A hench guy stood in front of him, towel round his waist, drops of water on his chest. The two men remained still for a moment, staring at each other. The other guy's gaze dropped from Wallace's face to the rucksack and rose again.

'Yo, do I know you?' he said, inclining his head with a half-smile.

'Don't think so,' said Wallace, looking down and crossing to the doorway. He'd never seen the brer before – not that he could remember, anyway. But the guy had seen him here. And that wasn't part of the plan.

Wallace crept to the back of the decrepit semi-detached house and surveyed the exterior from its overgrown garden. The brickwork was darkened with soot, and plants grew from cracks in the mortar. The ground-floor windows were screened off with MDF boards which had been heavily tagged with graffiti. He shook his head, taking it in. This wasn't how life was supposed to turn out, sleeping rough in an abandoned building with feds scouring the city for him. One of the windows looked as if it had been tampered with, like someone had already tried to get in. He went over to it and levered the board up. He worked it loose, creating just enough space to slip through without splitting the wood.

Inside, he paused and listened. There was a low gasp of air where the board had come away from the window frame, but no other sound. He stepped forward, footsteps echoing on the bare concrete. It was so dark that the walls were barely visible. Through a doorway, he could see slivers of street light from gaps in the window boards, like yellow needles piercing the shadow. He advanced towards them, finding himself in the front room. Should he have a look upstairs?

The breath came with a rustle of fabric. Wallace whipped round but the guy was on him, knocking him to the concrete. His shoulder smacked into the floor and the body was above him, rough hands clawing at his face, the stink of unwashed flesh filling his nostrils. Wallace shut his eyes and tried to bat away the jagged nails scratching around them.

'Money,' hissed the voice in the darkness. A hand clamped onto his neck, pressing on his windpipe and making him choke, while another hand grabbed at his rucksack. 'Give it!'

Wallace writhed under the attacker and felt the pressure on his neck lift. Now the guy was pulling at his bag, tearing it from him. Before Wallace could react, a kick connected with his groin, making him bellow in pain. He opened his eyes to see feverish hands searching his rucksack; then the silhouette of the Beretta appeared, aimed at him from a metre away. Adrenalin pulsed through Wallace's stomach; he'd forgotten to check if the pistol was loaded. And this guy was desperate; his hands were shaking. The brer probably hadn't had a fix in a while. Wallace had seen it plenty of times in his life.

'Where's the money?' came the rasping voice. Wallace still couldn't see his attacker's face properly.

'There isn't any, I swear,' said Wallace, raising his hands in submission.

'Liar!' The guy gave a single, hoarse breath, then gripped the gun tighter.

'Wait—' Wallace could just make out the finger squeezing the trigger. Instinctively, he raised both hands to his face.

*Click.*

The guy turned the pistol to inspect it, and in a second Wallace reacted. He grabbed the gun in both hands and twisted it hard left, hearing the snap as the guy's forefinger broke. He screeched and flailed his other arm at Wallace, who ducked as it swung overhead. Wallace let go and reached around the guy's back from the other side, gripping the gun where his attacker's finger was still trapped in the trigger guard. He pulled the man's arm back and up, twisting and lifting it until it popped out from the shoulder socket. The junkie screamed as Wallace relinquished his grip. Then he swung an elbow into the guy's head, sending him onto his back. Wallace straddled him, knelt on his arm and extracted the pistol, tossing it backwards. It smacked against the brick wall behind him and clattered to the ground.

Now in control of the situation, Wallace paused and took a few breaths. How dare this bitch jump him like that? How dare he pull the trigger? Who did he think he was dealing with? The rage began to flare. He stood and stamped down on the guy's face.

He stamped again, harder. Again and again.

Wallace stopped when he realised the guy wasn't moving any more. Suddenly, he was aware of the room around him, like he'd just woken up. He was breathing heavily, sweating, and even in the dim light, he could see liquid on his right shoe.

He knelt and put two fingers on the junkie's neck. Nothing. He shifted position slightly, and then he found it. The low thump of a weak pulse. Wallace hauled the guy onto his front and put him in the recovery position, so he wouldn't choke on his own blood. Then he snatched up the pistol and rucksack. Took a final look at the limp body of his attacker and headed out in search of somewhere else to sleep.

⁕

Now he'd had a chance to calm down, Zac was starting to think more clearly. Amid the confusion, there was one thing about which he was certain: the raid on the house had been a failure. He felt like a fool for getting his and Etta's hopes up. Though he'd called Etta straight away to tell her that Kofi wasn't there, the sight of her as he walked through the front door had hit him hard. It was almost too much to bear, seeing her deflated like that, the fight and vigour gone from her body. She'd hugged him briefly, then told him she wanted to be alone for a while and gone up to their bedroom. Even though they hadn't yet received further information about delivering the money, it was as if she'd already accepted defeat. The raid had been neither Zac's idea nor his responsibility, but he felt the weight of its empty outcome personally. There had been a chance to find Kofi – to get him back – and they'd missed it.

Alone in the spare bedroom, Zac looped the strap of the King Zephyr tenor saxophone around his neck, moistened his lips and began to play some slow blues scales. Sometimes, this was the only way he knew to relax, to think. Gradually, the notes began to form into 'Hard Time Killin' Floor Blues'. Zac could hear Skip James's haunting voice as he repeated the simple melody, its rhythm hypnotic. James sung about toiling in the slaughterhouse, asking how long the hard times could last and whether they would be the end of him. It wasn't difficult to work out why the classic song, now nearly ninety years old, had come to Zac.

As he settled into the music, Zac had to acknowledge that the raid hadn't been a complete dead end. In addition to the burner phone in the kitchen drawer, they had found a schoolbag in the cupboard upstairs; Zac had been able to ID it informally at the scene as belonging to Kofi. He'd wanted to grab it, to hold on to it, to bring the little Batman lunchbox home and put it on the counter where it belonged. But, for the second time that night, Connelly had held him back, making sure it was collected as evidence.

There were traces of blood on a radiator pipe in the bathroom, too. That was the worst part: knowing that Kofi had been hurt. The mixture of rage and despair had grown, taking hold of Zac, and Malik had needed to walk him outside to get some air. The bloodstains had been swabbed and would be sent for analysis along with a control sample of Kofi's DNA, taken from hair on his comb. But Zac didn't need to wait for the confirmation: Kofi had clearly been in the house. The question was, what did the fact that they had found the place mean?

Kaiser was not a person who made a lot of mistakes. Had he meant to leave the phone switched on at the address? Had he wanted them to find it? Was it a test, or an uncharacteristic error? Maybe it wasn't Kaiser who'd done it, but a more careless associate.

Connelly had informed Zac that the address was a Met Police safe house. He'd fought back the tears and instructed the Irishman to find out who had access to it. That represented a possible lead on Kaiser. And because Zac hadn't shared the ransom message with anyone except Connelly, even following the raid tonight, Kofi's disappearance was still classed as a missing person case and rested with Lewisham MIT. Zac wanted to keep the operation as close to him as possible. He still didn't know who he could trust. And now, of course, there was an extra danger: the chance that Kaiser would discover their attempt to rescue Kofi. His threat had been clear.

As Zac began to improvise around the song's main riff, his flow was broken by the beep of his phone. He stared at it for a moment. There couldn't be many people who would text him at 11 p.m. Zac grabbed it, swiped and stabbed at the screen. One new message, from an unknown number. He clicked into it. It was an audio file. He swallowed. Then he tapped play.

·

Kofi couldn't see anything. The blindfold was tight and pressed against his eyeballs. He couldn't move much either – same as in the little bathroom. And there wasn't a lot of sound around him. If he strained, he thought he could make out some traffic in the distance, but it came and went, leaving him wondering each time if he'd imagined it. That left his nose as the main source of information about his surroundings. And the smells in this new place were pretty strong: wood, paint and oil. It reminded him of the time he'd been to the big DIY centre on Old Kent Road with his dad, to get stuff for the house. He remembered complaining that he didn't want to go, that he'd rather stay at home and play *FIFA Soccer* on the PlayStation. But his mum had insisted that he help his dad. Now, he'd give anything to be there. It wouldn't matter if it was the most boring shopping trip in the world. Just as long as he could be with his dad.

A few heavy footsteps rang out, then the door creaked open and a gust of air came in before it slammed shut again.

'Someone's been a naughty boy,' said a voice. It wasn't the same man who'd brought him here. This was another person. But what were they talking about? Was it the stuff about the phone from back in the house? Kofi couldn't speak with the duct tape over his mouth.

'They tried to find you.'

Who had tried to find him? His mum and dad? The police? His mind was turning cartwheels as he tried to work out what had happened.

'And we told them not to do that.'

Kofi's heart started thumping in his chest. He thought of the message he'd recorded. The bit about his fingers. *All* of his fingers.

'So you're not going home just yet.'

Behind the duct tape, Kofi's lips had started to go all wobbly and he could feel tears being squeezed out of his eyes and soaking into the cloth blindfold.

'And we need to show your parents that we're serious.'

He heard the person getting closer to him, reaching for his hands, which were cuffed to a thick wooden table leg.

His fingers. They wanted his fingers. That was the punishment. He tried to say 'No', but it just made a stupid sound inside his mouth. He tried again, louder. And again. Then something connected with his head and it filled with pain, jolting sideways at the impact. The blow was hard enough for Kofi not to want another one. And he guessed that, somewhere nearby, the little black box with its devil horns was ready to be used on him too.

'Shut the fuck up,' said the voice. 'Do as I say.'

Kofi was dragged to his feet and marched a few steps until his ribs connected with what felt like a high table. The cuffs were undone and his right arm was pulled forward by strong hands. He tried to back away, but the body enveloped him, pinning him to the edge of the table.

'Don't struggle. You'll only make it worse.'

He felt himself trembling as his hand was clamped between two solid pieces of cold, flat metal. One of them was moving, getting tighter and tighter, pressing into his bones, squeaking as some wheel was turned. The pain was horrible and Kofi thought his hand might burst.

'Hold nice and still now,' said the voice, with a small laugh.

Kofi tried to stop shaking. Tried to picture himself as a superhero.

# CHAPTER EIGHTEEN

**Sunday, 26 August 2018**

Jones felt that if there was one positive to all the craziness of the past week, it was that she was, at least, discovering some new places in London. The latest was Herne Hill Velodrome, half a mile south-east of Brixton. As she turned off the quiet residential road and a thicket of trees gave way to the huge open-air cycling track, she felt a little stab of excitement. But it was quickly tempered by the recognition that her presence here signalled another betrayal of Boateng. Another betrayal of the best boss she'd had in her six-year career in the Met.

It wasn't difficult to spot Krebs on the track, her long frame bent over an expensive-looking racing bike, muscular legs pounding the pedals as she sped round. Jones walked behind the railings, managing to catch Krebs's attention as she whizzed through the bend. On the next lap, Krebs slowed and pulled in, hooking her handlebars over the railing. She clip-clopped up the steps to the quiet spot Jones had found on the top tier of the grandstand, by the finish line. In her Lycra gear, wearing a smooth, domed helmet and round mirrored sunglasses, the DCI had the appearance of a giant insect. What were those badass ones, the females that ate the males?

'Do you know the history of this place, Kat?' asked Krebs, unclipping her helmet and removing the shades.

Jones shook her head. 'No, ma'am.'

'Built in the nineteenth century. Good enough to host Olympic events, back in '48. The glory days, they were, before it fell into ruin.' She paused. 'Sounds a bit like the Met, doesn't it?'

Jones assumed that was a rhetorical question.

'But then,' continued Krebs, 'this great London institution was saved through partnership between the community and the authorities, and the result is what you see today.'

'The track or the Met?'

Krebs gave a small, dry laugh. 'Quite. You know, you're doing the right thing, Kat.'

Jones didn't reply. She let her gaze roam over the loop of tarmac and parched grass it enclosed. Everything that was meant to be green had turned brown after one of the hottest summers on record.

'So what's he been up to then?' asked Krebs.

It took a couple of minutes for Jones to fill her in on the trip to Tulse Hill police station, the story about Leonard Bray and the missing bullets, and Boateng's theory that this held the key to identifying Kaiser.

'But you didn't find anything in the storeroom?'

'Nothing by the time I left, ma'am. And I'd been there three hours, maybe more. We'd checked about half of the boxes. But Boateng carried on searching.'

Krebs massaged her forehead. 'Find out if he got anywhere, will you?'

Jones nodded. Maybe there was no way back from this position. Even if Boateng was cleared by an inquiry and allowed to carry on working in the MIT, could Jones sit next to him every day or work crime scenes with him, knowing that she'd sold him out to Krebs? Perhaps it was the beginning of the end for her in Lewisham. There was a moment's silence as she considered this.

'Will you brief the team about Kaiser being in the police, ma'am?' said Jones, eventually. 'I was just thinking… it would change the way that we work the case if everyone in Op Pluto knew.' What she really meant was that it would make her feel better about going behind Boateng's back. 'It might narrow down our suspect list.'

'Not by much,' replied Krebs. 'There are over forty thousand Met personnel, if we assume he's still in the police. He might have left. Been dismissed, retired, moved on.'

'Still, it could help us to profile, ma'am.'

A brief silence hung between them.

'You're right.' Krebs sighed. 'Did you know that last night, DI Boateng nearly wrecked an operation to find his son?'

'No, I didn't. I mean, I haven't spoken to him since—'

Krebs cut her off with a hand. 'Don't worry, Kat. It's not a test. I'm telling you this.'

'Right.'

'Do you think it's a coincidence that his son goes missing a couple of days after he starts to investigate Kaiser?'

The obvious connection had occurred to Jones.

'The premises they raided was a police safe house. Apparently, the son's mobile phone was active there, along with other… evidence. But Kofi wasn't inside.'

This was news. Jones wondered how Boateng and his wife were dealing with it.

'It's not an unreasonable assumption that Kaiser has Boateng's son,' Krebs continued. 'And if Boateng's son was being held hostage in a police safe house, then it's a simple step of logic to infer that Kaiser is in the police. So yes, I'll inform the team about that possibility during the afternoon meeting, for all the good it'll do us. I'll see you there.'

'Yes, ma'am.' Jones felt a wave of relief go through her. That was one less thing to cover up.

Krebs nodded at the track. 'Time for a few more laps before I head in, though.' She put her helmet and sunglasses back on. 'And don't forget to keep me in the loop about Boateng.'

By the time the DCI had reached the track, Jones's relief had already evaporated and been replaced with that queasy feeling in her stomach again.

●

Having skipped breakfast, Boateng was running on empty in every possible sense. He was back in Tulse Hill police station and had resumed the hitherto fruitless quest for any reference to the Leonard Bray investigation from four years ago. Ninety minutes of searching the boxes had revealed nothing, and he could probably only spare another half hour before he needed to report to the Op Pluto incident room for the overtime shift. He felt as if he were being powered by emotion alone: that strange, awful combination of anxiety and hopelessness, punctuated by the occasional scorching solar flare of anger. He needed to get it together.

After receiving Kofi's voice message last night, Boateng had simply cried. Big, guttural sobs that shook his body. He knew that traces of blood had been found at the house where Kofi had almost certainly been kept, and that cruelty to his son had caused that blood loss. But there was something worse about hearing his boy's voice: the tremor of fear as it caught on certain words, the pauses as he no doubt looked to his kidnapper for instructions. It had made the whole thing more real. That included the threats which Kofi had voiced, and the vague but terrible prospect of them being carried out because they'd raided the safe house.

Once he'd composed himself after listening to the message, he played it to Etta. He'd considered shielding her from it, but after the case last year, he knew there was no point. They needed to share this pain, help each other, and do what they could to get through it. He'd held her silently shuddering body as she insisted on hearing it again and again.

They'd slept fitfully, both aware that the forty-eight-hour deadline was up today and at some point they were likely to get the instructions about handing over the money and getting their son back. Boateng had drifted several times into a fantasy where Kofi had returned home and the three of them were having dinner together around the kitchen table. There were piles of chichinga – the spiced Ghanaian kebabs that Kofi loved – and juicy fried plantain. Then as much ice cream as any of them could eat. Maybe a film together, afterwards, cuddled up on the sofa. Kofi's choice – whatever he wanted to watch. Just a simple night together. Boateng cursed himself for the times he'd snapped at his son or scolded him over some minor infringement. None of that really mattered when you set it against life itself.

Boateng had found himself smiling at the thought of having Kofi home. But, each time, the dream had given way to a spike of murderous rage and the inescapable certainty that, given the opportunity, he would kill the person responsible for this.

He replaced the lid on the cardboard box he'd finished searching, shelved it and took another. Removing the top and starting to leaf through the documents inside, he found himself losing concentration again, as if his fingers were on autopilot, sifting the papers. Then he stopped as his subconscious registered the word.

*Bray.*

Boateng flipped back and checked, in case he was hallucinating. But there it was: a copy of a letter. The subject line read, 'Leonard Bray ballistics', beneath the logo of a castle turret and the words 'Fortec Labs Ltd', with an address in Bexleyheath, on the outskirts of south-east London. The message was succinct: three projectiles recovered from the scene of Leonard Bray's murder had been received by Fortec Labs. They would be analysed within a week and returned to Lambeth Major Investigation Team. Boateng frowned. Lambeth? Then he realised: serious crimes in Wandsworth would fall under Lambeth's remit. Not every borough had an MIT, so smaller and less populous districts would often pass murder inquiries to their bigger neighbours, where, unfortunately, such events were more common.

He felt a pulse of adrenalin at having found the trail. So, Wandsworth CID had sent the bullets that had killed Leonard Bray to a private lab for analysis. It wasn't an unusual practice, since the state-run Forensic Science Service had been shut down in 2012 for being too expensive. Ironically, it was tight resources in the Met's own facilities that had led to forensic services being outsourced, often at greater cost than if the work had been done in-house. And serious flaws could creep in while the evidence was outside of police control. Only last year, a scandal had erupted in Manchester when it was discovered that scientists in a private lab had possibly manipulated data on forensic samples, from potentially hundreds of cases across the UK – data on which convictions rested. It wasn't beyond the realms of imagination that the same thing had happened here.

Boateng was so buoyed up by his discovery that he almost missed the last line of the letter. The lab noted that the report and projectiles would be sent for the attention of a detective in Lambeth MIT. Boateng's jaw clenched as he read the name.

David Maddox.

•

'Recovered from Friday night, guys?' Jones hovered between the desks of Goodhew and Patel.

The young detective leaned back in his chair. 'I'm not drinking again.'

'I always say that.' Goodhew shook her head. 'Never works. Think I've got a two-day hangover.' She paused. 'By the way, how's Zac doing?'

'He's coping as best he can, I guess,' said Jones vaguely.

'Is he in today?' asked Patel. 'Haven't seen him much the last couple of days. I mean, obviously he's had other priorities.'

'Yeah, I guess he'll be here soon.' Jones checked her watch and then placed her hands on the backs of their chairs. 'So, same again next Friday night?'

They both laughed, but she was aware they all knew why she was there, reading over their shoulders. Both were on the Police National Computer, checking for records of anyone with a conviction for modifying a weapon. Jones hadn't escaped the graft; she was trawling the Met's Crimint system. As the three most junior members of the Pluto team, the work had fallen to them. And, as highest-ranking among them, Jones had de facto oversight of the search.

'Found anything?' she asked, trying to keep the urgency from her voice.

'Diddly-squat,' replied Patel. 'Some guys up in Yorkshire were reactivating antique weapons for a few years, but they're in jail now.'

'There was a guy from Tottenham converting athletics starter pistols to fire live rounds,' offered Goodhew. 'Looks like he's out now, but he was in prison for six years, so it's unlikely to have been him helping Kaiser.'

'Unless they linked up very recently,' countered Jones. 'Well, if it's any consolation, I haven't found much either. But there might be something useful there, somewhere.'

Patel gave a deep sigh and spun his chair to her. 'I don't want to be negative, Kat, but there's not a lot on here. And even if we do find someone – like this Tottenham guy – we're assuming that whoever's helping Kaiser modify the weapons has been caught for the same offence before.'

Jones tried to think of a reply that would help lift their spirits. Nothing came to mind. If even Patel was losing his enthusiasm, times were hard.

'I mean, it could be a self-taught bloke,' continued Patel. 'Or some guy who's never been on our radar. Then what?'

'Point taken, Raj. It's a long shot, like most leads in this operation. But we've got to keep working, turning over stones, and eventually we'll find something. This is a start.' She gave the pair each a gentle pat on the back before returning to her own desk. Another half an hour and she'd probably need to start bribing them with biscuits. She'd learned from Boateng that there was a direct correlation between comfort food and the willingness to put in the hard graft.

Jones had just started reading from the Crimint archives again when she noticed Boateng coming in. He hooked his flat cap on the stand in the corner and walked over to his seat, giving her a nod on the way. He still looked pretty ragged. His tiredness was apparent from the deep bags under his eyes, the slight self-neglect evident in his stubble and creased shirt. And yet there was something more purposeful about his movement this morning. Jones wondered what he'd been up to; she made a mental note to buy him a coffee later and get an update. Then she immediately felt rubbish for scheming against him.

'Right, listen up, everyone. Gather round.' Krebs clapped her hands and took up position standing in front of them as the team stopped work and rotated their chairs towards her. 'This is a special briefing, due to some new intelligence we've received.'

Jones saw Harper and Chambers exchange a glance. Maddox dropped into a seat beside Krebs.

'Now, you'll recall that DI Boateng's child has been missing for nearly four days. Last night, based on technical information, a raid was initiated by our colleagues in the MIT, supported by TSG, on a property in south London. They believed that Kofi Boateng – that's Zac's son – had been inside the house. Though there is still no clear evidence of a kidnap, we are drawing certain conclusions about the event, namely that Kofi was abducted. In the absence of any specific communication, however, the case rests with Lewisham MIT and has not been transferred up to the Kidnap Unit.'

Harper raised a hand. He frowned, but his brow didn't crease much. Jones briefly wondered if he'd had his forehead Botoxed. 'Sorry, but what's this got to do with our operation? Don't get me wrong, we want Zac's kid to come back safe and well, but our task is to catch Kaiser.' He cast around the room for support.

'That's my point, Kevin,' said Krebs, folding her arms. 'Given that DI Boateng knew about Kaiser from Darian Wallace, and considering the timing of the kidnap vis-à-vis Operation Pluto, we are working under the assumption that it is Kaiser who has abducted Zac's child.'

'Bit of a stretch, isn't it?' queried Chambers. He wiped a sheen of sweat from his top lip with the back of a finger.

'That's why I used the word "assumption", Will. What *is* evidence is the fact that the premises raided is a police safe house.' Krebs pursed her lips and scanned the group, letting the words sink in. 'We therefore have a new theory: that Kaiser is one of us. That he's in the police.'

Jones watched the range of reactions: shock from Goodhew, confusion from Patel, disgust from Maddox, suspicion from Harper.

Chambers's expression was one of disbelief. 'That's ridiculous,' he said.

'It's quite a difficult thing to accept, I know,' offered Krebs. 'But, at the very least, we believe that someone inside the police is helping Kaiser.'

'Zac,' said Harper, folding his arms, 'you got any ideas who that might be?'

'Eh?' Boateng scowled.

'I'm just asking.' Harper smiled innocently. 'Since you were the one talking to Wallace about it.'

'Thank you, Kevin,' said Krebs. 'Helpful comments only, please.'

'Where's the proof that Kaiser's police?' Chambers appealed with upturned palms. 'I know there were firms who were naughty boys in the nineties – early two thousands, maybe. South-East Regional Crime Squad, for instance, down the road in East Dulwich. But they cleared most of that up.'

'Obviously not all of it,' said Boateng, fixing Chambers with a cold stare.

'Wasn't just street level, either,' observed Maddox with a half-smile. 'The Met's very own finance director embezzled a few million quid before he was caught. Scumbag.'

Harper cleared his throat. 'Alright, look,' he began. 'You lot are on about it like he's someone we know. I've just got off the phone with our Czech counterparts. We've pooled our profiles, and based on combined expertise, we reckon that Kaiser is likely to be a foreigner. So, he's not going to be one of us, is he?'

'Sorry, Kev.' Boateng held up an index finger. 'Expertise?'

'Yeah, mate. Arms trafficking expertise, which is what I'm bringing to this outfit. I've studied the economics. It's a question of matching supply with demand. Most arms dealers don't work on their own patch. They usually don't even source the weapons on their home turf. They're brokers. So we reckon he's not British, and he probably ain't Czech either.' Harper interlocked his fingers and pushed his arms out. Jones could see the muscles moving under his shirt. He gave a gleaming-white smile, clearly satisfied with his analysis.

'But surely those theories aren't mutually exclusive,' said Jones tentatively.

'Mutually what?' Harper squinted at her.

'Well, you can be a foreign national *and* be in the police. Just happens that none of us is foreign,' she shrugged. 'PC Radwanska's from Poland.'

'Sergeant Idowu is Nigerian,' said Patel. 'Like, he's actually from Nigeria.'

'We've got a fella from Fiji in our team,' added Maddox. 'He's married to a Brit.'

'And our very own Pat Connelly's Irish,' offered Boateng.

'Exactly.' Jones nodded, grateful for the allies. 'Brexit hasn't happened yet.'

'Unfortunately,' muttered Chambers.

'Right,' said Krebs loudly, perhaps trying to halt any further development of that conversation. 'The point is, we need to start profiling inside the Met. Put your heads together and work out what sort of person might do this. Disgruntled firearms officers, ex-military personnel. Someone who knows guns.' She checked her watch. 'I need to get to a meeting.'

'I'm going to the gym,' said Harper. 'Need to let off a bit of stress.'

Goodhew raised a hand. 'What if we don't find anyone who fits the profile?'

Krebs arched her eyebrows. 'Then look outside the Met.'

Jones could almost feel the collective sigh of despair. Despite the intel on Kaiser's police link being shared, paradoxically she felt like they were further back than they had been before the briefing. There was a name for that, wasn't there? Socratic ignorance. The awareness of how little you know.

⁙

'Here you go, fella.' Connelly plonked the brown paper bag down in front of DS Nasim Malik, who sat engrossed in some data on his computer screens.

There was a second of surprise before the lad's eyes lit up. 'What's this?' he asked, though the sweet aroma and writing on the bag were all the information he needed to know.

'Cheeky Nando's,' replied Connelly. 'Sort of a celebration, I guess.'

Malik gave a lopsided grin. 'Legend.'

'Got to enjoy the small wins.' He removed his own chicken and chips and sat down next to Malik. 'But we've still got lots to do.'

His largesse wasn't due to his lack of time to make a packed lunch today, or the need for a morale boost. It was the result of a call which had come in, via Crimestoppers, first thing that morning. A member of the public – who wouldn't give a name or address – had seen a person they believed was Darian Wallace in a sports centre in Camberwell, late last night. Recognised him from the paper, they'd said. Connelly and Malik had immediately headed to the sports centre and retrieved the CCTV footage. Both men knew Wallace from their case last year and were able to identify him. Malik had been confident of the ID from the moment the figure had swaggered into the reception. 'I'd know that walk anywhere,' he'd said. They'd spoken to the young lass on reception and she'd confirmed that Wallace had come in just before closing time, saying something about leaving a bag in the changing rooms. Apart from the tattoo under his eye, she'd not noticed anything unusual about him, she said. People forgot stuff all the time and came back to get it. There was no point trying to get fingerprints or anything else from the changing rooms; hundreds of people passed through every day. It was the other potential follow-up that grabbed Connelly and Malik's interest.

Wallace hadn't been in the changing rooms long enough to take a piss, much less a shower. So he wasn't using the place as a public bathroom. That left two possibilities: either he was dropping something off, or he was picking something up. And since the management had been able to account for the contents of the lockers in use that morning, it didn't take the IQ of Darian Wallace to work out that someone had deposited a package for him. That meant he had help; the question was who from, and to what end?

It was a decent lead. Being able to put Wallace in a specific time and location meant that Malik and Connelly could mobilise every CCTV camera they could lay their hands on to track him into the sports centre and then away from it. It'd be a hell of a lot of legwork, but they'd drafted in others from the MIT to help with that, thankfully. And Connelly had followed his instincts a wee bit, too. He knew Wallace was on the run, without access to much. That suggested he might need to beg, borrow or steal to get the basics like food, cash and transport. So he'd asked Malik to take a look at local crime reports in the vicinity of the sports centre in a twelve-hour window around Wallace's visit. And that's where they were right now.

Malik had already torn open the brown paper packet and was using it as a plate while he chucked hot sauce over his chicken. 'I'd eat this every day,' he said. 'If I could afford it.'

'Aye, solid fuel, that is. Any likely candidates then? Or just the usual drink-driving and argy-bargy after kicking out time in the pubs?'

His young colleague paused with the sauce mid-air. 'Maybe a couple,' he replied, tossing the empty sachet aside. 'This one's weird. Check it out.' He clicked and indicated the screen. 'A 999 call from a payphone. Whispered voice says there's some guy injured in a squat. Gives the address, hangs up. Paramedics go round. They have to break in through the back, but inside there's a drug addict lying there. He's in a bad way. Unconscious but alive.' He gave Connelly a quizzical look. 'And in the recovery position.'

Connelly frowned. 'An attacker with a guilty conscience?'

Malik shrugged and grabbed a handful of Peri-Peri chips.

'How far away was the address from the sports centre?'

'About two hundred metres,' replied Malik with his mouth full.

'So Wallace leaves, looks for somewhere to crash, finds the empty house. Only it's not empty. He gets in a scrap and kicks the shite out of the fella. Then has a change of heart about his victim?'

'Doesn't seem much like him, does it?'

'You never know. Alright, let's plot the sports centre, squat house and payphone on a map. Three points gives us a possible route. And that narrows down the CCTV search by…' He tried to come up with a realistic-sounding percentage.

'Shitloads,' said Malik.

'Aye. Sounds about right.'

'Should we tell Zac?'

Connelly recalled his boss barrelling up the road outside the safe house operation, yelling at the top of his lungs. Remembered how he'd needed to manhandle Boateng – no easy task – out of the bathroom to stop him contaminating any evidence. 'You know what?' he replied. 'Let's leave it a while. Right now, we don't have anything serious to tell him. Don't want to set the hares running too soon, do we?'

# CHAPTER NINETEEN

Not for the first time that week, Susanna Pym felt well and truly out of her depth. For a start, she was in Peckham, a part of London she'd never visited, despite working just a few miles away in Westminster for the past twenty-five years. Then there was the venue. It didn't even have a name. But this was the only video games arcade she could find on Peckham Rye, so it had to be the right establishment. She couldn't have felt more out of place if she'd been on stage in a rap concert. And the cap, T-shirt, jeans and trainers she'd worn only added to the absurdity of her presence here. But she wouldn't have come if her job wasn't on the line. Taking a discreet look around, she entered.

The interior was so dark that initially she couldn't see her footing. Once her eyes had adjusted, she got a sense of her surroundings. Both walls of the narrow room were lined with whirring, bleeping and flashing electronic machines. She remembered visiting something similar on Brighton Pier about twenty years ago, when she'd taken the kids there on a washed-out summer holiday. But did these places still exist in 2018? Perhaps that was the whole point: it was 'vintage', or whatever young people called anything that was past its sell-by date. Ironic or not, there were no customers at lunchtime on a Sunday, and she was grateful for that.

A bar propped up the back wall. Behind it, a man with a Viking beard and shaved head was wiping down a row of unlabelled metal beer taps with hands covered in tattoos. Pym found his appearance unsettling, to say the least. Advancing further, she spotted a shock of red hair behind a table in the corner. Taking a final glance over her shoulder, she approached.

'Faye Rix?'

The woman looked up. She had an angular face, well-defined jaw and muscular shoulders. Up close, the effect was even more striking than it had been the first time she'd seen the journalist, outside the Home Office last week.

'Yeah,' replied the redhead, giving a dazzling smile and nodding to the empty chair in front of her. 'Grab a seat.'

'Do you mind if I smoke?' asked Pym. The nerves were killing her and she craved some nicotine.

Rix glanced at the barman, who nodded almost imperceptibly. He came out from behind the bar, walked to the front of the arcade and shut the doors.

'Closed for twenty minutes,' said Rix with a wink.

Pym turned, watching the barman return and disappear into the back room.

'Don't worry.' She gave an apologetic grin. 'He doesn't know who you are. Like most people around here.'

Pym extracted a cigarette and lit up, trying not to reveal her shaking fingers in the movements. She was breaking the law by initiating this meeting, but somehow that seemed OK. She'd already gone well beyond that with the bribery of her source. It was time to take control of the narrative, particularly now she was in damage-limitation mode. Once she'd become aware of the repeated failings of this Boateng character, it'd been an obvious choice as to whom to brief about it, off record. If anyone would do a proper job of exposing the cock-ups, it was the bolshie, aggressive young woman who'd had the balls to challenge her at the press conference. There was a quality the journalist possessed which Pym recognised in herself: ambition. So, she'd obtained the contact list from her media liaison team and searched through the names until she'd identified Faye Rix. The freelancer had a knack for uncovering police corruption. Coupled with some specific stories she'd written last year, it made her the ideal candidate for this little chat. The ideal person to take the spotlight off Pym and shine it on a suitable fall guy.

'You've got quite a reputation,' said Pym.

'All deserved,' replied Rix. She sounded like a character from *EastEnders*, but there was light behind her eyes. And when she blinked, Pym noticed how quick it was. She'd read somewhere that blink speed and frequency were indications of mental processing and therefore a proxy for intelligence.

Pym paused, took a long drag. The only sounds were a cacophony of tinny, repetitive jingles from the machines.

'And you're clearly quite well informed when it comes to the Met,' said Pym.

'I have my contacts.'

'How would you like the biggest story of your career?'

'I'm listening.'

'In the past seven days there's been a seizure of trafficked arms, resulting in two deaths; a search for their seller, which has uncovered bugger all; a witness offered a deal to cooperate on the case who died on remand; and an escaped murderer.'

Rix inclined her head. 'Yeah, must've been a busy week for you.'

'Quite so. Well, what if I were to tell you that there appears to be one person who is the common thread in this set of catastrophes?'

'I'd say that was unlikely to be a coincidence.'

Pym nodded and blew a jet of smoke sideways. 'My feelings exactly. The detective inspector in question has an excellent record of operational successes over twenty years in the Met. So when his name was mentioned to me by some of his own colleagues, I began to wonder. Is it a sudden outbreak of incompetence? A series of unfortunate accidents?'

'Or something more deliberate?'

'A bad apple in the barrel,' said Pym. She thought the phrase had been used before by the press to describe rogue officers in the Met. How many times made it a cliché?

'Bound to be a few, in such a big barrel.'

Pym cast around for somewhere to tap her ash and settled for her own cigarette pack. 'You've written about Zachariah Boateng before, haven't you?'

'Yeah.'

It was just one word, but Pym couldn't mistake the bitterness it carried.

'Would you like a chance to write about him again?'

'Sure,' replied Rix coolly, though Pym was starting to feel more confident now that she'd found this young woman's weak point.

'I'll give you a couple of days to do the homework on what I'm about to tell you. In return, I want you to promise not to run it until then.'

Rix sucked her teeth. 'OK. But where's my proof of your story?'

'You'll get it,' said Pym. 'Someone is working on that.'

'Sounds good to me.' Rix produced that wide, feline smile again, and Pym felt a strange desire to kiss her. Perhaps it was just the prospect of this woman saving her career.

●

'You OK, Zac?'

'Eh?' The question snapped Boateng out of his own world and back into the cafeteria. He nodded quickly. 'Yeah, yeah. I'm cool.'

His attempt at nonchalance had clearly fallen short of the mark. Kat Jones sat back in the chair and folded her arms.

'Come on,' she said. 'You haven't touched your coffee. And you're checking your phone every thirty seconds. Is it a lead on Kaiser?'

'Not exactly.' He'd been watching his mobile all day, a blast of adrenalin accompanying each notification, wondering if this was the one. But none of them had been the message he was expecting.

'Wallace?'

'Nope.'

She narrowed her eyes. 'What, then?'

He sighed, checked to make sure no one was in earshot and lowered his voice. 'Krebs is right about Kofi. He has been abducted. I can't confirm it, but I think it's Kaiser. You know what Wallace told me about Kaiser last year?'

'Sure. That he was in the police.'

'Exactly. So, we start working on Pluto, I'm doing my own thing with the Mensah lead, and two days later Kofi's gone.' He shook his head, closing his eyes as he became aware of a new feeling: regret. 'I pushed it – I pushed him – and now look what he's done.'

'You're sure it's a kidnap?'

Boateng clenched his fists under the table. 'Yeah. I didn't tell anyone except Etta. And Pat, cos he was running the missing person case.'

'Tell them what?'

'That he's demanded twenty grand to get Kofi back.'

Jones reeled back. 'My God, Zac.'

'And according to the message, the deadline's today. That's why I can't let go of my phone.'

'What's gonna happen?' she asked. 'Have you got the money?'

'It's at home.'

'Where did you get twenty grand? I mean, it's— Sorry, it's none of my business.'

Boateng spun his mobile on the table. 'We owe a few people.'

'Is there anything I can do?'

He managed the beginnings of a smile. 'Thanks, Kat. I appreciate that. I know Etta would too. But we're all set. Just got to play it low-key and we'll get Ko back safe and sound. I don't want the heavy mob coming in.'

'I could help you. Only me. No one else from Op Pluto.'

He shook his head. 'It's OK. Seriously. Although there is something you could look at on the Leonard Bray case.'

'Anything.'

He proceeded to tell her about the document from Fortec Labs confirming receipt of the projectiles from the scene of Bray's murder. Her eyes widened at the mention of DCI Maddox.

'Can you find out what the latest is with Fortec? I've had a quick look online, but I couldn't find anything recent. Maybe it moved, changed names, closed down.'

'Sure. I'm guessing you want that done discreetly.'

'Damn right. I don't want anyone else knowing about this. If we can find the last person to see those projectiles, we might—'

The beep from his phone stopped him dead. He flipped the cover off, tapped his PIN so fast he messed up and had to do it again, then opened the message. His heart suddenly felt as if it were the size of a kick drum, each beat reverberating in his chest.

It was happening tonight.

•

Darian Wallace checked that the pistol was inside the rucksack, then zipped it shut and set off. He pulled his hood up as he walked. It was going to be a long journey and he needed to get there before Boateng. At least he had some new clothes, bought with cash he'd taken out using the bank card Kaiser had given him. That'd confuse the feds if they were looking for the guy in the black T-shirt and jeans who'd visited the sports centre last night. It was inevitable that he'd end up on some cameras. This was London, after all; one of the most 'watched' cities in the world. But that shouldn't matter. He had a single job to do, some cash to collect, and then he was out of here. He just hoped that his actions last night hadn't given the cops enough information to find him.

Wallace had lain awake in Peckham Rye Park, wondering if he'd gone soft. Obviously, the best thing would've been to have avoided the ruck with the junkie last night altogether. But the guy had jumped him and gained the upper hand for a second before Wallace had got control of the situation. Thank God the Beretta hadn't been loaded. Otherwise it would've been game over.

The old Darian Wallace would've straight-up murdered that guy. Stamped on his head until there was nothing but mush left above the neck. Not gone easy on him, prevented him from choking, then called a damn ambulance... What was happening to him? Wallace tried to go back over his decision-making process. Something had stopped him ending that junkie's existence, such as it was. Not guilt; the brer got what he deserved for trying to shoot Wallace. It was something else that had caused him to save the guy.

In his days as a dealer, Wallace had seen enough people like that; hooked on the substance, doing anything to get it. Risking injury and even death. He'd never had an addictive personality, never been driven by anything stronger than his own will. In one sense, he viewed addicts as losers. Like his own dad with the booze. People who'd made bad choices and didn't have the willpower to stop. But on the other hand, he saw a kind of parallel to his own situation.

Like the junkie, Wallace was desperate. He'd do anything not to be locked down. Like the junkie, his drive was powerful enough to make him kill. He was on his way to do that right now. And, like the junkie, his chosen victim was largely innocent. Not blameless, but didn't deserve to die. Was that why he spared the guy's life? A kind of recognition. Not empathy, surely? On the road as a teenager, having no feelings towards other people had been a badge of honour. A cold heart was best; that way, nothing affected you. But now – he had to admit – things did affect him. His son affected him.

Something deep and unexplained made Wallace want to see Leon. To be around him, to look after him, to teach him and see him grow up. But no way was he doing that from inside a prison cell. OK, he'd taken a risk, using his son to escape, but the boy was unharmed and now they had a chance for a new life. One day he'd tell Leon the story and watch his eyes light up.

After he'd killed Boateng, he planned to take the money and get out of London. Maybe even out of the country. Could he take Leon and his baby mum, Jas, away with him? Somewhere no one would be looking for them, somewhere that didn't extradite to the UK. An island, maybe? No, he was dreaming. He'd have to get out first, then contact her and bring them wherever he'd gone. And that plan had its risks, too, if the feds were listening to her phone or whatever. He'd have to try, though. As much as he didn't want to watch his son grow up from prison, he didn't want to see him grow up via Facebook either. It shouldn't be a choice between his freedom and his son. Wallace was determined to have both. Someone like him shouldn't be denied those things, shouldn't have to compromise.

And that brought him back to the job he was about to do. He recognised that Boateng must be going out of his mind. If anyone snatched Leon, Wallace would do whatever was required to get him back. But he couldn't allow himself that empathy for Boateng now. Not when the future for Wallace and his family – Jesus, his *family* – depended on it.

As he strode on into the night, Wallace could feel the weight of the pistol against his back. It was his ticket out of here. And this time it was loaded.

·

Boateng parked his car on White Hart Avenue, a stone's throw from Belmarsh prison in Greenwich borough. The road was dark, with a handful of streetlamps on one side only. There was a timber yard to his left, and the rest of the street was lined with warehouses and depots. Everything was silent. He tried to focus on the details of his surroundings, telling himself that in an hour they could all be back home together, eating that meal he'd been imagining.

Boateng had anticipated somewhere isolated and low-key. Though he knew the time and rough area from the earlier text, the exact location had only been sent to him half an hour ago. There was no time to stand up the TSG, and he'd rather do the exchange personally than get Connelly, Malik or Jones involved. He couldn't take the risk. The presence of anyone else at the handover might threaten Kofi's safety. Nor did he particularly want to put his colleagues in danger. So, it was just him and twenty grand in an envelope, with only a can of CS gas and his bare wits for self-defence.

Exiting the car and following the map pin he'd been texted, Boateng realised that he needed to climb over a small gate down the street and enter what looked like a building site. The place was dead and he couldn't see any night watchman or cameras; not uncommon if there wasn't valuable stuff worth nicking. There were piles of chalk and sand, and girders and wire lying around. He checked his phone and tried to identify the place. Google Maps told him he was a few hundred metres east of Plumstead railway station, and close to the train tracks. Using the screen to navigate towards his destination, Boateng crossed the flat, open expanse of ground. He glanced side to side for signs of life or activity, but there was nothing. Approaching a long, low concrete roof where the pin had been dropped, the ground started to open up. Then it hit him: Crossrail. The vast project meant huge new train tunnels had been drilled beneath the city, but it was all still under construction. There was just one line south of the river, and the gaping entrance in front of him, six metres high, was the only point where it went below ground.

Boateng swallowed, his mouth dry. Was Kofi inside the tunnel? Was Kaiser with him? Staring into the darkness ahead, he felt his

stomach tighten and a tingle flutter through his limbs. He tried
to breathe deeply, stay calm, and think.

Now it was obvious to him why Kaiser had chosen this location
for the exchange. It was a piece of empty land, not covered by
CCTV, funnelling to a point underground and guaranteed to be
away from prying eyes. It also gave Kaiser a strategic advantage:
across the open ground, he could watch Boateng, check if he'd
brought backup and control the territory. And the terrain meant
Boateng had had to abandon his car and enter the area on foot,
limiting his movement.

He took a final glance back and stepped cautiously into the
tunnel. The only sound was his own footsteps echoing off the
smooth concrete walls. What little light came through the opening
faded to black a few metres inside. The air was cold and still.
Boateng turned a full circle but couldn't see or hear anyone. He
waited, his fear and frustration growing until he snapped.

'Kaiser!' he shouted into the darkness. 'I'm here! Come on.'

Silence.

'Where's Kofi?' yelled Boateng, his voice reverberating around
the cavernous space. 'Where's my son?'

Nothing.

'I've got your fucking money,' he spat. 'It's all here.' He bran-
dished the envelope and waved it, trying to provoke a reaction
in anyone who was watching.

A low hum rose from behind him, and as it became a loud,
insistent rasp, Boateng turned and stared out from the tunnel
entrance. A motorbike was approaching. As it got closer, he could
see there was one rider, all in black, with a tinted visor. The bike
was a big, powerful trail model with thick shock absorbers and
rough tyres. It came to a halt before the tunnel entrance, about
twenty metres away from Boateng. The rider remained on the
bike with the engine running, its guttural chug-chug amplified

by the enclosed space in which Boateng was trapped. Even at this distance, he could smell the engine oil and petrol vapours.

'Where is he?' screamed Boateng, his voice catching. 'Give me back my son!'

The rider cocked their head to one side, as if the display of emotion was a curiosity.

Boateng couldn't help himself. He began sprinting towards the bike, determined to rip the rider's helmet off and expose Kaiser. He'd only taken a few paces when the voice rang out from behind him, bouncing off the tunnel walls.

'Stop!'

Boateng froze and spun round. From the darkness, a hooded figure advanced and took shape. His brain frantically tried to process the details. But one thing stood out above all else.

There was a pistol pointing at him.

# CHAPTER TWENTY

Jones tapped her iPhone, glancing at the screen just long enough to register that there were no new messages. She hoped Boateng might call or text; something just to let her know he was OK and that Kofi was safely with him. It was 9.05 p.m. and Boateng had been told to get to the meeting place at nine. A lot could happen in five minutes. She wished she knew where he was. And that was nothing to do with spying on him. It was, she acknowledged, simply that she cared about her boss.

'Message from your boyfriend?'

Jones looked up to see Kevin Harper sitting back in his office chair, twirling a pen in his hand. There was a lascivious smile on his face as his jaws worked a piece of chewing gum. She didn't reply. It was the two of them and DC Raj Patel left in the Op Pluto room, putting in a late shift. Patel had his head down, clicking and typing, immersed in some search. His enthusiasm seemed undiminished by seven straight days on Pluto. Jones wasn't sure why he was still there on Sunday night, but she was glad of his presence; something about Harper made her uncomfortable.

Right now, she wanted to tell Harper to piss off. 'No, it's—'

'Wait.' Harper held up a hand, still grinning. 'You're gonna tell me you're single.'

Jones didn't reply.

'Hang on.' He pointed an accusatory finger at her. 'It's Porky Pig, isn't it?'

'Who?'

'Chambers. Chatting you up again. I saw him in the pub on Friday night – the pair of you doing shots.'

'No.' Her denial was swift, instinctive.

'Boateng then?' Harper wasn't giving up. 'I've noticed you two are pretty close.'

'Thanks, Kevin, but I'd prefer not to discuss my—'

'Just kidding,' said Harper with a wink. 'It's none of my business who you're shagging.' He stood up and crossed to her desk. Before she could formulate a way to pick him up on his choice of words, he spoke again. 'What are you working on?'

She could smell his aftershave and instinctively rolled her chair back a few inches. 'I'm extracting the actionable data from these source reports,' she replied coolly.

'From Porky?'

DI Chambers had supplied a wad of material that afternoon which he'd drawn together from informants – or Covert Human Intelligence Sources – across Trident, the Met's long-running programme to counter gang crime and gun violence. There were names, places, firearm makes and models, times and dates to be cross-checked. Goodhew – who was sensibly at home with her family – would go full steam on it tomorrow morning, but Jones wanted to make a start. Just in case there was something there; maybe even a lead that could help Boateng.

'Bit weird, isn't it?' Harper thrust his hands into his trouser pockets and rocked back on his heels.

'What is?'

'Well, we've been working on this op since Monday afternoon, and Chambers's main responsibility has been to obtain CHIS reporting. He's out there, creeping around, throwing money at his sources. There's nothing for six days. Then he drops this lot on us in one go and buggers off for a Sunday-night wank.'

Jones pushed her lips out. 'Maybe the intelligence came in from different handlers and he wanted to collate them first.'

'Why would he do that?'

'I don't know.' She shrugged. 'I don't work with covert sources. Perhaps he needed to check some details, get a couple of handlers to go back to their contacts. Follow up, whatever.'

'Maybe.' Harper nodded at her monitor. 'So, how good are the reports?'

'Haven't you read them?'

'Some, yeah. But I want to know what you think.'

Jones was mildly flattered. 'Well,' she said, bringing up a couple of windows on the screen and leafing back on her notepad. 'I think a few of them are almost useless. This one, for instance. The CHIS says that he thinks he heard someone mention a bloke called Kaiser or Keyser, and says he might be a Turk from Haringey who works in a restaurant in Wood Green and supplies the odd pistol to some of his mates who deal heroin.'

'What's so bad about that report?'

She pointed at the screen. 'Well, it's hearsay, for a start. The sourcing chain isn't clear or checkable. The restaurant isn't named. There are thousands of Turks who live in that area. It's miles away with no connection to south London. And it doesn't fit with what we think we know about Kaiser, namely that he's in the police.' She turned to him. 'Apart from that, it's gold.'

Harper raised his eyebrows. 'Have you considered that Wallace might've been lying about Kaiser's police link?'

'You're not the first person to make that suggestion.'

He nodded. 'OK, what else?'

She pulled up another report. 'This one's better. It's not about Kaiser, but it does describe a guy who, according to the CHIS, is modifying weapons in a garden shed.'

'Eh?' Harper cocked his head and pulled a face. 'Sounds unlikely.'

'Yeah, but there's a location: Dagnall Park. It's in Selhurst, Croydon. Bit of searching on the residents, Google Earth to pick out the sheds, go door to door, we could get somewhere.'

'Dagnall Park?' Harper sniffed. 'Might not be connected to Kaiser.'

'Even so, if it flags up some gun modification that'd be a result for Pluto. Proactive, upstream work? Top brass would be all over it. And the ways things are going, we might need to take whatever we can get on that front.'

'That's a slow-burn lead,' said Harper, shaking his head. 'No magistrate would sign off a warrant to search someone's shed on the basis of a single vague source report. Leave it.'

Jones slumped back in the chair. She knew Harper was right and that she was clutching at straws. She quickly checked her phone again: nothing.

'Let's face it,' continued Harper, lowering his voice. 'Chambers is firing blanks.' He chuckled at his own joke.

'At least he's producing some intel for us to work with,' countered Jones, feeling weirdly protective of the chubby, sweaty detective.

'Can we trust his product, though?' said Harper, glancing back at Patel, who was still ensconced behind his computer screen.

'What do you mean?' she asked.

'Well, when our paths crossed before, let's just say he had a nasty habit of making things up.'

Jones closed her notebook. 'You're going to have to explain that, Kevin.'

Uninvited, he pulled up the chair at the next desk and sat down, his knee a couple of inches from hers. 'You haven't heard the story then?'

'What story?' This rumour mill bullshit was starting to irritate her.

'Chambers has worked on Trident for years. When people are in a job too long, they start to take... shortcuts. Before I left the

Met, I heard about this one case where Chambers and his team wanted a guy in Kennington for firearms possession, alongside drugs offences. But he keeps himself clean and they can never catch him with anything on him. Chambers is getting more and more pissed off about it, thinks the guy's laughing at him. One day they go round to his flat for another of their pointless shakedowns. Next thing, the guy's dead. Chambers's story is that the fella pulled a gun on him and Chambers reacted first, shot him four times in the chest.'

'And you don't believe that?'

Harper bit his lip. 'Do you know what a first aid kit is?'

'You're saying Chambers could have saved the guy's life but didn't?'

'No, no. I'm not talking about anything medical.' He made quotation marks with his fingers. 'A "first aid kit". It's what you take out on a job in case you need evidence that ain't there. Normally it's got drugs in it – class A and B – a knife or two and a handgun. You take out whatever you need to make the scene fit. Magically, Chambers's dead man has a weapon in his hand.'

Jones was feeling very uncomfortable with this conversation. 'And what was questionable about that?'

Harper snorted. 'You have seen Chambers, haven't you? He's a sack of shit. A fat bastard with the reactions of a sloth. You're telling me he can put four bullets in a young, fit guy before that guy fires one single round back? No way.'

'How do you know this?'

Harper's lower lip curled down. 'Chambers isn't the only one with sources.'

'OK.' Jones waited, but Harper didn't elaborate. She didn't really want to know anyway.

'Did you watch *Macbeth*?' he said. 'The one with Fassbender in it.'

'Er, no. But I read the play in English class.'

'So, Chambers is a bit like that. Starts off with good intentions, but gradually gets pulled in over his head. The temptations are too much, and before he knows it, things are out of control.'

Jones thought about the play, Macbeth's wife encouraging him to commit murder. 'And why are you telling me?'

'I don't want you to put too much weight on what he says, that's all.' He stood up. 'Think I might grab a cheeky pint before I head home. Want one?'

Jones blinked. 'No, thanks. I'm gonna go through the rest of these reports then call it a night.'

'Another time then.' Harper rolled back the chair and gave her a pearly white smile.

She didn't reply.

•

Wallace stepped closer to Boateng, keeping the pistol aimed at his torso. He didn't know how this heater was going to fire, so he chose the biggest target. The fed looked like he'd seen a ghost. He raised both hands. Clutched in one was an envelope.

'Throw the money towards the entrance,' said Wallace, advancing in an arc about five metres away from Boateng until they were level. He could see Boateng's eyes were wet, but they were flicking around, like he was thinking. 'Just do it,' Wallace growled.

The copper seemed as if he was about to cry. 'OK,' he said quietly. 'Just tell me where my son is.'

Wallace jerked his head towards the motorcycle. 'He's coming. Once we've got the money.'

'I want to see him,' said Boateng, turning towards the tunnel entrance. 'Let me see him!' he roared at the rider.

'It don't work that way,' said Wallace. 'Cash first.'

Boateng's body was twitching. Was he going to try something?

'Do it,' commanded Wallace, louder now. He cocked the hammer back on the Beretta. The click echoed in the tunnel.

'Not till I see my son.' Boateng's jaw was set.

Wallace shook his head. The stubborn fuck. He glanced to the rider, who took out a mobile phone and tapped a text. A few seconds of silence followed before a beep sounded in Boateng's pocket.

'Better check your messages,' said Wallace. 'One hand only. Slowly, yeah?'

Boateng looked confused as hell. He reached down and extracted his phone. Stared at the screen for a moment. Then he let out a cry of pain like he'd stepped in a bear trap.

'You motherfuckers!' he screamed. 'You bastards!' There was spit at the corners of his mouth and tears in his eyes.

'Now you've seen your son, throw him the money,' said Wallace, the pistol sight still locked on Boateng in case he made a move. But the fight seemed to have gone from his body. He turned and threw the envelope towards the guy on the motorbike. Wallace still didn't know if that was Kaiser or one of his associates. Without switching the engine off, the rider dismounted, put the bike on its kickstand and walked over. Looked like whoever it was had a bit of extra weight around the middle. The figure picked up the envelope and, stepping backwards towards the bike, opened it and inspected the contents. Apparently satisfied, the rider got back on the bike and nodded at Wallace.

Wallace squeezed the trigger.

●

Boateng brought his hands up to his face and shut his eyes. The thought that came to him wasn't of Etta or Kofi or his own parents. It wasn't anything heroic or clever. It was only the recognition that his arms weren't going to stop a bullet and that raising them was a stupid thing to do.

He heard the motorbike engine revving outside.

Then a single dry click.

He opened his eyes. Wallace was staring at the pistol. Boateng registered the disbelief on Wallace's face as he racked the slide. It was stuck. He glanced up at Boateng, who took his chance. He threw himself at Wallace, closing the gap with quick strides and grabbing the weapon in both hands. Wallace's finger was still on the trigger. Boateng swiped his foot at Wallace's leg, trying to knock him off balance, but missed. Wallace managed to cock the hammer back and squeeze the trigger once more as Boateng pushed his arms aside. This time the bang was deafening, its aftermath drowning out all other sound with a high-pitched monotone, until Boateng heard the bike engine cutting through it. The rider was still there, in the tunnel entrance, watching them grapple over the weapon. Boateng swiped again and this time connected with Wallace's knee, knocking him to the ground.

But Wallace held tight to the gun. He pulled Boateng down with him and, releasing his left hand, aimed a hook at Boateng's head. Before Boateng could react, it connected with his cheek. The pain exploded through his face as he rolled onto Wallace, trying to get his weight above him. Boateng clamped his palm over the pistol slide to stop it firing again. Hot metal scalded his skin. The motorbike engine gunned once more and Boateng looked up to see the rider pivot the bike around on its front wheel and pull away.

'No!' he bellowed.

As Wallace struggled free, Boateng ripped the pistol from his hand. It smacked into the concrete, skidding away from them. Boateng snatched the CS spray from his pocket and fired it in Wallace's direction, but the younger man dived towards the tunnel entrance and scrambled to his feet. Clutching the CS can, Boateng rugby-tackled him, slamming them both into the floor again. As Boateng tried to aim the spray, Wallace kicked out and connected with Boateng's solar plexus. Winded, Boateng rolled onto his side, gasping. Teeth clenched, he hauled himself back up. But Wallace already had a step on him and was sprinting out from the tunnel into the construction site.

Boateng chased, his ribs burning. Wallace accelerated towards the bike as the rider looked over his shoulder and slowed down. Boateng gave it one last push, his legs hollow as he lurched towards Wallace. He was gaining on the pair when the bike stopped and Wallace leapt onto the back, gripping the rider's shoulders. Boateng launched himself forwards into the air, arms outstretched.

He just had time to see the puff of smoke from the bike's exhaust as its tyres bit into the ground and it pulled away, spraying him with chalk and grit. He crashed into the dirt as the motorbike roared off with Wallace on the back. By the time Boateng got to his feet, the bike had disappeared among the distant piles of building materials, its engine no more than an insect buzz.

Doubled over, Boateng sucked in a lungful of oxygen. Then, with every ounce of strength he had left, he stood up straight and screamed at the darkness.

•

Kaiser stood up and stretched out muscles that were sore and tight, as much from accumulated stress as from today's workout. Crossed the little office to where the whisky was kept on the side. Poured a generous measure into the crystal tumbler, added a single ice cube and rotated the glass, watching the ice turn clear and melt at the edges. A stiff drink was necessary to steady the nerves after everything had nearly turned to shit earlier. Kaiser took a large sip and felt the liquid flow down. The sensation was somewhere between pleasant warmth and uncomfortable burn.

There had been one major success from the night's events: twenty grand of Boateng's money was on its way to a man who had travelled in from Prague specifically to collect it. This man had no doubt spent most of the evening watching TV in a small room at the Woolwich Travelodge hotel, oblivious to the chaos unfolding a mile down the road from him in Plumstead. Perhaps it was better that their Czech visitor didn't know the details; all that mattered was that the cash was in his hands, and the debt for the Škorpions was paid. The guy would be back on the road to Prague first thing tomorrow morning without needing to extract his price some other way. One problem had been dealt with.

What couldn't have been foreseen, however, was Wallace's botched attempt at killing Boateng. It should've been simple enough. Apparently the Beretta had jammed and been dropped at the scene. Wallace had fired a gun before; he knew what he was doing. It was faulty equipment that was to blame. This cut to the heart of Kaiser's current difficulties. Across London, the Met had tightened up on firearms to the point where Kaiser was often forced to sell rubbish and low-grade converted weapons. The Quartermaster was supposed to apply his magic touch to the guns that came their way, but even his skills were limited when it came to shoddy raw materials. That was why Kaiser had been forced to expand the sourcing overseas, again. It was riskier, with the possibility of ending up in debt to serious people like the Czech mafia. They might think twice about resupplying now. It'd take some sweet-talking to strike a new deal. But that could wait.

Kaiser took another sip, the burn slightly milder this time. The whisky was starting to have its desired numbing effect.

The problems that remained for Kaiser were much closer to home. Boateng was still alive, and he would be more determined than ever to find his son. The boy was supposed to have been delivered back to his house after Boateng had passed the money over and been shot. But with the fuck-up at the tunnel, the plan had fallen apart. Kaiser didn't want to look after a kid who was of no further use but didn't want to have to dispose of another body, either. Something would have to be done with him, and with Boateng, too.

And that wasn't all. Operation Pluto was closing in, each lead they generated and every follow-up inquiry threatening to expose some part of Kaiser's operation or, worse, identity. The Pluto team was now working on the basis that Kaiser was in the police. Well, if that was what they were looking for, might there be a way to fix both problems at once? The implacable force of Op Pluto and the immovable object of Zac Boateng. That would draw things to a nice conclusion, after which Kaiser could lie low for a while and wait until everyone moved on. Then business could be resumed.

Making something out of nothing had always been Kaiser's gift, as had learning from mistakes. On the basis of those two principles, Kaiser began to think. A new plan started to take shape, better than the last. This time, it really would be done in one fell swoop.

Kaiser finished the whisky and set to work.

# CHAPTER TWENTY-ONE

**Monday, 27 August 2018**

The first thing Zac noticed upon waking was the smell of strong coffee. This was rapidly followed by the awareness of an almighty headache, alongside a series of acute pains in various parts of his body. Etta was perched next to him on the bed.

'How are you feeling?' she asked, extending a mug towards him.

Zac rubbed his face with both hands and levered himself into a sitting position. His cheek throbbed where Wallace had punched him. He remembered Etta patching his face up as he'd explained what had happened. He'd needed several drinks to numb his aching body as well as his skittering mind. Etta must have helped him to bed in the end; he couldn't remember falling asleep.

'Been better.' He groaned and took the mug. Sipped and burned his tongue. 'I'm sorry, love. I fucked up big time.'

She leaned in, cupped his chin and inspected the bruising. 'I'm just glad you're still alive. You could've died in that tunnel last night.'

He shook his head slowly. 'I lost all our money, too.'

She pressed her lips into a flat line before responding. 'Most of it wasn't ours anyway.'

'Damn,' he muttered, taking another sip of scalding coffee.

'I can't deal with much more of this, Zac.' Her voice was calm, but he could see her eyes were moist and there was a tremor in her hand as she placed it on the bed sheet. 'Our boy has been gone for nearly five days now. I feel like the world is falling apart. I didn't know what else to do, so after you fell asleep last night, I prayed.'

'But you don't—'

'Just…' She held up a palm. 'Listen. I'm not sure if anyone was up there to hear it, but afterwards, the idea came to me. And it was clear.'

'What idea?' His head was hurting.

'That we – you – need to tell your colleagues everything we know about this. No more doing our own thing. I know they threatened Kofi, but obviously we can't trust them. They tried to kill you, they took our money and they didn't give Kofi back. We don't know what kind of hell they've put our little boy through. And, whoever "they" are, they've got that murderer Darian Wallace working with them. It's too much for us – too much for you – to deal with alone. We need to ask for all the help we can get. You told me your colleagues were trying to find Kofi, that the MIT was looking for Wallace, and you've got this special Pluto operation team. Bring them all together, Zac. You're all working on the same thing.'

'But what if Kaiser threatens Kofi again? What if—'

'We've gone past that now. We just need to find him.' She gripped his arm with unexpected firmness. 'Find our son.'

For a moment, it looked as if his wife was about to burst into tears. But she set her jaw, swallowed, nodded and stood. Somewhere beyond his aches, pains, hangover and self-loathing, he felt her strength building him back up, making him ready for the fight.

It wasn't just psychological support he needed, though. After last night, Zac knew it was a question of physical protection, too. As Etta walked out of the bedroom, he leaned over to the bedside table. Pain shot through his ribs and chest as he reached for his laptop. Zac fired up the browser and tapped in the search term: 'military equipment websites'.

•

Connelly had woken at dawn and put in an hour with his plants before coming in to the Lewisham MIT office. It was going to be another long day, and he wanted to clear his head before starting. After having worked the whole weekend on Kofi's abduction and Wallace's escape, he'd felt the pull of the earth this morning.

The allotment gave him a sense of order and simplicity. Standing in it, he could see the boundary of the plot; clear lines a few metres around him. You planted, you fed, you watered, you protected, and at the end of it, you generally got some crops. They didn't always survive or thrive, but, in his experience, the success rate was a hell of a lot better than that of police investigations. And marriages. If only the rest of life was as straightforward as an allotment.

Never did that sentiment seem so true as now, rereading the email response from the Met's Estates and Facilities Team. The safe house on Romola Road had been on the Met's books for just over a decade. One hundred and twenty-four months, to be exact, during each of which it had been used by, on average, two or three operational teams. In some instances, the teams were repeat users, but the officers reserving the house for their meetings, sources or witnesses might be different. Needless to say, no one had booked it last week. That would've been too much to hope for.

Connelly couldn't help but feel deflated. He was looking at two hundred and fifty, maybe three hundred separate uses of the safe house since the Met had taken possession of it. Some of those instances would have involved multiple officers in the same team, any one of whom could have copied the keys and used it as a place to keep Kofi hostage. He didn't know where to begin. There wasn't any mention of the locks changing, to narrow down the access. He had to hand it to this Kaiser fella: the bastard knew how to cover his tracks.

Breaking his gaze away from the screen, Connelly began excavating allotment soil from under a fingernail with his biro lid. He tried to think of the best way to make sense of this mountain of data. Could he obtain the full personnel list from Estates and break it down by serving and ex-officers, or those who worked with firearms cases, perhaps? If he could show Boateng the list, would his boss be able to shed any light on it? Or would Boateng simply pick out the first name he knew and head straight round to interrogate the poor sod?

In moments like these, when there wasn't a clear answer, Connelly had a fail-safe course of action: brew some tea. Strong, sweet stuff, the kind that had fuelled generations of Irish. He pushed his chair back and stood.

'Pat,' said Malik, urgently. They'd each been so absorbed in their tasks that Connelly had almost forgotten the lad was there. 'Check this out.'

Connelly came and stood at his younger colleague's shoulder. The screen of Malik's laptop was divided into four. He tapped the top left quadrant with a fingertip.

'I put the three points where we believed Wallace had been onto a map. It showed him moving east, or south-east, from Camberwell, in the direction of Peckham. I got him on a council camera off a car park, then CCTV from the perimeter of Harris Academy school. Here's the last we see him.' Malik played the clip and Connelly watched as a figure, dressed the same as Wallace had been in the Flaxman Sports Centre, walked into the picture and out again.

'Nice work, Nas.'

'Then I lose him.'

'Shite.' Connelly bit his lip.

'For a few minutes,' resumed Malik, with a grin. 'Anyone's guess where he goes during that time, although I reckoned it's not back the way he came. So, I checked a few cameras I had access to, and look at this.' He played the clip in the top right quadrant. Someone, probably Wallace, approached a building, stopped in front of it – just out of shot – and marched off again less than a minute later.

'What building is that?' asked Connelly.

Malik raised his eyebrows. 'Barclays.'

'He took out some cash.'

'Reckon so,' nodded Malik.

Connelly got closer and squinted at the time stamp on the footage. 'At 11.42 p.m.'

'No one uses it for a few minutes on either side of him. Shouldn't be hard to trace the transaction.'

Connelly wiped a hand over his face. 'So, if we get the account details, we find whoever's helping him, and any other places he might've used it.'

'Exactly. Do you reckon he collected that bank card from the sports centre?'

'Aye, most likely. So you'll put the request in to—'

Malik leaned back in the chair and cracked his knuckles. 'Already done it, mate.'

Connelly let some of the tension drop from his shoulders as the smile creased his face. 'Right, lad. I'll put the kettle on then.'

'Three sugars, please,' said Malik.

⦁

Kofi flexed his right hand behind his back. The palm was bruised and sore where it had been squeezed in the vice yesterday. But he still had all his fingers. When his hand had been trapped, the metal jaws pressing into the bones below his knuckles, he'd thought that was it. That they were going to cut off at least one finger. But they hadn't. They'd just taken a photo, then unwound the handle and let him slip his hand out of the vice. Once it was free, he'd held it against his tummy with the other hand, as if that could protect it, until he was handcuffed again.

Kofi knew he had no chance against these people, if they really wanted to hurt him. They were bigger and stronger than him and, what was more, they had the nasty black box of electricity, with its spiky devil horns, in case he stepped out of line. He shivered, remembering the time he'd been hit with it. At least he hadn't wet himself when his hand was in the vice. That'd been so scary that he couldn't stop shaking, even when they'd put him back in the little room at the end of the workshop, and he was left on his own.

The man who'd brought him here had come in that morning and undone one hand from the cuffs. Given Kofi a bowl of cereal and told him to eat it quickly. While he was eating, the man had stood there huffing and checking his watch. Kofi wondered if he was late for work. When he'd finished the cereal, the man put tape back over his mouth and cuffed his hand behind his back again. He took out the bucket which Kofi had done a poo in as well as several pees.

The man had returned two minutes later and put the empty bucket back on the floor next to Kofi. It still smelled horrible.

'You're going to see your dad soon,' he said.

Kofi's heart leapt at the words, but the happy feeling vanished when he saw the man's crooked smile as the door closed. Back in near darkness, he could hear laughter rumbling through the wood before the padlock on the outside clicked shut once more.

•

'You could've died, Zac.' Jones shook her head, holding eye contact with her boss.

'Guess I was lucky Wallace was using this piece of shit,' he replied, gesturing to the battered pistol that lay inside an evidence bag on the table of the Op Pluto room.

'Why didn't you call me?' She kept her voice low, but she couldn't hide the urgency of her tone.

'I didn't want to get you involved in it.'

'I *am* involved in it,' she hissed. 'Remember?'

'If you'd been there, Wallace might've killed us both.'

'Damn it, Zac.' Jones shut her eyes, took a breath. 'You could've had a team for backup.'

'There was no time,' he protested. 'I had twenty minutes' notice of the location.'

'But you knew the general area. We might've been able to protect you. Maybe tail the motorbike away from the scene. Then lock the tunnel down, secure the evidence.'

'That's the only serious piece of evidence,' he said, wagging a finger at the gun.

'Who else knows about this?' she asked. 'You can't keep this quiet. You need to—'

'OK, OK.' He held up his hands. He sighed, and just for a moment, Jones thought he looked ten years older than his forty-four years. Then he sat up straight. 'I'm going to give the team a full briefing on it. Kofi's kidnap is linked to Wallace as well as Kaiser. All of us on Op Pluto should be working together on it, with Pat, Nas and the rest of the MIT mob down the corridor.'

'You sure?'

'Yup. Etta had some words with me this morning. Twenty of us have got more chance than just me, even with you helping.' He smiled and, despite her anger at his recklessness, Jones couldn't help but smile too.

'We'll get Patel to run the details on the Beretta here,' he continued. 'See if it's been on our radar before.'

Jones took up her notepad and pen. 'What about the rest of the forensics? There might be tyre tracks and footprints outside the tunnel; fibres; maybe CCTV and ANPR to pick up the bike. Gunshot residue on Wallace's clothes, when we find him, and—'

'Whoa.' He half-raised both palms. 'Hang on, Kat. Yeah, maybe that stuff was there at ten o'clock last night. But Crossrail is a working building site. I guarantee there are forty guys trampling all over it right now. Forget the bike. The plate will be stolen or cloned, and I'd bet a month's wages the guy knew what roads to take to avoid number plate tracking. And as for Wallace, he's savvy. He'll ditch those clothes the first chance he gets.'

'So, what, we're just giving up on those leads?'

'No, we're concentrating on the high percentage ones.'

'The Beretta that Wallace fired at you?'

'That, and the other solid lead.'

Jones frowned. 'Which is?'

Boateng paused, then took out his mobile phone. 'The only other person who's seen this is Etta, so far.' He swiped and tapped and turned the screen towards her.

She gasped and noticed Chambers and Goodhew look up from their desks. In the photograph was a small, black hand. It was being held in a metal workshop vice, wound so tight that the skin was bulging around the base of the fingers, which curled over as if trying to protect themselves. Her reaction was visceral, disgust quickly replaced by anger at whoever would torture a child.

'It's horrible, I know,' said Boateng. 'Took me a while to be able to look at it. And every time I do, I want to murder the person who did that.' He sounded so matter-of-fact, Jones wondered if he was serious.

She blinked. 'I realise this is part of the case, Zac. But why are you showing me?'

'He swiped outwards on the screen with forefinger and thumb. Look closely,' he said, handing her the phone. 'It was taken in a workshop. There's stuff in the background. Maybe it's this guy we've been looking for who modifies the guns. If we find his shed or whatever, we can match this up to it. I've passed the number to Connelly, but I'm guessing it's another burner. The scene, though,

Kat. That's the evidence. Kofi is in that workshop. Section 47, ABH, against a minor. That's a charge right there, if you find the…'

Jones had stopped listening. She was zooming, moving, searching. She didn't know much about tools or workshops, but a familiar shape had caught her eye.

'Look at this,' she said, making a couple of small adjustments then rolling her chair alongside his and holding the phone up so they could both see it.

Boateng peered at the object. 'It's something metal. A piece of specialist kit, maybe?' He pinched the screen to get the full view again, tilted it.

Footsteps approached behind them and Jones instinctively hid the phone.

'Jesus Christ,' exclaimed Chambers. 'Is that what I thought it was?'

Boateng turned to him. Anger at the intrusion flashed across his face before giving way to resignation. 'Yeah, Will, it is,' he sighed. 'It's Kofi.'

'Shit, man. I'm sorry.' Chambers tugged his polo shirt loose at the armpits and stood there.

'I'm gonna brief everyone on it at the meeting,' said Boateng. 'You know, when we're all in.'

'Yeah, course.' Chambers sniffed. 'Anything I can do, you know, just…'

'Cheers, Will.'

'What do you think the metal thing is?' Jones asked Boateng.

'Well, it's like a rod, with a groove all the way down, but I don't—'

'Can I see?' asked Chambers, who was still behind them. 'I mean, you are going to share this with us, aren't you, Zac?'

Jones hesitated and glanced at Boateng, who nodded once. She held the screen up to him. Chambers took the opportunity to lean in close to her. She could smell his body odour. Since it wasn't even 9 a.m. yet, she guessed that either he wasn't wearing a clean shirt or he hadn't showered. Or both. She'd taken a breath through her mouth and was about to ask him to move back when he stood up straight and gave them a grin of satisfaction.

'It's a gun drill,' he said authoritatively.

She rolled her chair back slightly to look up at him and put a little more distance between her nose and his armpit. 'Which is…?'

He tutted. 'It's a type of bit. OK, imagine you're drilling a hole in a long, solid object. Like a piece of metal for a gun barrel. You've got to remove the stuff you're cutting out as you drill in, right? Like a tunnel. So, a gun drill has a gap all the way down it. You push air through as you drill, and it blasts the debris out the back. Simple.'

Boateng nodded at her. 'Told you it was specialised. Nice one, Will.'

'Pleasure.' Chambers stood there. Then he frowned. 'You think it's Kaiser's workshop?'

Jones shrugged. 'We don't know.'

Chambers pointed at the phone. 'Can you send me that?'

'Everyone will get access to it,' said Boateng flatly.

'Alright, good,' said Chambers. He looked from Jones to Boateng and then, when neither of them said anything more to him, he shambled out of the office. Jones guessed he was heading for the cafeteria and one of the greasy bacon sandwiches he seemed to live off.

Boateng watched him leave before swivelling back to her. 'What did you think you saw?'

'This,' she replied, zooming in again to reveal a diamond printed on the metal, another two sharp triangles meeting it at the tip.

Boateng moved it around on the screen, then shook his head. 'What is it?'

'Mitsubishi,' she said, leaning across and clicking her mouse. She opened Google and tapped the word in. 'See?'

'How did you get that from a third of the logo?'

Jones shrugged. 'My mum drives a Shogun. But they make all kinds of stuff. Including machine parts, I guess.' A bit more googling and she quickly established that, among many other products, Mitsubishi manufactured gun drills. And they were only available directly from Japan.

'Genius,' said Boateng, the smile creeping up his cheeks. 'Can't be too many people who've imported one of them into the UK.'

'Probably not,' acknowledged Jones, allowing herself a smile too.

                                        ●

Wallace had got to the shop on Deptford High Street as soon as it opened. 'Shop' was probably the best description for the Bangladeshi-run place, where he now sat quietly in a corner. Calling it a travel agency would miss out the second-hand mobile phone section of the business. Calling it a telecoms shop wouldn't do justice to the currency exchange services on offer. And calling it a money transfer agency would ignore the print and copy facilities. The family who ran this enterprise had something for everyone, including a couple of broadband-connected PCs for anyone either too poor or too shady to use the internet on their own devices. That suited Wallace just fine.

After the fuck-up last night in the tunnel, Wallace had been unceremoniously ditched in Shrewsbury Park near, ironically enough, Shooter's Hill. He was still none the wiser as to who the guy on the bike had been. He didn't think it was Kaiser, but casting his mind back to the time he'd bought a heater, he wasn't sure he'd *ever* met Kaiser. It made sense: why risk exposing your face to customers when you could pay someone else to do that for you? If anything turned nasty, it wasn't you in the firing line.

This theory was supported by the fact that, right now, his contact with Kaiser was taking place via Google Hangouts, the messaging feature of their Gmail accounts. ColonelKurz21 was online when Wallace had signed in, and had directed him to the private chat. Kaiser had simply written:

*You fucked up.*

Wallace's palms felt a bit clammy. *Not my fault*, he typed back.

*Why isn't Boateng dead?* came the response.

*Beretta was a piece of shit*, replied Wallace. *Jammed on me.*

There was a pause before Kaiser wrote: *Did you test it?*

Wallace was getting pissed off. *How am I meant to do that in a city?!*

Another pause. *QM assured me it worked fine before he passed it on to you.*

Wallace shook his head. Obviously the guy who'd supplied it wasn't going to take the blame, was he? Then Wallace recalled the fight with the junkie in the empty house, the pistol being thrown backwards and smacking against the brick wall. But maybe it wasn't that impact that had caused the problem. There were other, more likely reasons: the piece had a refitted barrel and was practically an antique.

*That thing was older than my granny*, typed Wallace.

There was no reply.

Wallace knew he had to stand firm. He wrote: *Where's the rest of my money?*

The response came quickly. *You'll be paid via the card when Boateng is dead.*

Sucking his teeth, Wallace typed: *Give me a proper tool and I'll do it.*

*I'll send you direct to the shed to get a new one.* Kaiser gave Wallace an address on Dagnall Park. He didn't know the road, but the postcode was Croydon. *At 5 p.m. today,* added Kaiser.

Wallace messaged back to say he'd be there and assumed that was the end of the chat. He'd just started wondering how he was going to fill the day, and whether he'd need to walk to Croydon, when another message arrived from Kaiser.

*There's someone else in the shed I need you to deal with. Call it a 2-for-1 offer.*

Wallace read the rest of the instructions. Then he sat back, took a deep breath and wiped his palms on his trousers.

# CHAPTER TWENTY-TWO

Try to be in the moment. That was what Etta always told him after she'd been to a mindfulness session at work. Easier said than done, though. Every time that Boateng wasn't thinking or doing something specific on this case, his thoughts ran to Kofi. And those thoughts would quickly generate a storm of emotions so visceral that he felt as if his entire body was being taken over by some alien force. He'd spent so much time over the past week in the company of rage, sadness and anxiety that they just seemed normal now. Sometimes, Boateng wasn't even sure of the order this process took. He might become aware of a low-level, bubbling unease in his stomach and guts, a restlessness, and then he'd think of Kofi: where he was being kept, how he was being treated, what hardships the kid was enduring. Boateng couldn't help but blame himself. It was his tenacity that had pushed Kaiser to use Kofi as a bargaining tool. If he'd just left it alone… But Boateng knew that wasn't him. How much was his stubbornness going to cost him and his family? He tried to dispel the rumination and bring his mind back to his senses: the suburbs flashing past, the feel of the steering wheel in his hands, the sounds of the Ray Charles track which Jones had requested.

'Good find, wasn't it?' Jones swigged from a water bottle. 'By the ballistics guy.'

'Yeah,' replied Boateng. 'Patel played a blinder.'

The young DC had taken the Beretta straight to the ballistics lab on Lambeth Road this morning. It was a bright idea, since there had been no obvious serial number on the outside of the weapon to trace. An expert there had identified the old Italian pistol immediately and, taking ten minutes out from another job to sit with Patel, had explained that the 1930s models often had unusual markings. It hadn't taken long for him to discover a handful of seemingly random letter-number etchings on various parts of the weapon, some hidden and only visible when the pistol was stripped. Patel had scoured the databases for Berettas and found an old model with the same markings recorded. It had been seized in a drugs bust in the east London borough of Newham two years earlier and then sent to the Met's firearms disposal depot for destruction. Somehow, it had ended up in the hands of Darian Wallace last night.

'He'll go places with initiative like that,' said Jones. 'Patel.'

'Like out of the Met, to a job with half the stress and twice the salary.' Boateng managed a smile. It was a common situation these days in the police: bright graduates coming in, outperforming the old guard on energy, creativity and brainpower, then leaving within two or three years to join a law firm, the civil service fast stream, a security company or even, in a few cases, go into politics. 'Don't go getting any ideas,' he added. Boateng knew the Met was lucky to have kept Jones for six years, and that her father's tragic death in the line of duty was the bedrock of her motivation to serve. They couldn't take her for granted.

'You know what it means?' she asked, breaking the brief silence. 'The fact that the Beretta was sent for destruction.'

Boateng nodded. 'Wallace was right.'

•

Jones had a sense of déjà vu as she watched Terry bowl across the warehouse floor towards them. He raised a hand of greeting at her, which became a handshake when he got closer. It clearly didn't take much to win him over. He then thrust his hand towards Boateng and simply said, 'Terry.'

Boateng hesitated a fraction before accepting. 'Have we met?' he asked.

'Don't think so, mate,' replied Terry cheerfully before turning back to Jones. 'This the same business you were here about last week then, is it, love?'

'Perhaps we could speak in your office?' she said, glancing at Boateng.

Walking beside Terry, Jones heard a clanking sound and looked up to the mezzanine, where a metal floor stacked with storage boxes ran in a broad U-shape parallel to the walls, just below the little windows. At the top of a set of stairs leading up from ground level, Gaz – or maybe it was Joey – was unpacking a wooden crate.

'New arrivals,' said Terry, pointing upwards. 'My boy's sorting out a load we took off a ship coming up the Thames Estuary about five years back.'

'We?' Jones wasn't quite sure who Terry meant.

'Yeah, us. The Met. I'm in the police, too, you know. Civilian, obviously, but it's all part of the same team, innit?' He winked at her.

'Why's it taken five years for them to get here?' she asked.

'Boat captain's just lost the second appeal on his sentence, so he's going down for the rest of his term now. And they don't need the firearms as evidence no more. So, we chop 'em up.' Terry rubbed his hands. 'Cuppa tea?'

Ten minutes later, having combed through his files, Terry turned to his guests, triumphant.

'Here it is,' he said, slapping the paper with the back of his hand. 'Beretta pistol, 1934 model. Yup, definitely destroyed, twenty-fourth of May this year.' He listed the markings, then turned the document over as if that would explain the mystery. But the reverse was blank.

'So how do you account for me finding it in a Crossrail tunnel last night then?' asked Boateng.

'I can't.' Terry shook his head, blinking. 'I'm stumped.' He ran his index finger down the details, mumbling to himself. 'It's my signature here,' he concluded. 'I can't remember that exact one – we get so many – but if I did the form, then I must've watched Bertha eat it myself.' He passed the paper to her, sat down and stroked his belly.

Boateng frowned. 'Sorry?'

'The cutting machine,' explained Jones. 'If we ask nicely, maybe Terry will show us on the way out.'

The foreman slurped his tea. 'I'd love to.'


Back in the Pluto incident room, Jones put both elbows on the desk, leaned forward and massaged her eyes with the heels of her hands. She was in one of those late afternoon lows, and it wasn't just the dreary process of unpicking Chambers's glut of source reports that had flattened her mood. It was the fact that, just moments after wishing Boateng good luck with the lead she'd found him on Fortec Labs, she had trotted down the corridor like a good girl to Krebs's office. Talked her through the whole thing and received a metaphorical pat on the head. Krebs might as well have given her thirty pieces of silver.

Jones rationalised it to herself with the argument that it was safer all round if someone had oversight of Boateng's plans, particularly after what had happened last night. Technically speaking, he hadn't hidden the fact that he was going out now; it just so happened that everyone else was working on other stuff and the Fortec lead hadn't been briefed to the team yet. But even as she spilled the beans to Krebs, a little nagging voice was telling her that Boateng might be right, that he was on to something.

Why wouldn't Wallace be telling the truth about Kaiser executing Leonard Bray? His intelligence on Kaiser obtaining weapons from the destruction depot had already been proven right earlier today, though it was still a mystery how the Beretta had slipped out of there and into Kaiser's possession. Its destruction was so recent that Terry had, eventually, even located security CCTV footage of it being cut up. The wall camera was a little way off, but the distinctive shape of the pistol was clear enough and the time stamp matched Terry's documentation. Jones had hoped Boateng would offer an explanation, but he couldn't.

Opening her eyes again, Jones spotted Goodhew crossing the room towards her. The slump of her shoulders gave Jones the message before the analyst placed the sheet of paper on her desk.

'Nothing, I'm afraid,' said Goodhew.

'That was quick.'

Goodhew arched her eyebrows. 'Mitsubishi couldn't get us the info fast enough. Their UK office made some calls to Japan and then did the checks right away.'

'Guess they're worried about negative publicity,' suggested Jones. 'What did they say?'

'Eighteen Mitsubishi gun drill bits imported to the UK in the past ten years,' said Goodhew, gesturing to the printout. 'And none of their buyers is known to us for modifying weapons. No connections to Op Pluto, Darian Wallace, or Kofi.' She shrugged. 'They haven't got a single criminal conviction between them.'

Jones began reading the list of names and addresses. 'One of this lot knows about the drill bit in that photo. Our next task is to profile each of them and see where that gets us. Age, occupation, people they live with – whatever you can find.'

'Sure.' Goodhew paused. 'Is Zac here?'

'No, he's out.' Jones didn't want to say any more. 'Why?'

'Just… I thought he'd want the update, given that it's about, you know, his son.'

'Don't worry, I'll pass this on.'

'Also, I was thinking… What if the original importer sold the bit online? On eBay or whatever.'

'Good point. Try a search for that, too. Then, if these profiles don't give us anything to work with, maybe we just call them up and ask if they've still got the bit. And failing that, we go back further than ten years.'

'OK.' Goodhew sighed gently. 'I'll get onto it.' She glanced almost imperceptibly at her watch.

Jones spotted the movement. 'I can do it, if you need to be heading off? Or we can ask Raj.'

Goodhew smiled. 'Thanks, but I already called the nursery about a late pickup. My husband's leaving work early to collect Holly.'

'Is that OK?'

'Yeah, no dramas. I'm into this. And it's not like Pluto's going to run forever, is it?'

'I seriously hope not. This is really good work, Amy. Keep it up.' Jones took a final glance as she handed the paper over. It took a couple of seconds for her weary brain to register the street name at the bottom.

'Wait!' She snatched it back and checked.

*Dagnall Park.*

The same street as the gun modification shed mentioned in Chambers's source report.

Jones jabbed a finger on the address. 'This is the one,' she said, suddenly energised. 'Get everything you can on the Dagnall Park address.' She leapt up, scooting her chair back so fast it tipped over. The others in the room stopped what they were doing and looked at her.

'Where are you going?' asked Goodhew.

'To brief Krebs, then the MIT. If there's a chance Kofi's there, we've got to hit the place right now.'

'Don't we need a warrant, or—'

Jones shook her head. 'There's no time, it's threat to life…'

The rest of her explanation about priority was lost as she dashed through the door and down the corridor.

•

As Boateng took the A2 south-east from Lewisham, he reflected on the letter which he'd found in the Tooting police station archives. In 2014, Fortec Labs Ltd had received the bullets from Leonard Bray's murder scene and were due to analyse them before sending them back to Dave Maddox in Lambeth MIT. At first, Boateng had refused to believe that Maddox could have been responsible for anything dodgy. He and Boateng had crossed paths a few times, and on each occasion he'd found the DCI to be a bit blunt but generally effective. OK, so Maddox was a copper who didn't much like going the extra mile when the task in question was someone else's responsibility. But who wasn't like that after twenty years' service?

Still, he hadn't asked Maddox about it straight out, partly due to the general suspicion he'd built up since Wallace told him that Kaiser was in the police. But mostly it was because Leonard Bray's murder was the only thing he still hadn't briefed everyone else in the Op Pluto team about, apart from Jones. He would, of course, but first he wanted to follow it up personally – ask the scientists who'd actually dealt with the case. The only problem with Boateng's plan was that Fortec Labs didn't exist any more. Or rather, it didn't exist under that name.

Jones had dug around in Companies House, comparing the details of Fortec Labs with other similar firms. It hadn't taken her long to discover that four months after Fortec had been dissolved, a new firm was incorporated with two of the same company directors, half a mile down the road from Fortec's old premises. If Theta Scientific Solutions Ltd, or TSS, was the resurrection of Fortec, then Boateng hoped they could perform a miracle for him. One that might lead to Kaiser.


'So, how come you guys changed names and all that?' asked Boateng casually, as he took a seat opposite Dr Ondrej Setkov, the director of TSS, who had also run Fortec. He was a slim, fit-looking man, probably in his forties. Boateng guessed he spent his spare time cycling or swimming; something involving physical endurance.

Setkov adjusted his glasses and cleared his throat. 'We had some, well, unfortunate incidents occur at Fortec Laboratories.' His accent bore a trace of what Boateng guessed was his Eastern European place of birth.

'What kind of incidents?' asked Boateng. In his pocket, he felt his phone vibrating with a call and he reached into his jacket to silence it.

'It was all cleared up at the time,' said Setkov breezily, spreading his hands.

Boateng waited.

'Some, ah, evidence which we had received went missing,' continued Setkov. 'Of course, we often didn't know what criminal proceedings the items related to, because that was sensitive. Our job was simply to run our tests according to the client's brief and report the results. Objectively,' he added.

'Right,' said Boateng. He thought of the story he'd once heard about a parachute school which had rebranded and moved a mile up the road after one of their chutes had failed to open. 'And missing evidence was bad for business, I'm guessing.'

Setkov cocked his head. 'That is an understatement, Inspector. Business wasn't just bad; it dried up. We had no choice but to start a new company with a new name, though we did not receive any further work from the Metropolitan Police after that.'

'I'm sorry to hear it.' Boateng couldn't know if Fortec was knowingly behind the missing evidence or not, but he needed to keep Setkov sweet for the request he was about to make. 'So, what do you think happened to the evidence?'

'At that time, we were doing so much work for the police, it was very difficult to keep track of everything. We had good systems, but there were many people coming and going. Couriers, detectives, technical staff. When there was a priority case, the order of our work would shift at a moment's notice and the investigator would sometimes come to collect the results and evidence personally.' Setkov shrugged. 'We figured that was safer than using a private courier company. And since the police was the client, we were happy for them to do that. Most of the time there were no problems. But after we had two or three of these incidents, people started to ask questions.'

Boateng's phone vibrated against his ribs and he silenced it once more.

'Can you check your records for a job from 2014, please? I'm wondering if it was one of those incidents.' He began giving the details of the Leonard Bray case but stopped himself midway through when he saw Setkov shaking his head. 'What?'

'I am sorry, Inspector. We no longer have that information. It was destroyed. Some individual police teams or boroughs may have kept their copies, but we have nothing from that time.'

Boateng felt as if a weight were bearing down on him, squeezing the energy from him. Another lead on Kaiser; another dead end. But he fought back the disappointment and tried to think; there had to be something. 'What about the lab technician who analysed that sample? Firearms projectiles in 2014. Were you involved in—'

Setkov shook his head quickly. 'No. My area is DNA. But if it was ballistics, then the work would have been done by Eric. He was our only ballistics technician.'

'Eric who?'

'Eric Morton.'

'And is he here?' Boateng gestured outside the small office in the direction of what he presumed were the labs.

'He retired last year. I think he had a good pension plan.'

A small sense of hope began to grow within Boateng. This lead was still alive – just. And it was still worth keeping off the record. Maybe he could try speaking to this Eric Morton guy straight away. 'I'll get one of my colleagues to find his home address. But I don't suppose you'd know where I might find him right now?'

Setkov gave a thin smile and leaned back in the chair. 'Eric is an angler. We're not really in touch, but last he told me, he was spending all his time with the fish.'

Boateng frowned. 'Outside of London, I'm guessing?'

'No. He always went to a place near his home. South Norwood lake.'


As Boateng walked back to the car, he checked his phone. Six missed calls from Jones, three voice messages – presumably all from her – and a text from a number that he recognised immediately.

It was the same phone that had sent him the picture of his son's hand in a vice.

•

Wallace found the right number on Dagnall Park and stood in the driveway for a moment, studying the unremarkable red-brick semi-detached house. Not particularly old, but not especially new either. Thick net curtains in all the windows, a neat little hedge and some flowerbeds at the front, wooden fence down the side. Anyone passing might think it was the home of a small-time accountant or office manager whose gardening hobby was as dull as his working life. No one would guess that this place was the hub through which hundreds of guns passed on their way to the streets of London and beyond. Not in a million years. Remarkable as that was, Wallace didn't want to hang about to consider it any longer. There were one or two other people walking further down the quiet street, a couple of cars passing, and at 5 p.m. he guessed it wouldn't be long before people started coming home from work. More potential witnesses putting him here. He made his way up the path.

Pressing the latch on the tall side gate, Wallace found it open, just as Kaiser had told him it would be if he arrived on time. He slipped through and closed it behind him. Parallel to the house, a motorbike rested on its kickstand under a tarpaulin. Not seeing or hearing anyone, Wallace lifted the tarp and glanced at the bike underneath. It was a trail model, same colour and style as the one he'd escaped the building site on yesterday. The number plate was different, but there was chalk ground into the tyres, which Wallace recognised as the same colour and texture as the material left in the soles of his trainers last night.

The 'shed' Kaiser had told him to visit looked more like an outhouse: a large, robust structure which dominated the garden and backed onto a clump of trees beside a railway bridge. As he approached, a burst of high-pitched mechanical whining pierced the suburban silence, followed by another. Wallace swivelled to scan the rear of the house. There were no signs of life; much like the front, the lights were off and net curtains drawn. The Quartermaster was clearly a man who liked his privacy. Wallace knocked on the outhouse door and heard a sound from inside, like metal clunking on wood, before a voice spoke.

'Who is it?'

'It's the postman,' said Wallace, aware of how awkward he sounded. 'Got your council tax bill.' That was what Kaiser had told him to say. A prearranged code like some kind of James Bond bullshit. Except James Bond wasn't quite so well armed as this brer.

'I've already paid it,' replied the voice.

Just as Wallace was about to knock again, thinking he'd got it wrong, he heard two deadbolts slide back and a big lock turning. The solid door opened and a chubby face appeared with a stupid grin.

'Only joking, son,' said the man. 'Get inside.'

Wallace stepped through into a spacious workshop. A large bench ran down one side and the centre of the space was filled by a broad wooden table, the top of which was a foot thick. Wallace saw vices, drills, two lathes and a machine that looked like a microwave. Tools hung from boards on the walls. There were metal lockers, plastic tubs full of bits and pieces of God-knows-what and a big safe in the corner.

'Thanks for last night, yeah?' Wallace sniffed. He didn't like being in anyone's debt.

The brer scratched his gut, his smile gone. 'You were meant to have killed him. You might've got us both in some very deep shit.'

'Yeah, well.' Wallace shot glances around the workshop. He noticed a padlocked door at the back and gestured to it. 'What's in there?' he asked.

'Mind your own business.'

Wallace bit his lip.

'What went wrong then?' The man smirked. 'You never pulled a trigger before?'

'The piece jammed.'

The guy looked straight through him, his eyes beady and cold. 'You blaming me for that, are you, son?'

Wallace didn't appreciate his tone. Back in the day, he'd hurt people for less disrespect than this fat fuck had just shown him in the space of thirty seconds. A little rage bubbled up and Wallace forced it back down. 'Nah, course not.' He blinked, smiling. 'Must've been my bad.'

'Damn right.' The man inspected the blade on a power saw and shifted it across the workbench. The thought occurred to Wallace that you could cut up a person with one of those.

'Boss says you've got a new one for me, though.'

The man nodded, then walked around the bench and picked up a pistol. 'This is a Browning Buck Mark, OK?' He was talking like Wallace was a moron. 'I sawed the barrel down and threaded it for a suppressor, see?' He held up the tip, then screwed on a metal cylinder that doubled the weapon's length. 'I'm quite proud of that one,' he smirked. 'Even if I say so myself. Accurate over twenty-five yards or more, and about a silent as you can get. Takes .22 ammo. I'll get you some.'

Wallace watched the guy cross to one of his plastic tubs, extract a box, pop the magazine on the Browning and load it. He replaced the full mag, racked the slide and stood staring at Wallace. They were a few metres apart. After the morbid image of the power saw, Wallace suddenly felt a sense of dread seeping up from his guts. Had Kaiser set him up? Was this how it was going to end, shot in a garden shed by a fat man in Croydon? He should've seen this coming, after the brer in prison had died last week… Wallace glanced back at the doorway. If he threw himself at it now, he could just—

'Here you go, son.' The guy was holding it out to him. Wallace took a breath, tried to slow his heart rate. He wiped a clammy palm on his top and then took the pistol from the Quartermaster's outstretched hand.

Wallace wrapped his fingers around the grip, felt the weight. 'Now I just need to test it,' he said.

# CHAPTER TWENTY-THREE

The Pluto team's first job had been to seal off Dagnall Park at each end with local uniformed officers, such that the cordons were not visible to anyone inside the target premises. Deploying at such short notice meant that they were without the heavy mob from TSG or a specialised Tactical Support Team. But Krebs and Maddox weren't taking any chances, so they had to wait until an armed response vehicle arrived before the door went in. It was the minimum level of protection needed for an operation with suspected firearms threat.

Crouching behind a high brick wall just outside the property, Jones tried to steady her breathing. She was wearing body armour and carrying CS spray but, without a Taser, she'd be one of the last in. If this was the location where Kaiser was modifying his weapons, they had to be prepared for the occupants to be armed. The memory of having a gun pulled on her last year by a murder suspect was still fresh, as was the fight-or-flight reaction it had produced in her body. But that might not be the only risk here: if Kofi was inside, there was every chance that a hostage situation could develop if they didn't play it right.

Connelly, Malik and two other MIT detectives were with them; altogether they were ten strong, forming two groups of five. From the Pluto team, just Goodhew – as a civilian without arrest operations training – remained back in the incident room. Boateng was the only other absentee, though Jones had tried her best to get hold of him. His lack of response suggested he was into something important. Several people had already asked where he was; Jones had kept silent. Harper had even made a joke about finding Boateng inside the shed. She hoped he'd retrieve her voicemails and hustle down here before it was all over. Especially if his son was inside.

Ahead of Jones, Malik had his Taser drawn, as did Chambers. Maddox was unarmed but controlling the Airwave radio handset, communicating in whispers with Krebs's group, who had approached the house from alongside the railway lines at the bottom of the garden, using the trees as cover.

A low engine hum rose and fell. Jones heard car doors open and close and looked behind her to see three ARV officers, each carrying a full-size MP5 across their chest with a pistol in their hip holster. They joined the group behind the wall and Maddox began updating them.

'No sign of activity in the house,' he said quietly. The unit buzzed in his ear, its volume down. 'Same at the back,' he said, relaying the message from Krebs, then listened to another crackle and murmur from the Airwave. 'Lights are on in an outbuilding, though. Two small windows at the rear.'

The ARV officers conferred, and one set out to loop around the back. Two minutes later, a message came through to Maddox's radio. The firearms officer was in position with the second group. The ARV leader at the front of the house moved forward, conferring with Maddox before taking the radio from him and whispering some instructions into it. Then he signalled towards the house.

'We're going in,' he said.

Maddox motioned Chambers and Malik to advance ahead of him, and they were off, Jones walking quickly in a stoop behind them. They moved silently to the side gate. Maddox carefully pressed the latch, and it opened. Chambers followed the ARV officer through, with Malik closely behind him, Taser ready. They passed a motorbike under a tarpaulin and Jones briefly thought about Boateng's account of the previous night at the tunnel. She could feel her heart pounding against her ribcage.

They crept down the side of the house. Jones's senses were on full alert, every sound intensified. She tried to minimise the noise of her own footsteps. A train rumbled in the distance and a crow was cawing in one of the big trees behind the outhouse. She saw Connelly and Patel emerge from either side of the large shed. Maddox pointed at the door, and Connelly nodded and crept around. Krebs followed the Irishman, her face taut and drained of colour. Chambers adjusted his grip on the Taser. Malik took up position on the opposite side of the door to Connelly. The ARV officer was directly in front of the door, his MP5 raised. Harper carried the Enforcer, the red battering ram that could take a door clean off its hinges. The air seemed to hang perfectly still. Then Maddox chopped his hand and Harper stood, wound up and hammered the Enforcer through the lock. Connelly and Malik were through and shouting, with more barked instructions as Patel and Chambers piled in after them.

And then there was silence.

'Clear!' came the cries from inside, followed rapidly by Connelly's voice.

'Over here,' he yelled.

Jones entered behind Harper and Maddox. Krebs was last in. Immediately, Jones could smell the gunpowder, its scent lingering in the unventilated workshop. There was another odour too, something more organic. On the far side of a large central unit, Connelly stood staring at the ground, several of the others beside him.

'Is this our weapons guy then?' asked Harper.

'Could even be Kaiser,' offered Chambers.

Skirting the workbench, Jones saw a body lying on the floor. There was a dark stain in the timber around its head and shoulders.

'Stay back,' ordered Krebs.

Jones stepped sideways to get a better view. As Connelly knelt to check the pulse on the carotid artery of the body, Jones rapidly concluded two things: one, the amount of blood and number of gunshot wounds she counted made it extremely unlikely that this man was still alive; and two, despite the hole in his face, she recognised him.

'Christ,' said Maddox, glancing from the body to Jones and back.

She felt as if everything was being sped up, her mind racing to process the information. Sweeping her gaze around the workshop, she spotted tools, boxes and a vice. It looked like the one in which Kofi's hand had been trapped. DNA might confirm that. On the side bench, she noticed a large cube that resembled a cross between an incubator and a microwave. It took her a moment to register, then it made sense. But before she could voice her thoughts, Maddox was gesturing to another door at the back, which was padlocked shut. It looked like a storeroom. Harper came over and the two of them listened at the door, Maddox sniffing and wrinkling his nose.

'Anyone in there?' he called. There was no reply.

The ARV officer stood ready with his weapon trained on the door. Then he nodded, and Harper took a step back before throwing the Enforcer at the padlock.

Jones watched them all reel back slightly at the smell from the tiny space before entering. She approached too, covering her nose. The sight inside was pitiful: a cramped room with a little window high up, its frosted glass admitting a few rays of early evening sunlight. There was a bucket to one side, which smelled as if someone had defecated in it quite recently. Apart from that, it was empty.

As Krebs shouted something about scene of crime officers and everyone getting out, Jones continued to stare at the cupboard that, perhaps only yesterday, had almost certainly been Kofi's prison.

She was glad that Boateng wasn't there.

•

Susanna Pym took a sip of her gin champagne cocktail and quickly concluded that it didn't merit the £19-a-glass price tag. But she hadn't chosen the Coburg Bar in order to get value for money. The dimly lit downstairs watering hole at the Connaught Hotel provided a good place to talk discreetly, particularly at the corner tables, where large wing-back armchairs tended to shield one's conversation from nosy neighbours. The other advantage was that, with its primarily international clientele of Arabs, Indians and Russians, there was minimal chance of anyone here recognising her. It wasn't as if she were Foreign Secretary. Not yet, anyway.

She kept her head down, scrolling through Twitter on her phone and monitoring the reactions to her own tweets earlier that day as well as anything else she'd been tagged in. It didn't make for the most inspiring reading. Left-wing people were still up in arms about the shooting of Aaron Collins last week. For goodness' sake! The chap had fired on armed police officers. Had he expected a gentle slap on the wrist in return? There were demands being made for body cam footage to be released, insistence that the Met prove Collins was a threat at the precise moment they opened fire.

Before her ire could rise any more, Pym registered something in her peripheral vision. Her guest had entered and was navigating across the bar towards her. He took the armchair opposite Pym and sank back into it with a groan. She hadn't even greeted him before a waiter appeared at his shoulder and asked what he'd like to drink.

'Beer,' said the man.

'What kind of beer, sir?' asked the waiter, tactfully. 'Would you like to see the menu?'

'Just give me a lager.'

'We have the Schiehallion Pilsner, it's a really beautiful Scottish craft—'

'Fine.'

'Very good, sir.' The waiter gave a small bow before departing.

'Long day?' Pym arched an eyebrow.

'We caught another murder this evening. Connected to the operation.'

'My God.' She leaned in, then remembered to lower her voice. 'Who?'

'Twenty-eight-year-old man from Croydon named Gareth Riley. Known to his friends as Gaz.'

Pym expected her guest to elaborate, but he didn't. 'Come on then. The suspense is killing me.' She paused; the metaphor wasn't deliberate. 'What's his connection to Pluto?'

'He was modifying weapons in a big shed at the bottom of his mum's garden.'

'Kaiser's weapons?'

'We think so. He worked in the Met's firearms destruction depot, and it seems he may have been taking his work home with him.' The man paused as the waiter came over and carefully placed the beer on their table. Waving away the glass, he took a long swig from the bottle and let out a breath of satisfaction afterwards.

'Needed that,' he said.

'Taking his work home *how*?' asked Pym.

'Stealing weapons from the depot then redrilling their barrels. Upgrading them or whatever and selling them on. There are even one or two people on our team who think Gaz Riley could be Kaiser himself. Their theory goes that he tried to do someone over on a deal and got shot, maybe even with one of his own weapons.'

'I thought Kaiser was supposed to be in the police.'

'Well, this guy was.' He shrugged. 'He just wasn't a police *officer*. Civilian technician, I think his official job title was.'

'So?' She gripped the cocktail glass tighter and could feel her toe tapping on the carpet. 'Is it him?'

The man shook his head and drank some more beer. 'I think Gaz Riley was involved with Kaiser. It fits with the source reporting. He may even have kidnapped a kid. But I think Kaiser is someone bigger – maybe someone older, more experienced. Someone with the international connections to import firearms, too. Right now, I couldn't guess much beyond that.'

'So we haven't got our man yet?' She tutted. 'Do you know what I want? I want your team to catch someone red-handed with a big stockpile of guns in their home for us to lay out in front of the press and say look, this is a bad person and now we've arrested them.' She spread her hands in the imaginary news headline. 'Then I want to appear on the radio, the web or preferably the TV, talking about all the wonderful work the Met and the NCA have done together, and turn the public mood around. Get those bloody crowds off the street outside Lewisham police station. Take away their ammunition.' Another poor choice of metaphor. 'I just want somebody we can call Kaiser. At this point, anyone will do, frankly. That'll take the heat off me. Off us.'

'We'll get there,' said the man. 'But there's one less bloke making guns now at least.'

'I suppose that is a success. If you have hard evidence that he was doing that.'

'He had ammunition, gun parts, a couple of replicas that had been converted and a 3D printer, which we're analysing now.'

She took a sip of her cocktail. 'Small scale, by the sound of it. But it's still a good story, apart from the fact of him being murdered. I'd sooner have had an arrest, you know. Who killed him?'

'We don't know. Kaiser, perhaps. A rival gunsmith. An unhappy client.'

'Hm. I'd rather not make a song and dance about a murder. Looks like the streets aren't safe.' There had already been rather a large brouhaha in the news about London having a higher murder rate than New York City earlier that year. Even though that appeared to be a statistical anomaly, which had evaporated after a month, the numbers did overwhelmingly suggest that violent crime in the capital was on the rise over the past year or so. And, if that trend continued, ultimately only one person would be held responsible: the Minister for Policing. Yet another reason for Pym to lose her job. She felt the muscles in her neck and shoulders contracting. 'What was Boateng's role in this?'

The man frowned, took another swig of beer. 'He wasn't there. No one knew where he was. Bit weird. Particularly since it's his kid that might've been kept in that shed.'

'What?'

'Yeah, his kid went missing. Maybe he was following up on that.'

'He's a bloody loose cannon!' she spluttered. 'Nobody knows what he's up to. I'd be kicking him off the Pluto team, if he wasn't going to sacrifice himself so nobly for the cause.' Her mouth puckered with delight.

The man sighed. 'You'll be screwing over a good copper if you take him down. It'd be the end of his career.'

Pym placed her glass down on the table harder than she'd intended. 'And what about *my* career? What about yours?' she hissed.

He drained the bottle and belched softly, but he didn't reply. Pym knew she was on to something here. Gone was the man's usual confidence, and she could tell she'd pushed him out of his comfort zone with the dilemma about this Boateng fellow.

'Look,' she said, with a wide smile and all the reasonableness she could muster, 'I'm not saying anyone has to screw him over, and you certainly wouldn't be associated with it. We just need an insurance policy for both of our careers if we fail to achieve our objectives. Which, I must say, is looking increasingly likely with each day that passes on this disastrous operation.'

He shook his head, deflated.

'Have you brought it or not?'

He clenched his jaw. 'I'm not happy about this,' he said. 'It's not how I work.'

'You'll get some extra for it.' She extended an upturned palm towards him.

Reaching into his jacket pocket, he produced an envelope and gave it to her. 'I've printed off the decision logs, and there's a couple of incident reports. Including one he briefed us on today. You'll see.' He pointed at the envelope. 'A firearm was discharged in a Crossrail tunnel last night. Boateng was there. And so was our latest murder victim, Gaz Riley, apparently. Or at least his motorbike was.'

'Boateng in the middle of it again? And yet, you say, he was the only one not at the gun shed today?'

'That's about the size of it.'

Pym thought for a moment. 'You don't suppose…' She shook her head. 'Could it… I mean, is it possible that Boateng is Kaiser?'

The man grunted a laugh, shook his head. 'I bloody well hope not.'

'Well, whether he is or not is one thing. Whether he *should* be Kaiser is another.'

'Eh?'

'Boateng is our fall guy, and—'

'Your fall guy,' he insisted.

'Whatever. He's the fall guy, and we also need someone to be Kaiser.'

'You want to frame him as Kaiser? You're mad.'

'Deals with both problems in one fell swoop, wouldn't you say?'

He didn't respond.

Pym tucked the envelope into her handbag. She'd select the best bits and then pass them on to the journalist Faye Rix, as and when it suited her. As the man mumbled his goodbyes and stomped out, probably in search of a boozer more suited to his tastes, Pym felt a little surge of excitement. If Operation Pluto succeeded, she'd be the golden girl, taking full credit for the multi-agency initiative and cementing her position close to the PM. If it failed, however, she now had the evidence to hang it on this Boateng chap and let him take the blame. Pym finished her cocktail and allowed herself to relax a little as she signalled for the bill.

She was back in control.

※

Jones stood up straight, rolled her shoulders and looked her old adversary face-on. She wasn't backing down. This time last week he'd got the better of her. He may have won that battle, but the war would be hers. She knew it. And she had a good feeling about tonight; she was going to beat him. She'd decided that it was a 'he' when she first saw the ten-foot wall on the housing estate in Vauxhall. When she'd started training, earlier this year, a wall run that high seemed impossible. Now she was on the verge of cracking it. She pictured the wall as a stubborn, aggressive guy. Someone who wouldn't give an inch to her, whether personally or professionally. She'd encountered enough men like that. Giving it that character made her want it even more. To 'break' the jump, as the Parkour Generations guys often said. The coach had told her to trust her instincts. Right now, though, she was having some trouble with that.

Her instincts told her that Boateng's line of inquiry on Kaiser could be the right one. After his visit to TTS – formerly Fortec Labs – Jones had been excused from the immediate follow-up on the quartermaster's shed. She was dispatched under Krebs's instructions to interrogate Boateng, 'in the nicest possible way', to find out what the meeting had yielded. Boateng, who clearly still trusted Jones and felt that she was onside, had duly briefed her over the phone on the conversation with Dr Setkov and the plan to track down Fortec's retired ballistics analyst, Eric Morton: the fisherman who Boateng hoped could explain what had happened to the bullets that killed Leonard Bray. Morton seemed like a decent lead and Jones thought Boateng was right to be cautious, to keep the investigation into the missing projectiles quiet. Wallace had been on point about the Met's firearms depot – maybe he was right about Kaiser murdering Bray. And about him being in the police, too.

Now she was in two minds: should she continue briefing Krebs and protect herself from any fallout around Boateng's actions, or repay his trust and leave her DCI in the dark from now on? Why was Krebs so interested in every twist and turn of Boateng's investigations, anyway? Jones wished she could ask her dad's advice. He'd know what to do.

She prepared herself to attempt the wall run again, shaking out her fingers and bouncing on the balls of her feet a few times. She looked up at the top. Closed her eyes for a moment. Then she took a half-step back and propelled herself forwards, gathering speed in a sprint at the obstacle. She took off from her left foot like a long jumper, kicking off the wall with her right foot and stretching upwards, her hand fully extended. She felt as if she were hanging there, weightless for just a second, before three of her fingertips caught the top of the brickwork. Her body slammed into the wall, but she stuck the grip, throwing her left hand up to catch the top. Steadying herself, she half-walked, half-dragged herself up and over. Before she knew it, she was standing on the wall. Her legs were wobbling slightly.

Jones let out the breath she hadn't realised she'd been holding in.

Then she became aware of the clapping, cheering and whooping from below.

Zac watched his wife pounding the hell out of the boiled yams, ramming the pestle down into the mortar again and again. Bash, grind, scrape, repeat. Her teeth were clenched, her forearms stiff. He stirred the pot of Egusi stew – a Nigerian recipe from Etta's mother – and threw some salt over the tilapia fish he was frying alongside it.

'You alright, love?' he asked.

She blinked, nodded quickly.

'Thinking about those texts?'

Etta wiped her eyes on the shoulder of her T-shirt. 'Mm.'

The first message that had arrived earlier that evening from the unknown number – presumably written by Kaiser – had seemed positive enough: *You'll get your kid back if you do what I say.*

Zac had replied to ask why he should trust the sender this time. The response had been as swift as it was cold: *You have no choice.*

There was a choice, though. Zac still believed that. He could find Kofi and Kaiser first. Zac had been briefed on how close they'd been at the quartermaster's shed, and he'd told Etta, sparing her some of the worst details. Kofi had been there, and almost certainly Kaiser, too. He had replied to the second text to ask if Kaiser wanted more money.

*No*, came the reply. *I want you. Don't need to tell you what happens if you speak to anyone about this.*

But he had spoken to others about it. Etta was right: they couldn't do it alone.

'I did what you said, by the way.' He flipped the fish over in the pan.

She stopped pounding and looked at him. 'You told them what happened last night?'

'Yup. And I got the OK from Krebs to link up the investigations into Kofi and Wallace with our operation.'

She smiled, for a second, then it was gone. 'I'm proud of you,' she said. They both went about their cooking tasks for a minute.

It had been Zac's idea to make a solid, comforting meal for them to have together. They both needed to keep their strength up. 'African steroids', his old man used to call yams. They did actually contain steroids, just not the bodybuilding ones. But Dad swore they made you big and strong. More than that, cooking together was a good way to keep their minds occupied; Zac knew that there wasn't much more he could do tonight, so it'd be better to get some rest. He had the feeling that tomorrow would be even longer than today.

'Quiet without them, isn't it?' he observed, glancing around the kitchen. 'If Amelia was still here she'd be telling us something new that she'd discovered. She'd be half shouting to be heard over Kofi.'

Etta pressed her lips together.

'And Kofi would be rampaging around with his toys, pretending to be a superhero,' he continued, dumping a bagful of spinach into the stew and stirring it in.

She let out a small laugh. 'And you'd be trying to tell him he had to go and brush his teeth.'

'He wouldn't listen, obviously.' He chuckled, shook his head. 'We'd have to resort to bribery.'

'You'd crack first,' she said.

Zac lifted the fish out of the pan and set it to one side. Then he stepped across and put his arms around Etta from behind. Planted a kiss on her neck and rested his forehead on her shoulder. She put down the pestle and clasped his arm to her. Just in that moment, he felt safe. He hoped she did too. But he knew it was an illusion. They were both thinking about that phrase from the text message, the one that contained every possible threat and no explanation.

*I want you.*

# CHAPTER TWENTY-FOUR

**Tuesday, 28 August 2018**

Wallace lay still and stared up at the tree canopy above him. Morning light filtered through the leaves, and he could feel the air warming already. Brockley and Ladywell Cemeteries wasn't a bad place to sleep. In fact, it was a damned sight safer and more comfortable than some of the places he'd slept over the past few days. Not least that empty house with the mad junkie inside…

Some people might've got creeped out lying in a graveyard, six feet above a load of rotting corpses. Not Wallace. And that was nothing to do with being hard or anything like that. It was about how you saw death. Wallace had inherited his mum Leonie's pragmatism when it came to the end. 'Me soul gwan fi heaven,' she'd say. 'So me nah care what 'appen to me body.' He'd heard other Jamaicans say similar things; an uncle had once told him he wanted to be buried in a cardboard box, so his family could spend the money for a coffin on decent rum instead. Wallace reckoned that their attitude came from a combination of deeply held faith about the afterlife and the awareness that life itself was cheap and fragile. Though Wallace had never lived in Jamaica, he had the same awareness.

A couple of times, growing up, he'd thought that his dad might actually kill him. The violence was pretty constant when his dad was there. But it was the booze that made him unpredictable and dangerous. The idea that he might start a beating and not know when to stop, not be able to stop... Both Wallace and his mum experienced that fear enough times. Sometimes, he wondered whether the reason his dad was so fucked up was because he hated *himself*. If you didn't love yourself, how could you ever show love for another person? And what were you without self-respect?

With each passing day, Wallace felt like his self-respect was being eaten away. Some of that came from living like a tramp. Most of it was the result of being ordered around by Kaiser, which reminded him of his dad. Wallace's present lack of power fed his desire to rebel, like he'd always done. To say *fuck it*, I'm doing my own thing. But he knew that would be suicide. Kaiser's reputation was solid: screw him over and you die. It was that simple. Wallace didn't know how far Kaiser's network extended. He didn't even know if Kaiser was at the top of it. He just knew that someone would come for him if he backed out of the deal.

What angered Wallace the most, though, was the fact that he needed Kaiser. He needed that money, and there was no easier, quicker or better way to get that amount of cash. He needed the money to escape to somewhere he could bring Leon and Jas. And Reece, he guessed. Wallace wasn't going to lie: he wasn't up for raising another man's kid. But Reece was alright, and he knew Jas wouldn't come away without him. And without Jas, he wouldn't get to see Leon. Of course, it was a risk leaving the country – he might not see his kid ever again – but no way was he spending the rest of his life in prison, either. So, it was a risk worth taking for his freedom, for the chance of a new start.

That new start began with Kaiser – whoever that really was – and with the money for killing Boateng.

At least he knew that his gun worked this time.

Jones had felt a buzz from the moment she woke up. It had lasted through her shower, breakfast and bus ride in to Lewisham. And she was pretty sure it wasn't just the lingering satisfaction of cracking the wall run last night at the parkour class. It was the sense that they were getting somewhere: the net was tightening on Kaiser, and they were closer to finding Kofi. Yesterday's raid on the weapons shed in Croydon would be a massive setback for Kaiser. Now, they had to build on that momentum.

There was more activity than usual when Jones walked into the Op Pluto office just before 9 a.m. Connelly and Malik were both there, talking to Boateng. Malik raised the coffee pot when he spotted her. She didn't need a verbal invitation. Grabbing a mug off her desk, she headed over.

'Nice job finding that shed, Kat,' said Malik, pouring her a cup of his customary strong brew.

'Aye.' Connelly swigged his tea. 'Grand work, so it was.' He looked like he meant it.

Feeling embarrassed, she mumbled something about Good-hew's research and Chambers's source reports as she concentrated on adding the milk to her coffee.

'Still, it needed someone to see the whole picture.' Boateng nodded at her. 'We've chucked a big old spanner in Kaiser's machine now.'

They murmured their agreement and drank together.

'So, you missing us then?' asked Connelly, his bushy eyebrows arched.

'Not really,' replied Boateng.

'Same here.' The Irishman grinned. 'Well, Nas is missing you, Kat. You've broken his wee heart by leaving us. Right, Nas?'

'Piss off, Pat.' Malik gave Connelly a joshing punch on the shoulder.

They all laughed, but Jones was aware that no one had mentioned the elephant in the room: Kofi was still missing. She couldn't begin to imagine what Boateng and his wife were going through. A brief silence developed, and Jones started to wonder if she should fill it. Then Krebs swept into the room with Maddox in tow and clapped her hands.

'Gather round, everyone,' she called.

The Pluto team plus their visitors from MIT assembled in front of a pair of whiteboards. Some rolled chairs across, others stood. Harper was sharing a joke with Goodhew, while Chambers spun on his seat and picked his nails, a strip of bare flesh protruding below the hem of his polo shirt. Patel was checking something he'd written in a notebook. There were others from the MIT: a couple of detective constables and two more analysts, all working with Connelly under Krebs's overall command.

'Yesterday we had a bit of success,' began Krebs, gesturing to a set of photographs pinned to the board with little magnets. 'A joint Pluto and MIT team raided this garden shed in Selhurst, Croydon at 1810 hours. We discovered a body inside, which we have identified as Gareth Riley, an employee of the Met.'

Some of the MIT staff who hadn't been there exchanged whispers.

'It was clear that these premises were being used to modify weapons, as part of what we believe to be Kaiser's arms supply network,' continued Krebs. 'The initial lead on the property was provided by one of Will's sources' – she nodded at Chambers – 'while the exact address was the result of painstaking and inspired work by Kat.'

Jones felt herself blushing and glanced over at Goodhew. 'Amy did a lot of that digging,' she added.

'Well, ultimately it's a team effort, of course,' replied Krebs, giving Jones a broad smile. She went on to describe the equipment found inside the shed, listing gun components, ammunition and tools. 'A quick analysis of the 3D printer retrieved from the location has suggested that it was being used to print replicas of weapons. We believe that these copies were being switched with real firearms by Riley at the Met's destruction depot, which is where he worked. The replicas were destroyed and logged. The real arms were probably then smuggled out of the depot and modified in the shed, most likely by Riley, to remove traces of their origins or make them live again, before being sold onto the streets of London and elsewhere in the UK. The previous night, we know Zac was the victim of an attack by Darian Wallace using one such firearm. Fortunately, that gun didn't go off and Wallace fled the scene on a motorbike, possibly driven by Riley.'

'Luckily, Zac is OK,' said Maddox. 'But what's also—'

'Just remind me again,' interjected Harper. 'Why was Zac in that Crossrail tunnel on his own with Wallace?'

'I was trying to find my son.' Boateng spoke in a low, steady voice.

'With no backup?' said Chambers.

'I briefed all this in yesterday,' replied Boateng. Jones could see he was holding in his frustration.

Harper turned in his seat. 'Yeah, but, have you told us *everything*, Zaccy boy?'

Boateng glared at him. In the brief silence that followed, Jones noticed that Krebs was still watching Boateng.

'OK, let's get back to this,' said Maddox, stepping forward and indicating a mugshot of Wallace on the second whiteboard. At least one person was showing some leadership. 'We're going to hear more about Wallace in a moment. What's relevant to Pluto is that, before he escaped, Wallace told Zac about this supply line to Kaiser from the Met's firearms depot. Given his record, there were a few sceptics, myself included. But with the pistol from the tunnel attack, and our discovery of the shed, he's been proven right.' He paused, scanning the group and noticed Boateng's raised arm. 'Yes, Zac?'

Boateng lowered his hand and cleared his throat. 'Wallace also told me that Kaiser was in the police.'

There were some sharp intakes of breath. Jones thought back: she'd known since day one of Pluto that Wallace had told Boateng that Kaiser was in the police. Krebs had briefed the Pluto team to that effect on Sunday, though it was speculative, based on the likelihood of Kaiser kidnapping Kofi, and Kofi having been held in a police safe house. But she didn't think Boateng had openly shared this information with the rest of them before. And he certainly hadn't talked about Leonard Bray. Jones guessed that was the trump card he was keeping up his sleeve.

Maddox frowned.

Krebs shook her head.

Harper folded his arms and turned to Boateng. 'Forget to tell us that last week, did you, Zac? Jesus.'

Chambers raised a hand. Ran his tongue over his lips before speaking. 'When was his information from?'

Boateng rubbed his chin. '2012, when he met Kaiser.'

Some more murmured conversations broke out and Jones saw Chambers nodding sagely. 'So,' he said, 'Kaiser could be someone who left the police any time after 2012.'

'In theory, yeah,' replied Boateng, though Jones noted the caution in his voice as he addressed Chambers. She recalled what Boateng had told her about Chambers working on the investigation into the death of his daughter, Amelia, around that time. The investigation that had gone nowhere.

'This is bullshit.' Harper shook his head.

'OK,' said Krebs, raising her voice and sweeping a hand through her bob cut. 'Let's keep that in mind for our profile. Now, we need to bring this chap in for questioning.' She sidestepped slightly and tapped a photograph that Jones recognised as Terry.

'Terrence Riley, known as Terry,' continued Krebs. 'Gareth's father, and the foreman of the Met's firearms destruction depot for the past eight years. Dave and Kevin are going to lead that interview today – treading carefully, of course. His son was murdered yesterday and there's nothing yet to suggest that Terry knew what Gareth was doing. Terry didn't live at the Dagnall Park address. He and Gareth's mother are separated.'

'Twenty quid says he was in on it too,' said Chambers with a smirk.

'Forensics may throw up some other leads from the shed in due course,' replied Krebs evenly. 'Now, you should all be aware that we have linked Op Pluto with the separate investigations by the MIT into Kofi Boateng's disappearance – which we now believe to be a kidnap – and the escape of Darian Wallace. We believe that Kaiser is behind the abduction of Zac's son, and that Wallace is working with Kaiser.'

'And who let him out?' asked Harper. 'Maybe we should be asking Zac who Kaiser is.'

Boateng rose quickly, his chair shooting backwards. 'You got something to say to me?'

Jones watched him glaring at Harper, his chest heaving, jaw set. When Boateng lost it, he could be scary. But Harper just smiled, his lips moving as he chewed some gum.

'Zac.' Krebs put her hands on her hips.

Boateng flicked his eyes from Harper to her and back, then seemed to relax. He tugged at his shirtsleeves and slowly sat down.

'This is a stressful time for all of us,' said Krebs. 'But we're not going to help our chances of wrapping up Op Pluto if we're fighting among ourselves.'

Harper stared at the carpet, but Jones could see he was still grinning. It irked her that he was outside their chain of command and thought he was above any of them. She wondered if he was so cocky within the NCA, where he was answerable to the brass.

'On the subject of Darian Wallace, DS Connelly has some new information for us. Pat.' She extended a hand and the Irishman stepped forwards, glancing at some notes which Malik had given him. He moved a couple of spare magnets and pinned up a wide-angle black-and-white image of a man in a hooded top. Part of his face was obscured, but Jones saw the resemblance to Wallace immediately.

'Right,' he began, looking around the room. 'Well, shortly before midnight on Saturday, this person – who we strongly believe to be Wallace – visited the ATM of Barclays Bank on Rye Lane, Peckham, and used a card to withdraw five hundred pounds. Given the time stamp on the security camera, we've been able to trace the account that the money was taken from. Nas received confirmation of the details first thing this morning.' He glanced at Malik, nodded. 'Wallace took the cash from a Met Police account.'

Krebs moved to inspect the photograph. 'We're sure that's Wallace?' she asked.

'Aye, ma'am, pretty sure. Nas tracked him from the sports centre in Camberwell where there's a clear facial ID from their CCTV, as well as the receptionist confirming he visited. That's where we think he picked up the gun he tried to use on Zac, by the way.'

'What information did you get on the account?' said Maddox. 'The Met has a hell of a lot of them.'

'Finance came back to us just before this meeting,' replied Connelly. 'They said it's an account used to pay CHIS expenses.'

'No way,' blurted Chambers. Jones could see the sweat on his forehead. 'Those transactions are covert. They're not made with the Met's name all over them. Can you imagine that showing up on someone's bank statement? We wouldn't have any sources left – they'd all be dead.'

'It was covert,' interjected Malik. The assembled group turned to him. 'It was in the name of a human resources company. When we traced that on our systems, it showed up in connection with CHIS payments.' He glanced at his notes. 'Specifically, on Trident.'

Harper leaned back in his chair and folded his arms. 'That's your team, isn't it, Will?'

Chambers swallowed. 'There are Trident teams all over London. We've probably got ten, twelve bank accounts for our ops in Southwark alone.'

'We'll need to establish who had access to that card,' resumed Connelly, scanning their faces.

'Very good, Pat,' said Krebs. 'Alongside the safe house, it confirms what we thought about Kaiser being in the police and, by extension, what Wallace told Zac.'

As Connelly returned to his seat at the back, Maddox stood and distributed actions for the day: forensic follow-up on the quartermaster's shed, including phone and financial records for Gareth Riley; interviewing Terry from the firearms depot; tracing those with access to the bank account used by Wallace.

As the meeting broke up, Jones heard Connelly and Malik begin telling Boateng something about the safe house. She was scooting her chair across to find out more when Krebs called her name. Jones turned and the boss beckoned her over to the whiteboards. No escape.

'Any update?' said Krebs quietly. 'On his visit to the lab?'

Jones glanced back at Boateng, who was still deep in conversation. Now was the time to make her decision. If she told Krebs about Eric Morton, the retired ballistics analyst, she'd be giving away Boateng's last secret. If she didn't, who knew how much damage it might do to her career when it came out in the wash.

'Well?' Krebs leaned in. Jones felt as if the room had suddenly got smaller. She had to be quick. She went with her instinct.

'Nothing, ma'am.'

'What, there's no update? He hasn't been there?'

'No,' replied Jones. Her heart was beating so strongly she felt sure Krebs must be able to hear it. 'I mean, yes. He went there but it was a dead end.'

The DCI straightened up and pursed her lips. 'So there's no more follow-up from Fortec? Nothing more on Leonard Bray?'

'No, ma'am.'

Krebs nodded, and Jones was grateful when she broke eye contact to scan the room. 'Very good, Kat. You've done exceptionally well on this operation.'

'Thank you.'

'Anything else comes up, you'll keep me in the loop.' It was a statement rather than a question.

'Of course, ma'am.' Jones forced a smile and went over to join the others, her heart still thumping.

⁕

Kofi was grateful that, for the first time since he'd been taken from the school, he'd been allowed to sleep lying down. Not that he'd got much rest last night, though. The comings and goings he could hear at this new place seemed to be constant. And they all sounded the same. A knock at the door, sometimes the buzzer ringing, then footsteps entering, a brief conversation and the door shutting again. The man who lived here had a lot of visitors.

He'd only caught a few glimpses of this man, the same one who'd brought him here. He was old, with a beard and long hair pulled back into a ponytail. He had a spider's web tattoo over part of his face that made him look scary. Kofi didn't know who the guy was. He had no idea where he was, either. Same as when he'd been taken to the shed, he'd been put in the boot of a car and driven here. When he'd arrived, he'd been taken through a hallway, past a lounge and into a back room. The door was locked, and he had fresh tape affixed over his mouth and wrists, but at least he could walk around. After five days of sitting down, that was like a Christmas present. The windows in the back room were blacked out, except for a narrow strip at the top where the light came in. So he knew it was daytime now.

Kofi could hear a lot of noise outside. Doors, footsteps, voices, cars. It sounded like where his friend Neon lived, so he guessed he was probably on an estate. Somewhere that there were always a lot of people around. Then he heard the front door shut and everything went quiet. It was the first time the door had closed without the buzzer going or a knock first. Had the guy gone out? Kofi got right up to the door, pressed his ear to it. He couldn't hear anything. Waiting there for what seemed like ages, he had an idea.

If he shunted the small table across to the window, he could get up onto it and look out. Then, at least, he might be able to find out where he was. Maybe even get someone's attention. He held his breath and put his ear to the door again, just to be sure. It was silent. In his mind, he pictured the Black Panther escaping from captivity and being the hero. He began to heave the table across the room. It was heavy and difficult to move on the thick carpet, especially with his wrists tied. But, with a combination of hands, elbows and hips, he got it there.

Kofi sat on the table and brought his feet up. Then he pushed off against the window and stood. But he still couldn't see out. He stepped from the table onto the narrow sill and reached up to the window latch. If he could open it, perhaps he could pull himself up and get his head through. He might even be able to climb out. His legs were shaking as he reached up for it.

Then he heard a key turn in the front door. Frantic, he tried to step back onto the table but missed his footing, losing his balance and tumbling to the floor. He put his hands out to catch himself and thumped into the carpet. Pain shot through his arms as he tried to get to his feet, but the lock was already turning, and before he could move, the door flew open and the man with the spider's web tattoo stood there. His face was screwed up, his eyes dark.

'What the fuck do you think you're doing?' he barked.

'Nothing,' said Kofi immediately, his voice muffled by the tape. He stood up straight, his hands and shoulders aching really badly. He felt as if he were about to start crying.

'Kaiser told me you might try this,' said the man. 'I said you wouldn't be so stupid. But clearly you are. So, now you've got to learn.' He walked off, returning a moment later with something in his hand that Kofi recognised all too well.

The little black box.

Kofi stayed still as a statue, though he could feel his body trembling. 'No. Please. Don't,' he tried to say, the words unclear.

Advancing towards him, the man flicked a switch on the side of the box. He snarled, and Kofi could see that his teeth were dirty.

'You won't be trying that again,' he said.

●

If it hadn't been for the view of the Crystal Palace transmitter tower and the London Overground train that had just thundered past, Boateng might've thought he was in the middle of the countryside. South Norwood lake was the largest body of water for miles in any direction; an oasis lined with ancient trees and bordered by playing fields. He could see why Eric Morton chose to spend his time here. But the effect was illusory; the urban sprawl of Croydon resumed just a street or two away.

He hadn't contacted Morton before coming here, preferring instead to keep the inquiry low-key and take the chance of not finding him. Leonard Bray's murder was the one thing Boateng had kept just between himself and Jones, and his gut feeling said that was the right call. He just hoped this didn't turn out to be a complete waste of time. Boateng had googled Morton and found his picture on the website of a forensics conference from a few years ago.

Circumnavigating the lake, he had a couple of false starts before an elderly fisherman pointed him to a clump of trees across the way. Rounding the bend, Boateng found a grey-haired man in a fleece sitting on a canvas chair and gazing out at a float whose bright orange tip bobbed and glowed on the water.

'Eric Morton?'

The guy snapped his head round, confusion creasing his face for a moment. 'And you are?'

'Detective Inspector Zac Boateng.' He flashed his warrant card and received a nod of recognition from Morton, though he was still eyeing him warily.

'How can I help, Inspector?'

'Zac,' said Boateng, stepping towards him. 'Any luck yet?' he asked, pointing to the float.

'Sod all,' sighed Morton, shifting his attention back to the lake. 'Some monsters in here though, somewhere down there. Carp and pike, mostly.'

'Pike? Those are the evil-looking bastards, aren't they?'

Morton smiled. 'Bastard to catch, too.'

Boateng studied the grey water. The visibility was a few inches at best. 'Tell you what, I could do with a day like this.'

'Beats working.' He indicated his sitting position. 'Technically, they call this a sport.'

'That's my kind of sport.'

Morton chuckled briefly. 'What's this about then, Zac?'

'You used to work in Fortec Labs?' Boateng kept his tone light, friendly.

'I did. I was in the Met's labs for twenty years before they shut the place down in 2012. Whole bunch of us out of a job. I started working with Setkov at Fortec after that. We handled mostly Met contracts anyway, so it wasn't like the work was changing much.'

Boateng caught something in his tone. A hint of regret. 'Something else changed?'

'Bloody right it did.' Morton shook his head briefly. 'The pace of it doubled and the level of organisation halved. Coppers were coming in left, right and centre demanding results, analysis, return of items there and then. It was a nightmare.'

'Sounds chaotic.'

'We lost a few bits of evidence and a couple of big cases collapsed. Our reputation was done. We were lucky to avoid legal action.'

Boateng nodded. 'So Setkov set up a new outfit.'

'And I retired.' Morton spread his arms. 'I mean, come on, this isn't bad. Better than the stress of the lab, anyway.'

Boateng murmured his agreement. 'Can I ask you about a case, please, Eric?'

Morton blew his cheeks out. 'You can try... Once you're out of the job, though, you wouldn't believe how quickly they blur together.'

'I bet.' Boateng wondered if it'd be the same when he retired. Probably not. 'This is a case from 2014. A guy called Leonard Bray was murdered on a building site. Three projectiles were recovered from the scene and sent to Fortec for ballistics analysis.'

Morton narrowed his eyes, but there was no spark of recognition.

'Wandsworth CID sent them to you and requested they be returned to a DI David Maddox in Lambeth MIT. Only they somehow never made it there. And without a weapon to connect the bullets to, the case wasn't even taken on by the Crown Prosecution Service.'

Pushing out his lips, Morton began to nod slowly. 'Yup. They thought it was us that lost them. But I swore blind they'd been collected. Just, it all happened so quickly that it didn't get recorded, and then it was our word against the Met's. All got a bit nasty and eventually the whole thing was dropped.'

'They were collected, you say? Who—'

Boateng was interrupted by a screech from Morton's fishing rod. The float had vanished and line was spooling out into the lake.

'Shit!' cried Morton, leaping from his chair and grabbing the rod. He clamped a palm over the reel and the tip bent sharply over as he raised it, almost doubling back on itself. 'He's a big lad.' Morton grunted and heaved, his feet sliding in the gravel. Then the line went slack and the rod straightened out. 'Damn.'

'Unlucky,' said Boateng.

'Thought I had him,' grumbled Morton, winding the tackle in. He opened a plastic tub and stuck a couple of maggots on the hook before casting back out again. Boateng watched the bait sink into the darkness.

'You were saying,' resumed Boateng, 'that someone collected the Leonard Bray projectiles.'

'Yeah.'

'Courier?'

'No. Detective.'

Boateng could feel his pulse rising. 'Don't suppose you remember the name?'

Morton grimaced, then shook his head. 'No, sorry.'

Kicking a small stone into the water, Boateng fought back his disappointment. The lead couldn't end like this… Then the idea came to him. Maddox was meant to have been the recipient of the returned projectiles. He took out his phone and swiped to the group photograph which Jones had sent him of the team night out last week. He rotated the picture and held it out to Morton. 'Was it this guy who collected them?'

Morton studied the screen. 'That's the one.' His response was swift, confident.

The stab of adrenalin hit Boateng as he zoomed in on the image. 'This bloke, yeah?'

'That one.'

Boateng glanced at Morton. 'Definitely?'

'I never forget a face.' He pointed to the screen. 'He collected the Leonard Bray bullets. Denied it afterwards, of course. Blamed it on us. And there was no way to prove otherwise. But a hundred per cent, it was him.' Morton tapped the image.

He wasn't pointing at Maddox.

# CHAPTER TWENTY-FIVE

After he moved to London from Ireland, and before he joined the Met, Connelly had worked in the building trade. Started out as a labourer, graduated up to plasterer's mate, eventually becoming a plasterer himself. Some people thought there weren't any transferable skills between plastering and the police, and they'd be right. It was the mindset that was transferable. You hacked away at something, got under the surface, excavated and found out what was really there. Then, with a hell of a lot of patience and hard graft, you smoothed it over and made it presentable to your customers. If you'd done a decent job, they'd have no idea what kind of mess had been there before you sorted it out.

When he'd asked Boateng to come into the MIT office, Connelly hadn't had the finished product. But what he and Malik had found when they'd chipped away had been so significant, he had to tell his boss. Boateng had been down in Croydon somewhere, but he promised to come straight in on his return to Lewisham. Now, as he watched the fella march across the open-plan office, Connelly wasn't sure he knew how to break the news.

'Alright, lads,' Boateng greeted them. 'What've you got?'

'Grab a seat, boss.' Connelly shunted his chair nearer to Malik's desk and picked up a wad of paper. 'We wanted you to know about this before the next team briefing.'

'Appreciate it.'

He placed the documents on the desk and jabbed a biro at them. 'This is the list of all personnel who had access to the safe house on Romola Road, where Kofi was kept.'

Boateng stared at the paper. He swallowed, nodded. 'Go on.'

'Pretty much all the local MITs are on there, but I thought it might be useful to divide the list by serving and ex-officers, you know, so that we didn't miss anyone who left the Met.'

'Good idea. And?'

Connelly took a deep breath. Glanced over his shoulder and kept his voice low. 'There's a name which comes up time and again between 2009 and 2014, from the vice team. Ex-officer.'

Boateng looked squarely at him.

'Kevin Harper,' said Connelly.

'Hm.' His boss wiped a hand over his face as he thought. 'Could be a coincidence, of course.'

'Aye, could be. Tell him what you found, Nas.'

Malik pulled up a record on his screen. 'I was checking out the bank card that Darian Wallace used to withdraw cash in Peckham. Initially we thought about doing a block on it, stop him taking any more out. Then we decided it was better to let him carry on, see where it led us. There's a thousand-pound limit anyway. He took out another five hundred quid last night in Ladywell.'

'OK,' said Boateng.

'We went back through the debit card's history. It was one of a bunch approved eight days ago for source payments and related expenses on Operation Pluto. The request for those cards was made by another bloke we know.' Malik ran a hand over his neat beard.

Boateng was silent, his eyes wide.

'Will Chambers,' said Malik.

'Harper and Chambers.' Boateng bit his lip. 'Fits with something I just discovered. Great work, boys.' He clapped them both on the shoulder and started to get up.

Connelly placed a hand on Boateng's arm. 'Hang on. That's not all.'

His boss sat back down, leaned in.

'There's one more name that features in both records. Someone else who used the safe house. And who authorised the money to Chambers's bank cards for this operation.' Connelly cleared his throat, realised his foot was tapping on the carpet. 'It's the reason we wanted you to hear it first, boss. Without anyone else here.'

'Who?'

'It doesn't necessarily mean that—'

'Just tell me.' Boateng's tone was hard.

Connelly exchanged a glance with Malik, then held Boateng's gaze as he spoke.

'Krebs.'

⁕

As Boateng walked to his car, he took out his mobile and called Maddox.

'Zac,' said the DCI. 'You OK?'

Boateng sniffed. 'Apart from the obvious stuff, yeah.'

'Sorry about those dickheads in the meeting. Don't let them get to you.'

'Cheers.' He sighed. 'It's all good.'

'Harper and Chambers seem to have some kind of comedy double act going on.'

'I thought they couldn't stand each other.'

'Chalk and cheese, right? At first, I was like, great, more politics.' Maddox grunted a laugh. 'But now they've got one another's backs, like old mates. Can't work it out, to be honest.'

'Me neither,' replied Boateng, though the same thought had occurred to him. He hesitated. 'I wanted to ask you, Dave. Same sort of lines.'

'Yeah?'

'Do you think Krebs is acting weird?'

'Weird how?'

'I feel like she's watching me all the time on this op. I mean, I know there was the Wallace escape, and the buck kind of stops with her, but it's more than her normal level of scrutiny. Has she said anything to you?'

'Nothing specific, beyond the Wallace stuff. Could just be the politician in her. It's not easy to stay operational at DCI. She's dealing with the top brass on this, and obviously she wants to come out of it looking good. You know what she's like.'

'Yeah,' acknowledged Boateng. 'I do.'

'Do you want me to have a quiet word with her?'

'No, just…' Boateng didn't know how to express it.

'Sort of keep an eye on her, yeah?'

'Something like that.'

'Alright. Where are you now?'

'I'm going to offer my condolences to Jermaine Mensah's mum.'

As he drove towards Brixton, Boateng turned off the car stereo to let himself think. Was it a coincidence that Krebs was involved with the safe house and the bank cards – both of which appeared to have been used by Kaiser? Maybe. It seemed as if half of the Met had been in the safe house, and Harper was on that list too. Hell, Lewisham MIT was probably on there. Boateng himself could've copied the keys if he'd wanted to. And as for the bank cards, Krebs had operational oversight of Pluto; she'd obviously have authorised them. Boateng found it hard to imagine her knowing that Darian Wallace was on the other end of the ATM. And yet something niggled at him.

His psychology degree had taught him to be aware of confirmation bias: the tendency to look for what you already know – or think you know – and cherry-pick the evidence to suit your existing theory. In this case, Boateng had to acknowledge that it hadn't even crossed his mind that Kaiser could be a woman. Last year, Wallace had said it was a man who'd sold him one of Kaiser's guns. That didn't mean that the street vendor was Kaiser. And Boateng had to concede that he didn't really know Krebs that well. Yes, they'd worked together for three years, but he barely saw her outside of work. She kept her private life private, and he'd always respected that. Who really knew what any of their colleagues got up to once they left work?

But corruption? That was something else. He shook his head at the absurdity of it. Krebs was ambitious, but he couldn't see her breaking the rules. Couldn't see her even assisting someone like Kaiser, let alone *being* Kaiser. Perhaps he was better off focusing his attention elsewhere. Like on Will Chambers.

Chambers was the one who'd actually held the bank cards, who could have distributed them how he liked and failed to report it when one went missing. And, more importantly, he was the detective that Eric Morton had pointed out from the team photo. The one who'd collected the projectiles that had killed Leonard Bray, before they'd been analysed. Boateng drummed the steering wheel. He didn't like Chambers; the guy had been part of the team that had failed to catch his daughter's killer six years ago. Incompetent and lazy at best, corrupt at worst. But was that history skewing his judgement, too?

Then he recalled his conversation with Connelly and Malik. What if Kaiser was more than one person? Two individuals, with different abilities and networks, who together played the role of 'Kaiser'. Both male, or a man and a woman, perhaps… They divided the tasks, each avoiding too many coincidences or contacts for anyone to pin the arms dealing on them. Boateng ran with the thought, wondering how the partnership could have developed. Would it be a relationship of equals, or was there one dominant individual, an 'alpha', giving the orders to a downtrodden, submissive 'beta'?

Boateng couldn't make sense of it, even with the silence to think. So he turned the music back on and concentrated on his destination. Minutes later, his phone beeped with the arrival of a text. He got a brief stab of adrenalin, but as he checked it he saw it was just the notification of a delivery. His next-door neighbour had signed for a package on his behalf. It was from the military kit website.

Gloria Mensah's flat was on the first floor of a ten-storey block on Loughborough Road, right above a twenty-four-hour launderette. Boateng could feel the vibrations from the machines below as soon as he stepped into the narrow hallway.

He removed his flat cap. 'My deepest condolences, Mrs Mensah. Thanks for making the time to see me.' He'd called ahead to introduce himself and explain the visit.

'Welcome,' replied Gloria, but her voice was hollow. 'Come through.'

When she moved aside, Boateng noticed a large crochet Bible verse on the wall: 'Be strong and courageous. Do not be frightened, and do not be dismayed. For the Lord your God is with you. Joshua 1:9.' The threads were frayed and faded; it had clearly been put up a while ago. He wondered what the past week had done to this woman's faith.

Music grew louder as he walked into the living room. In front of the TV, a girl with her hair styled in two large Afro puffs was dancing in time to a video game, following the moves on screen. She stopped when she noticed Boateng. He thought back to the tattoo he'd seen on Jermaine Mensah's forearm.

'Hello. Are you Effi?' he asked.

She nodded, then glanced from Boateng to her mum and back.

'Darling, go in your room for a while,' said Gloria. Effi groaned but paused the dance game and did as she was told.

'I've got a son about her age,' said Boateng gently, as he heard Effi's bedroom door click shut down the hallway and some muffled music start up.

'I had a son.' Gloria sank into the sofa. Boateng could see that her eyes were wet. He didn't want to push too quickly. Taking a moment to study the room, he counted at least a dozen photographs of Jermaine and twice as many sympathy cards. Below their feet a machine went into spin cycle and the floor began to shudder. The Mensah family weren't living here by choice.

He sat down on the edge of the sofa and turned towards her. 'I had a daughter, too,' he began, not quite sure where the disclosure would take him. 'She would've been fifteen now.'

Gloria nodded absent-mindedly, then snapped her head and looked right at him. 'What happened to her?'

'She died six years ago.'

'Lord have mercy.'

Boateng bit his lip. After a few seconds, he spoke. 'She was murdered.' He hesitated. 'I know what you're going through.'

Gloria's nostrils flared. 'They said my boy died from drugs.' Her fists were clenched.

Interlocking his fingers, Boateng leaned forward. 'I know. But I think there might be more to it than that.'

She sat forward. 'What do you mean?'

'Your son was a good kid, Mrs Mensah.'

She nodded once, as if that was stating the obvious.

'I think he had some friends that were involved in some bad business, and he got mixed up in it,' continued Boateng. 'He made a mistake, and he was trying to set it right. But he made an enemy in the process.'

'Are you saying someone *killed* my boy?'

Boateng cleared his throat. This wasn't the official line, but she deserved to know. 'Not just that, Mrs Mensah. I think the same person might have been involved in my daughter's death, too.'

He paused, but Gloria just stared at him. Her lower lip was trembling.

'Last week, they abducted my son. And I mean to catch them,' he added, feeling himself well up. He blinked, fought back the emotion; he didn't want to cry in front of her. She needed to see that he was in control. 'That's why I wanted to speak to you here, now. I've got to ask if there's anything you can think of – anything at all – that might help us work out who could have done this to Jermaine.'

Gloria continued to hold his gaze. Then she screwed her eyes shut and began to sob. Big, powerful sobs that shook her body. Boateng edged closer. He could feel Gloria Mensah's pain. The urge to help her was overwhelming, but he wasn't sure what he could do. What he could say. Suddenly, she reached out with both hands and wrapped her arms around him, leaning in and resting her head on his shoulder as she wept.

'My baby wouldn't hurt anyone.' Her voice was a strained whisper.

Boateng placed a palm on her back. 'I know.'

She sniffed, took jagged breaths. 'I can't think of anything else to tell you. I told the police officer everything.'

'The Family Liaison Officer?'

'No, the detective that came here. The day Jermaine was arrested,' she added.

Boateng stiffened. He knew that the FLO would have been to visit Gloria and Effi on the day Jermaine died, to break the news. But he had been arrested three days before that, held in custody at Lewisham.

'What time did they come round?' he asked.

'In the morning.'

'Can you remember exactly when, Gloria?'

She let go of Boateng, wiped her eyes with the back of her hand. 'Early. I hadn't gone to work yet, and my shift starts at eight. I'm a cleaner at the hospital,' she explained. 'So it would've been about seven thirty. I'd been awake since the first phone call, though. Worried sick.'

Boateng calculated. Though news of a shooting had filtered into the twenty-four-hour news during the night – causing protestors to mass outside Lewisham station before they'd arrived at work – names hadn't been released until later that day. Boateng knew he was the first detective involved in the case, and there was no record of anyone visiting Jermaine Mensah's family.

'What did this detective want?'

'To search Jermaine's room. Asked me all sorts of questions about what he'd been up to, who he'd been with. Did he have any other phones, that kind of thing.'

'Do you remember the name, Gloria?'

She shook her head, sighed.

Boateng thought about what Eric Morton had told him. Then he took out his phone, tapped and swiped to the photo of the team night out. 'Can you see detective who came to visit you in this picture?'

Gloria scrutinised the image, zooming in and checking each face in turn. Then she handed the phone back to Boateng. 'That one,' she said confidently.

He looked at the screen. 'You sure?'

'I'm sure.'

Boateng pocketed the handset, noticed the tremor in his fingers. He had to make a phone call.

◆

Wallace stood high up on the walkway, staring down at the low-rise block in Camberwell. He'd been up here for nearly two hours, watching. Normally, he wouldn't stay in the same public place

for more than a few minutes, if he could help it. Better to stay
hidden. But with his hood up, and just one person – a shuffling
elderly woman – having left through the nearby front doors since
he'd arrived, he felt safe enough. Besides, this was important. He
needed to see his son again. And it had to be now.

Earlier today, an email had arrived from ColonelKurz21 with
some instructions. And not just the time and place at which
Wallace was to execute Boateng. He'd kind of got his head around
that task. It was the extra request – or 'order', as far as Kaiser was
concerned – to kill that had shaken him up.

Boateng's kid.

Wallace remembered lying in hospital last year, cursing the
name of Kofi Boateng. The young boy whose snitching had
surely played a part in him going to prison. At the time, Wallace
would've clapped him and his father for nothing. Enjoyed it. Back
then, though, Wallace didn't have a baby. Now, he thought about
his own son, growing up. Was it fair to kill a kid that, basically,
had nothing to do with guns and drugs and murder? Who just
happened to be related to someone who was part of that world?
Should a boy whose life consisted of school, football and video
games have to pay someone else's debts? Wallace knew for sure
that he wouldn't be happy if that was *his* son's fate…

Movement on the ground level caught his eye. He glanced
down and there they were. Jas, her sleek hair back in a tight
ponytail. Reece, holding her hand, a toy dangling at his side. And
there, strapped to Jas's chest in a sling, was Leon.

Wallace couldn't see any details at this distance. Couldn't see
the big eyes or the tiny fingers or the funny little tufts of hair.
But still, he felt something aching inside him. A desire to go
down there right now and just take them all away with him. A
desire to be a *family*. Even as he thought those words, Wallace
experienced a feeling of disgust. When had he ever wanted that?
He was a lone wolf, a shark. A predator who didn't need anyone

else. Other than the bond to his mother – which was as good as gone now she was in a care home, losing her mind – that had never been his life. And maybe it was better if things stayed that way. He always screwed up relationships, got into beef, pushed people away. Without fail. Why was he kidding himself that this would be any different? If he got out, though, he could send money, keep an eye from a distance. Kind of like he was doing now.

He watched Jas pause a moment, scanning the paths around her between the blocks, as if she knew someone was there. Then she hitched Leon up on her chest and tugged Reece's hand as they set off together towards the main road. Wallace was left up on the walkway, staring down as his family disappeared around the corner of a building.

He snapped out of the fantasy and back to his current choice: the one that would determine more than just his escape from Britain. It would influence how, when and where he saw his son in the future. And, with Kaiser pulling the strings, the choice was black and white. To kill or be killed. A zero-sum game of life and death.

Wallace checked the time on his burner phone. Nearly 6 p.m.

It was time to go to work.

•

The plan was coming to fruition. Kaiser had accessed the building with a swipe card in the name of someone who didn't exist, switched off the CCTV and brought the boy inside. Collecting him from the dealer's flat, the kid had looked shit-scared. What had the old guy with the spider's web tattoo done to him? Kaiser had lent him the stun gun in case he needed to keep the boy in line, and had collected it back along with the kid. Hopefully, it had been nothing more sinister than a few jabs with that… Well, it didn't really matter anyway. By around 9 p.m., an hour from now, it'd all be over.

Kaiser had to face the fact that, after years of success, it was time to step away from selling guns. It'd been a good run, but with the Pluto investigation there was just too much scrutiny. Too much chance of exposure. They'd already tracked down the Quartermaster, busted his shed. So Kaiser had lost the capacity to modify weapons, and with it the ability to break the link between a weapon and its past. And that was the unique selling point for the London market. Kaiser had then taken the decision to get rid of the Quartermaster; he was of no further use and there was too much chance of him grassing once he'd been caught. Wallace had obligingly whacked him before he'd had the chance to snitch. Of course, the same principle applied to Wallace. That was why – once Wallace had taken care of Boateng and his kid – Kaiser would have to deal with Wallace, too. After tonight, there would be no loose ends. No one looking for Kaiser. With the evidence that they'd find on Boateng, the Met would quickly draw a neat and tidy conclusion: that Boateng was Kaiser. That assumed everything went to plan, of course, which was why Kaiser was here personally.

Stopping the arms deals would cut off the extra money. Halt the bonus to Kaiser's meagre public-sector salary. Temporarily at least. Eventually something else would take its place. Adam Smith, one of Britain's greatest economists, had been a believer in contraband. He'd said that the only laws smuggling broke were the laws of the land. The laws of market forces, however, meant that smuggling wasn't just logical – it was an optimal solution to market interference by authorities. Human nature meant there was always demand for things like guns and drugs. Stuff the authorities didn't want people to have. And if the demand was there, then anyone willing to risk supply would turn a profit.

Kaiser glanced across the room at the kid, gagged and bound to a chair, fear visible on the parts of his face not covered with duct tape. The boy for whom Boateng would clearly do anything. Now was the moment to put that to the test. Extracting the burner phone, Kaiser tapped out a text to Boateng and pressed send.

# CHAPTER TWENTY-SIX

'I'm *this* close.' Zac held his forefinger and thumb an inch apart. He'd just filled his wife in on the phone call he'd made after leaving Gloria Mensah's flat. 'I think I know who Kaiser is. Now I need proof.'

Etta prodded the microwaved jollof rice around her bowl. Neither of them had had time to cook tonight. And neither had the appetite to eat much. 'What we need is Kofi safe here with us,' she said quietly.

He pressed his lips together, nodded. 'This is the best way to find him, trust me.'

Elbow on the table, his wife rested her forehead on her knuckles. Zac hated this. Hated seeing their family breaking apart. Hated seeing the woman he loved in this state. Hated thinking about what was happening to their boy. He felt the rage seething within him again, the heat being turned up on a furnace somewhere inside.

Then the beep of a text sounded across the kitchen.

Zac got up and went over to the side, where he'd left his phone. He knew that a few of the team were still in the office, including Jones, Connelly and Malik. An hour ago, they'd told him to go home, eat something, see Etta, get some rest if he could. Maybe it was a final update before they, too, headed home. He grabbed the handset.

It was a message from the burner. He glanced at Etta, opened it.

*If you want your son back come to firearms depot now. No backup. One whiff of another officer and your boy dies.*

His throat felt suddenly tight, constricted, as if he couldn't breathe. Tears pricked his eyeballs as he took the phone over to the table, showed Etta. She studied it, placing her hand over his.

'Time to go and get our son back,' he said firmly.

She squeezed his hand, nodded. 'But you need to tell the others.'

'I will.' He put his arm around her.

Then he stood and went upstairs to get the package he'd collected from the neighbour half an hour ago.

Leaving the house a few minutes later, there was no question who Boateng would call. He'd dialled Jones's number before the front door had even shut behind him. He popped the doors on his car and got in as she picked up.

'Zac, what's going on?'

'You still in the office?'

'Yeah,' she replied. 'Why? Is—'

'I've just got a text. From Kaiser.' He clamped the phone between his ear and shoulder, started the engine and threw it in gear. 'Telling me to meet at the depot.'

'The firearms place?' Boateng could hear the alarm in her voice. 'But why does—'

'I've got some idea,' he said, pulling out into the road. 'But that's not important. The only thing that matters is getting Kofi back.'

'OK,' she said immediately. 'I think Pat and Nas are still here. I'll grab them, plus some others, and we'll—'

'Listen, Kat. Kaiser said any sign of backup and Kofi's dead.'

There was silence on the other end. Boateng accelerated, heard the engine strain and shifted gears.

'Kat?'

'What do you want to do?' she asked.

'I want you guys there. Just be as discreet as possible. I'll go in, see what Kaiser wants from me and stall for as long as I can.'

'Are you carrying anything?'

'CS spray,' he replied. 'That's it.'

'What about a firearms team?'

Boateng checked the mirror. With Kaiser likely to be carrying a weapon, he knew the risks. 'Yup,' he said eventually. 'Bring those guys. Quick as they can, yeah?'

'Got it. We'll make sure no one can leave the premises.'

'Alright, see you there,' he said.

'Just, be careful, Zac. Don't do anyth—'

He rang off. Then he moved out, overtook a bus and slammed his foot to the floor.

⁘

Ten minutes later, Jones was in a pool car from Lewisham station, speeding south-east towards the depot in Bromley with Malik at the wheel and Connelly in the back. All three of them wore Kevlar body armour over their tops and the two guys had Tasers; Jones made a mental note to do the training so that she could carry one. She'd just been patched through to the Met's communication centre. An operator picked up and Jones gave her name, rank and badge number.

'Requesting immediate assistance,' she stated, as Malik pulled onto the South Circular at Catford. Neon-lit convenience stores and cheap takeaways flashed past under the street lights. 'Armed response.' She gave the details: situation, address, personnel. The child's life at risk.

The voice on the other end repeated the information back to her and then went silent. Jones could hear keys clacking. 'There's one Operation Viper unit in Vauxhall which might be able to get there.'

*Vauxhall?* It'd take them twenty minutes to get to Bromley. At least. And what did the operator mean by "might"?

'There's no one closer?' she asked, glancing over her shoulder at Connelly, whose brow was tight with concern.

'Most of the armed response teams are off duty today,' replied the operator. 'They've all just worked three days straight at Notting Hill Carnival.'

Jones knew the biggest street party in Europe had its fair share of violence – the seas of people giving cover for gangs and individuals to settle scores – but she hadn't anticipated its effects on the readiness of firearms officers.

'Shit. OK, what about these guys in Vauxhall? Can they get there?'

'Hold for me, please.'

Jones kept the phone to her ear. 'Nearest ARV is in Vauxhall,' she whispered.

'Jesus,' sighed Connelly, slumping back in his seat.

Malik flexed his hands on the steering wheel, weaved between two vehicles. A horn sounded behind them and faded as they raced on. The operator's steady breathing was audible on the line. The seconds before she spoke again felt like minutes.

'DS Jones?'

'I'm here.'

'I confirm that the ARV is deploying to your stated location. ETA is fifteen minutes. We'll dispatch local units from Bromley to assist.'

Jones reiterated the threat to Kofi. 'Make sure you tell them no blues and twos. OK?' She hung up.

'ARV on the way?' said Malik, keeping his eyes on the road.

'Yeah. Fifteen minutes, they said.'

'From Vauxhall to Bromley?' Connelly leaned forward between the two front seats. 'That's ten miles. We'll be lucky if those boys get there in twenty, twenty-five minutes.'

Jones looked back at him. He was right. And she knew what that meant.

They'd have to act before the armed response arrived.

·

Boateng parked outside the depot and scanned the street around him in the small industrial zone. It was dark and quiet, but he could make out some low light inside the building. The place where his son was being held. He wanted to rip the fence open and break his way straight through, but he forced himself to slow down as he approached the gate on foot. Kaiser was someone who thought things through. Who didn't make a lot of mistakes. He inhaled deeply through his nostrils and pressed the buzzer. Moments later a soft click sounded and the outer gate opened. Boateng only knew of one entrance to the building: the door they'd used the time he'd come here with Jones. He considered trying to find another way in, but he wasn't even sure if there was a second entrance. In any case, if Kofi was in there, he couldn't risk surprising Kaiser. For now, he had to play the game and improvise until backup arrived. He hoped Jones and the others would be just a few minutes behind, and that they'd have the nous to cut their engines long before they reached the depot. That would be the surprise for Kaiser.

The door to the building was locked. Boateng peered through a narrow window into the half-light but couldn't see much in the entrance. He slapped his palm against the door and heard the echo inside. After a few seconds there was another click, and the lock popped. Boateng swung the door open with a squeal of hinges and crept into the silence. He stepped carefully, eyes adjusting to the gloom, alert to any movement or sound. Blood was thumping in his ears.

A metallic scrape came from deeper inside the warehouse. Following the noise, he rounded a corner and continued, the floor opening out as he reached the gun destruction area. The first thing he saw on his left was the huge yellow machine that Terry had called Bertha, its steel jaws raised as if expecting dinner. Then, as he stepped forward, there, under a spotlight to his right, was Kofi. His son was strapped to a chair with duct tape, his mouth also covered. As they saw one another, Kofi's eyes bulged, his little arms and legs pulling at the restraints. It was more than Boateng could take.

'Kofi!'

Everything else went from his mind and he began sprinting towards him. He'd gone just a few metres when the shot rang out, deafening in the enclosed space. The high-pitched tone filled his head.

Boateng froze. It took him a moment to register that neither he nor Kofi had been hit. Unable to discern the origin of the echoing shot, he scoured the walls. In the wide recess of shadow between his son and the cutting machine, barely visible, his gaze alighted on a human form.

The figure stepped out from the dark towards Boateng. But all he could see in those first few seconds was the gun aimed at his chest.

# CHAPTER TWENTY-SEVEN

'Take your phone out slowly and throw it over here.'

Boateng flicked his eyes from the pistol to Kofi and back, then did as he was told.

'It's OK, mate,' he said to Kofi. 'What do you want?' he demanded, hearing the tremor in his own voice. It was anger distorting the sound of his words, not terror.

'Like I said in the text, I want you.'

'You're Kaiser,' stated Boateng, his theory confirmed.

DCI David Maddox took a couple of steps forward. 'I have used that name, yeah.' He brought the heel of his shoe down hard on Boateng's phone with a crunch of glass and plastic.

Boateng stared at the smashed mobile. Any chance of reaching the outside world had just vanished. 'Let my son go, Dave.'

Maddox glanced at the boy. 'Not yet.'

The words gave Boateng some hope. But he had to buy time. 'Why did you take him?'

'At first, I thought ransoming your boy back to you was a good way to get the money for my missing Škorpions.' He kept the pistol trained on Boateng's chest. 'Face it, Zac. Your kids are – were – your weak point. I knew you'd pay up and do everything off the books. Problem was that you started investigating, too. That's when I realised I had to get rid of you.'

'Motherfucker,' spat Boateng.

'Then, once you'd told the Pluto team that Kaiser was in the police, I thought of a new use for you. You can be Kaiser, and then everyone will stop looking for him.'

Boateng wanted to charge at Maddox, smash his arrogant face and then choke him. But with a gun pointing at him, those would be suicide tactics. There had to be another way. The distance was too great to use the CS spray. He needed to keep talking.

'Are you mad? No one will believe it's me,' countered Boateng.

'No? The guy who's been going steadily off the rails for the past few years, since his daughter died, investigating on his own? They'll believe it alright.' Maddox held one side of his jacket open to reveal some papers. 'I've got stuff here saying that you were the one working with Riley to steal weapons from this place. That you were the one sourcing guns overseas. And that you staged the kidnap of your own son to make yourself look like the victim.'

'Bullshit,' growled Boateng.

'They'll find the burner phone on you to prove it.'

After a couple of seconds, the implications of that line dawned on Boateng. *They'll find...*

'Not forgetting your role in the escape of Darian Wallace,' continued Maddox. 'Who you've been working with all along.'

Boateng ground his teeth, his breathing heavy. But he had to keep his anger under control. Had to keep Maddox talking. 'You were using Chambers. Since he was in your team at Lambeth. He looked up to you. You got the safe house keys off him when he was at Lambeth MIT, and the bank card from Op Pluto to pay Wallace.'

Maddox sniffed. 'Glad to see you've worked something out.'

'Were you going to let him take the blame for Kaiser as well?'

'Nope. Will was far more useful to me working gang crime in Trident. He was putting customers my way without even realising it.'

'Fucking corrupt scumbag.'

'Ouch.' Maddox winced.

There was more. Boateng could mention how Chambers had told him earlier by phone that Maddox had sent him to collect the Leonard Bray bullets from Fortec. Or he could tell Maddox how Gloria Mensah had identified him as the detective who'd come to her house the morning of her son Jermaine's arrest, before anyone else could have known he was involved. But he knew that was, at present, circumstantial. He needed concrete evidence; without that, he was just bluffing. Worse, he didn't want to put Gloria and Effi in danger. A feeling of despair shot through him. Was this what his efforts would come to? Working out the identity of Kaiser – the man responsible for half of the gun crime in London – only to lack that ultimate proof? And the final nail in Boateng's coffin was Maddox's plan to frame him as Kaiser.

'You had Jermaine Mensah murdered in prison,' stated Boateng.

'People take overdoses all the time inside,' replied Maddox.

'He wasn't a drug user. You had someone feed him enough methadone to kill him.'

Maddox shrugged. 'Blame yourself, Zac. You were the one who was trying to cut a deal with him. The worst part about it is that the kid couldn't have identified me. The best he could've given you was Gaz Riley, who you found anyway. So think about that. He died for nothing.'

Boateng was furious. 'You think murder is a fucking game?' he bellowed. 'You've destroyed Gloria Mensah's life! When you went round there to—' He stopped himself, realising he'd said too much.

Maddox frowned. 'What's she been telling you?' Then it seemed to click, and he nodded to himself. 'Looks like I'll need to take care of her too.'

'You bastard!' yelled Boateng. He knew he was losing it, that Maddox was winning. He wrestled with the fury, looked at his son. Tried to focus, to keep talking. 'Why would people believe you, if you claim I'm Kaiser?'

Maddox gave a crooked smile. 'Multiple sources. I've supplied some material to the press, via an influential associate of mine.' He chuckled. 'They'll get these papers, too, once you've signed them. Your admission of your own guilt should be enough. Signatures and whatnot.'

'Why the hell would I sign anything for you? Admit to any of your crimes?'

'Because your son's life depends on it.'

●

Kofi's heart had leapt when he saw his dad come in. Finally, he was going to be allowed to go home. To do all the normal things he loved doing: kicking a football around, playing on the PlayStation, watching his favourite TV programmes. Things he wouldn't admit to his schoolmates that he loved, like being read a bedtime story by his parents or giving them a hug. Things he hadn't been able to do for nearly a week while he'd been tied up in strange houses and a tool shed. It was all going to be over. He was so happy. Then the man who'd brought him here had appeared and pointed the gun at Dad.

They had talked about people Kofi didn't know. Now, the big man with the gun was saying something about Kofi's life depending on it. He didn't understand. Depending on what? Something his dad needed to sign?

Kofi heard footsteps from the other side of the warehouse. He looked past his dad to where a man in hoodie had just stepped out. Kofi hadn't even known he was there. He must've been hiding before Kofi had been brought in. As he got closer and his face caught some of the light, Kofi held his breath. His stomach started to turn over and, for a second, he thought he was going to be sick. It was the man from last summer. The young, light-skinned one with the hollow face, like someone had sucked the air out of his head. His eyes were small and cold. And he was holding a pistol. It was aimed at Kofi's dad.

He watched his dad turn, raise his hands and say, 'Darian, please.' That was the guy's name, Kofi remembered. Darian Wallace.

Now the tall guy who'd brought Kofi here was placing some papers on the massive yellow machine, spreading them out. He put a pen next to them and told Dad to sign. Dad swore at him – words he'd told Kofi never to use. Then Dad was turning back to Darian and trying to talk to him, telling him they could work it out. Darian didn't say anything; he just kept the gun pointed straight at Dad.

Suddenly, the tall man walked right over to Kofi, so close that he could smell him, and held the gun out. Right at his face. Kofi screwed his eyes shut. But he could still see that last image on the inside of his eyelids: the black hole at the end of the pistol. It seemed huge, bigger and bigger as he pictured it in his mind. He tried to make a noise, but the tape was too tight over his face.

Kofi could feel himself starting to shake, like he'd done in the spider-tattoo man's flat when he'd brought out the little black box, and like he'd done when they'd put his hand in a vice. He tried as hard as he could to shift his body, but he couldn't move his limbs, and the chair was too solid, too heavy.

'Sign them, Zac,' he heard the man say.

•

Wallace looked down the barrel of his heater at Boateng. The cop was about to lose it. That was understandable; there was one piece pointing at him, another at his son's head. And he was being told to sign away his reputation in exchange for his son. There was no question he'd do it – if there was anyone Wallace had met in his life who put his family first, it was this fed from Lewisham. Wallace had to respect that. His mum was the same,

and now he had his own son, Wallace could see where it came
from. But whatever he did, Boateng wasn't getting out of this.
Wallace knew that once he'd signed, both he and his kid would
be killed. The thought flashed through his mind that the event
would leave him – Wallace – as the only witness to Kaiser's plan.
Was Kaiser really going to let him just walk away? Still, he kept
the muzzle trained on Boateng's chest.

Detective Inspector Zachariah Boateng. The man who had
caused him so many problems, whose tenacity meant that Wallace
had ended up back behind bars, unable to see his mum, unable
to take what was rightfully his. As much as he respected some of
Boateng's values, he *hated* the brer. And he was being paid decent
money to pull the trigger with Kaiser's assurances of remaining
anonymous and immune.

Wallace glanced across to Boateng's kid, wrapped to the chair,
squirming behind the unyielding duct tape. Then at Kaiser, who
stood next to the boy, pistol pressed to his tight Afro curls. A
faint noise came from outside the depot, catching his attention
for a moment. He stiffened, blinked, straining his ears. But there
was nothing more. He shifted his focus back to Boateng. But this
time, he wasn't looking at the sights on the top of his piece, lining
up the shot. He was looking into Boateng's eyes.

In those moments, Wallace saw the things he'd seen so many
times before: desperation, pleading, weakness, the confusion of
a trapped animal that was about to die. The desire to stay alive
but the lack of power to change anything. And he recognised that
same desire in himself, and that same lack of power, ultimately.

'Sign the fucking papers,' said Kaiser, louder now.

'Please, Darian,' said Boateng.

Wallace made a tiny movement of the gun towards the papers
laid out on the machine. 'Do what he says, yeah?'

'OK, OK.' Boateng sidestepped towards the machine, picked
up the pen. Scanned the text, shook his head. Began signing.

Wallace tightened his finger on the trigger.

He'd waited a long time for this.

●

Inside the depot's perimeter, Jones whispered her instructions to Malik and Connelly. Connelly was her senior in experience, but right there and then, Jones knew that she was in charge. Her drive to help Zac, to find Kofi and catch Kaiser, was as strong and clear as anything she'd felt in her career so far. She had already led the three of them up and over the outer fence. Malik had landed heavily on the other side, but after they'd held still for a while, Jones was convinced they'd got away with it. They were treading such a fine line: getting the backup in place for Boateng without alerting Kaiser and compromising Kofi's safety any further. Kaiser wasn't a person who acted impulsively; the decision to bring Boateng here was deliberate, but Jones couldn't yet work it out. It had to be some kind of set-up, something to do with the firearms. She just knew they needed to be on their guard.

With the armed response still five minutes away, Jones had made the call to go in. The main entrance was locked, and breaking in would be too obvious, too dangerous. So, while Connelly covered the front, she and Malik moved as silently as possible around the building. They found a fire exit on the opposite side of the warehouse to the main entrance. It was locked, too. She told Malik to wait outside the back door, aware that all he and Connelly had were Tasers. The electroshock weapons were good in most circumstances, but not much protection against bullets. She had to get inside.

Tracking to the side of the building, she spotted a patch of light high up on the wall. Peering at it, she realised that one of the small windows was open a crack, its angle catching a security spotlight from the neighbouring warehouse. Jones stood back, assessed her options. She heard raised voices. They were coming from inside the depot. Now was the time. This was the decision dad would've taken.

Stepping back to give herself the run-up, Jones took four quick steps towards the wall and launched upwards, kicking off and stretching with her right hand. Her fingertips grazed the sill and slipped off. She felt the instant where her body stopped going up, the fraction of a second before gravity began to pull it back down. Without thinking, she threw her left hand at the sill and caught it, her legs swinging wildly to one side. She stuck the grip.

Jones hauled herself up with both hands, walking her feet up the wall. Holding tight with her left hand, she began to ease the window higher with her right, the gap widening until she reckoned she could squeeze her head and shoulders through. Her left fingertips were screaming with the tension and pressure of her weight pulling back, but she stayed firm, gritted her teeth. Jones got her right arm inside and clamped the window sill with the crook of her elbow, just as her left-hand grip broke. Then she was up and inside, lowering herself carefully down onto the mezzanine level. Her adrenalin was pumping, but she tried to keep quiet.

Following the voices, Jones crept around towards the rear stairs that led to the ground floor. She heard Boateng say something indistinct, then another voice in reply, louder. She recognised it, but surely it wasn't… Manoeuvring herself down towards the lower level, Jones eased herself sideways. She couldn't risk being seen.

Making the slightest of movements, Jones peered around before drawing back to cover. She couldn't believe what she'd just seen. Moments ago, she'd heard the voice of Darian Wallace. But when she'd caught a glimpse of Kofi, taped to a chair, it wasn't Wallace standing over him with a pistol. The adrenalin sparked again for Jones, coursing through her limbs as she tried to process the sight of DCI Dave Maddox. And work out what the hell she could do to help.

Then she heard the gunshot.

# CHAPTER TWENTY-EIGHT

Boateng hit the deck as the shot rang out behind him. Instinctively, he covered his head with his hands, pressed himself against Bertha. Sound filled his ears and made his head vibrate. At first, he thought he'd been hit, but he couldn't sense the same searing pain he'd felt last year. He tried to think. Kofi. It didn't make sense; he was signing the papers, so why had Maddox fired?

Boateng rolled over, looked up from the floor. Tried to understand what was going on. Maddox was staggering forward, still gripping the pistol in his right hand. His left was clutching the side of his stomach, the white shirt soaked red where blood was seeping through it. His eyes were wild, mouth open. To Boateng's right, Wallace stood, his weapon aimed at Maddox.

'Drop the gun!' barked Wallace.

Maddox grimaced, raised his left hand in a partial surrender. Then he whipped the right up and fired off two rounds. Wallace spun with the impact, squeezing the trigger and letting off another shot that went somewhere up into the mezzanine. Boateng heard it ping off metal and watched as the two wounded men faced each other, roughly thirty feet apart. Between them, on the far side, he could see Kofi. The lad was trying to move in his chair.

Boateng scrambled to his feet as Maddox bellowed in pain and raised his pistol once more.

Spurred into action by the chaos unfolding just metres away from her, Jones crept down the metal stairs until she was so close to Kofi that she could almost reach out to him. The kid was shaking and hyperventilating. Noticing the movement, Kofi turned to her. She placed a finger over her lips, motioned him to stay calm.

Craning her neck around to take in the main space, she watched Maddox raise his gun again, taking aim at Wallace. Jones could see that each of them had been hit and was struggling to move. Maddox fired again a split second before Wallace pulled the trigger. The noise was deafening as both weapons went off several times, a couple of shots zinging around and connecting with the stairs. Jones ducked and just had time to see Wallace slump to the floor as Maddox stood watching him before she registered the heat in her own arm and glanced down to see she'd been clipped above the elbow. The small wound felt as if it was getting hotter and hotter, and blood was oozing from it into her top. She didn't even think about stopping herself before she yelled at the pain.

Hearing the sound, Maddox turned and began lurching towards the stairs where she was half hidden. He lifted the gun once more, his gaze unfocused. She couldn't tell if he was aiming at her or Kofi. But she wasn't taking the chance. She stood and lunged towards the boy, arms out, as Maddox swung the pistol, tracking her movement. He steadied himself for a shot as she stood in front of Kofi.

'Dave!' she screamed. 'What are you doing?'

Maddox grunted, tensed his arm and shut one eye.

Then Boateng crashed into him from the side, tackling him to the ground. He grabbed Maddox's wrist and beat his knuckles against the floor until his grip on the gun broke and it spilled from his hand. Jones sprinted to them and grabbed the pistol. Maddox and Boateng were locked together on the floor. For a second, she wondered if she could shoot Maddox, but she'd only ever fired a gun once before, and he and Boateng were grappling so tightly she couldn't be confident of hitting her target, especially with the pain in her arm. The priority had to be Kofi. She tucked the weapon into her belt and retreated to where he sat, checking his restraints. There was no way she could break the duct tape and she didn't have the tools to cut it. So she began to drag his chair towards the fire exit.

'It's going to be alright,' she heard herself telling him. 'We'll get you out of here, Kofi.'

As Jones reached the door, sweating and heaving, her arm bloodied, she glanced up. Maddox and Boateng were still wrestling, neither man in control. Behind them, she saw Wallace lying there, his top soaked with his own blood. He was twitching, still alive. And the pistol was in his hand.

•

The thought had occurred to Boateng, in the years he'd known Dave Maddox, that he wouldn't ever want to be in a fight with the guy. The DCI was built like a rugby player and, at six foot four, he had about six inches of height on Boateng. Even with a bullet in him, he was one strong bastard. Now Boateng was scrabbling to get the upper hand, to find some way to subdue him.

Shifting to get the angle, Boateng gave Maddox a shameless knee to the hip area, where he'd been shot, producing a roar of agony. He followed that up with a couple of quick punches to the face, but stuck on the ground, he couldn't generate any power. Maddox shook off the blows and ducked his head, letting go of Boateng's shirt collar.

Finally, Boateng was able to move. But before he could slide sideways to line up a proper strike or reach the CS spray canister in his pocket, everything stopped instantly as a heavy shock rattled through his body. His spine curved outwards, throwing his head back. The pain overwhelmed him and he was immobilised, powerless to stop it.

Then he was being pulled up by his collar again. Maddox hauled him across to the cutting machine, jabbing him every couple of seconds with the stun gun that had appeared from his pocket. The shocks felt as if they were flaying his skin and twisting his insides. Between each jolt, Boateng fought to snatch a glance across at the stairs. Kofi and Jones had gone. Had she managed to get his son out? The idea came to Boateng that, whatever happened to him here, Kofi would be safe, taken back to Etta. He felt a glimmer of relief before the next jolt of electricity paralysed him. But he couldn't give up.

Backup had to be arriving soon…

'Sign,' commanded Maddox as he forced Boateng against the machine. The papers lay on top of it.

'Just listen, Dave, we—' Boateng couldn't finish his sentence before another electric shock snaked through him, making his legs buckle. He held tight to the machine, kept himself standing.

'Fucking sign,' Maddox repeated.

There was no point trying to negotiate or resist. Not when Maddox had the stun gun. 'OK, I'll do it.' Boateng wiped away involuntary tears. Hands shaking, he lifted the pen and took the second document. Maddox was watching him, the stun gun poised to bite again. Boateng could see he was wincing every so often at the bullet wound above his hip, still patting and pressing it with his left hand as his gaze moved between Boateng and the documents. Boateng tried to calculate whether he could get the CS spray out before Maddox was able to hit him again with the stun gun. Maybe if he was distracted by his wound… Boateng signed the next document without even reading it and reached for the third.

Then the gun blast exploded in his ears and Maddox disappeared from his peripheral vision. Boateng spun towards him, glancing up to see Wallace still lying where he'd fallen some twenty feet away, the pistol wobbling in his hand, blood pooling under his body. He looked at Boateng but didn't fire again. Boateng didn't need another invitation.

He gripped Maddox's hand with both of his and plunged the stun gun into his chest, causing the big man to spasm and jerk. Maddox let go of the stun gun and it clattered to the ground. Boateng saw that Maddox was bleeding from the leg where Wallace had shot him, but somehow, he struggled to his feet, gasping, and came at Boateng again.

Maddox reached into his jacket and produced a six-inch hunting knife. Boateng just had time to register the curve and serration of the blade before it flashed towards him. He weaved backwards but stumbled into the machine behind him. The knife slashed his forearm as he raised it to shield his face. Boateng felt the cut on his skin but there was no time to check the wound. He had his back to the machine and couldn't retreat further.

He was trapped.

Steadying himself, his eyes lifeless, Maddox wound up for another stab. Boateng reached into his pocket for the CS spray, but he was too slow, fumbling the grip. The blade connected with his stomach, its tip piercing his clothes. Boateng felt the blow in his abdomen as Maddox's full weight drove the knife forwards.

Then it stopped. Maddox continued to push, growling with the effort. Seconds later he seemed to realise the futility of his attack, the force of his arm dropping as he focused on the blade's impact point. The hunting knife was embedded in a dense layer of Kevlar mesh, part of the covert body armour that Boateng had worn under his shirt. Maddox looked up and for a second his eyes met Boateng's. Then Boateng unleashed the CS spray into his face. Maddox gasped, choking, squeezing his eyes shut and thrusting the hunting knife at Boateng again. Instinctively, Boateng dodged it and grabbed Maddox's sleeve, twisting and using the momentum to pull his arm through into the machine. He pinned Maddox's hand on the cutting plate and leaned on his arm. Boateng tried to reach the buttons at the side. If he could lock Maddox's arm in the machine, he'd be safe. But he couldn't reach the controls without letting go of Maddox. The DCI was trying to free his arm, still gripping the hunting knife.

Boateng threw his leg out with a grunt, stretching and kicking at the end of the movement. The tip of his shoe connected with the button and the machine whirred to life, its hydraulics hissing as the first claw came down. At the last second, Boateng released his grip on Maddox's arm, pushing his elbow forward until the hand with the knife was fully inside the machine.

'Fuck!' screamed Maddox. Like a wild animal in a snare, he swung his body round, flailing his legs at Boateng. For a moment, Boateng thought it was over and Maddox was beaten. Then Maddox reached into the machine with his other hand, took the hunting knife from his pinned arm and turned back to Boateng.

Maddox swiped with the knife but Boateng stepped away. Then he saw Maddox wind his free arm back. He was going to throw the knife. Boateng dived for the control panel and hit the second button as Maddox's free arm reached its full extension. He saw the blade glinting and hurled himself to the deck as Maddox wheeled his arm forward. The knife clattered off the wall above him as the second mechanical claw hissed and began its descent. Maddox jerked his head at the noise. 'No!' He was trying to arc his foot towards the big red stop button at the base.

'Zac!' cried Maddox. 'Do something!' He swung a shoe towards the button again, grazed it without pressing it. 'Zac!' His voice was high-pitched, desperate.

The claw was halfway down.

Boateng did nothing. He heard the pop as Maddox somehow found the strength to wrench his own shoulder out of its socket. But his arm was still trapped in the machine as the second claw reached it. Boateng watched as the blade connected with Maddox's forearm and, after the briefest of pauses, sliced right through it. The bone cracked and splintered like a piece of wood. There was a thud as the limb hit the base of the machine.

Maddox produced a noise like nothing Boateng had heard before, his body contorting before slumping to the ground, blood pumping out from his severed arm. The horror paralysed Boateng for a moment. Then he heard a gasp from behind Maddox and remembered: Wallace.

As Boateng looked at Wallace, a hand reached out and gripped his leg.

'No, Zac,' growled Maddox. 'Save me.'

Boateng stared at him. At Kaiser. The man who had caused so many people – his own family more than most – so much pain. The choice was an easy one. Without a word, he ripped his leg free of Maddox's fingers.

Moving across to Wallace, Boateng saw how much blood he'd lost. The light in his eyes seemed to be fading and his face was pale, but he focused on Boateng as he knelt next to him.

Wallace made a small choking noise. 'Help,' he whispered. He let go of the pistol and Boateng found himself clasping Wallace's hand. It was getting cold, the pulse slow and weak.

He never imagined he'd be in this position, but Boateng had to acknowledge that Darian Wallace had saved his life. Without the shot he'd managed to make, Boateng knew it could be him dying now, not Maddox.

'There's backup coming,' he told Wallace. 'Sit tight, yeah?' He looked over his shoulder towards the fire exit. 'Kat!' he yelled. 'Anyone!'

'Nah,' Wallace grimaced. 'Not me. I'm gone. My son, my baby mum. Help them.' He swallowed effortfully. 'Please, Zac.'

Boateng didn't know what to say. Had Wallace given up already? Did he know he was dying? Was it a trick? This was the man who'd tried to kill him a few days ago…

'I've got something for you.' Wallace groaned, his speech slowing.

'What?' Boateng searched his face. 'What've you got?'

'Proof. Kaiser.' Wallace coughed. 'His email.' He managed to whisper the details; Boateng committed them to memory.

Boateng studied the young man, once a killer, now suddenly vulnerable, and spoke two words he thought he'd never say: 'Thanks, Darian.'

'Just... my boy, yeah? Make sure he's OK?'

'I promise,' said Boateng. He felt his throat tighten as he gripped Wallace's hand. For a few seconds the only sound in the warehouse was Wallace's laboured breathing.

Then a hammer blow came from the front door, followed by the cry of 'Armed police!'

'Here!' shouted Boateng in response. 'Get a medic! Somebody help!'

# CHAPTER TWENTY-NINE

**Friday, 31 August 2018**

The three of them sat close together in the waiting room. Zac had his arm around Kofi, the lad sandwiched between him and Etta. Kofi was reading a *Black Panther* comic book that Zac had bought for him, partly to prove that the superhero did exist when he was young, long before the film. They had arrived early for their appointment with the Child and Adolescent Mental Health Service's specialist trauma team. Zac swivelled his head and gazed out of the window. Looking at the tranquil garden of Maudsley Hospital's Michael Rutter Centre, the events of the past few weeks seemed somehow distant, intangible. And yet their effects on Zac, Etta and Kofi were very real.

Physically, Zac had got away pretty lightly. He'd needed a few stiches in his arm to close the wound from the hunting knife. The Kevlar body armour he'd ordered online had protected his stomach from what could've been a fatal stab; instead, its only trace was a bruise at the point of impact. Compared to the two men who didn't survive the night, that was nothing. He'd experienced flashbacks, too: intrusive images of certain moments from the depot, each triggering a mini panic attack. Some related to him: the memories of being electrocuted, of seeing the knife blade move towards him, of Maddox's lifeless eyes as he lunged with the intention of killing him. Other flashbacks were about Kofi:

304                          Chris Merritt

watching the poor kid squirming in the chair to which he'd been strapped, the terror in his eyes, the incomprehension of why this was happening to him. Those ones were worse.

Zac knew that Kofi was experiencing the same kind of symptoms, but more acutely. It was those psychological effects that brought them here today, for an emergency appointment with the country's top child trauma professionals, who would make a thorough assessment of Kofi's state of mind and determine what treatment was needed. The past two nights, Kofi had wanted to sleep between his parents, and they'd let him. Zac couldn't imagine trying to cope with the after-effects of abduction, captivity and physical abuse at any age, let alone eleven years old.

It broke Zac's heart to think that it was his job, his choices and actions, that had led to Kofi's kidnap and imprisonment for six days. Though his overriding feeling was relief, he held himself responsible for the ordeal his son had been through, for the nightmares that had woken the lad every night since the depot. He stroked Kofi's head. At least they were here now, and able to get help. Zac knew that the symptoms of post-traumatic stress were some of the most treatable of any mental health problem, and that gave him hope that Kofi's suffering would be temporary.

He also knew that, while they were here, the rest of the Op Pluto team would be digging, analysing and joining the dots on the electronic evidence that Wallace had given them with his dying breaths. High-level sign-off had granted them access to the ColonelKurz21 email address. The account's sent messages contained evidence of conspiracy to murder, but Maddox had good security awareness and had only used the address to communicate with Wallace.

Further technical analysis, however, had shown several other email addresses accessed from the same IP address, which corresponded to the house where Maddox lived alone. Those contacts had sparked leads and provided evidence that was being followed up now. Further arrests were planned, and Harper had taken some foreign contacts back to his colleagues at the NCA for investigation with international law enforcement partners as distant as Turkey and Latin America. Zac was wondering if they'd find anything that related to his daughter's death, though it would only be a formality; in every other way, justice had been served. Dave Maddox was lying in a mortuary, his network in pieces, with gun supply in London heavily disrupted. For now at least.

Maddox's crimes had cost him his life. Zac didn't know what exactly had led him to turn corrupt. With some officers, it was a slow and steady slide into criminal behaviour, the opportunities and immunity of the Job proving too much temptation. And once you'd crossed a line, done something you shouldn't have, further steps were easy. Zac understood that well; he'd broken the rules enough times. But that was different, he assured himself: Maddox was abusing his power for personal, criminal gain, while Zac's decisions were about his family, about serious crimes that had gone unpunished. They were two totally separate causes. Weren't they?

He recalled Malik's stories, passed on from his parents, about the things that had caused them to flee Iraq. Police wearing balaclavas in public: unidentifiable, unaccountable. Kidnapping, ransoming, extorting. Murdering their rivals and enemies and dumping the bodies anywhere they liked – in the canal, the desert, or just a skip at the end of the street. Knowing they'd never be caught. Zac couldn't really imagine living in a society like that. Most people took it for granted in Britain that, nine times out of ten, if you took a problem to a police officer, they'd try to help you. They might get stuff wrong, be overwhelmed with stress and paperwork, or have their personal bigotries – especially back in the day – but, by and large, you could trust them to uphold the law, not break it. Dave Maddox was abusing that trust and had been doing it for years. Boateng thought about the operation name: Pluto. The god of the underworld in classical mythology.

Had Maddox chosen the name personally, believing he was some kind of untouchable, godlike figure?

When Sir Paul Condon had been commissioner in the nineties, he'd estimated that half of one per cent of the Met was corrupt at some level. That didn't sound like much. But, in a force of forty-three thousand officers and civilians, it equated to just over two hundred people. Zac didn't know what the stats were today, but Maddox had to be at the extreme end of that group – an outlier even among the criminals that wore uniform.

The image of the DCI being carried out of the depot popped into his mind. How they'd collected his arm from inside the machine, laid it next to him on the stretcher in case it could be reattached in hospital. They never got him that far; he was already dead. So much for the god of the underworld. Boateng knew that Maddox had intended to frame him as Kaiser. He assumed the rest of the plan was to have Wallace shoot him dead, then for Maddox to murder Wallace and make it look as if he and Boateng had killed each other – a criminal partnership gone sour. He didn't want to imagine what would've happened to Kofi… Maddox had nearly got away with it, but it was that same arrogance as those balaclava-clad Iraqi police officers that had undone him in the end. The arrogance to think he could deceive and manipulate everybody around him, including Wallace, into doing what he wanted. Wallace had obviously realised that. Maybe he, too, thought he'd get away with his escape from prison.

'Kofi Boateng?' The voice was soft, calm.

The three of them looked up towards the doorway, where a woman in her thirties with round glasses and a friendly smile stood, holding a clipboard. Zac glanced back to his son.

Kofi nodded. 'Yes,' he said quietly.

'I'm Dr Bremner. Would you like to follow me, please? We're just down the corridor on the left.'

They stood, and Zac rubbed his son's back. 'Come on, mate,' he said.

Kofi rolled up the comic and went forward to meet the psychologist. She and Kofi walked side by side, Dr Bremner asking him questions about how far they'd come and whether he'd got a day off school.

Zac and Etta linked fingers as they followed just behind.

•

Almost eleven days to the hour, Susanna Pym found herself back in the anteroom at Number 10. This time, she relaxed into the armchair and admired the artworks. She had no need for the frenzied use of an iPad today; a trawl through the media this morning had shown that coverage of the Met's operation to tackle gun supply was overwhelmingly positive. Of course, the *Guardian* was asking about root causes, social determinants, that kind of thing – that was par for the course – but others lauded her efforts at the helm, steering the ship safely through turbulent waters and other nauseating metaphors. Faye Rix had written a particularly encouraging in-depth piece that almost made it look as if Pym herself had unmasked a corrupt senior police officer, keeping hundreds of guns off the streets of Britain. It was good to have another ally in the press, and Rix was worth the price of the odd exclusive.

It was also rather nice to be free of DCI David Maddox: the man whose rough appearance belied his deviously sharp mind, and whose Machiavellian skills would probably have made him a successful politician. She did wonder, naturally, if any evidence of their past quid pro quo favours would surface as his life was picked apart by investigators like this Boateng fellow. She'd been completely wrong about Boateng: duped, of course, by Maddox. It frightened her how easily she'd decided to hang the whole bloody mess around Boateng's neck, let him take the fall for everything that had gone wrong. But the main reason she was scared was because it showed how easily someone might do the same to her.

Pym turned slightly to take in another multimillion-pound painting. What a fool she'd been! Putting Maddox in charge of Operation Pluto, meeting him in secret and thinking it would give her the inside track on a high-profile investigation. Instead, all she'd done was give the fox the swipe card to the chicken coop. For the past few days, she'd puzzled over her inability to see through Maddox's deception. It had even made her question whether she was really cut out for the manoeuvring required at the top table.

Then the media coverage had started to pick up and the praise began to flow: an escaped murderer caught (and killed); an arms-dealing police officer exposed (and killed); weapons off the streets; and protests at the police shooting dissipating. Everything was moving in the right direction, leading Pym to make a decision: not to question her own judgement or even get out of the game, but rather to tighten her grip, build new alliances, anticipate being screwed over. Perhaps this Boateng chap was someone to be in touch with…

'Minister! How are you?' Donald spread his hands, the greeting unnecessarily effusive. Mindful of his dismissive manner last week, Pym gave him a cordial but restrained response: he needed to know his place. She had the feeling that, now, she could outlast this obsequious little shit.

Down the corridor, Donald knocked firmly on the large door and then opened it to admit Pym, bowing with a little flourish as she passed him on the way in. Pym ignored him and instead focused her attention on the prime minister, who was up and walking towards Pym, her arms outstretched as if they were relatives – ones who liked each other.

'Sue!' she cried. 'Do come in.'

Pym briefly considered telling her that it was Susanna, not Sue, but thought that might spoil the moment.

'How marvellous to see you.' The PM beamed. 'Congratulations.'

Pym smiled back, savouring the absurdity: she was being congratulated for appointing a psychopath to lead a task force investigating his own arms dealing. Allowing herself to be drawn into the embrace, she caught the faintest whiff of lavender. She'd never noticed that before.

She'd never been this close to the PM.

# EPILOGUE

## Monday, 1 October 2018

Boateng and Jones flanked Commissioner Cressida Dick in front of the Met Police coat of arms on the wall and held up their framed commendations for the cameras. The commissioner placed a hand on Jones's shoulder and did the same to Boateng. She seemed genuinely delighted, and when she'd given a little speech, she was all over the details. She even pronounced his surname right. It was the first time Boateng had met her. He had to admit, he felt like a fanboy. And he knew Jones would be thrilled. If her old man could see her now…

He smiled and peered through the cluster of flashbulbs to where Etta and Kofi stood, both dressed up for the occasion. The pair of them looked so smart. He'd put on his dress uniform; it wasn't often that kit got an outing. Luckily it still just about fitted him. Etta was thrilled and had taken a half-day off work; Kofi had been allowed out of school early to come, too. The lad was doing well. He'd had four sessions with a psychologist and his progress was noticeable. Barely any nightmares, settled into his new school. His previous fears seemed to have gone; he'd even told his dad he wasn't nervous about the bigger boys any more.

Life was getting back to normal for Etta; she'd resumed her boxing classes as well as mindfulness at work. Those were two things Boateng knew she loved but which she'd been reluctant to do soon after Kofi's return, when they'd all just wanted to spend extra time together at home. His wife was much happier in herself, the torment of that week in August gone but not forgotten.

'OK, thank you very much, ladies and gentlemen,' Commissioner Dick told the photographers. She shook hands with Jones and then Boateng, congratulating them once more on the award for extraordinary bravery in the line of duty. 'We need more officers like you two,' she said. Boateng replied that it had been a team effort. He glossed over the fact that it was Maddox who'd been in charge of the team.

As Krebs made a beeline for the commissioner, Boateng headed towards his family. All three of them were grinning like idiots. He plucked two glasses of fizz and an orange juice off a tray as he passed one of the waiters.

Etta gave him a big kiss as he handed out the drinks, and they clinked a toast together.

'Do I get champagne, Dad?'

'No, mate. You're too young.' He took a sip. 'It's prosecco anyway. You wouldn't like it.'

Etta laughed and raised her glass. 'I'm so proud of you, love,' she said.

Boateng put his arms around her and Kofi. 'At the risk of sounding cheesy, it's me that's proud of you guys. Warriors.' He squeezed Kofi's shoulder. 'Especially you, Ko.' The two of them crossed their forearms over the chests like the Black Panther. Kofi spilled a bit of orange juice and burst out laughing. Boateng trod it into the dark carpet and winked at his son.

He became aware of a presence at his shoulder and turned instinctively. It was that new Minister for Policing he'd seen on the TV. The one he'd read about on the Met's intranet. Sue Pym, wasn't it?

'Detective Inspector Boateng,' she said with a wide smile. 'Can I call you Zac?'

'Sure.' Boateng took a bigger sip of his drink. 'This is my wife, Etta, and my son, Kofi.'

'Lovely to meet you all. I'm Susanna Pym. May I offer my heartiest congratulations, Zac. You and your family have been through a great deal these past weeks.'

He hesitated. How did you address a minister? Was it ma'am or Minister?

'Yes,' he said, eventually. Glanced from Pym to Etta and Kofi, then back. 'We have.'

'Well, I'm still relatively new in this job, you know,' continued Pym. 'And I could certainly do with an experienced officer like you to consult once in a while. A sounding board, if you will. When I need a little help.'

'Right.' *Sounding board?* Boateng wasn't sure what she was talking about.

Pym cleared her throat. 'Well, I don't want to intrude on a family moment.'

'Not at all.'

She fixed him with a level gaze. 'I hope I can call on you when the time comes.'

'Of course.' Boateng shrugged. 'I mean, I don't know how—'

'Wonderful.' The smile lingered on Pym's lips. 'I have your number.'

# A LETTER FROM CHRIS

Thank you for reading *Life or Death*, the third book in the Zac Boateng series.

If you're interested to know more about the novels, please join my mailing list. You can unsubscribe from the updates whenever you like and your email address will never be shared.

*www.bookouture.com/chris-merritt*

When I was twenty-five, I watched through a helicopter window as a man on the ground below put a gun to someone's head. Fortunately, he didn't pull the trigger, instead bundling his victim into the boot of a car and kidnapping him. Thanks to the efforts of the British Army, he was found alive and freed. This was Iraq in 2006, and the armed man was an Iraqi police officer whose intention was to ransom the abductee back to his family for a few hundred US dollars. As Zac tells us in *Life or Death*, the police there were in the thick of criminal activity at that time.

In Britain, we generally take it for granted that we can trust the police. As Zac notes, they have their biases and bigotries, and they make mistakes, but most of the time they'll do what they can to help. *Life or Death* is a story about what could happen when someone in the police chooses to use his or her access, power and privilege for personal gain – often at the expense of others. Some officers in the Met have gone down that road. It's a terrifying prospect, and worthy of a story that provides Zac with an adversary of extreme personal significance.

Though *Life or Death* picks up some of the unfinished storylines from the first Boateng novel, *Bring Her Back*, a YouTube video also helped spark the idea for this book. In it, the Met Police showed their firearms destruction depot and, most importantly, the large yellow cutting machine that I dubbed 'Bertha'. When I saw this monstrous device slicing a shotgun in two, I thought, 'Imagine getting your arm trapped in there…' That's the way my imagination works. Call me twisted.

Much has been written in 2018 about violence, murder and gun crime in London. Statistics appear to show that all three of these offences are on the rise. While we do need to exercise caution when interpreting the data, there is clearly a problem. Serving police officers have told me that the austerity and budget cuts of the past decade are to blame, reducing the Met's capability to disrupt the importation and conversion of firearms. Having worked with the aftermath of two shootings as a psychologist in the NHS, I've seen how the impact of such traumas goes well beyond the immediate victim. Let's hope we can make the capital safer, even if that would put Zac and his team out of a job.

As usual, I've travelled around London ferreting out interesting locations for this book. Londoners will be familiar with the giant (still unfinished) Crossrail tunnels, like the one in which Wallace confronts Zac. They may be less familiar with the 1948 Olympic velodrome tucked away behind some trees in Herne Hill, or the video games arcade in Peckham. Every place in *Life or Death* is authentic, with the small caveat that the wall Wallace escapes over is on the other side of the road to Ruskin Park; I hope readers will allow me some artistic licence in the service of drama. The Parkour Generations training sessions attended by Kat Jones are real, and I thoroughly recommend taking one of their classes if you want a totally new way to see the city.

If you enjoyed *Life or Death*, please do leave a review online. Feel free also to drop me a line via Twitter or my website. There, you can find out more about my other work on psychology, some of which features in the Zac Boateng novels.

Thanks again for choosing to read *Life or Death*, and if you haven't read the other two Boateng books then please take a look: *Bring Her Back* and *Last Witness*. I have many more ideas for stories in the series, so keep in touch for further details!

Best wishes,
Chris

 @DrCJMerritt

www.cjmerritt.co.uk

# ACKNOWLEDGEMENTS

Huge thanks to my editor, Helen Jenner, at Bookouture for seeing *Life or Death* all the way from basic concept to the story you've just finished reading. Her input at both the planning and editorial stages improved it greatly, as did the first reading of Kate Mason (no surprises there). I'm grateful to my agent, Charlie Viney, for his continued support, enthusiasm and advice. A long-time resident of south London, he knows the locations I write about almost as well as Zac Boateng. To the Bookouture team, whose hard work behind the scenes is appreciated every day – thank you, Jennifer Hunt, Alex Crow, Noelle Holton, Kim Nash and Julie Fergusson. Voice actor Damian Lynch has done an incredible job narrating Zac and his world for audiobook, while Dan Battaglia and Alex Hargreaves at Audible have handled the production and management of the audiobooks with aplomb. Paula Cuddy and Robert Murphy at Eleventh Hour Films are plotting to bring Zac to your screens – their originality in preparing *Bring Her Back* and *Life or Death* for TV deserves to be realised.

I am indebted to Amy Gorman for sharing her experiences of working in the Met, especially on kidnaps, for this story. Thanks also to Sarah Stephens, and to another former Met officer who served in the NCIS (which after several mergers, two name changes and much rearranging of furniture became the National Crime Agency). Their stories provided the backdrop of Operation Pluto. Firearms details in the book are accurate thanks to the expertise of Bomber and Starfish from the City of London Police.

Fortunately for the people of London, it's only their humour that's wide of the mark.

In researching police corruption for *Life or Death*, I drew heavily on the work of Graeme McLagan, whose book *Bent Coppers* details the history of corruption in the Met and the efforts to combat it. Frightening, compelling and at times comical, it's well worth a read.

Most of the hand-to-hand combat in the novel – including Wallace's sleeper hold, aka the 'lion killer choke' – is drawn from the Brazilian jiu-jitsu classes of Roger Brooking, with whom I had the pleasure to train a few years ago. On a less painful – though spicier – note, Yusuf Muhammad and Dan Quarshie kindly shared some culinary aspects of their West African heritage with me. I'm still waiting to be invited for jollof with their parents.

Printed in Great Britain
by Amazon